THE
SOUND
OF
Diamonds

Hold to hope

Rachelle Rea

Steadfast Love 1

THE
SOUND
OF
Diamonds

RACHELLE REA

WhiteFire Publishing

This is a work of fiction. All characters and events portrayed in this novel are either fictitious or used fictitiously.

THE SOUND OF DIAMONDS

WhiteFire Publishing
13607 Bedford Rd NE
Cumberland, MD 21502

ISBN: 978-1-939023-60-5 (digital)
        978-1-939023-59-9 (print)

To my grandfather, Richard John Detwiler (1941-2011)
For once asking me, at a book fair you and Grandma took me to,
where I'd like my book table. Thank you for believing in me.

Gwyneth

Chapter One

Leiden, the Low Countries, the Netherlands
23 August 1566

A crash shook the nun's cell I had called my own since seeking refuge in my mother's homeland. My gaze snapped to the door. A sister screamed somewhere within the convent. Glass shattered. The rumbles of men's dark shouts arrowed fear straight into my heart.

A man burst into the cell, the door banging against the far wall. My breath seized in my throat, for I recognized that red hair and those fearsome brown eyes. Devon Godfrey, known to most as Dirk.

I lunged behind the only chair. "Come no closer!"

"Fear not, milady." He stepped toward me, his masculine voice speaking English words familiar yet foreign to me after months in this place where I heard only feminine voices speaking Dutch. "I mean you no harm."

My gaze latched onto the dagger strapped to his baldric. I fought the urge to shriek. No harm? He meant me no harm? He who killed my parents before my very eyes!

"You lie." I dared a quick glance around, searching for a weapon of any sort. Seeing naught but the chair I stood behind, I bemoaned the Spartan nun's cell. "Why would you rush in here if not to do harm?"

His gaze imprisoned mine. "I came to rescue you."

"From what?" This was not what I expected. The only thing I needed protection from was the man in front of me. He was why I was here, now, in this vile land full of Protestant heretics. We had met only once, on the night my parents died, but I knew all I needed to know about him. For he had done the deed.

He stretched out both hands. "Milady, I know you have every reason to fear me—"

"I most certainly do." The whisper slashed through his half-formed

sentence. A frisson of fear crawled up my spine.

His eyes narrowed. "You must trust me. 'Tis the only way we shall survive this night."

The sound of glass shards pelting cold stone clapped my ears. Voices, looming louder and louder, assaulted my mind. Sisters' voices. Women I had lived with for months now, ever since my parents died. I should have been able to discern to whom they belonged, but the cacophony of noise denied me that privilege.

A large hand clamped on my upper arm. I tried to wrench away, but the hard fingers held fast.

"Release me!" I struggled against him, to no avail. Through the lenses of my spectacles, I met Dirk's gaze. His dark eyes revealed one emotion—determination.

"They approach. This group seems especially violent. We must be away." He dragged me toward the door.

"Who approaches?"

"The mob."

Horror spun through my stomach like a winter storm. "A mob? Attacking the convent?"

Dirk pulled me into the narrow hallway. The heady odor of tallow candles filled my nose. Speckled light danced on the cold walls, but darkness drowned me—my mind as much as my eyes. How had he found me? Uncle Oliver had agreed I would be safe here, in the Low Countries, in this convent hidden away in Leiden. He had protested against the notion of my hiding so far away—even in the land of my heritage—but my insistence that Dirk could never find me here had been enough to convince my uncle.

Yet here Dirk was, with a firm grasp on my arm, leading me to who knew what.

"Wait."

He ignored me. I dug the heels of my leather shoes into the floor. His head whipped around so fast I reared back. For a moment, I was thankful for his hold—surely the swift movement would otherwise have sent me stumbling. My gratitude fizzled when I caught a glimpse of the fury in his gaze, illuminated by the meager amount of candlelight that graced the hallway. Had that same fury painted his face as he plunged a dagger into my parents' backs?

"We have no time."

My ears rang with the clamor that grew louder every second, reminding

me that the convent was even now being overrun and raided by a violent mob. "I demand to know where you are taking me."

"Foolish woman." He tried to pull me forward but only succeeded in dragging me. "By the time I told you, they would be upon us, and we would be dead." His look bade me believe he spoke the truth, but I shook my head. How could I be sure of aught he said?

I could not. Not ever again. Not after what he had done. "I doubt I will be any better off in your bloodstained hands. You murdered my parents." I spat the words.

A sigh spilled from him, and the flickering candlelight flashed upon a sliver of pain in his eyes.

Before I could scoff at the pretense of remorse, a scream from somewhere behind us reached a painful pitch before cutting off. My muscles seized. Dirk yanked my hand so hard it seemed he nearly severed my arm from its socket. I lurched forward. He flung me toward the wall then followed me into a small alcove I had not seen before. Tears pricked my eyes as I took a shuddering breath. I knew the owner of that scream. Sister Margried. Such a sweet soul. Always ready with a kind word and gentle smile.

So unlike me.

She and Sister Agnes and I were the only English women here; both had taken me into their care when I arrived. Margried, only two years older than my own eighteen years, had become as close as a sister to me. Where were they?

I did not realize I was squeezing Dirk's hand until the diamonds on my rosary pressed into my other palm, alerting me to the tightness of my fists. When I tried to pull away, he refused. Prayers surged from my heart in a torrent.

How long we huddled there in that tiny space, I did not know. No other screams shook my soul, but breaking glass, thundering shouts, and maniacal cackles of laughter gave rise to a realization. The threat of the danger sucked the air from my lungs. This convent in Leiden—the safety it promised was now like every other promise. Broken. I wished I could cover my ears to drown out the reality. I pictured glass becoming shards after falling to the floor. Pottery shattering into thousands of pieces.

The truth hit me with such force I almost gasped aloud. Rumors of the violence had made the sisters and me wonder if the chaos would reach this province, this convent, this so-called sanctuary where I was supposed to be safe.

What bitter irony. Uncle Oliver had agreed to my coming here where I could recover from my grief, where I would be protected, where I could consider entering the convent as a postulant—a pursuit impossible in Protestant England. Instead, the man I had hated ever since the night I met him, when I saw him standing over the bodies of my parents, a dripping dagger in his hand, had crashed into my life again. Stood beside me. Even claimed to be my protector.

While the Beeldenstorm riot raged all around us.

The Calvinist preachers throughout the Low Countries had stirred up those disloyal to Catholicism. It had begun in Poperinghe on the fourteenth of August: raiders had entered the churches, torn out the organs, removed the sacramental altars, broken windows, destroyed paintings and statuaries, stolen the plate and vestments and anything popish.

No. No, he was wrong. That could not be what was happening. "This is not a church, but a humble convent!"

"Nevertheless, these men seem intent on destruction. Come. We must get out of here." He tugged on my hand, trying to pull me in the opposite direction of the clamor. But, unable to push the scream I had heard from my mind, I halted. He released my hand and gripped my upper arms, his brown eyes boring into mine. "Do you not realize what is happening? How can you ask me to wait?"

"I refuse to leave my sisters behind."

He let go of me as if my gown were on fire. "Sisters? Have you taken vows?"

"*Nee*, I have not."

A low growl escaped from his chest as he clasped my fingers once again and led me down the hall, to our left, toward the noise. A metallic odor stung my nose. My stomach rolled. Surely it could not be... but it was. The same smell I had encountered that fateful day months ago when my parents had died. Blood.

No longer did shouts cascade through the air. Even the sounds of destruction—screams, thuds, shattering glass—seemed softer, fainter. I chanced a whisper. "Margried."

Dirk tightened his grip on my hand in obvious warning. I did not care. What did it matter if I perished here in the convent at the hands of my enraged countrymen?

Better that than breathing my last at *his* hands.

"Margried." The feeling fled my fingers as Dirk squeezed them, but a

low groan answered me.

"Margried!" I wrenched away from Dirk, into the room to my left. Dropping to my knees before the still figure, my hands hovered over her, unsure of what to do. Was she in pain? Was she dying? *Nee*, I refused to entertain that thought even for a moment. I brushed away the hair that had escaped from her wimple, revealing eyes that widened with fright as they looked over my shoulder. "'Tis well. I am here."

"As am I." Sister Agnes emerged from a shadowed corner of the chamber, a rag in her hand. "Lady Gwyneth, what are you doing here?"

My gaze sought my friend, lying on the floor, obviously weak and injured. I glanced back at Sister Agnes. The older woman knelt at her sister's side and pressed the damp cloth to Margried's forehead.

"I am staying with you two."

An annoyed groan rippled through the room, but it was not Margried's. It was a distinctly masculine sound. Coming from a distinctly masculine creature. "There is no *staying* to be done. By any of us."

When he scooped Margried into his arms, the girl's eyes went wild with fright.

Sister Agnes rushed toward him. "Sir, unhand her immediately! 'Tis most unseemly!"

"I mean no harm, but we must be leaving. All of us."

Sister Agnes's mouth fell open. Those words again. *No harm.* Once more my heart did not believe him.

"Are you coming or not?" Dirk pierced me with a look that said I was to follow or he would carry *me* out of the convent also. He darted to the doorway, looked right and left, and ducked out. I grabbed Sister Agnes's hand and stepped after him. He headed to the right once more, to wherever he had been leading me before.

"Do you know this man?" Sister Agnes's question hung in the air of the hall.

"Aye." *Do not ask any more questions. Especially not whether I trust him.*

"How?" Sister Agnes could always be counted upon to be contrary.

A sigh ruffled through me. When I inhaled again, the scent of tallow candles warmed my insides. "His family is friends with mine." Although *he* was not. Not any longer.

Another voice entered my ears, speaking the Dutch of my mother. Or shouting it, rather. I spun in time to see a burly man with a torch in his hand turn the corner of the hall. We locked gazes, he looking as surprised to see me as I no doubt looked to see him.

"Take her." Dirk set Margried on wobbly feet in front of me. Agnes and I clasped the other woman in both our arms before she collapsed against us. Her groan sounded in my ear as I turned back to the flickering torchlight. The faint smell of smoke wafted over me. Dirk crashed into his adversary, causing the torch to fly over both of them and land in a doorway. Flames licked up the wooden door.

Dirk and the Dutchman wrestled for but a moment before the man's head cracked against the floor and his eyes rolled back. Dirk rushed toward us and took Margried in his arms once more. "Come quickly. They will be after us in a breath."

Sister Agnes gave no protest. She flew after Dirk, her habit embracing the narrow confines of the hallway like a bat's wings. I chanced one last look at the man lying on the stones and the fire claiming the doorway behind him. Somehow I knew he lay unconscious, but not dead.

The convent erupted in shouts. Footsteps pounded behind me as I sought to run faster. They followed us. My countrymen. Men with whom I shared a heritage. But it mattered not. I was Catholic. They were Protestant. Thus, I was the reason for their fury. They were here to purify the convent's grounds of what they called graven images. *Heretics.* Anger convulsed inside me with the ferocity of a storm-tossed sea.

"Run, milady!" Agnes's call broke through the sound of my own breathlessness. My lungs heaved for air. How long did this hall stretch?

The shouts behind me grew louder. I looked over my shoulder. The man nearest to me grinned, his teeth gleaming in the light of his torch. I swallowed my scream at the terror that filled me. I fixed my gaze straight ahead, and a burst of moonlight sparked in front of me. A door had been opened to the outside. My soul dared to hope I might come out of this alive. I must. Sister Agnes and Margried needed me. They knew not to what villain we had entrusted our escape. I must survive this, if only to warn them that we could *not* trust him.

My eyes adjusted to the brightness to see that Margried no longer jostled in Dirk's arms. He no longer ran. Instead, he stood by the door, reaching toward Sister Agnes, coming toward him. Where was Margried? Surely he had not tossed her aside in order to run more swiftly? My fury threatened to bubble over as I watched Sister Agnes leap through the open door. Did she so willingly desert her sister?

"Gwyn!" I heard Dirk shout and met his gaze, suddenly angry at his calling me by my Christian name—and shortened, at that. Then I trembled at the fear in his expression and tumbled to the floor. Shrieking, I batted

away the hands of the man who had grasped my gown and pulled me down.

"Where is your habit, sister?" The grinning man spat the last Dutch word. "Could it be ye are a lady sequestered here?"

"No matter!" A younger man barreled toward us, his jowls bouncing. "I say we kill her!" The torch he carried blazed as he waved it and leered. He intended to use it as a weapon, and the thought of that fire lighting my skin sent a new strength streaming through me. But despite my struggling, the grinning one held me fast.

Wees gegroet Maria, moeder Gods—

"Release her!" Dirk surged forward and sent a fist into my captor's jaw. The man's grip loosened, and I wrenched free. When I looked up, Dirk had sent the man flat on his back.

Cacophony ensued. More men emerged from I knew not where, but they obviously fought on Dirk's side. One with shaggy brown hair leveled the one intent on murdering me with the torch. I scrambled back and tried to gain my feet but tripped over the boots of another. He looked down at me, chagrin on his face, as if sorry he could not help me rise.

"Gwyn, get out!" Again with his chopping off my name. Dirk freed his dagger and used it to cut through half the torch in the hand of a roaring man. I tossed a look behind me. Where was out? Through the door, of course. I lunged in that direction then cried out as something yanked off my wimple. Fingers fisted into my hair as I fell to my knees. My hands lifted to my forehead, where surely my blond locks were being torn from the roots.

"The more ye struggle, the worse it'll be for ye."

Gasping, I twisted on the floor, my knees collecting bruises as they banged against the stones. A cackle sounded in my ears. Horror streaked through me as a grimy face with blackened teeth neared.

"Full of fire, are we?" Noxious breath swirled in the air before my nose. His free hand disappeared into his pocket. The blade glimmered as it slid free.

A yell from behind the man caused us both to look up. Dirk met the man's dagger with his own, tossing the smaller weapon across the stones with one swipe. The man's grin vanished.

"Let go of her." Dirk's dagger rose to rest against my captor's neck.

Fingernails trailed over my scalp as the man grasped my hair more firmly. He flicked his wrist with a savage throw that sent me reeling backward. Shards of pain caused the moonlight from the door to narrow

into stars before my eyes. I reached a hesitant hand to the back of my head, regretting it the moment my light touch doubled the discomfort. I slid my fingers beside my skull and felt the sticky droplets.

Was this how I would die, then? In the middle of a battle during the Beeldenstorm, my own blood streaming around me? I fought the dizziness, but the shouts continued to fade.

A form dropped beside me. Dirk's expression remained as stony as the floor on which I lay as his gaze went to my blood-red hand.

His features softened then hardened again, this time into an expression I dared not believe. *Concern?* He looked past me, calling for his men, but it took all I had just to keep my eyes open. My ears refused to invest the effort into listening to his words. My mouth felt fuzzy, but I tried anyway. "Margried?"

I had seen Sister Agnes exit through the door Dirk had opened, but where was Margried?

His two men were there, then, hovering over me from their full heights. How was it that I, no petite woman, felt so small compared to these men? *I am lying on the floor.*

The brief words the men exchanged around me failed to penetrate my mind as I struggled to make sense of why I lay there. What had felled me? I could not remember. I needed to remember. More so, I needed to stand. I shifted in an attempt to rise.

Dirk must have surmised my intent for he tunneled his arms beneath me. When he lifted me, my head spun even more. Nausea swept over me in a deadly wave and not just from my head wound.

I lay in the arms of the man who had murdered my parents.

Completely unable to do anything about it.

Dirk

Chapter Two

I cradled her to my chest and prayed she could not hear my heart pounding inside it. Of course, her eyes had closed and she did not appear to be hearing anything at all at the moment. Which was why my heart raced like it wished to escape from my ribcage.

"Will she live, do you think?"

The frankness I usually appreciated about Ian only gave rise to anger at his question. My jaw tightened. "Aye."

His brows rose as his gaze lowered to my shoulder. I merely turned away, toward the door, not needing to look. I could feel the blood from her wound seeping into my shirt. And it frightened me to no end. This was not according to plan. There had been no intention on my part to ever feel fear for her. To ever feel *anything* for her.

She, a woman I had met only once before, was a means to an end, a pawn in the plan that would redeem me. Take her from the convent. That had been the goal for the day. If I saw her safely home, mayhap that good deed would be enough to, at the very least, cast doubt that I was the one who had murdered her parents.

The plan had escalated into much, much more.

Bodies littered the hallway, some gone, some groaning. Other raiders would soon join them. We needed to be gone by then.

Without a word, I strode from the scene. Gwyn and getting her to safety were my only priorities. Her and the two sisters now in my charge. I still could not believe she had spun away from me and into that room without heed. She could have been killed if a raider had been lying in wait for her. The thought brought my gaze to her once more. She moaned softly against my chest as she bled into my shirt. I clenched my jaw against the sound but still felt the trickle that warned her injury was serious.

The cool of the night greeted me before I fully emerged from the convent. Cade appeared beside me as I stepped through the door. Our gazes met. For there before us stood the nun Gwyn had called Agnes. She had one arm wrapped around the shoulders of the younger one whose name I could not recall. In her free hand she held a short dagger—if it could indeed be called a dagger. It more resembled a kitchen knife.

Whatever it was, she pointed it at me.

"Come no closer!" So she spoke English. Gwyn had chosen this convent strategically, then. So close to the shore, it appeared it was a favorite of English women, for both the nuns before me spoke my language. Agnes's features froze as her gaze darted to the bundle in my arms. "What have you done to Lady Gwyneth?"

I exhaled. "Naught but rescue her from raiding villagers."

"How badly is she injured?"

I glanced down, my throat seizing at the way long golden lashes fanned across the face of the girl I held. Such a pale face. She was losing blood. "Badly. Now will you put that down? We must be away from here."

To my surprise, Agnes obeyed with mouth closed. She shifted to tuck the knife into the folds of her habit. The movement jostled the younger nun; she tipped to the side. Agnes reached for her, and they both started to go down.

Cade surged forward, caught the nun before she hit the ground, and lifted her into his arms. Agnes gave him a long look before stepping back, as if satisfied enough by what she saw in his expression to trust him with her sister.

"Let us go."

"Go where?" Agnes shot me an uncertain look.

"Away." Noting the way her face reddened, I glanced at the man to my left. "Ian, lead us."

Ian gave me a curt nod and forged a path away from the fiery convent toward the moonlit woods. I nodded for Cade to go on ahead. The young nun's eyes, wide with wariness, met mine over his shoulder then dropped to Gwyn.

Agnes went next, and I thanked God for one woman able to walk on her own. I glanced down at the one I carried and pulled in a deep draught of air, nearly choking on the acrid smell of smoke filling the air around us.

Gwyn's brows knit together, but she slept. Free from the pain, I hoped. For now. *Please, Lord, will You heal her?* As I faced forward again and followed in Agnes's footsteps, I accepted our unexpected company. Mayhap it was best this way. Gwyn might be more comfortable with two other women present—presumably, friends.

If we could keep them all safe.

Ian and Cade stepped through the trees with the stealth of predators on the prowl. Ian kept one hand on the baldric crossing his chest. There was no one I would rather be following through the Low Countries than these two trusted friends.

They had been there for me through the darkness. Cade had known me since I had chosen the scoundrel's way—and, after my father's death, when I turned from that path. Ian we had met shortly after. These were the men who guarded my back.

In contrast to their trackers' silence, Agnes crashed through the overgrowth like a drunken man. Autumn's blanket of leaves protested her harsh treatment. As if my thoughts summoned her attention, she flung a look at me over her shoulder. "I know not your name."

I had not met many nuns, but this one defied all my expectations. Despite the tension radiating through me, I could feel a smile tug at my lips, but I refused to give it lodging. How much had Gwyn confided in the sisters with whom she sought safety? If she had told them all about that night we had first met months ago, then the sound of my name would not be welcome. "You need not know it."

The older woman stopped walking and crossed her voluminous sleeves, the motion adding to the bat-like appearance her habit lent. Her eyes narrowed. "I need to know who you are if I am to entrust our care to you."

A low chuckle sounded from ahead of me. I passed her and shot Cade a look as I did so. The chuckle died as he snapped his gaze forward again.

"I am a friend."

"How can I be sure?"

I expelled a sigh and again breathed in air tinged with smoke wafting from the convent. "Is not saving your life from the mob incentive enough?"

Her footsteps began again behind me. Wise woman. She knew it would be foolish to let us leave her behind alone in these dark woods not far from a fiery convent filled with raiders. Even so, I had every intention of allowing her to do so should she wish it. I already carried one woman in my arms.

Gwyn chose that moment to moan. My stomach flipped at the sound. When her eyelids fluttered, it flipped again.

"Halt!" I threw the whispered word at Ian. Cade stopped and turned to face me. I laid Gwyn on the leafy ground with all the gentleness I could manage.

She opened her eyes and looked straight into mine, pulling in a gasp at the same time. Her green eyes shuttered closed once more behind her glasses.

"Milady, how fare thee?"

"Lady Gwyneth!" Agnes flew to her other side and knelt. She grasped one of Gwyn's hands in hers and her lips moved. Praying for her?

I moved my hand behind her head. She opened her eyes as I felt the wound. The smile Agnes had tempted me to show earlier burst into fullness as Gwyn glared at me. A good sign. She was not as weak as I feared.

My fingers probed the dried blood but came away clean. "The bleeding has stopped."

Gwyn's gaze narrowed on my shirt. "Staunched by your shoulder, no doubt." Something unidentifiable flickered in her eyes. Just as swiftly as it had appeared, though, it was gone. Her gown rustled as she struggled to rise.

I pressed her shoulders down again. "Ian, how much farther to the river?"

"How do you feel, milady?" Agnes asked.

Ian glanced ahead then back to me, his brows pulled together. "Another hour of walking at this pace."

"Well. I feel well." Her voice sounded weak, trembling.

I nodded and slid my arms beneath Gwyn again.

"Nay." She struggled against me. "I can walk on my own."

"I sincerely doubt that."

"Why not allow me to try?"

I hoisted her higher as she kicked her legs weakly. "Because you would slow us down."

She stopped moving. The moonlight refused to cause a glare off her glasses, so I received the full brunt of her glower.

"Are we being followed?" She glanced over my shoulder, her nose wrinkling with fear.

"Nay. Not yet." Did I believe we would be followed? Mayhap. Mayhap not. No need to ignore the advantage of the trepidation in her expression, however. If apprehension caused her to trust me and allowed me to carry her, then I would exploit it. And deal with the guilt later. For guilt did attack me when her green eyes widened and her nose wrinkled further.

"'Tis well, Lady Gwyneth." The soft voice of the younger nun brought my gaze to her. "God is with us and will protect us."

Gwyn relaxed as she took a deep breath. I kicked myself mentally. And why had *I* not employed the devout argument? Instead, I had alarmed her. *Lout.* I had to remember I dealt with women at the moment. Not a band of men. Not the servants of a keep.

In a way, remembering would be easy. I allowed my gaze to travel the length of Gwyn's flaxen hair. The silky strands that had come loose from the knot at the back of her head played on my arms. So light against my skin. Almost white in the moonlight. It had been that hair that had caught my attention upon our first—our only other—meeting. The night she grew to hate me.

'Twas that night I sought to make restitution for.

"Let us go then." At my words, Cade and Ian turned and started walking. Agnes walked slightly in front of me, but only slightly, as if she wanted to be able to keep both Gwyn and the younger nun in sight.

Lord, I am sorry. I had intended only to keep Gwyn safe. My motives had been true. Yet the fact that I had fallen into the mire of deceit and sought to manipulate her emotions did not sit well with me. That was the way I had managed situations for most of my life. A habit I was trying to change by the power of the Savior who had gripped me not quite a year ago. How easily I fell back into my old ways.

"Sister Agnes." To my amazement, Gwyn's voice soothed the spinning of my guilty thoughts. Should not her voice, the voice of the one I had hurt, have deepened the regret? Indeed, I had hurt her far worse than feeding her fears this night.

"Lady Gwyneth? Are you well?" Agnes fell back to walk beside me, her gaze never leaving Gwyn's face.

"I am well." The same answer she had given before. I did not believe her. "How was Margried injured?"

Agnes's lips pursed.

"Sister Agnes?"

I willed the nun not to answer her, not to cause her anxiety.

"She..."

Disagreeable woman.

Margried's soft voice spoke from a few feet ahead, where she looked over Cade's shoulder. "'Tis well, Sister Agnes. You may tell her."

I cocked a brow at the cryptic statement and noticed that Gwyn did the same.

Agnes nodded. "We were in the chapel, praying, when the mob arrived."

Gwyn gasped. "Did they see you?"

"Aye and nay."

"Whatever do you mean?"

"We were not alone." Agnes's voice dropped to a whisper. Gwyn's gaze swung between Agnes and Margried and back again. For one brief moment, she even tipped back her head to look at me.

"Many sisters sat praying when the doors thundered open. Angry men, torches held high, burst in."

The sound of a strangled sob pierced my soul, and my gaze met Margried's. Tears ran down her face. Ian gave me a shattered look but kept walking. I agreed with his unspoken decision to keep moving. If there was anything Agnes needed now, it was the slight distraction that searching for a spot to place her feet provided. The same was probably true of Margried needing now the shelter of Cade's arms. I was unsure how I felt about the way Gwyn stiffened as I thought that.

"What happened?" Gwyn's eyes softened behind her glasses.

"They struck down almost all of us. Margried and I escaped, but not before she fell upon her arm."

The horror of the truth seemed to strike Gwyn and everyone else into silence.

Except Cade. "Which arm?" When Margried continued to weep softly into his shoulder, he whispered the words again, patient. "Which arm?"

She sniffed, looked up, and touched lightly the arm that lay against him. Inside of a second, he lifted her away from him, turned her body, and positioned her against his chest once more with her injured arm no longer crushed against him. Her sobbing picked up in pace.

One glance at Agnes revealed that her troubled gaze remained fastened on the forest floor. A lone tear sparkled in the moonlight as it traveled down her cheek.

I looked at Gwyn. Stoic, she did not cry, nor did she say a word; she only stared up at the sky. I risked turning my gaze upward. The jagged branches of the trees, cushioned by the soft foliage of late summer, formed a canopy above us that allowed snatches of moonlight to filter through. What did she see?

And why did she not cry? I thought of my mother and youngest sister and knew they would have dissolved into puddles over hearing of lesser tragedies. Why did I care about the way she reacted? Was it mere curiosity, surprise that she seemed to take the relaying of the deaths of her friends better than many men would?

Who was this woman in my arms?

Gwyneth

Chapter Three

Pulling in a deep breath, I attempted to calm the nausea swirling in my stomach. Tentacles of anger tightened around my insides, assuaging the ill feeling but only adding to the unpleasantness. Faces of the sisters I had come to know during my stay at the convent revolved around my mind. I forced my eyes open, told myself to focus on other things besides the faces of my dead friends. I would pray for them later.

The chill night air belied the fact that summer had come upon the Low Countries mere months ago. Yet this was how it always was, cool, and the closer one was to the sea, breezy. Not unlike England at this time of year. Unlike España, or so Uncle Oliver had told me when once he returned from a visit there with his wife. He had gone years ago, during the summer. The innermost cities of España choked the throat with heat and slicked the forehead with sweat. Though I had never been there, he had often described the place for me so that it seemed as if I had.

England was my home. I had lived there for all of my eighteen years, save the months I had spent in Leiden. I had left only because I had met Dirk. On the same night I had lost both my parents.

I looked up at him now. Red curls fell over his forehead, making him appear very much a rugged man of self-rule. "Where are you taking us?"

His eyes, the color of loamy ground, stared down into mine. I swallowed at the burst of fear that exploded in my brain and forced my expression to be hard, rocky, unrevealing.

"To the river." He slanted his gaze forward once more.

"Does this river we are walking toward have a name?" I looked ahead. Margried rested against one man's shoulder, while the other man forged the path through the woods. A swell of panic abated when I saw that Sister Agnes walked beside Dirk.

"The Rhine."

I nodded, taking that in. "And after that?" If I were alone, I would insist he release me now, and I would run away, as far as I could. I would not get far, that much I knew. Somehow, though, I would make him miserable until he grew tired of chasing me. But I had the sisters to think of. Sister Agnes could probably outrun me—it would not be hard to do. But Margried…with her injured arm, I could not expect her to last long.

"Rest now."

Anger bristled down my back as I stiffened in his arms. "I demand to know what you intend to do with us."

A sigh billowed from his lungs like air from a blacksmith's bellows. "By what right?"

Rage spun through me. "By what right? How dare you! You expect me to do as I am told and allow you to abduct me without so much as asking where you are taking me?"

His eyebrows lifted in a look of amusement, only fanning the flame of my fury. "I do."

"You insolent, overbearing—"

"Watch yourself, milady, there are holy women present."

My mouth dropped open.

"I will tell you our final destination soon enough."

"By that you mean I will know once we have arrived."

A chuckle rumbled throughout his large frame and into my bones. "Mayhap I will keep it to myself till then."

A whimper snapped my gaze forward. Margried arched her back. The man who held her maintained his hold on her, but the shuddering breath she drew attested to her pain.

I fixed my gaze on Dirk. "Well, how much longer till we reach the Rhine?"

"Ian?"

The leader turned his head to smile at us. I bit back a smile of my own. The flash of Ian's teeth lent him a boyish look that was both endearing and encouraging. Why, he had to be little more than a lad! Which slashed him off my list of threats, and made a successful escape attempt even more likely. If Dirk merely left me and the sisters in Ian's care, while he and the other brown-haired man went off to hunt or do whatever it was that men did in the woods at night…. It just might work.

"We have reached the river."

A small sigh escaped Sister Agnes.

I pushed away from Dirk's shirt. "Let me down. I can walk from here."

He frowned. "Are you certain, milady?"

So we were back to *milady*, then. "Most assuredly certain."

His brows rose as that humorous glint in his eyes reappeared. He swung his arm from beneath my knees and plopped me on the ground, keeping both hands at my waist. "Can you stand?"

I blinked several times to erase the extra image of him that swam before my eyes. He must have noticed my failure at focusing on him, for he moved closer. Quite of their own accord, my hands fluttered to his shoulders, my fingers resting on the course cambric shirt covering the wide expanse.

"Lady Gwyneth?" Sister Agnes's worried expression peeked at me from beside his arm.

"I am well."

Dirk's shoulders rose and fell beneath my hands. "Why do you keep repeating that when there is not a shred of truth in it?"

The extra Dirk vanished as the real one crystallized before my eyes. "Why do you care when you have abducted me not to further truth but to satisfy—to satisfy—?" My clouded brain refused to come up with a sufficient reason for his actions this night.

"I saved your life from the Iconoclastic riots, milady. Is that not enough to secure a small sliver of your trust?"

"*Nee.* I insist on knowing what your motives are. Why did you abscond with me?"

A vein in his jaw ticked as his teeth clenched. "Are you steady now?"

I nodded. "Aye."

He stepped away from me, and surprise streaked through me at how suddenly the night's chill swamped me. At that moment, a breeze rushed between us, picking up the hair that had escaped from my knot. I brushed strands from my face. A breeze. A sea breeze.

My fingers froze. The Rhine. I gasped, glanced at Sister Agnes, and then took a step toward Dirk. I scanned our surroundings. Dark woods. Hard-packed forest floor, as if we were on a well-worn path. Ian and the other man, who still held Margried in his arms, skittered their gazes toward each other and refused to meet mine.

As did the man in front of me. I jabbed my finger into the baldric crossing his shirt. "West. You are taking us west. Toward the sea." Another finger jab. "Do you intend to take me by ship back to England? Well, go ahead! I am sure that many an English nobleman would be delighted to see you!"

He caught my palm in a vice-like grip just above the dagger strapped to his baldric. His chest heaved once. His eyes blazed. He seemed to stretch and grow until he towered over me, my height inconsequential. Not enough space existed between us. His dark glare suffocated me. Had he given my parents the same sinister look before he murdered them?

"Aye. We are going west. Toward the sea."

My voice lowered to a whisper. "And to England?"

He spun away. "Cade, Ian, take the women to the river." One hand reached up to rest upon the trunk of a thick tree, as if he were exhausted by our exchange.

Margried's whisper did not penetrate my mind enough to make out her words, but the next moment she had found her footing on the forest floor. Cade motioned her to the right. Sister Agnes followed. Cade sent me a pointed look, and I turned. But not before I glanced once more at the man who now leaned on a tree for support.

That look in his eyes haunted me. At first, I had been so certain it was pure evil, a menacing, murderous glare. But he reacted almost as if it were…pain.

"Come, milady." Ian touched my arm for a brief moment then fell in step behind me. As if I would have gone anywhere but the river. I wanted as far away from Dirk as I could manage.

The trickling brook that greeted us seemed far too peaceful for the circumstances. The events of the night hung on my limbs. The intrusion of *him* into my cell, the sickening realization that the riots had come to Leiden, fear for Margried and Sister Agnes's safety, the terror of being attacked in the hallway…

At the river, I sank to my knees beside Margried and Sister Agnes. I cupped my palms to hold the precious water and looked at my rippling reflection. After I washed my face, I stared at myself in the river. Unable to see much, I wondered how I appeared. I had no cochineal and beeswax with which to paint my lips. No rouge, either. I looked less a lady and more like…what I was. An Englishwoman seeking refuge. Some refuge.

Sliding my narrow sleeves up my arms, I plunged them into the water to ruin my reflection. I was grateful of a sudden for the shift in fashion over the last decade; freeing my hands would have been difficult if I wore the trumpet sleeves popular a few years ago. The delight of feeling clean again distracted me from the headache that threatened to split my skull in two, though it came raging back when I finished and shook my arms of excess water.

A frown took over my face as I watched Sister Agnes scrub at her own

hands. Again, the night's dealings swept over me. Fights. Battles. Death. One glance at Margried revealed that she was gazing across the Rhine. She had cleaned her forehead so that only a thin cut remained visible. As she cradled her injured arm in one hand, her lips moved.

I looked toward where Cade and Ian stood. They were within hearing distance, but their eyes stared to either side, away from us. My shoulders slumped in relief at the modicum of privacy they allowed us, and I reached up and loosed the rest of my hair. My wimple had been lost when the man had grabbed me, and the men were not watching. This was no time to cling to a vestige of modesty.

I dipped my hand into the water again and again and washed the dried blood from the back of my head. The wound had swollen. I measured the bump to be about half the size of my palm. It stung and ached, but I was well.

"Margried, how is your arm?"

The young woman startled and caught her lower lip between her teeth as she met my gaze.

"Margried?" Sister Agnes reached out. With reluctance, Margried relented and pulled back the wide sleeve of her habit.

I gasped, and my hand flew to my mouth. My ears picked up a rustle, and I turned to see one of the men—was it Cade or Ian?—take a step forward, his gaze fastened on Margried's left arm. Dark purple and sallow bruises dotted pale ivory skin. The moonlight danced across fingerprint marks, telltale signs of a struggle.

The wince crossing Sister Agnes's face mirrored Margried's own when lifting the sleeve even higher revealed a bruise circling Margried's elbow, twice the size of the cross on my rosary. I reached for it now.

"I am well. Merely sore."

Sister Agnes ignored Margried's whisper and probed the outlying edges of the discoloration with tender fingers. Only when her fingers ventured further, into the center near the elbow, did Margried groan.

Sister Agnes released her. "Much damage, mayhap, but I can feel no broken bones."

"Praise the Lord for that." Margried's smile transformed her face. She truly was a beauty, with those luminous blue eyes and her black hair hanging free.

"It will heal slowly. You must be careful with it for several days, Margried." Sister Agnes settled the younger woman's sleeve over the bruised elbow with gentle hands. I shot a glance at the two men watching

us. Why could they not stand several more feet away? If they did so, I might be able to talk with the sisters about the next "several days." We needed to develop a plan if we were to escape from Dirk and his men.

And another thing, why did both of his men have to have brown hair? It made discerning between the two of them doubly difficult. *You are weary, Gwyneth.* And asking pointless questions. I had much reason to be weary, however. My thoughts turned to the women beside me. So had they. "Sister Agnes, do you sustain any injuries?"

She scoffed. "Nay, those angry Dutchmen were far too slow for me."

Margried's face sobered in an instant. Tears pooled in her eyes. Knowing that her thoughts had turned to those we had left behind, I rose and shifted closer to her. Putting an arm around her, I leaned my head against hers.

She folded into my embrace, and her hand reached out to Sister Agnes. The older woman's lips tightened as if she restrained the urge to weep, but she clasped Margried's hand, nonetheless.

Sister Agnes reached out her other hand to me. "What a picture the two of you make." I had never heard her voice so low. "With your hair as black as ink, Margried. And yours as white as wheat in the moonlight, Lady Gwyneth."

I smiled. "As poetic as a bard, as always, Sister Agnes."

The nun snorted. "As if I should ever wish to emulate that worldly caste."

I let go of Sister Agnes's hand and pulled away from Margried slightly so as to be able to take off my glasses. Closing my eyes, I rubbed the bridge of my nose, then let my fingertips roam to rub beneath my eyes. I sighed as relief from my headache settled over me like a warm blanket. The thought of a blanket reminded me of how cold August nights could be in the Low Countries.

"Are either of you cold?" I opened my eyes to the blurry forms of the two women.

"Not I." Sister Agnes's tone sounded as if the admittance of such a thing could count as a sin.

"Nor I." Margried's voice held a trace of a smile. Did she think the same of Sister Agnes?

"I believe I shall try to wash my hair."

Sister Agnes's brows rose, but she nodded.

Margried chuckled. "You do have a bit of a rat's nest atop your head, Lady Gwyneth."

I rolled my eyes and tossed a wry grin in her direction. "Would you care to join me?"

"I think I shall put it off another night." She lifted her arm. "Until I am less sore."

"Probably a good idea." Sister Agnes cracked a smile.

"Will you hold my glasses, please, Sister Agnes?"

"Of course."

After I handed the spectacles to her, I knelt at the edge of the river once more and plunged my hands beneath the silvery water glinting in the moonlight. I had not noticed how chilly the water was before. No matter. I could hurry. My fingers tunneled into the knots at the ends of my hair. Gradually, I worked my way up until droplets of water spun from each tendril.

Every few seconds, I glanced at the shadowy forms of Sister Agnes and Margried. In a way, I was responsible for them. It had been I who had alerted Dirk to their presence. It had been I who had insisted we go after them when I had heard that ghastly scream. If I had left them there, would they be alive now? My heart ached as I thought of the many who had not been saved.

Did it even matter? Could I possibly expect Dirk to treat my friends well? My teeth clenched as I yanked on an unruly knot at the nape of my neck, aggravating the bump gained from my fall. What did he intend to do with us? With me?

He had killed my parents almost right in front of me...how long until my blood stained his hands, as well? A shiver raced over me as I remembered that night we had met, the night they had died.

Satisfied that my hair was at least moderately clean, I turned around with my mouth opened in order to release some remark to Sister Agnes and Margried. The words promptly died on my lips as my gaze latched onto a dark figure.

Tall and imposing, he stood towering over me. I had known such a sensation precious few times in my life. Most women—and some men— could not rival my height.

It had to be Dirk, but I refused to squint to make sure. Would he laugh at me if he knew I struggled to see him? I had experienced that before, from my uncle, and had no desire to hear that humiliating sound again.

Determined to put an end to my disadvantage, I scrambled to my feet. One rounded toe of my shoe caught in my skirt, and I pitched forward. Dirk caught me easily, his palms wrapping around my bare wrists. The size of his hands made my forearms resemble thin twigs.

I jerked away from him, and he let me. I hated to admit it to myself, but it was true. There was no way I would have been able to get away if he had not wanted to release me. I could feel his gaze burn into the top of my head, but I would not give him the satisfaction of meeting it.

"Cade, Ian." His deep voice rumbled between us. "Take the sisters back to our camp."

I froze. What was he thinking? Why did he command his men to escort Sister Agnes and Margried? Why did he wish to be alone…? I forced myself to take a deep breath. Why did he wish to be alone with me? The rustling of leaves burst into my ears from several feet away. *Nee.* I could not be left alone with him!

I took one step—just one—before Dirk captured my wrist once more. "I need to speak with you, milady."

Jerking away from him, I slid my sleeves down my wrists. Never again would he touch my bare skin. "I need to be with my friends. They have been through a terrible ordeal this night."

"So have you. They shall be all right for a few moments. Cade and Ian will take good care of them."

"'Tis most improper."

He remained silent at that, and I knew why. Naught had been proper about this night. *Except…*that first man that Dirk had felled at the convent—he had left him senseless, but alive. My brow furrowed. Why had Dirk not killed him?

I smoothed my forehead and assumed a blank expression. "I must stay with them." My voice sounded weak in my own ears. I could not tell him the true reason I needed to get to Sister Agnes. Just for a moment. Just enough time for her to hand me my glasses. For without them, I could barely read the expression on Dirk's face, not the emotions in his eyes, much less the hidden meaning underlying his words. And that put me at a distinct disadvantage.

Dirk

Chapter Four

"Nay." I ran my fingers through my hair and looked into the heavens. *Lord, can You please help me get through to her?* "I mean you no harm, but I need to speak with you alone."

She shuffled her feet as if searching for more secure footing, and I narrowed my eyes. Why did she not look at me? "Milord, please—"

"Dirk."

She stiffened. I released her arm and immediately regretted it. Had her pulse been quickening?

"I do not wish to speak with you."

My neck craned back. I supposed I deserve that. "Be that as it may, I wish to speak with you."

Her shoulders straightened, and I noticed her fingers formed fists at her sides. Was the woman bracing herself? I wanted to expel an exasperated sigh.

Instead, I clawed at my swiftly dwindling composure. "Lady Gwyneth, I mean you no harm."

She flew at me, one fist flattening at her hip while she poked me in the chest with a pointer finger. *"Nee!* You keep saying that, but no matter how many times you repeat it, I cannot believe you!"

"Cannot or will not?" I stayed where I was, neither moving a muscle nor pushing away the finger she insisted on jabbing.

As I stared down at her, the remembrance of that first night washed over me. The forest fell away, and I stood in Barrington Manor. Seeing her for the first time. One glimpse and I had detected something different about her. Haughty air. Cold green eyes. Yet something about the way she at once reached for the cross at her neck and swallowed... As if as taken with me as I was with her.

I knew from that first moment that she thought me below her. And she was right.

Though I had not seen her since, now she was wrong.

"Both." She withdrew and, as if she had read my thoughts, reached for the rosary at her neck. The diamonds sparkled as her fingers played with them. At last, she lifted her head. I almost wished she still stared at the forest floor; the sorrow on her face threatened to undo me.

"Whether or not you trust me, milady, your life is in my hands."

"You think I have not realized that? Have not been plagued by the thought since you first burst into my chamber?"

My lips released a haggard sigh. "What have I done this night except try to keep you alive?"

She crossed her arms over her chest, blocking me out in more ways than one. "It is not what you have done this night."

Pain lanced through my chest. In no other manner could she have as satisfactorily plunged a sword into my gut. Lest my mind journey back once more, I clamped the door shut on the memories of the night we had met and dropped to sit beside the river. I gazed into the flowing water and picked up a leaf. Twirling it between my fingers, I looked up at her. "I refuse to get into an argument with you about that."

"What is there to argue?"

I did not do it, Gwyn. But I could not say that. "There are more pressing matters to discuss."

"What could be more pressing than the murder of my parents?"

A growl emitted from my throat. "Confound it, woman, sit down so I can tell you what I'm trying to say."

She flinched and sank to her knees beside the river.

I winced. "You have naught to fear from me… I will *never* raise my hand to you, no matter how furious I am with you."

There. I saw a spark in her eyes. She hid it again beneath an expression of impassive disbelief, but I had no doubt that what I had seen was the first chip of the wall between us tumbling to the dust below. Progress.

Her mouth pursed, released, and tightened again as she stared straight ahead. Did she hold back words, tears, or both? I may have never seen her cry, but I had certainly seen enough crying women to know that the sight undid me.

Best to say it quickly and get it over with. "The reason I came to you this night was to get you out of Leiden. It is not safe here for a Catholic."

She snorted. "My religion is illegal in England as well."

My brows rose, and my mouth twitched, amused at the unladylike behavior. "But it will not get you killed."

"How did you know I was here?"

"I have my ways."

"Do you?"

"Your uncle did not exhaust himself trying to keep your haven a secret, milady."

Her face paled, but it could have been the moonlight. "He never dreamed you would follow me here."

I threw the leaf into the river. "*He* should have followed you here. The Low Countries are no place for a lady in times such as these. Certainly this should have been his last choice for a haven."

"I did not wish to stow away in some peaceful hamlet. I wanted to get as far away as possible from you."

I pulled in a deep draught of air, wanting to call her uncle ten times the fool. Did Barrington truly think to abandon an innocent woman to the fate that was sure to await her in a place as roiling as the Low Countries? How dare the man let his niece out of his sight if he really believed someone—I—had murdered her parents?

"You have stated your reason for abducting me. I am out of Leiden. Will you now leave me here?" The hope in her voice astounded me. Did she wish for me to abandon her in the middle of the woods?

"I did not abduct you, milady. I rescued you from a convent under siege."

"Het maakt niet uit."

My eyes popped open wide, for that was one of the few Dutch phrases I knew and that she would say it now... I wanted to roar, but I forced my tone to remain evenly pitched. "Of no import? Would you rather I have left you with the Dutch with their torches and death threats?" I regretted the words when I saw the look streaking across her face.

Her eyes widened, and I expected tears to glisten there. Again, she surprised me by maintaining her composure. Yet her features gave voice to her thoughts. My raising my voice at her only fed the fire of fear burning within. A fire I now wanted to put out.

I told myself to close my eyes, to stop this outrageous *compassion* for her from growing. She was a means to an end. Return her, and it might be enough to arouse doubt as to the allegations against me.

Then she reached up; I expected her to play with that cross again. Instead, her fingers probed the back of her head. A head crowned with

glistening golden hair.

"I would rather you leave me now."

My head cocked. "Is your hair wet?"

She gathered a handful and wrung it out. Streams of water ran down her hand. "Are you just now noticing that?" Her grin stretched.

My mouth dried. I blew out a breath. "My plans are not to leave you here by the river, despite how much you seem to prefer that possibility."

"Is it a possibility?"

I glanced askance at her. "Nay." A niggle of suspicion shot through my mind. Why did I get the feeling she was looking right through me? "My plan is to return you to England."

Her face softened for one swift second before hardening into the stubborn expression I had grown accustomed to in only these short few hours. "Why?"

"Why do you think?"

She turned her face away, giving me a view of her profile. Pert little nose. Long lashes. That damp hair that hung like a curtain across her cheek.

"I know not what to think." She reached for the rosary at her neck.

Compassion surged within. She looked so small and frightened. Frightened of me. Alas, that it had come to that. "Lady Gwyneth."

Her gaze swung my way, again with that distant look.

"I will say it one final time. I mean you no harm. I intend to return you to your uncle as soon as I possibly can. Sooner, if the weather cooperates."

A long moment passed as she took a deep breath.

"I do not expect for you to believe me straightaway."

"But you expect me to believe you at some point?"

"Aye, even if it is the minute you again see Barrington Manor."

The wrinkles in her forehead smoothed as if the worry drained from her. Did it? Or was she toying with me, attempting to assume a façade in order to fool me? I shook my head at the thought. Gwyn had the most expressive face, giving away her every thought. She would never be able to hide anything. As if to confirm what I already knew, her features contorted in a look of pain.

"Milady? Does your head pain you?"

The grimace only deepened. "I am well."

I cocked a brow. "Did you have one of the sisters examine your wound?"

"*Nee.*"

"Then let me."

She visibly stiffened. "'Tis not necessary."

"Head wounds are always to be taken seriously, milady." Anxiety pinched in my gut at the thought that her wound might be serious. In the middle of the woods, in the middle of the night, what hope had I of procuring her anything more than my meager knowledge of the healing arts? I shifted to my knees and reached out a hand to that glorious hair.

To my surprise, she jerked. Eyes wide with fright, she leaned away from me. The bodice of her gown heaved up and down once, twice, as she fought for breath. My teeth clenched. My hand dropped. "When we return to camp, have one of the sisters inspect it."

"You dare command me?" She closed her eyes. "'Tis not that."

My eyebrows pulled down. "'Tis not what?"

"Where I cracked my head."

Utterly confused, I waited for her to go on. My sisters had oftentimes done this, spewed words that had no coherent meaning whatsoever. It was best just to wait for the whole story.

"'Tis merely a headache." She lifted her hand to her face and wiped a tear from her eye. Nay, 'twas no tear. She rubbed underneath her eye as if applying balm.

"But a headache not caused by…"

"*Nee.*"

I craned my head back and closed my eyes. *Of course.* "Do you have these headaches often?"

"Quite."

"Are they borne of the spectacles you wear?"

Silence met my query. Then in a voice as soft as the summer wind, "Yes." Her shoulders suddenly straightened, and her chin jutted out. "How deep do you think it is?"

I pulled my gaze away from her eyes, wondering the same about those luminous orbs, and glanced at the river, where she had trained her gaze. "Very." And I wondered whether I spoke of the water or her eyes.

She nodded.

"Why do you ask?"

A shrug formed her only answer. My gaze scanned the ground around us. "Milady, where are your glasses now?"

"Sister Agnes has them."

Aha. Did her reluctance to be left alone with me involve more than just fear of me? For some strange reason, the very possibility sent hope cascading through my soul. "Milady…" I gentled my voice. "Can you see me?"

She scoffed. "Of course I can see you."

But that suspicion that she only looked *through* me rather than *at* me grew as she flicked her gaze to focus somewhere past me. "Now it is my turn not to believe you."

Her eyes shone like emeralds as anger filled them. My chest constricted at the thought that she had probably never seen her face without those glasses in the center of the image. She lived her life unaware of the startling beauty she possessed.

What if six decades earlier Michelangelo had never decided to lay on his back and bequeath splendor to the Sistine Chapel? No one would have ever known the beauty he put there.

Her brows furrowed, and the wrinkles resurrected on her forehead, causing her to resemble a little girl in a pout, lessening the similarity to the Sistine Chapel ceiling. "Believe as you wish. I can see you quite well."

The temptation to hold up two fingers and ask how many she saw proved weaker than my desire to preserve her dignity. Humiliating her after the night she had been through would probably not be the best way to garner her trust. If indeed I could *ever* garner her trust. It surprised me how much I wanted to.

Still, I could not resist a few more probing questions. "What does 'quite well' mean?"

Did I detect a twitch at one side of her mouth? "*Dat gaat je niks aan.*"

I guffawed, tipping back my head to release the laughter in the direction of the heavens. *Lord, if I am going to survive the next few days, I am going to need an ocean-full of Your strength.* "It most certainly is my business, milady. *You* are my business."

"I do not wish to be."

"I do not wish for you to be, either, but my honor demands I cannot leave you here in this volatile land."

The smile I had suspected she would soon sport vanished immediately. "Your honor? I rest little hope in your honor."

I sobered. "I pray you can come to, Lady Gwyneth." After rising from the hard ground, I reached out a hand to her. This time, to my relief, she did not jerk away. The fearful look in her eyes, however, stung me as if she had. Then her fingers lifted. Just before she allowed me to help her stand, I saw them tremble.

Gwyneth

Chapter Five

Warmth assuaged the ice of my hand, chilled by the water and pure fear. Dirk's fingers clasped mine in a strong grip, and he hauled me to my feet. Too fast. The emotions flowing through me like the Rhine stopped cold as I stumbled. I fell forward into a chest as hard as stone, and the breath left my lungs. His hands in mine set me at a safe distance and released me.

My cheeks burned, and I knew they blossomed like the dull red of his hair. How many times would I trip into the man? This made, what, the third time this very night? First in the convent when his hold kept me from falling, and the second time just an hour past, before he had disclosed his intentions. This was going to be a long trip back to England.

"You have told me where you intend to take me, but you have not told me why."

How many times during our conversation had I longed to read the expression in his eyes? Too many to count. Yet never had I wanted more to see him clearly than in this moment. Had revulsion filled his gaze at our contact? Did his eyes darken with anger now at my implied question?

For the first time, it was not fear of him that made me long to know—it was curiosity.

"Do you truly wish to know, milady?"

The jolt of lightning I had felt fizzled, and the uncertainty returned. A murderer. A madman. A miscreant. He was all of these monikers and the many more I had called him in the months since my parents' murders. I must keep reminding myself who he was, *what* he was. "I do."

"You will not like it." Did I detect a trace of a grin in his voice? "Honor."

"You are right," I said. "I do not like it."

"Only because you assume I have none."

"You are right again."

A gentle chuckle flowed out of him, blending with the rushing of the

35

river and the owl's call. "You admit it?"

In spite of myself, I smiled. I drew in my lips, erasing the expression. But he had not missed it. Somehow, I sensed that. "Will you release me to return to the camp now?"

"Of course." He took my hand and tucked it in the crook of his arm.

So he knew. Knew I struggled without my glasses perched on the bridge of my nose. My knees quaked as we walked. I made out the lines of trees and heard the sound of the river water receding as our footsteps drowned out most other sounds. Except for the occasional thrum of a frog or call of a cricket, I heard nothing.

He could be leading me anywhere. The thought brought my panic to the forefront of my mind and caused prickles to sprout on my arms. I refused to tremble, though, lest he feel it in my fingers. I would give him nothing.

But he already had something—knowledge that I always tried desperately hard to keep secret.

My vulnerability weakened me in his eyes, I had no doubt. Made me seem the dependent woman who could not fend for herself. If it served my purposes, mayhap I would allow him to continue to think that for a time.

How I hoped no malicious tree root would claw at my feet and cause me to trip. I paced my steps after Dirk's as best I could. The trust I had to place in him goaded me.

"Milady..."

His voice had softened, the gruffness I had heard when I had annoyed him back at the Rhine all but gone now. We left the word behind, hovering in the air as we stepped forward. He said no more, but I heard the echo of his unspoken *I mean you no harm.*

I resisted the urge to roll my eyes. How many times would he repeat himself?

A laugh grated on my ears. It belonged to one of Dirk's men. Cade or Ian? Cade, I thought. Their voices were more easily discernible than their thatches of brown hair. Why did the man laugh?

"We are here," Dirk whispered. He need not have. I shot a glare in his general direction, broke away from his arm, and took a step toward Margried and Sister Agnes, huddled beneath a tree. I stopped when I noticed Cade stood near them. Why?

"Cade." Dirk's rumble made the man turn.

I resumed walking and shot a glance at the other side of the tree at which the horses stood. I blinked. Horses? Was my mind imagining...? *Nee,* those were true horses. Stomping, snorting horses. Where had *those* come from?

Dirk's voice rumbled behind me. "I see you were successful, Ian."

I came to Sister Agnes and Margried at last. "My glasses?"

Sister Agnes fumbled in her habit for a moment then held out her hand.

I held up the lenses to my eyes. Securing the arms around my ears, I looked at Dirk.

His eyes latched on mine, and I swung my gaze to the horses again. Beautiful creatures, all six of them. One spotted and speckled, each of the others rich hues of brown and black. It had been months since I had ridden. I wanted to climb on the back of the one with wild eyes and multicolored hair. I could be far away in seconds.

Ian's head bobbed from behind the far horse's flank. "They were waiting for me, just like you said. Harnessed and ready."

A grin split Dirk's face.

Horror cascaded through me. Ian surely had not *stolen* those horses, had he? I doubted he could have—the man was tall, but gangly, as if fresh out of boyhood.

Margried leaned toward me. "You are well?"

I nodded. "He wanted to tell me where we are going."

"And where are we going?" Sister Agnes's lips tightened into a thin line.

"England."

Margried's eyes grew round. Sister Agnes's lips flattened further. "England?"

"He intends to return me to my uncle."

Ian walked toward the center of the camp, close to the invisible dividing line betwixt us women and the men. I instinctively stiffened, then relaxed. I felt far less vulnerable with my glasses on my face. The round lenses allowed me visibility of even the smoothest edges of Ian's young, rough-hewn face. Somehow, being able to discern the smile curving his mouth soothed the anxiety pooling in my stomach.

Dirk stepped forward also, to the center of the camp where a pile of supplies lay. My gaze dropped. My brow wrinkled. How had I not noticed that pile before? Had Ian pilfered those things, too?

Only Cade hung back, his arms folded against his chest, his legs crossed at the ankles as he leaned against the trunk of a tree.

"Milady, may I interest you in a blanket?" The grin on Dirk's face made my brow arch.

Of a sudden, icy panic dribbled from my heart into my bloodstream. *Nee, Vader God. Please not that. Not that.* Yet a sliver of fear inched its

way into my insides. Despite my earlier arguments to the contrary, did Dirk have enough honor not to…ruin mine?

As if sensing the direction of my thoughts, his smile slipped. A weary sigh pulled from his broad chest, and he picked up a blanket from the pile. He filled his arms with a few more and walked toward me, an almost disappointed look crossing his features. Features as chiseled as the day I had first met him months ago. Framed by fiery red curls.

"Try to get some sleep." The night air embraced his whisper and stole it away just as quickly as he formed the words.

Before I could think of anything to say, he walked on, leaving me there with two blankets in my arms. He handed Sister Agnes and Margried two each as well then crossed the invisible divider into the men's side of the camp. I turned toward Margried and cocked my head when I found her holding Cade's eyes with her own. She broke the contact with him and, avoiding my gaze, blushed.

"Did he say what he intends to do with us?" Sister Agnes wasted no time in kneeling on the ground and laying out one blanket. She looked at me, curiosity—and apprehension—increasing the wrinkles around her eyes.

I kept my voice low. "You and Margried? Not yet."

She sighed. "Well, I do hope he takes us with you."

I almost dropped my blanket. "Why would you hope that? This is the man… "

Sister Agnes stared up at me from her makeshift pallet. Suspicion caused her eyes to narrow. "Lady Gwyneth?"

I shifted my eyes between the two women. "He is the reason I am here." I watched Margried drop her blanket even as I clutched my own closer.

Sister Agnes's gray eyes widened. "He is the one who…?"

I nodded, waiting for them to react, to rage at him. But that was what *I* would have done.

Margried only knelt and smoothed the wrinkles from her blanket. When she looked up at me, she whispered, "I do not wish to be separated from you, Lady Gwyneth."

I closed my eyes. "Nor I from you." I opened them again. "Neither of you."

Low whispers from the three men drifted over to us on the breeze. Of what did they speak? Did Dirk even now disclose to his friends that I struggled without my glasses? Mortification sparked in my cheeks. I busied my hands by picking at the blanket I had laid on the ground.

"The riots have spread all over the provinces, Lady Gwyneth," Sister

Agnes said. "It is not safe for any Catholic to remain here. Regardless of who he is, we should trust him to see us home."

Home. They wanted to return to our birthplace. My thoughts of myself—and how I did not want to trust Dirk whatsoever—shamed me. "I understand."

"'Tis not that I fear death, mind you."

"I would never suspect that of you."

"Fleeing to England, however, will allow us more freedom."

One corner of my mouth rose. "Catholicism is still illegal in England. You will not be able to practice freely, and you may yet face prejudice."

Sister Agnes chuckled. "Better that than what we would face here."

"Mayhap this is God's plan." Margried lay down on her pallet and pulled her other blanket over her habit.

My eyes widened. The events of the last few months rolled through my mind. My parents' murders. Running from the only home I had ever known. Arriving in a strange land, albeit the land of my mother's birth. Living in the convent—a life so different from the one I had led all my eighteen years. "Why do you say that?"

Margried gazed up at the starry sky. "Mayhap we can serve Him better in England, a land where peace reigns."

"Peace in theory, because Protestantism is preferred." But the words I muttered did not hold my thoughts. Margried's talk of God's plan… She meant it could be His plan to usher these two, His faithful daughters, out of a land of violence and danger and into safety. I could live with that.

What I could not live with was the thought that it had been God's plan to steal my mother and father, my home, all I had ever known, from me.

I took off my glasses and lay down.

"Are you comfortable?" The words wafted over from the men's side.

I ceased stretching out my long legs onto my blanket. It had been Cade's voice. This did not surprise me. Of the three men, he seemed the most compassionate. Neither Margried nor Sister Agnes answered, and I did not know what to say. A tense silence settled over us as I squinted into the darkness.

"Aye."

I wondered how much of a chance Margried's small voice had in being heard by the men.

Drawing in a deep breath, I attempted to settle in to sleep. I did not intend to rest. I expected to lie awake, mulling over all that the last few hours had brought.

"Lady Gwyneth?" Margried whispered.

"Margried?"

I turned over an inch, trying to avoid putting the side of my head with the swollen knot on the ground. I had forgotten about Dirk's request to have one of the sisters examine the wound. Oh, well. It would keep.

"Does your head pain you?"

Did she refer to the wound I had just been thinking of or the nightly headaches that plagued me? "Very little. And your arm?"

"Very little."

The corners of my mouth turned up at that. Very little, indeed. That bruise on her arm was monstrous. I snuggled back into the blanket, amazed at how I wanted to laugh at our evading the truth about our pain.

I moaned and tried to roll over, but the hand on my shoulder refused to relent. I scrubbed at my eyes with one hand then peeked out below my palm.

A small gasp escaped me as I scrambled back. Dirk withdrew his hand, but remained crouched beside me. "Time to wake, milady."

"'Tis not even morning yet."

"Be that as it may, we must be going."

I squinted up into the predawn glow. For a moment, my breath caught at the colors the night had awakened. I reached for my glasses, and the colors became even clearer. Coral, sapphire, and diamond hues streaked the sky as if painted there by the finger of God.

Dirk moved away, and my gaze followed him. He bent at the knees beside Margried. I flung back my blankets. "Let me."

He nodded and returned to the men's side of the camp.

"Margried." I touched her shoulder, and her eyes opened, as if she had not truly been sleeping. Had she? "Did you rest well?"

One corner of her mouth quirked. Amused, was she?

That only amused me. "Nevertheless, we must go."

"Go where?"

I shot a glance at Dirk, whose back was to me as he stood beside the speckled horse. "I know not."

"I will wake Sister Agnes." While she did, I bundled my blankets in my arms. The blankets Dirk had given me. I touched the cross at my throat.

The diamonds' edges pressed against the tender pads of my fingertips. *Hope sounds like this.* Diamonds I had plenty. Hope I had little.

Especially here, now, at the mercy of a murderer.

Cade walked over, his hands busy with a satchel from which he pulled a few rocks. "Something with which to break the fast, maidens." He waggled his eyebrows.

Mine rose. I saw Margried blush. Did he really mean…? The rock he dropped in my hand crumbled slightly. "What is this?"

Sister Agnes smiled. "A biscuit, Lady Gwyneth."

Margried giggled at the look I gave Sister Agnes. "Here, allow me to fold your blankets while you eat it."

"Fold my…" I eyed the itchy pile of warmth in my hands. Had I not folded them already? She took the bundle from my arms, and I watched her deft fingers snap the folds and line up the creases. Where had she learned that?

Not in the nobleman's castle in which I grew up. Nobleman's castle, indeed. Barrington Manor was no mere castle. It was a powerful, privileged estate, etched into the land on which my family had resided for generations. Well, part of my family. Though my grandfather had been an Englishman, my grandmother had been a Spanish widow when Grandfather married her.

Barrington Manor was inhabited by a mish-mash of heritages. My mother was a Dutch woman who had immigrated to England in pursuit of religious freedom. My father, half English and half Spanish, had fallen in love with her and her quiet ways. My family tree had been as poorly formed as the biscuit I turned over in my hands.

"Best take a bite before it takes a bite out of you."

I glared at Dirk but he only turned away again, a smirk on his face.

I chewed the rock-biscuit as best I could and took the crisply folded blankets from Margried with a grateful expression. I had realized I was spoiled when I arrived at the convent and had been forced to become accustomed to the Spartan cell I called my own…but no one had ever told me my blankets were untidy.

Now I wondered what the other nuns had thought of me. *Nee.* I refused to think of the women who had not survived the raid.

"Milady, come hither." Dirk did not even turn from the horse by which he stood when he called me. Not the pretty horse, either.

Lifting my chin, I obeyed. Reluctantly.

"This mount will be yours. She is gentle and will not give you much distress, I pray. You do know how to ride?" Finally, his gaze met mine. A cool expression filled his brown eyes.

"Where did you procure these horses?"

He sighed. "So you do not know how to sit a horse?"

"Did you steal them?"

He looked up as if beseeching heaven for strength. I refused to let my smile reveal itself.

"Nay, I did not steal them." His gaze flicked, and I turned to see Ian standing beside another horse. Talking to Sister Agnes, whose mouth pinched in a thin line as if she sought to absorb every word he said.

"Did Ian steal them?"

"Ian."

Ian looked our way.

"Did you steal these horses?"

Ian's brows rose. Surprise lit my insides. I knew what that look meant. *Nee.*

"Nay, of course not." He looked at me, but I swiveled back to face Dirk.

"Where did they come from?"

"I have my ways."

'Twas the same thing he had said last night about knowing I had come to the Low Countries. I sighed. "I will listen now."

Dirk scoffed. "I doubt that."

"I do not lie."

His gaze narrowed, and I gulped, suddenly wishing I could rescind the words that a moment ago I had meant with all of my being. Now, pinned beneath his dark-as-dirt eyes, the sudden urge to squirm fought to overcome my willpower. I straightened my spine and refused to flinch as his penetrating look probed deep. For a moment, it seemed as if he saw my soul. Was he pleased with what he found there?

I shook the thoughts from my mind.

He nodded. "Neither do I, milady."

A thousand refutations wrestled with my tongue, fighting for release. I held them back and pressed my lips together. But they swirled within my mind even so.

"Do you know how to ride?"

"Aye."

One corner of his mouth tipped. "Ride well?"

I gave him a curt nod.

"Astride?"

My shoulders straightened. "I know how, but why—?"

"I planned for fewer riders and saddles, and sidesaddles proved hard to come by."

With a pop, my lips parted. "Are you saying—?"

"Since you know how to ride so well, you shall direct him yourself." He flashed me that devilish grin and strode away. Toward the spotted and speckled horse, I noticed. So that one belonged to him.

Margried consented to Cade helping her mount; Sister Agnes allowed Ian to assist her. How did my nun friend know how to ride? I sighed.

Dirk reappeared, but I did not meet his eyes. Refused to, actually. What had happened in that one moment in which his eyes held mine? I knew not. And I did not care to think about it.

I let out a shriek when he clasped my waist in his firm hands. "What are you—?"

He plopped me onto the bare back of the mare and stared up at me. I swallowed hard. Fought my uncertainty. *Let me go, please.*

He released me as if he had heard my unspoken thought. I busied myself with smoothing wrinkles from my skirt. The night spent on the ground had wrinkled my gown, but that mattered little. I looked at the sisters. I must worry about them, above all else. Margried caught my eye and gave me an encouraging smile. I tried to return it but feared I managed little more than a grimace.

Which was probably the only facial expression I would have for the rest of the day, if Dirk truly intended to take us all the way to the *Kanaal*.

Dirk

Chapter Six

We pushed our horses hard for several hours, and I could not help but wonder how the women would take to the long ride. If we rode for a day, we would be sure to make Scheveningen Port by nightfall. Perfect. Yet if there was one thing I was learning about having Gwyn in company, it was that things often evolved far from perfectly.

I could not shake loose the image of her tangled in blankets, hair awry, fast asleep. I had not wanted to wake her and disturb her rest, but something in her face had tugged at me, made me think it would be a mercy to release her from the bondage of her dreams. Ludicrous thought, no doubt induced by my obligation to get her up and moving so we could depart.

I glanced back. They all seemed to be holding their own. A smile stretched across Gwyn's face, even. For some reason that surprised me. I did not truly believe her when she had attested to knowledge of horse riding, but here lay proof. She guided her mare to lope beside Margried's with such skill that Margried's mount followed the lead of Gwyn's horse.

The innocent look on her face turned my thoughts to the moment after I had awakened her, when she brought her fist to her face and opened her eyes. For one second, those green irises had been as lucid as the sea at first watch. Free. Without fear. The sight had given me hope that she would look at me with that expression thereafter. Then distrust had shadowed her expression. Time to stop those foolish thoughts.

I held up a hand. My fingers pulled on the reins, and the speckled mare came to a stop. I turned. Everyone else had halted their horses. Except Gwyn. As she rode up beside me, her mare's great sides heaved. Flecks of sweat sparkled on the hem of Gwyn's gown.

"Milady?"

"I came to tell you I am not running away."

My brows rose as I watched her dismount without aid and straighten her skirts as she made for the woods. I shook my head at Cade and Ian as Margried and Agnes followed her.

Ian's brows furrowed. "Should we have let them go all at once like that?"

Cade snorted. "Did we have much choice?"

The women soon returned; the sun shone down on us as we chewed biscuits even worse than those with which we had broken our fast. If one believed Copernicus, then we—this whole world—revolved around the sun. Yet little mattered more to me in this moment than the five people who surrounded me. My gaze latched on Gwyn as she took off her glasses and pinched her nose with two fingers.

Agnes turned her head to look over her shoulder more than once, and the motion trained my eyes on her. "Does something trouble you, Sister Agnes?"

She shifted, but her wimple did not. What did they put in those things that made them so stiff? "Nay. But I thank ye for asking."

Gwyn's gaze pinned on the woman. Did she bristle at the nun speaking so politely to me? I could hardly blame her for that. Few would hesitate to take the same stance. Had I not failed my father, caused my mother too many tears, even harmed my sisters' chances for good matches? My endless list of foolish deeds stretched before me like the road we traveled today and even farther…

"You look behind you."

Agnes finally turned to look at me. "Merely missing what lies behind."

"Lady Gwyneth has no doubt told you my plan is to escort all of you to the shore."

Margried bit her lip then released it. "And across the *Kanaal*?"

"If you wish."

Agnes's brows almost disappeared inside her wimple. "If we wish?"

Cade cleared his throat. "We will not force you to board the ship—"

"Ship?" Gwyn's voice hit a high note.

I shot a glare in Cade's direction. The man had the decency to redden.

"What sort of ship?" But the suspicious tone warned me Gwyn had already deciphered the next part of my plan.

I saw no reason to delay the inevitable. "A Sea Beggar ship." The sort named for a disparaging remark that had been made to Margaret of Parma, the Spanish king's regent, about the Protestant rebels in the Low Countries captaining and sailing them. *Do not trouble yourself over those beggars,* or some such. Trouble, indeed. They were yet another facet—the

Beeldenstorm was another—of the religious rebellion Gwyn loathed.

The remains of the biscuit Gwyn had been working on flew from her fingers and in my direction. She rose from her seated position and put her face close to mine. "A *Watergeuzen? Un mendigo de mar? Un barco protestante? Un barco hereje?*"

"*Sí.*"

I could tell I had caught her off guard. I was still trying to figure her out, but it seemed that she fell to speaking Dutch when upset or saddened… and Spanish when angry or impassioned. And the last thing she had expected was for me to respond in kind.

The pause did not last long, however. She resumed her tirade, storming around the patch of forest we had claimed as our own for the hour. Her skirt whirled around her in a wrinkled circle as she swung this way and that. She even occasionally punched the air with her fist.

When I managed to draw my eyes away from the display, I stored in my mind the looks on Sister Agnes's and Margried's faces. Patient. Withdrawn. Even, in Sister Agnes's case, a mite bored.

So Gwyn acted like this often, then?

She stopped of a sudden and stared. With her hands planted at her hips and eyes blazing, she could have passed for any enraged señorita on the streets of Spain. Except for the fact that her hair shone golden in the sun and every Spanish lady I had ever met had hair as dark as sin.

Not this one, though. The hair of an angel befit her. She was devout. Devoted to her God. Religious from every edge. She huffed and reached for the cross at her neck. Her Spanish transformed into English. "What are you thinking? Are you mad? They will never let me on the ship if they know I am Catholic and therefore all that they are fighting against."

Next she swung an arm in the nuns' direction. "They will certainly never allow the sisters on the ship."

I did not answer.

She tilted her head back and examined the summer sky. "Do you plan to sneak onboard under cover of night? What will you do when we are discovered?" She stepped closer to me. "And we will be discovered. For you cannot possibly expect me to—"

"Aye."

She blinked. "*Nee. Nee,* I refuse. And the sisters will certainly refuse."

Realization dawned on Agnes's face. "How can you ask us to lie?"

Shock lit Margried's eyes. "Even to procure our safety, the cost of sin is not worth it."

"I am not asking you to lie."

Gwyn sighed. "What then? To hide ourselves the entire voyage?"

"I will lie for you. You need only play along."

An inexplicable emotion eased across her features. The fight seemed to drain from her even as her eyes refused to weaken their hold on mine. I knew the precise words she was remembering.

I do not lie, she had said.

Neither do I.

Yet here I was, willing to break my word to her and my word to my God that I would never again decry the truth. Not only willing, but *intending* to do so. Planning.

I swallowed, shaken to the core. Yet my resolve did not crumble, even when Gwyn dropped her gaze to the ground and reached for the rosary at her neck once more. Not even then.

"There is no difference. You are asking us to lie by omission. Passage—even our lives—is not worth it."

It was worth it to me. I had to. *I must.* To protect her. To see her to safety. Away from the Low Countries and those who would not hesitate to harm her. 'Twas the only way to restore my reputation. I would deal with the consequences later.

"I know what I said, milady, but this is necessary."

She slashed her hand between us. *"Nee,* it is not. How can you say that? To say that is to go against your honor."

A small smile cracked my lips. "I thought I possessed no honor?"

She cupped her elbows with her palms and turned away, looking at her friends, the sisters. She looked back at me. "You must have some. You saved us last night."

I nodded. "And an honor it was."

"Why throw that away now?" Her hands dropped.

I stood, not liking that she had turned from speaking of her own refusal to sin to how my honor demanded my refusal. This was not about me. That was the point. "I am not throwing it away, but salvaging it."

She did not understand, not yet. Mayhap she never would. But I must do this anyway. Return her to safety. It was the only way I could ever hope to clear my name with those who had witnessed my reputation torn to shreds.

The only way to restore my name was to ruin it again. With an abduction. With a lie. I could have laughed at the irony if Gwyneth's face had not held such sorrow. Margried's face also drew down with mourning.

A breeze stole over the treetops, making the branches, lush with leaves, sway.

Rising to her feet, Sister Agnes looked at me, eyes grim. If she had appeared disappointed, she could not have socked me in the gut more effectively. For she did not look disappointed. She looked unsurprised. As if she expected no better from the likes of me.

"Come. Let us ride."

Gwyn shook her head, not in defiance of my order, but in disappointment. Why did that cause my heart to leap within my chest as it had when I carried her in my arms last night? The same strange hope surged within me now. Instead of the delight of holding her, it was the thrill of knowing she had thought better of me. Instead of the stark fear of knowing she bled into my shirt, it was the ache that stemmed from knowing I had let her down.

I touched her arm. "Lady Gwyneth."

Her chin lifted. "Milord."

"Dirk."

She heaved a sigh.

"There is no other way, milady."

"There you are wrong. There is always another way."

I cocked one brow. "Oh? Is it possible, then, that there is another way that your parents perished?"

Shock and sorrow collided on her face in a blend I hoped never to see again. The agony that streaked through me seemed a small echo to what caused her face to crumple. No tears gathered in her eyes, but her sharp wrench away from my hand spoke enough of her grief.

I raked my hand through my hair and motioned Cade and Ian to the horses. As I watched Margried rush to embrace Gwyn, my foolishness slapped me anew. Choice words burned through my mind and I fought to keep them behind the barrier of my clenched teeth. What had possessed me to dredge up the woman's grief, yet fresh, and throw it in her face? How dare I?

I turned away, trusting one of the other men to see her safely on her horse. Did I dare delegate her life, as well? Did I dare leave, thereby ending the suffering she went through for having to endure the likes of me? Dare entrust Cade and Ian with the charge of seeing the woman—*women*, I corrected myself—across the Channel?

Nay.

If I must, I would pass the duty on to them. But while I yet lived, the obligation was mine and mine alone. I dared not bargain with her life, even with the two men I trusted most.

As we rode away, I had to force myself not to push the horse beneath me to a faster and faster pace. But I was done with running. By God's grace, He had saved me. Transformed this hardened sinner into a man bent on doing things God's way.

Why, then, am I willing to lie?

Because I held more regard for Gwyn's life than my own. More desire to see her returned to the family she had left than to ever be reunited with mine. The thought brought pain, but the truth of it seared into me. This was no longer entirely about regaining my honor. This was about getting Gwyn to safety.

If that required throwing away what little honor I had left, so be it.

Later, as the sun started its descent, I slowed our pace. When the great shining orb dropped below the horizon and the darkness hemmed us in, I kept us going. The sea was not far now. The salt-laden breeze wafted over us every now and then. "Keep close." I tossed the two words over my shoulder, turned back around, and swiveled to look back once more. "Is everyone well?" Addressed to all, the words were meant for one.

And from the look on her face, she knew it. Gwyn's anxious expression shone from beneath her round lenses, even in the fading light. Nods reassured me, but hers look haunted. I longed to draw us to a halt, but at the docks, Captain Tudder waited. He had given me his word he would not cast off until midnight. Although I did not doubt we would make the deadline, that afforded us precious little dawdling time.

Lord, will You please help her trust me?

Gwyneth

Chapter Seven

I blinked up at the stars, pinpoints of vivid brightness. We had been riding an entire day, and now it was well into night. Would we ever stop? Weary, that was what I was. If my body had not been screaming it for several hours, the pointless questions swimming in my mind now confirmed it. My head bobbed, and I shook myself. I could not fall asleep. If I did, a tumble to the ground from the back of this tall horse would surely follow.

"Lady Gwyneth." The rumble of Dirk's voice sent uncertainty crashing through me. From my place directly behind him, I coaxed my horse to ride alongside his beautiful speckled one. Brown eyes bore into mine. "When I ask you this, take me seriously."

I cocked one brow, but the effect might have been lost in the darkness.

"Do you need to ride with me?"

Swallowing my refusal, I eyed his horse's head. Strong and sure, the great beast led the way with conviction. The speckled coat dazzled the eyes, but as much as I wanted to ride the magnificent creature… *"Nee."*

"Are you certain?"

"I am well."

His mouth tipped upward. "I sincerely doubt that."

I trained my gaze straight ahead. "How much farther?"

He scanned the path. Or whatever trail we followed. Truth be told, I could discern no visible path whatsoever and had given up on trying to find one long ago.

"A mile, mayhap two. The smell of the sea is already in the air."

I turned to look at him again. "I cannot—" My entire body went rigid as my eyes followed the thin shaft that passed in front of my face. The arrow had sailed past not an inch from my nose.

Dirk leapt into action, freeing his dagger from his baldric and

50

moving his horse in front of mine in one swift move. "Thieves!" His yell reverberated through the forest and through my ribcage, sending fear spiraling into my stomach.

From the left, the same direction from whence the arrow had come, figures on horseback spewed from the massive mouth of the forest. Shouts and calls rose in a din that my ears could not decipher. I watched Dirk engage with a man twice his size in girth. Their daggers clashed with a clank.

My horse stepped backward, and I laid a gentling hand on her withers. "Easy, girl."

A scream cried for my attention. I shot my gaze to my left, where a terrifying sight met my eyes. "Sister Agnes!" I hurried my horse forward, into the fray. Desperate prayers poured from my heart, and I let out a cry as I watched the sister struggle. A burly man had her wimple in his hand.

"*Katholiek!*" He shouted insults as he tried to pull her from her horse.

Margried and I got there at the same time. "*Nee!*" I put my horse between his and Sister Agnes's.

The man's eyes glowed nearly yellow and widened with surprise at the Dutch word spilling from my mouth. "*U bent Nederlands.*" *You are Dutch.*

His huge hand reached for my arm, and I realized my mistake. *Too close. Gwyn, you got too close.* I cinched my heels to my horse's flank, but he was faster than my commands to my mount. Sausage fingers clamped around my upper arm, and he tugged.

"*U bent Katholiek!*"

I pulled against him, but his strength surpassed mine. As I started to slide, I sent a frantic glance over my shoulder. Margried and Sister Agnes contended with another enemy now, turned away from me and oblivious to my plight. I had naught on me. Not a blade, nothing. So I did the only thing I could do. I pulled back my other arm and punched the villain full in the face.

Shock washed over his features as he released me to grasp his nose. Revulsion pooled in my stomach. Had I broken it?

"Gwyn!"

My eyes shot to my right, and I saw Dirk turn his horse toward me. Angry obscenities brought my focus back to the man in front of me. Why had I not fled when I had the chance? I dug my ankles into my horse's side, but it was too late. The man had a grip on me again, this time on my waist.

I lashed out, caterwauling and clawing at his hand. But he would not let go. Blood dribbled from one of his nostrils. The swelling had already

begun. One jerk, he let go, and I was falling. My horse neighed in panic. What if the mare ran? Would I be trampled? Had that been the evil man's intent all along, to pull me from the horse's back and watch me be crushed to death?

An arm as strong as a tree trunk scooped beneath my ribcage. *Whoosh.* My lungs relinquished every ounce of air, and I caught a glimpse of black ground, green-treed horizon, and star-blanketed sky as I was lifted, lifted, lifted.

A choked sound escaped me as my body collided with another. I swiveled my neck and saw Dirk's anxious expression meet mine. How had he gotten his horse to me so fast?

Screams sounded all around us. We passed two crumpled bodies lying on the ground, motionless. My eyes latched on Cade's form, battling with a brute while shielding Margried behind him.

I pulled in shallow breaths, desperately trying to restore my air supply, but Dirk's arm clamped around my stomach, making the task difficult.

The beautiful horse came to a sudden stop. Unprepared, my body lurched forward then back, held by Dirk's relentless grip. My breathing stuttered in my ears, and I saw black spots. "Dirk." His name came out as a wheeze.

He adjusted me in front of him, and I understood why he had held me with his vice-like arm. I had not truly been on the horse until now, rather merely draped across his side, secured by naught but his arm. The black spots receded as I sucked air, replaced by a paralyzing terror as the sounds around me died.

Dirk's hold loosened, but he wrapped his other arm around me. I touched my face, amazed my glasses had stayed on during our mad dash.

"Cade!" Dirk's chest rumbled beneath my back, and the blush began as I realized how close we were. I was in his lap. "Ian!"

A strangled cry came from somewhere behind us. I jerked to look past Dirk's shoulder, but Ian was fine. He stood over a still figure. I gulped. The owner of that cry was gone.

"Sister Agnes!" My scream sounded labored.

"I am well. We are both well."

I swiveled to see both Sister Agnes and Margried standing by a horse without a rider. "*Dank je, Vader God.*"

"Aye. Thank You, Lord."

I looked up at Dirk, and warmth filled me at the expression on his face. His brown eyes liquefied with relief, awe, and something else I could not quite identify. "Thank you for saving me."

He nodded. One red lock swayed onto his forehead. He said nothing, yet said so much with his eyes. I did not want to translate, so I slid from his embrace, from his horse, ignoring the trembling in my limbs. I rushed to my friends. Wrapping my arms first around Margried, then Sister Agnes, I silently thanked God again for sparing us.

"Are you sure you are well?" we asked over and over again.

When we stepped away from one another, I noticed Cade and Ian both tied an extra horse to their own mount's reins. I went to stand at Dirk's side where he positioned the supplies more sturdily on his speckled horse's back. "How many were there?"

A heavy sigh released from his chest. "Five."

"Is there a village nearby? Do we need to take them to a magistrate?"

His eyes met mine. "Nay, Gwyn."

I put a hand to my throat and worried my rosary between my fingers, realizing what he meant.

"Are you well, milady?"

"Yes."

He stared down at me, as if searching my eyes lest the answer I had spoken did not match the answer in my gaze. I swayed on my feet. "I do not lie, remember?"

He nodded. "Do you need to ride with me?"

I glanced away, expecting to find Margried and Sister Agnes standing in a huddle where I had left them. Instead, Ian helped Sister Agnes onto her horse.

And Cade helped Margried onto his. *His.* So Cade had posed to Margried the same question to which Dirk now awaited an answer. And she had answered in the affirmative.

I brought my gaze to his. Opened my mouth. All my life I had thought I was independent. Grandfather had called me headstrong. He had told me I reminded him of the feisty Spanish señora he had married. I was everything like my grandmother, nothing like my timid mother.

Or was I?

Standing there before Dirk, the realization that I was completely at his disposal washed over me like an ocean tide. I relied upon him. I had done so for the last day ever since he and the mob had descended upon my saintly sanctuary.

I gasped in a quick breath and managed a nod in his direction while studying the toe of my shoes. Gently but firmly, he planted his hands at

my waist and lifted. I gasped again, this time at the tenderness of my skin that his touch evoked. He saw my wince. "Did I hurt you?"

I remained silent.

The darkness of the forest did not conceal the bodies lying mere feet from us. I closed my eyes to the sight. He set me on his horse sidesaddle and stared up at me until I was forced to look into his eyes. His fingers tunneled through his thick red curls. "I am sorry for causing you pain."

Sticky silence stretched between us as my eyes widened at his words. A thousand retorts played at the corners of my mind. I could reply to that one soft statement in so many ways. Hang out his stained record to slap him in the face. After all, I knew of some of the nefarious deeds he had committed in his younger days.

And of the one deed he had committed so recently that had ruined my life forever.

Why should I not? He was at fault for stealing those two precious people from me. He was the reason I had fled to the Low Countries and remained sequestered here for months, clinging to a safety I had never possessed.

My breathing became rapid as I stared down into his brown eyes. I memorized the curve of his jaw, the straight line of his nose, the dark brows that contrasted with his fiery hair. There was naught of the wolf in him in that moment.

That was why I could not say even one word of derision, though I knew he deserved worse than words. I was strangled, choked by the knowledge that no matter what he had done to those I loved, he had saved me. Did I not owe him an ounce of gratitude for that?

The thought rankled. Nonetheless, I held my tongue and acknowledged that now, in this one moment, nothing could be appropriate save silence. The time for accusations would come. The time for justice would come. Later.

He nodded and swung up behind me. Once again, I sat in his lap. I felt him turn, look back at the others. He exchanged a few words with Cade and Ian, and we moved. The horse's muscles bunched beneath me as if fearful of another attack.

"Will others find us, do you think?" I whispered the words, aware of the fear crackling in them, unwilling for any of the others to hear.

Gwyneth, you fool. Had I truly just revealed weakness, wariness, to the one man I could not trust? Had I truly just been *vulnerable* with him? *Willingly?*

"Nay, they seemed like a lone bunch. A mile and we will be at the sea."

"Where you will lie." Coldness I did not feel crept into my voice. But I could not have this… *camaraderie* between us.

What was wrong with me? I was beyond weary, that was what was wrong with me. I was tired and torn and feeling the effects of being dragged across a province or two in one day.

"Aye, for your safety." His words sounded as stone hard as mine.

Good. Despite his words, I knew what his tone meant. Distance. A reminder of just who could not rely on whom here, now. The last thing I needed was to be confused about who I could trust.

That could prove deadly. After all, it had once before. With this same man.

Dirk

Chapter Eight

I had hurt her. I knew I had. The acknowledgement seared through my soul as prayers spun from my silent lips. Escapades from years gone past could not compare to this. I had been unruly then. Rebellious. I had possessed a wild streak that had caused annoyance, grievances, and untold amounts of frustration.

But never had I harmed a woman.

Now my savage grip on Gwyn had most likely given her a stomach bruised black and blue.

Where had those thieves come from, anyway? How dare they intrude on the last leg of our journey and attack the women, defenseless as they were? I allowed the anger to churn through me although I knew it was useless. It only compounded the guilt and shame I would feel later. So as we rode to the sea in silence I did my best to ignore the woman in front of me and prayed for forgiveness.

Calm finally settled over me about the time sleep seized Gwyn. I strove to coax my steed to be steady, even as we continued on our way. Gwyn had gotten precious little rest in the day she had been in my care and had suffered much.

My fingers itched to smooth back the blond hair laying all a-tangle on my chest and probe for the goose egg she surely had. Had she asked one of the sisters to look at it yet?

Should I relieve her of her glasses? Would she sleep better free of them? But where would I put them?

My arms hemmed her in, holding the reins on either side of her and preventing her from falling off. She shifted against me. I swallowed hard.

A soft moan escaped her lips, sounding like the mewling of a lost kitten. My stomach twisted. Did she have nightmares? Should I wake her?

I glanced behind me, as if I could find the answers I sought there.

Margried's bright blue eyes stared straight ahead, though weariness pulled at them. Sister Agnes seated her horse as if she were accustomed to doing so for half the day. Cade quirked a brow at me, and Ian rubbed his jaw, but I turned forward again before either could say a word.

A shudder passed through Gwyn and into me. She whimpered once more. I pushed the reins into one hand and touched her shoulder. "Milady." The whisper did nothing to rouse her.

Mayhap I should let her sleep, even this way. Troubled rest was better than no rest at all, was it not?

I settled for stroking her shoulder, hoping it would calm her. Even so, just when I thought she had been comforted, she let out a moan. Abandoning my prayers for forgiveness, I beseeched God for her peace.

The still of the night cloaked us as we journeyed toward the coast. My gaze scanned the trees to the right and left of us. I willed the quiet to continue. The last thing we needed was another party of renegade thieves to appear. This close to the port, I doubted it, but one never knew. Desperate times…

When the smell of salt grew stronger and I could hear muffled voices ahead, I glanced back again. Agnes's stiff wimple had been tilted in the scuffle, and Margried had not had hers since I had first picked her up. I glanced down at Gwyn, huddled against my chest. Her hair shone silver in the scarce midnight moonlight.

The nuns still looked like nuns, however, in their long habits. Mayhap, though, the austere black would pass for the current fashion of dark gowns. Gwyn, on the other hand, looked like a loose woman with her hair unbound. The thought caused me to cringe. The voyage across the Channel would last until morning, and I had no desire for the women to worry about aught but sleeping whilst the hours passed.

A crisp breeze caressed my face, and I knew the time had come. The hand that had been rubbing her shoulder cupped her upper arm. I leant down and whispered her name in her ear. She did not stir. "Time to awaken, milady."

'Twas what I had said to her long hours ago. My heart started to pound, and I wondered if, after all, that would be what awakened her.

Would she grace me with the same trusting look she had given me when I had shaken her awake before? The thought dried my mouth.

She pulled in a shuddering breath. Her eyelids fluttered. They shuttered closed again. The trees in front of us thinned. I had not much time. "Milady. We approach the coast."

Her lips parted as her eyes opened. She was the most beautiful sight I had ever seen as she looked at me wonderingly, sleepily.

Just as before, the bars around her soul clamped down again, forming a barrier between us that I knew was impossible to scale.

"We are close?" She blinked, and I knew the moment she realized how she had leaned into my chest to gain her rest this night. She pulled away and stiffened her spine as with a wooden rod.

"Aye, milady. Not far now."

"Not far until what?"

"Not far until we somehow make you look presentable."

Shock sent her jaw swinging open. Hurt lit in her eyes, and I regretted my choice of words. Then the lioness appeared. "How dare you say such a thing when it is you who have insisted on dragging me through the province the entire night?"

"I did not mean to imply—" Truly, I had not. A more beguiling sight had never before been seen than her, hair mussed, cheek wrinkled from where it had lain against my cloak.

"Of course you did not. You only meant to inform me I look a fright."

"Milady—"

"I daresay you are probably correct." She smoothed a dainty hand across the top of her head, patting down the stray hairs. When her palm passed, they sprang alive again. I could not help it. Truly. The smile burst onto my face before I could stop it.

Her eyes blazed. "And just how do you intend to allow us to freshen up?"

"I…" My voice trailed off as I gazed into the distance. My smile had not died. What was the use in trying to hide it now? She had already seen it. "I thought women knew how to do such things themselves."

To my amazement, she hesitated. Unsure, I assumed, whether or not to take that as a compliment or take me to task for giving her so little to work with in conditions such as these.

"You are right." Her green eyes sparked. "We do."

I pulled up my horse, hearing Cade and Ian and Sister Agnes do the same behind me. I dismounted and lifted Gwyn to the ground, noting her grimace. She linked arms with Margried, and the three women stepped into the slight shelter provided by the sparse curtain of trees. Cade, Ian, and I stood shoulder to shoulder, our backs turned to where the women had disappeared to. A great deal of rustling went on behind us.

I squinted, searching for distraction. The thin trees before us gave no hint of what lay in front of them, but the faint sounds of a dock in the

middle of the night assailed my ears. The creaking of hulls of ships. The groan of ropes tugging against the tide. Snores of a watchman or two. Trills of laughter, no doubt the result of a bottle of spirits. And lots of rustling.

"Cade, after the women return, you will take the horses to the tavern one by one and tie them up. Make as if to go in the door each time so that if anyone is watching, you appear a customer." A swift nod told me he would do what I had asked. As if I had needed the assurance. I had known Cade since boyhood. Trusted him like a brother. He and I had grown into rebellion together and for years had sought only our own amusement. But we had always been there for each other.

"Ian, you will stay with me and the women." I had only known Ian for a little more than a year, but still some friendships rooted deep.

No other sounds passed between us men as my ears tuned in to the frantic rustling coming from our rear. The call of a bird pierced the night air. The rustling abruptly stopped.

Never had a fiercer urge to turn consumed me, but I resisted the temptation. "Milady?"

"We are well, but not quite ready." Gwyn's voice, with a hint of laughter in it.

Out of the corner of my eye, I saw Cade's mouth twitch.

"You may turn around now." Agnes's gruff voice brought my neck around fast.

Ian disguised a chuckle with a snort, but Cade released a full-out guffaw.

Gwyn, casting a half-hearted glare in Cade's direction, dipped into a curtsey before us. Her blue gown remained wrinkled and well worn, but her hair had been successfully pinned with a piece of fabric the women had pilfered from…somewhere. As she rose from her curtsey, I found myself wondering where they had gained the material to construct that flimsy head covering. It did not look as if it would last long. But long enough, if we were lucky.

My gaze tore from Gwyn's when a titter spilled from Margried's lips. Though her beauty was of a darker sort than Gwyn's, the woman possessed a pretty face. As I looked between Cade and Ian now, that fact worried me. I could not allow either of my best friends to fall in love with a nun, after all.

Though she looked anything but a nun now. Somehow, the three women had removed every vestige that made Agnes's and Margried's habits *habits*. The dark fabric remained dark, but the billowing sleeves had been trimmed and thinned until now the gowns resembled slightly

too large dresses with old-fashioned trumpet sleeves.

Perfect. Captain Tudder would not spare the three women a glance until we were safely aboard his ship. He was oblivious to women. More so than most married men I had met. Once aboard his vessel, the women would be safe, I had no doubt.

Well, I had not *much* doubt. My gaze halted on Gwyn once more. "You have done well." The wrinkles of sleep had been erased from her cheek. I mourned the loss. They had made her look young, innocent.

Her gaze rammed into mine, and my ears refused to decipher the rumbling of voices beside me. I knew that both Cade and Ian spoke…but who was I fooling? She still looked young and innocent.

The thought slammed through my chest with the strength of a sword. I had to protect her. I had to get her out of here. Out of this land of violent men who might share a heritage with her but who would kill her in cold blood if they knew she was Catholic. Such was the nature of this time of religious upheaval in which we lived. Catholicism was not even legal anymore in the land to which we were returning—not since Elizabeth had become queen decades ago.

"I thank you." She broke eye contact, releasing me.

"We must be off."

All three of the women turned toward the horses.

"Nay. We will not be riding."

Gwyn's brows knit together. "What do you mean we will not be riding?"

Sister Agnes cocked her head and looked from the horses to me. "Why not?"

Cade strode toward the horses. "'Tis nearly time to board the ship."

Gwyn's gaze flicked past me to the thin trees that hid the port from view as if she searched for the ship of which Cade spoke. "The Sea Beggar ship." Her whispered words freed from her eyes the mirth of moments ago.

Ian shook his head. "We cannot take the horses with us."

I met the eyes of each woman in turn. "You will remain silent while I discuss the details of our passage with the captain."

Sister Agnes and Margried nodded at once. Gwyn looked hesitant. Of course.

I took a step forward. Her green eyes lifted to mine. A storm brewed within them. I was not surprised. I knew what she thought of the untruth I planned on telling. But she could not see this was best—if not right, still best. And the only way to secure her safety.

"Will you remain silent, Lady Gwyneth?"

She adjusted the glasses perched on her pert nose. Emerald eyes looked into mine, grave and serious. "Aye."

The argument hovering on my tongue hitched in my throat. The whisper tore from me before I could halt it. "Why?"

"I must trust you. You have earned that much from me." She studied the hem of her gown.

Well. I looked to Cade and nodded. He gathered the reins of my horse in his hands.

"I will miss that one."

My brows rose as I looked down into Gwyn's face. "You will?"

"Aye. Such a pretty horse."

A laugh bubbled in my throat. "Ian, let us get these women safely to the docks before they miss any more of the horses."

Gwyneth

Chapter Nine

The putrid smell of unwashed bodies sank into my nose as Ian and Dirk herded us through Scheveningen Port. The stench overwhelmed, but more shocking to my sensibilities was the crowd. The moon hung high in the sky. It was the dead of night. So why all these people milling around?

A hand thrust toward my face, and I flinched away from the string of shining pearls dangling from it. Words in Dutch proclaiming an exorbitant price hawked in my ears. Dirk spun the hand away and pulled me forward with a gentle tug on my arm.

I could not justify what the man had wanted *in gold* for the necklace. "What he demanded is ridiculous!"

Dirk spared me a quick glance over his shoulder. "You look a lady who can pay." *Oh.* But what explained the expression on his face? His features pulled taut as if he worried. Did he?

Words in various languages assaulted my ears. It was as if our presence brought the market to life. Or *my* presence.

Margried and Sister Agnes and I had labored over making Sister Agnes's wimple look less nun-like and more befitting of a lady. Mayhap we had done our job too well. My presence enticed every overpriced offer of goods and baubles for a mile.

Then, blessed relief. The smell of the sea grew stronger. The sounds deepened in my ears. No longer did merchants shout over one another to make known the worth of their wares. Instead, the groaning of giant ships in the port filled my senses. With it, the lapping of waves against the hulls. And the slapping of the wind, warning of a storm, in my face.

I glanced back at my friends to see how they fared. Margried tried to tuck back tendrils of black hair that had pulled free from the knot at the base of her neck. Sister Agnes's eyes flitted everywhere, as if trying to take it all in. How long had it been since the sister had been near the port?

Probably not since she had crossed over from England.

Of a sudden, the irony of the situation struck me. Three Catholics, English-born, in the Dutch convent closest to the coast—and therefore convenient for Margried and I, at least, who had run away from home. We all now relied on three men—themselves sons of England—to see them to their homeland once more. Different circumstances had pulled us here.

Sister Agnes's, the least complicated. She had been devout from birth, I imagined. Had longed to devote herself to God for all of her days since childhood, she had told me. I believed her. Though her tongue was as sharp as the wind whistling in my ears, she made the perfect nun. Consistent. Reliable. Faithful. Even her very name meant pure, holy. Since England's convents had died at King Henry VIII's hand, she had gone to the Low Countries.

Margried had escaped from a tyrannizing father who had wished her to marry a man twice her age. She always shuddered when she spoke of the man, but she had never told me his name. I grimaced at the mere thought of facing such a thing. In the Low Countries, she sought refuge.

And then there was me.

Of all of our stories of how we had come to be at the convent at Leiden, mine seemed the most succinct in my mind. After my parents had been murdered, I had fled to the land of my mother's birth for sanctuary. The end.

Until, of course, a certain man had changed all that.

I looked down at the wood upon which we now walked. Dirk had released my arm a while ago, after we had departed the clamor of the market. He glanced back now as if to study the condition of the people who followed him. Avoiding his eyes, I threw my gaze behind me. Sister Agnes looked stoic. Margried's eyes stretched wide in wonderment. Curious, I turned back and stared past Dirk.

A gasp tore from me. The epitome of heresy settled in the choppy sea before my eyes. A Sea Beggar ship. A symbol of the fight to make Protestantism the faith of the Low Countries.

The king of España fought against the cause. Why the Spanish king ruled the Low Countries was strange in itself—control had passed to the Hapsburgs, Philip's family, through an inheritance not a century before. Years ago, King Philip II had made Margaret of Parma regent over the Low Countries, but the fervor for that blaspheming traitor, Luther, and the religion he had stirred up gained traction in the provinces.

Thus, the rebellious Sea Beggar ships.

'Tis but a few hours, Gwyn. You can endure a few hours. Aye, of course I could. I stared up at the vessel we approached.

"Milady." Dirk's eyes, when I looked at him, were serious. The thin line of his mouth betrayed his tension. "Stay behind me."

And stay silent. I remember. I heard his unspoken reminder as if he had whispered it into the increasing wind. I heard it better than I would have if he had, mayhap. The wind kicked up the sails of the great vessel. They snapped above and before us. Uncertainty churned in my stomach, and we had not even boarded yet. Would we board soon? Or would we wait upon the docks whilst Dirk and the captain talked?

I tried to imagine the captain. Dirk had not described him; I would have been surprised if he had. Men did not think of such things. Though they usually supplied a name, and this Dirk had not done that either.

A picture of a swarthy fellow with greasy hair and grimy neck entered my mind. Mayhap with tobacco-blackened teeth. Big and burly, his voice would no doubt match his form. Gruff. Grating. Ingratiating, intent on the sack of gold Dirk would pay when he deposited us on the other side of the *Kanaal.*

The man that walked up to Dirk met none of my expectations. Clean-shaven and on the whole *clean,* his eyes skimmed over us. Not a glimmer of greed in his gaze. "Dirk."

"Tudder."

That was all the greeting the men exchanged before walking off, seeking seclusion. I glanced back at Ian, who crossed his arms and widened his stance, taking his duty of guard seriously. Not a touch of surprise streaked his features.

Which confirmed my shocked suspicions. That *Tudder* fellow was the captain of the Sea Beggar ship. And with well-groomed hair and a lean, fit frame, he was everything I had *not* expected. His teeth even gleamed white.

And Dirk was about to lie to him.

For me.

Dirk

Chapter Ten

"I thought you were bringing me one woman."

I ran my fingers through my hair. "We acquired the others along the way." *Technically the truth.* Tudder need not know that we acquired the others along the *hallway.*

"How's that?" Tudder's eyes narrowed.

I knew what he was thinking and I did not like it. "Rescued them."

One of his black brows rose.

"Will you grant us passage for them?"

"Don't see as I have much choice."

I grunted, not liking where this was going. A tentative deal was all that stretched between us, as tenuous as the lines holding the sails snapping above us seemed to be. Tossed by the ferocious wind, the lines battled to hold the sails to the ship. But I knew those ropes to be far stronger than they appeared. I stared into Tudder's hazel eyes. "I will increase the amount of gold."

"Of course you will."

One corner of my mouth twitched, detecting the humor in his tone. But just as quickly and easily as the expression of mirth had found lodging on my face, I let it slide once more. I named a price in ducats, and after a moment, Tudder shook his head.

"Tudder."

He only smiled. "Our friendship is too old to haggle over."

"Exactly. I insist."

He changed the subject. "You almost missed your chance. My men have already readied her for casting off."

Accepting he would not allow me to pay him, I glanced at the silent ship. My eyes made out the form of one man who looked to be on watch duty. The silent deck confirmed his words. The sails still snapped above me in the wind. They had been let out to catch the breeze that now reigned in the air as a bluster.

A lesser captain would have seized the opportunity to sail in that strong sea air. This was the Tudder I remembered. "I thank you for waiting."

"I thought you said you would have one more man." Tudder's voice posed a statement, not a question. I looked back at the group of women I had left with Ian only a few feet away. As I watched, I saw Cade slither into the group as silent as a sunrise. So that was who Tudder had been talking about.

Cade's eyes were hard as flint, as if...I searched his face and the realization hit me. *As if disapproving.* Disapproving? I clenched my hands. Of what did Cade have to disapprove in me?

I flicked my gaze to Gwyn. She watched me, her expression blank.

"One thing more."

I turned to face Tudder again and waited, not liking the sound of the man's tone.

"Who are the women?" He chuckled. "The older one has an air about her."

I blinked. Water churned not six feet away from us against the stomach of the ship. I wished for naught else but to board her. Me and the others with me. One second ticked off as I hesitated. Two.

If I lied, Tudder would see through it. But the man trusted me and, if he suspected I deceived him, would trust I had my reasons. Which only made me want to tell the truth, I realized.

Lord, what to say? That did it. Invoking the name of the Lord provided the impetus I needed to make the infuriatingly *right* choice.

I chanced another glance at Gwyn and looked into her eyes. If I lied for her, she would be safe. If I lied for her, she would understand. To my surprise, both mattered equally to me.

"Two of them are nuns, Tudder."

He blinked, his eyes widening for a moment as he digested those five brief monosyllabic words. "Nuns?"

"Aye." *Might as well tell all.* "We rescued them, along with the lady, from a convent in Leiden."

His chin lowered as he regarded me from under raised brows. Whether he was more surprised by the truth—or the fact that I had disclosed it—I could not tell. "You are aware of the type of ship I sail, Dirk?"

"Aye, I am. As are they." I tunneled my fingers through my hair again. A Sea Beggar ship. A symbol of the rebellion. The Sea Beggars had looted many a Spanish galleon, swindling from the hold gold and riches brought over from the New World, bound for Spain. They were a source of great pride for their fellow Dutchmen, a blast of courage. Probably provided enough gumption to incite the raids blazing across the Low Countries even now. The raid that had brought three women into my hands.

A smile cracked Tudder's lips. "I do not know what you are about, my good man."

"I am about procuring passage across the Channel."

"You say they know this is a Sea Beggar ship."

"Aye."

"And they are still willing to sail upon her? Are they converted?"

I chose to answer his second question. "Nay."

Tudder's smile disappeared, but his eyes still revealed good humor. "I will indulge you this once, my friend."

Gratitude sluiced through my veins, and I resisted the desire to shoot a victorious glance at Gwyn and the others. She would be happy to know I had neither buried the truth nor stooped to deceit. Would that elevate my honor in her eyes?

A chuckle pulled from my chest as I clasped hands with Tudder, sealing our deal.

If it did, I would not mind. Mayhap then I would *have* honor in her eyes.

As he released my hand, Tudder gave me a meaningful glance, and I steeled my expression, wondering how much my chuckle had divulged. I glanced up at the sky. Dark clouds now hid the moon. A pang of unease stole through my gut.

Tudder motioned behind me. "Retrieve your companions and board. We set sail forthwith."

I nodded. "I thank you."

A small grin split the man's cheeks. "A most interesting predicament you have found yourself in."

I shook my head. *You have no idea.* "Indeed."

Gwyneth

Chapter Eleven

I met his gaze each time he looked my way, but my ears, trained to be sensitive to sounds of every shape and style, could discern little of what the men were saying. I did, however, hear the captain ask about "the women."

He is lying. I wanted to scream the words. I wanted to find paint and splatter the incriminating letters across the hull of the heretic's ship. I wanted to write them in the sky with bolts of lightning.

But I did none of that. I could say those three small words, if I so chose. I could march up to the captain and whisper them in his ear, watch his face go numb as he realized what I was revealing. I could hold my chin high, square my shoulders, and look him full in the face, no matter how improper the pose might be.

Watch him squirm as he realized I was a true child of God and he was not. Nor would ever be. Then the question needled into my brain. *Why?*

Why did I care whether Dirk lied to the captain or whether the captain knew the truth? Did I not consider myself above him? Above both of them?

As a daughter of the Church, a devout member of Christ's devoted, why did I concern myself with these men, both of whom I knew to be liars, cheats, and blasphemers, if not in character then by association?

I looked at Margried. Her drawn forehead attested to her concern. She was no more comfortable with this deception than I…yet she made no sound. Sister Agnes's lips pressed into a narrow line, and her eyes sparked with displeasure. So we all agreed that we disapproved of the goings-on between Dirk and Captain Tudder. And we each silently agreed, also, to do naught about it.

My stomach cramped in knots as I listened to the lapping of the water against the hull of the ship. The vessel loomed with the sinister scowl of something that plotted against me. Mayhap it did. Did it intend to sink in the middle of the Channel and convey me to the bottom? Did it plan on dragging me down and drowning me itself?

I shook my head to clear it of the pointless questions. The voices stopped for one long pause, and I sent a plea toward heaven. *Thy will be done.*

A whoosh of salty sea breeze flung part of my makeshift wimple into my face, and I flinched, wondering if the finger of God had concealed my eyes for that brief moment. I pulled the fabric from my glasses.

Dirk strode toward me. Was it my imagination or had some of the lines from his face smoothed out? He seemed less concerned, less weary, less burdened somehow, as if the talk with the captain had eased a load from his shoulders. Had it?

His gaze swept all of us and landed on me. "It is time to board." He looked to Cade. "Did all go well with the horses?"

Cade gave a slight nod. "Aye."

I frowned at the tension threading the air between the two men. My gaze settled on Dirk. "Are you ever going to tell us exactly where those horses came from?"

Dirk grinned. "A friend of mine."

I raised a brow and crossed my arms. "Is that so?"

"He is a farmer."

"Does this farmer-friend have a name?"

His grin dissipated. "You ask too much, milady. It is time to board the ship and rest."

I? Ask too much? After all he had asked of me? To trust him? To flee with him? Not to flee from him? To ride on his horse with him? To consider him a man of honor?

I shook my head. "I doubt any of us will have much rest this night."

Margried touched my arm. "Why is that, Lady Gwyneth?"

Dirk's eyebrows collided as if to echo her question.

I looked up at the sky. Even pointed a finger in that direction. "A storm approaches."

Dirk

Chapter Twelve

Blast, but the woman was right.

A glance at the sea only confirmed it, and a scan of the sky revealed ever darkening clouds. Was it safe to take the women onto the water in the soon-to-burst storm? I looked to my left, back at the port that should have slept but never did. Heard the faint sound of coarse voices hawking wares. Remembered the angry light in the eyes of the mob and the thieves who had come after Gwyn.

There was no safety here. This was no haven. Even onboard ship during a storm, we stood a better chance. "We board."

Gwyn held back, so Cade lifted Margried into the swing first. Margried's breath caught, and he said something soft that made her smile and made me frown.

With her safely over the side, hauled over the railing by Ian, who had already climbed up the ladder for that express purpose, Cade turned. Our eyes met. Cade usually wore a wide grin, always laughter resided in his eyes. Mayhap that was why the look he gave me now made my gut churn.

I could count on one hand the number of times Cade and I had been angry with each other. Though we always reconciled in the end, not being able to guess the reason for his anger now bothered me.

Gwyn waved Agnes ahead of her, and my eyes narrowed. I stepped closer to her, lest it be her plan to bolt from the docks in hopes that we would merely leave her behind. As if I would even entertain the idea.

She noticed my nearness and looked up at me. The lenses of her glasses sported a small fracture. From the fight in the woods? I almost winced at the memory of clutching her against my horse's side, knowing my brutal grip would bruise her. I almost let slip a question of how she fared. But that would be indelicate. She would only glare. Not like I had never had that happen before.

"You seem pensive again."

I looked down at her. "Again?"

She shifted her weight from one foot to the other. "You seemed almost calm merely a moment ago."

"Almost?"

"Well, no need to be surly about it."

"Lady Gwyneth?" Cade held out his hand to Gwyn. I took a step to intercept, forcing him back. And helped Gwyn onto the swing myself.

I put one foot in the lowest ladder rung. An elbow nearly jostled me from my position, but I held fast and put two or three rungs beneath me, between Cade and me.

"What was that all about?" Gwyn, sitting comfortably, was at eye-level.

"What?"

"That shove he just gave you." She looked bemused, which, in an odd way, I was grateful for. Her insistence to have the other women go ahead of her had put two thoughts into my mind: she planned to run or she feared being aboard the ship. And I disliked the idea of her fearing being aboard the ship.

Her laughing eyes snuffed out the idea. Then I realized *that* might mean she had intended to flee. I did not like that any better. "That was not a shove."

"Oh? What was it?"

Mercifully, the crewmen hoisted her higher at that moment. I almost lingered on the ladder, tempted to do so to escape her tongue for but a moment, when I remembered there were now three women on the deck. And only one Ian. And, though I trusted Tudder, I did not know Tudder's crew.

I scaled the rest of the rungs with ease and landed on the deck with a *thump.* A matching *thump* and Cade stood right beside me. *Well.* So he had been right behind me. He had most likely heard every word between Gwyn and me.

The deck vibrated as members of the crew scrambled around us, readying to make way. Captain Tudder strode forward, his boots smacking the wide planks of the deck, his stride accustomed to the motion. "Timothy here will show you to your quarters."

A lithe young fellow with a straggling beard that looked as if he had grown it to prove he was old enough stepped into view. He gave me a quick nod and stepped to the hatch. One long leg disappeared.

"Wait." Gwyn's voice brought me to her side in an instant. She had paled.

Timothy stopped.

I angled my body to give us a modicum of privacy. "What is it, milady?"

"I—" She looked down. "I do not wish to go below just yet."

"But you said yourself that a storm approaches."

"I am aware. I still wish to remain above for a while."

I sighed, unsure why she seemed insistent. Turning, I looked at the other women. "If you wish to go below, you may." My gaze swept Ian and Cade.

When both Margried and Sister Agnes moved to follow Timothy down the hatch, Cade and Ian trailed them. I put a hand to Gwyn's elbow and steered her toward the railing, as out of the way of the scurrying crew as I could manage. Shouts from Captain Tudder boomed in the air, yet I did not miss the boom that had not stemmed from his lips. Thunder.

She was right. Of course, I had known it as soon as she had said it and I looked at the sky. But some part of me had still wished that the storm would pass, that the Lord would breathe and blow it away, down the Channel toward France or Spain. Portugal, even. Anywhere but here, in the strip of sea between England and the Low Countries.

I turned to see her staring out over the water. She raised a hand to her forehead, and her fingers fluttered over her skin. A headache again.

"If you go below, I will see you have a cool cloth for your head."

Her gaze skittered from me back to the sea. "I want to stay above a while."

I lowered my voice. "Why?"

"It will be the last time I see this land."

I rocked back on my heels. "You cannot be sure of that." The words wavered on the air, encased in the salty sea breeze, and plunged into the water below, inadequate.

"Be that as it may, I would like to watch."

I swallowed the smile that would only enrage her. Watch? Even in moonlight little of the shore would be visible. But with the clouds blocking even such meager light…

"You do not have to stay." Her faint whisper pulled me in until I was aware of naught but her. Fair hair. Pert nose. Luminous eyes. Slender fingers playing with that diamond-studded rosary.

"I will stay."

"Why?"

Because there was nowhere else I would rather be. But I could not say that. "To keep you safe."

Her eyes left the shoreline and turned to encompass the crew, running and rushing back and forth, preparing to head out to sea. "I daresay I am safe enough now. They do not notice me."

No man was fool enough not to notice her. I gripped the railing and watched my knuckles whiten. And so we sailed. Pushing off from the port, away from the docks, ropes loosening, hull creaking. The water grew fiercer, churning like butter beneath a milkmaid's able hands. Still, minutes passed, and Gwyn said naught about going below.

"Milady, you need your rest."

She swiped at her forehead again as if she could wipe away the ache. My hand itched to take those glasses from her and try to loosen them so as to alleviate her suffering. But if I did, she would be unable to find her way, and I might have to carry her below. Which, on second thought, was not entirely an unpleasant prospect.

She took a deep breath. "How long will we be aboard this ship?"

"Naught but a few hours."

"I can rest later."

"When we reach the shore? It will be morning then, and we must travel."

She moved closer to the rail, leaning over it, peering into the depths below. "Will you steal more horses?"

I scowled. "I did not steal—"

The grin she gave me almost sent me to my knees. Same with the giggle that spilled from her lips. She looked back down into the water. "My uncle calls this *el Canal de la Mancha,* the Channel of the World."

"My mother calls it 'The Unfortunate Voyage.'"

She turned to me, leaning one hip against the rail. "Why is that?"

"She is not a sailor." A plop of rain hit my cheek, and I brushed it away.

"The water does not agree with her?"

"She does not agree with the water."

She rewarded me with another giggle. "What is your mother like?"

I pondered the woman before me a moment more before my thoughts turned to the one I had not seen in nearly a year. "She has red hair."

"So that is where yours comes from."

"Aye. But her gray eyes went to my sister, Susan. She is also tall, unlike Susan. She snorts when she laughs."

Gwyn's jaw fell open before she closed it behind her hand. "She sounds like a wonderful woman."

"She is. If not for any of the reasons I mentioned, then for enduring what I have put her through."

I saw her stiffen. Watched her eyes turn solemn. With my gaze, I followed the path of her fingers from the rail to the diamonds at her neck. She was remembering, remembering the rake I had been, remembering that I would always be her enemy. *Lord, this is not fair.*

"What was your mother like?" I did not expect her to respond. I expected her to turn away or ask to go below, anything to escape my company. But I had to try. Had to ask just one question, to try to preserve what had coursed between us a moment ago. I had enjoyed it, the easy banter, the sharing... I wanted it back. She took a quick step to the side, away from me, and I waited for her to walk away.

What I did not expect was the wobble of her chin. The deep breath she tucked into her lungs.

Idiot. How could I have asked her that? She believed I had murdered the woman I now asked about. *Foul lout unworthy to walk the earth...*

"She was nothing like your mother."

I froze, my muscles seizing into position as I stood cemented to the swaying deck. A raindrop slid down my cheek, but I did nothing to halt its progress. The sound of the waves smacking the side of the hull seemed louder as she allowed the silence to stretch between us.

"She was a small mouse, tiny and timid. And afraid. Afraid of... everything. 'Twas where she came from, I suppose. The hard life she had here before marrying my father and moving to England."

I dared not say one word. I especially did not dare lay my hand atop hers on the rail as I desired to do.

"Grandfather used to wonder how I was so unlike my parents. Said fire is not the healthy product of timidity and laughter."

Fire. Her Grandfather had been right about that. She was a lioness. But now, staring out over the expanse of the vastness of this strip of choppy sea, so narrow yet seeming so wide, Gwyn more resembled a wounded kitten.

"Milady, I—"

"*Nee.*"

The flash in her eyes only kindled the surge of protectiveness that had sparked with her words a moment ago. The lioness had returned, but she was still wounded. *I did not kill them.* "You must listen—"

"I do not wish to hear it, Dirk. I cannot—"

A great crack of lightning lit the horizon and, knowing what was coming, I rushed to Gwyn's side. If only I had not.

She tore away from me and closer to the rail just as the thunder shook the ship. She cried out, but not from fear. From pain. She put her hands

to her ears as if the unearthly sound were too much for her.

The rain began in earnest, drenching everything, causing a pounding in my ears, and obscuring my vision. I knew what was coming. *Help me, Lord!*

I reached for her as the roll of the waves against the opposite side of the vessel crashed into the hull. She cowered away from me, lost her balance, tripped. I let myself slide, trusting the violent, crazed, dangerous pitch of the waves and the leaning of the ship and even the slant of the rain to propel me to the rail and to Gwyn.

Another strike of lightning split the sky and illuminated the fear on her face. Her hand cast for mine and mine for hers. The tips of our fingers touched. A scream tore from her mouth as she slammed into the rail and away from my hand.

"Nay!" Panic clawed the cry from my throat as I stumbled, powerless to get to her. She plunged over the side and into the roiling sea.

Gwyneth

Chapter Thirteen

I heard myself fall. Air rushing by my ears. In my ears. Through my ears. I heard Dirk's cry. His anguished voice. His terror. And that was what set my heart to racing even faster than my body now racing toward the water.

Then I heard nothing but wetness. My gown and kirtle immediately tugged me under, heavy and made heavier by the water. I had never thought of water as heavy before. But now as it pushed me, pressed in on me, and plunged me deeper, ever deeper, I thought I would never again think of it as anything else. *So heavy.*

And cold. I had not felt the night's chill while standing upon the deck with Dirk. Was it his presence, his smile that had warmed me or merely distracted me from the cool of the evening air? *So cold.*

A massive pull of the water and I was sinking downward, on the verge of forgetting what *light* and *warmth* and *upward* even meant.

Would I never again know anything but this crushing weight, debilitating cold, downward pull?

Nee. I refused to surrender to my demise yet. Not just yet. I flung out my arms, moving my torso, feeling the pull of the bruises left over from the thieves' attack and Dirk's saving me from that fall. As I kicked my legs, I remembered him doing it again at the rail of the ship. Trying to save me. Rescue me. It had been a valiant effort. Why had he failed?

I forgot. Just as I had feared I would, I forgot. What light was. What warmth was. What *up* was. What was I doing? Was this my time? *Moeder. Papa.* Would I go to them?

A heave of panic sent my lungs reaching for air. But there was no air. I had forgotten that, too, and water filled my mouth. Salty water that made me want to retch. But there was nowhere to retch. Nowhere at all. Except blackness and darkness and coldness and down. Always down.

My chest hurt. I let go, or rather I felt myself forced to let go. My limbs

refused to obey. My lungs filled with the water I had tried unsuccessfully to spew from my mouth.

So heavy.

So cold.

Hopelessness—that was all I knew. All that banged on the walls of my heart...but I would not give in. I thrashed in the water, feeling nothing but heavy and cold and dark and everlasting *down*.

Would I see heaven now? Would I be reunited with my parents? God seemed far away...where was He? I had faithfully served Him...where was He now?

How could there be anything but this awful darkness?

Heavy...cold...

Down. Darkness.

Dirk

Chapter Fourteen

I could have sworn the world stood still. The rain stopped. The thunder silenced. The lightning seized mid-arc. But it did not. I knew it did not. I told myself it did not.

And that gave me precious little time.

Men shouted and called and screamed as the deck continued to pitch in the wild waves. The same wild waves that held Gwyn in their watery depths. Pulling her down. Drowning her.

Nay! I would not let that happen. I ran to the center of the deck and started unwinding rope from the mainmast, pushing myself to move quickly. Tudder appeared beside me. "Get below, man!"

"Gwyn fell!"

Even in the raging wind and rain, I could see the blood drain from his face. "Fell?"

"Fell!"

He swiveled away and started spinning shouts into the air above the noise like only a sea captain could do. More men joined me at my task and within a moment the rope was unwound and being tied about my waist.

How many heartbeats had it been? How many moments had passed? An eternity. Panic clawed at my chest, twisted my stomach, and turned my body to lead. Shouts and unintelligible words assaulted my ears from every side. Another crack of lightning split the sky. The storm thundered. *Too close.*

Lord, please, help me save her. Prayers pitched from my throat in silence as sounds surged upon me from every side. Finally, bound to the ship by the rope, I ran to the rail. I hoped and prayed the rope would allow me enough room. If not, I had a dagger in my boot. I would not hesitate to cut my lifeline to get to her.

But then I would not be able to bring her up. Nonsense. I could find

the rope again. I had to. I must. I would.

I dove. The icy water sent prickles over my body, and I prayed for protection for Gwyn against the mind-numbing cold. She had been immersed in it far longer than I.

Kicking my legs, I swam lower, knowing she was lower, deeper, farther down. Throwing my arms out in every direction while still trying to swim, I caught nothing. A cry of panic lodged in my throat, but I did not release it. Merely rationed the air I had stored in my chest.

I could see nothing at all. The darkness of the sea combined with the darkness of the night combined with the darkness of the storm spelled doom. My fear for Gwyn compounded. She could not see perfectly in blinding light…what must she be feeling here, now, somewhere near, unable to see anything?

I gained momentum, allowing the icy water to swing me ever downward. *Lord, please, help me save her.*

She was here. She had to be here. Somewhere near. My whole body jerked as my hand brushed what seemed to be fabric. Gwyn? I dove after it. And the rope tugged.

Without hesitation, I pulled at my boot. Freed the knife. Said a prayer. Cut the rope.

I dove lower, hoping against hope, praying harder than I'd ever prayed before.

Then I felt it. Sweet Hallelujah, I felt it. More fabric. What had to be the hem of her blue gown. *Gwyn!* All of my senses screamed for air, for relief. What must she be experiencing, having been without air far longer than I?

I clutched a handful and tugged. I could almost hear the ripping, severing me from her. *Nay!* Instead of tugging, I followed the fabric swimming below. It was still being pulled down by the weight of the gown and the weight of the water. Without letting go, I grabbed my knife again.

Miracle! I touched her arm, trailed my hand to her shoulder, felt her hair floating all around my fingers.

The truth struck me. She did not move. In all the time I had held her gown, held her arm, held her shoulder…she had not moved.

Please, God, please, God, I'll do anything. Anything! Save her!

Tucking her body into mine, pressing her hard against my chest, I started kicking with all I was worth, but as I had known it would be, it was not enough. So I slashed at her dress, as cautious as I could be not to cut her.

I released swathes of fabric to billow beneath us and disappear. Layer

after layer gone. My kicking seemed to finally make a difference and we began to rise. My lungs screamed at me for air, and I thought my head and chest would burst from the pressure, the need to breathe.

Where was the surface? Where was the surface? The surface…

I blinked, clenched my teeth, anything to keep unconsciousness from pulling me down. Her hand shifted against my stomach. *Anything, God!*

That small shift of her hand compelled me to kick faster, harder. I saw the wobbly, rippling light that meant the surface. We broke free.

I opened my mouth and pulled in air mixed with rain mixed with fear. For she had not moved again. Drawing in shallow breaths, I kept her head above water and tried not to panic at her listlessness. *Lord, save her!*

"Gwyn!" Where I got the breath to shout, I did not know. I looked around. A new fear assailed me. I could not see the ship.

"Dirk!"

I swam to see behind me. The ship! My eyes strained against the pelting rain to take in a form standing on the rail. Had that been Cade's voice?

The figure dove into the water. I pulled against the current, dragging Gwyn against me, to meet him. I saw the rope around him snap taut before he reached me. I kicked faster, trying to get to him, knowing he could not get to me. To my surprise, I watched him unwind the rope from his waist. What was the fool doing? If he released that rope, we could all be lost!

Then I realized his intent. The truth spiraled through me, circling my stomach, my heart, my soul, as I readied myself for what he meant to do. He threw the rope in my direction.

I reached up a hand.

And missed.

Kicking furiously, I lunged toward where the rope—that coiled salvation—had disappeared beneath the frothing waves. My fingers brushed it, clasped, caught.

The cold slowed my motions, but I managed to wrap the rope around Gwyn and me. Lashing her to my chest, securing her there. Safe. Nay, not safe. Not yet. Not until she awakened and I knew she was well. Not until her lips bloomed rosy red once more and scowled at me. Rain slanted against my vision and plastered my hair to my head and her hair to my shirt. I clung to her with one arm, willing any warmth I had left in my body to seep into hers.

"Ready!" The wind and a boom of thunder swallowed my shout. "Pull us up!"

I grunted as the rope lurched. It tightened around us, and I prayed I had left enough room for us to breathe. The members of the crew hauled us through the water. The rope pulled taut, lifted from the waves, and we streamed closer to the ship, closer. My legs gave up the fight, and I swam with one arm, trying to get us back as fast as possible.

"We are almost there, Gwyn. You are going to be well." I whispered the words into her hair, willing her to hear me. Awaken. Groan. Anything. *Anything, Lord.*

A moan released from her lips. I closed my eyes, praising God beneath my breath. "You are going to have my head for destroying your gown, are you not? Well, you must awaken first." I watched, but her eyelashes did not flutter. I clasped her closer as we came almost to the hull.

I shot a glance behind me. Where was the man who had given us his rope? I hoped he had not given us his life as well.

Out of the water we rose. Out of the cold. Out of the waves. I clutched the rope with one hand and held Gwyn to me with the other. She never moved. Not once. But I could feel her breathing. Her back rose and fell slightly against my hand. Her breath fanned my neck. "We are almost there, Gwyn."

I could hear the men now. "Heave! Pull! They be close!"

Arms and hands, a multitude of them, on my shoulders and back, pulled us up and over the rail. I was propped on my feet, but my legs gave way, and I crashed to my knees on the deck before anyone could stop me. I cradled Gwyn in my arms, taking the brunt of the fall myself.

Then they were there. Shouting and pulling. The members of the crew. Ian. Untying her from me.

For one precious moment, I would not let her go.

I released her, watched Ian pick her up in his arms, disappear down the hatch. And I stumbled to my feet. Captain Tudder leaned close, a strike of lightning flashing and revealing rain streaming down his face. "Get below!"

"There is still a man out there!"

Thump.

"Steady, men! Pull!"

What had that been? I swayed like a drunk to the side and clutched the railing. Peering beneath me, I could see Cade looking up at me, hands wrapped around the rope. So it *had* been him out there, in the sea.

"Hey! Tell them to pull straight."

And it had been he who had made the thump against the side when the crew had pulled him up and into the side of the hull.

A smile cracked my lips. Rain chapped the skin. "You deserve to have

81

your head bashed for that fool act out there!" Untying his rope to give it to me. I shook my head. The brick-brain!

Thunder rumbled above us. Cade was level with me now, eye-to-eye and grinning. "Felt like letting you go first is all. Mighty nice night for a swim."

I chuckled. "Are you well?"

He climbed over the side and let go of the rope. "Why wouldn't I be?" But I saw the red marks on his palms before he let them fall to his sides. He sobered. "How is she?"

That was what I intended to find out as I turned from him and hastened down the hatchway. Darkness consumed me immediately. The thick air clogged my throat as I stumbled into the walls and doors of the narrow hallway. I winced when crash after crash clapped my ears as a result of my own clumsiness. My legs still believed themselves to be underwater.

I did not even know which chamber Ian had taken her to. And I was making far too much noise to be able to hear the voices of the nuns. My feet halted in the middle of the hall, and I listened. To the creaking coming from the hold. To the shouts of the men above me on deck, fighting the storm.

To a moan coming from a door to my right.

I did not knock. I did not even reach for the knob. I merely burst in. Which reminded me of the moment in which I had done the same to her cell at the convent in Leiden days ago. Such a look she had given me then! A mixture of panic and hatred and fire that had sparked something in my soul I had not been able to surrender since.

She had hidden behind the chair. As if the meager barrier it offered was better than nothing. I had never before sunk lower than I had in that moment.

I had sunk to nearly the same depth when I had crouched above the body of her father, blood dripping from the knife—the very blade I had pulled from Barrington's chest—in my hand, and looked up to find her in the doorway.

The look of betrayal she had given me had rocked me to my core. A mere shadow of the scathing look she had given me in Leiden. Now, as I surged toward the bed, I realized *this* was the lowest I had ever been. For I had almost lost her—and I knew it.

I longed for a fiery look from her. Any look from her. The two nuns moved away, clearing my view. Still trying to catch my breath, I stared down at her. Hair aswirl about her heart-shaped face. Brow smooth of wrinkles of worry. Pale. So pale, save for the blue tinge to her lips, the almost purple tint at the tip of her nose.

"She sleeps," Margried said.

"I can sit with her." Surely they were exhausted from our traveling. They did not go far, only to the corner. I cared not if they watched; I sank to my knees beside her, grasped her hand, and brought it to my cheek. It was cold to the touch, but my fingers searched for and found a faint pulse. Alive.

My eyes closed. *Thank You, Lord. Thank You.*

Now if only she would awaken. Let me see her eyes, her smile, her glare in the flickering candlelight. The truth brought my eyes flying open.

I am falling in love with her.

Gwyneth

Chapter Fifteen

Darkness pulled at me. So weary, I could not open my eyes. Too weary to even lift my hand. No matter. What would I reach for?

My senses swam in a sea of confusion. For I could breathe. I pulled in deep breaths of crystalline air. So light. So warm inside my chest. Penetrating to the farthest reaches of my heart.

If I could breathe, then why did I feel as if I were still underwater, at the mercy of the current, at the mercy of the storm?

Lost between two worlds, I hovered, unsure of what to do. I wanted to awaken, open my eyes and see the bright, bright world. But what if it was not bright? What if it was dark? What if the nightmare of being tossed in the *Kanaal* was true and opening my eyes would be to return to being conscious of not being able to breathe?

So I stayed there, in between, hovering, wondering, confused and frightened.

A whimper pulled from my chest without my permission. I heard it, ashamed. I was not meant to be afraid. I was meant to be sure, saintly, about this thing called death. But I was not.

All I knew was fear. And that made no sense. For I was Catholic, a true daughter of the Church. It made no sense, no sense at all.

If hope sounded like diamonds, then what did redemption sound like? Mayhap the cry of seagulls flapping their wings in the morning breeze. Certainly not the creak of a wooden ship, crack of lightning bolts, or cramps of a stomach full of saltwater.

My right hand was too heavy to lift. Besides that, it was warm, and I was so cold. It was that warmth that finally convinced me to try to open my eyes.

But not yet. I was not brave enough for that yet. Still, I entertained some hope that I was not underwater anymore. If I was not, I was not sure where I truly was. But with the sound of hope, the sound of diamonds, coursing through me, I lifted my left hand. Reached for the rosary at my neck. Willed my tongue to unclamp from the roof of my mouth.

"Gwyn?"

Why did that voice invade my dream or whatever this, this place, was? Dirk Godfrey, my enemy and my savior, both. My friend. It was with that realization that my eyes fluttered open. *My friend?*

He knelt beside the bunk in which I lay, his brown eyes looking at me as if I were an angel or an apparition. Mayhap both. "Gwyn."

The world shifted, and I realized I was below, in the belly of the ship. My left hand clenched around the rosary. Below. The one place I had not wanted to go. My gaze traveled to where my right hand lay, warm and safe in Dirk's large palm. I looked up at him, attempting a glare.

He only smiled. Which made no sense.

And he did not let go. So I tugged my hand free. I missed the warmth. I watched his smile slip slightly, but his joy was evident. Joy? Over what? Me?

I attempted to shake my head to clear it, when I realized the monstrous ache that weighed down my face, my neck, my hair. Unbidden, a groan pulled from my chest.

Dirk spun away, and I examined the dark curls mussed on his head. They looked as if he had run his fingers through his red hair a thousand times. I had noticed that he resorted to the habit when frustrated. What had given him cause for concern tonight?

The pieces of the picture of the night shifted into place after fragmented place.

He turned back and laid a cool cloth on my forehead. "Here." Relief swirled from the coolness to reach the dark places that contained the strongest ache. An ache that came not only from it being night and my having worn my glasses all day long.

He still knelt beside me. I realized just how close he was. Close enough for me to see him, truly see him, without my glasses. Close enough to measure the planes of his face. Close enough for me to see joy dancing in his brown eyes.

Close enough even for me to see a small scar at the side of his right

eyebrow. I opened my mouth to ask him about it but only succeeded in gasping in a few short breaths.

"Wait. Do not try to speak just yet." He rose from my side, and I looked up at the ceiling. The rocking of the ship intensified.

He dropped beside me once more, this time with a cup in his hands. Tipping it to my lips and sliding one arm beneath my shoulders, lifting, he helped me drink the cool, clear wine.

"Easy." He pulled it away before I could finish it. I gave him my best smoldering look.

His smile only widened. "For the last hour, I have longed for you to look at me like that."

The ship pitched to the right, and I jerked, afraid I would fall from the bunk. He grabbed my hand again, seemingly unaffected by the motion.

A cold sweat broke on the back of my neck.

He saw my look, interpreted it, and slid a bucket into my lap in the nick of time. When I had disposed of the saltwater I had consumed while immersed, he disappeared with the bucket and returned with another cool cloth.

"Where…Margried, Sister Agnes?" My voice sounded raspy, and I wondered if that result was more from embarrassment or the scratch of the salty sea I still tasted in my throat.

"Resting." He nodded toward the corner of the room. A shadow bathed the space he directed my gaze toward. Did the women sleep on the floor there? I squinted, unable to see.

Unable to see much of anything. I gasped and half sat up. "My glasses!"

He gently pushed me back down. I let him, since my headache had increased tenfold.

The room tipped beneath my dull vision. "Dirk, my glasses…" A low moan escaped me.

My situation had just become so much worse. Now I was not only in the belly of a Sea Beggar ship that might or might not capsize at any moment, forced to trust the one man I had hoped to never meet again, the one man I should *not* have trusted for any reason.

Now I could not see, either.

I pictured my glasses at the bottom of the sea, settled into some sandy spot that cleansed the lenses. Why I would have imagined them sparkling clean in such a place, my mind refused to tell me.

"I am sorry, milady. I did not see them."

My gaze focused on Dirk. His tone of voice sounded almost…

repentant, contrite. "You did not see them?"

He shook his head. That made me smile, somehow amused. Until I noticed he held my hand again. I tried to pull away a second time. But he would not surrender the contact completely. I eyed him.

He did not seem to mind. "Gwyn…"

I wished he would not do *that*. Say my name in such a way that made warmth cascade through my insides, made my heart fold in on itself.

Made me feel as if I could trust him.

I had been doing too much of that lately, I realized. Surely it was not healthy, good, or even right. He was a murderer. Moreover, he had murdered the two most precious people in the world to me. And he had fled from the scene like the dastardly villain that he was.

I had to remember that. As much as I detested the idea, I had to conjure the image of him kneeling over my dead parents, knife in hand. My loathing for the remembrance caused my fingers to tighten on the counterpane, my lips to thin into a narrow line.

I darted a glance at the corner, where Sister Agnes and Margried supposedly slept. He had not lied to me about their presence, had he? If so, if they were not truly in this cabin with us, that meant we were alone. And I was weakened by my fall overboard. Cold and weak. Completely vulnerable. Compounded with the lack of my glasses, the truth of how helpless I was sent waves of fear through me.

He saw it. I knew the moment he saw, sensed, smelled my fear. For his fingers relaxed around mine, though he did not release them. His head dipped, and he expelled a heavy sigh. And, seeing him like that, I supposed I owed him something. "I thank you."

He looked up.

"For saving me. Again."

Near the scar I wanted to ask him about, a vein below his right eye twitched.

"You did dive in after me, no? I assumed when you said—"

"I did." His eyes darkened.

"Oh."

"I am sorry. About your glasses."

I tried to pull my hand away, but my efforts were futile. Tried to pull my gaze away from his but failed at that, too. The joy had all but disappeared now, the space stolen by a dark shade that reminded me of the spiced chocolate my uncle had once ordered from España for the birthday of my aunt, his wife who had died, pregnant, in the plague outbreak that had

also taken my grandfather. So much death.

I had faced my own this day.

"It was dark down there." I shuddered at the memories assaulting me.

His forehead wrinkled. "Are you cold?" He laid a blanket overtop me before I could answer. Then I realized it was not a blanket, but a man's cape. His. I buried both my hands in its folds so that he would not reach for my fingers again.

He noticed and, from the hurt look in his eyes, interpreted the reason behind it. Just as the ship rolled to one side, he stood. He took a sliding step that made me envious of his balance.

Ignoring the voice inside that said I should not, I burrowed my arms deeper beneath the second layer of warmth. If I closed my eyes, mayhap he would leave. Or at the very least waken Margried or Sister Agnes so that they could sit with me while he slept a few hours. He needed to sleep. I watched him scrub his face with his palm and tilt his chin toward the ceiling.

"You should get some rest."

He smiled an exhausted smile. Exhausted, no doubt, from rescuing me. How many times would the man do that?

The course of my thoughts took a new turn, and I bit back a gasp as I slid toward the wall and away from Dirk. How many times *would* the man do that…before he ceased? Before he left me to my own devices? Before he shrugged me off as no longer his concern, no longer in his care?

Before he abandoned me?

I was entirely dependent on the man who had murdered my parents. Stark panic welled inside, and I snaked one arm up to the collar of my gown and grabbed the rosary. Started saying hurried prayers as if the ship were going down. Even the sudden gratitude that my rosary had survived what my glasses had not was not enough to still the fear.

My eyes flew to Dirk. With his face still turned to the ceiling, I thought I saw his lips moving. A gasp escaped me. Was he *praying*?

He must have heard my intake of breath, for he opened his eyes and stepped closer. Then he looked down at me, sorrow lining the corners of his eyes in an expression I had seen him wear only a handful of times. The expression he wore every time the subject of my parents arose between us and I accused him of doing the foul deed that fateful night months ago.

"Are you well, Gwyn?"

What could I say? How could I answer in such a way as to put that tone from his voice? For I wanted to, I realized. Not just to appease myself, so that he would say naught and leave me be to get warm and to rest…but so that *he* could rest and no longer look so troubled.

But I could not twist the truth and lie. Not as he had done on the docks with the captain who even now labored above us to save us from the storm. The storm!

It was not an untruth that I feared the storm…in fact, the mere thought made my gut churn, and I hoped I would not have need of the bucket again. Appropriately, a crack of lightning flashed a meager amount of light through the porthole and into the cabin. Not enough, however, to my dismay, that I could discern whether the shadows in the corner bore the names Margried and Sister Agnes.

"I am concerned about the ship." My voice sounded small. "How it bears up beneath this storm."

He took a step toward me then stopped. "This vessel will be fine, I assure you. She is sturdily built and commanded by a worthy captain."

"A relief that is, to be certain."

"But you are not relieved?"

How he saw through me. "Not wholly. Such facts as those have proven naught against the hand of God in the past." I had said too much. My gaze veered away from his.

"What do you believe about the hand of God, milady?"

So it is milady again. Good. No more Gwyn. The last thing I needed was to hear my name on his lips once more, although merely the silky tone of his voice sent that familiar warmth spiraling through me.

I fought against it, but I was too cold to resist any flickering bit of warmth, whatever the source. I hated how weak that made me feel, dependent not only upon him, but for the very sound of his voice. "I believe that He is sovereign."

He nodded, and my shoulders stiffened with incredulity. Was that nod one of agreement? But how could Dirk believe the same as I?

"What do you believe about the hand of God?" I spat the question at him, fully aware not only that my voice sounded caustic—so different from his patient tone—but that I *wanted* to sound that way.

"The same. And I believe this summer storm will blow over within the hour."

He saw my mouth open, and his voice rose slightly before I could speak. "But if it be His will that it does *not*, I believe God will see us to His heaven."

I played with the cape he had laid over me, feeling a sensation other

than cold: unease. I did not want to be having this conversation with him. I did not want to be having *any* conversation with him.

Especially one about the sovereignty of God. "You believe that?" The question spilled from my mouth before I could stop it or shroud it in an icy bitterness that would defy the trembling of my tone.

"Aye. With all my heart. As I believe He has put us together for a purpose."

Angry, I swung my legs over the side of the bunk before I could think better of it. My feet hit the icy planks of the floor. I stood, shocked to notice the swathes of my blue dress that trailed the floor. "You cut my dress."

Before he could reply, the ship chose that moment to groan and list to the right. I slid, but I did not mind, for the sway of the storm sent me right into Dirk, the man who dared guess the purpose of God. I pounded both of my fists on his chest over and over. He let me.

This was the man whose voice I had not heard say even one word on the dark night we had met. This was the man who had murdered my parents in their own home on the same night. This was the man who had left me alone with their bleeding bodies while he ran away.

He put his arms around me, splaying his fingers across my shoulder blades.

I remembered.

I stopped hitting him. I remembered the safe feel of his arms around mine, remembered him whispering something against my hair while we had bobbed in the churning sea. The ship tilted again, and the cabin, oddly, righted itself in my topsy-turvy dizziness. Dirk's arms tightened, increasing the awareness of what I had not known I had been aware of. His rescue of me. "Did you say something?"

He looked at me quizzically.

"When we were in the water? Did you say something?"

"I said you were going to be well."

I blinked up at him, amazed that he had let me leave the bunk and strike him like some termagant. I looked at my fists against his chest. My lungs played tug-of-war with my throat of a sudden, and my breath came in shallow gasps.

My eyes flooded. Rippling beneath my watery gaze, his face softened. "You are going to be well, Gwyn." So we were back to Gwyn again. "Whether this ship goes down or we make it safely to shore come morn."

I raised my fists and struck him again, but not hard. "This is not about the ship!"

"What is it about then?"

A lone tear slid down my cheek. The sensation was strange. I had not cried since I knew not when. It was the tender touch of his thumb that undid me. He wiped away that single tear, but it was only the firstborn.

Visions of that night months ago, the picture of my parents lying in pools of their own blood, assaulted me. I covered my face with my hands and stepped back, away from him, but he was there. Strong arms going about me. Just as if I were in my father's embrace again as a little girl, but deeper, *more*, somehow. And for the first time, I was cold no longer.

I amazed myself at my supply of tears. For someone who had almost drowned in a body of water, I *was* a body of water. I lost track of time as I allowed the rivers of mourning to trace my cheeks and my fingers. Dirk tucked my head beneath his neck and rocked me back and forth. It was far more soothing than the rocking the ship had been doing of late.

Another thing that amazed me was that I let him. I let him comfort me while I wept over the very crime he had committed.

Dirk

Chapter Sixteen

I stroked her silky hair as I had longed to since I had first seen it unbound, free, and damp by the river. Soft beneath my fingers, like corn silk fresh from the field, it was all I had expected it to be. Except, of course, the scent of salt clung to it. So I rocked her, standing in the cabin Tudder had appropriated to the women, letting the reality of the storm and the nuns in the corner and my telling the truth and the ache of almost losing her all slip away. Nothing else mattered except seeing her through this.

Had she not cried once since that night? The suspicion almost sent me reeling with her in my arms. The faces of my mother and sisters flashed through my mind. Lady Rohesia Godfrey was a woman who loved to laugh and smile, but she could weep with the best of them. And the best of them would be my sister Susan. She cried at everything.

But Gwyn had never teared up in my presence. Not when she had learned of the deaths of her friends at the convent. Not when I had shouted at her in the forest and that look I never wanted to see again crossed her face. Not when we had been attacked hours ago.

Not once.

Gradually, her wracking sobs transformed into soft gasping breaths, then hiccoughs, and finally, every few minutes, heartbroken sighs. Heartbroken. An appropriate word for what she was. I could not even fathom how devastating the loss of both parents must be. I had lost my father, aye, but to illness. Lung fever. I closed my eyes as I remembered stepping into his darkened chamber with my brother, Harold, at my side to receive his blessing…and say farewell.

She had never had that farewell. My throat thickened. "Gwyn, I am so sorry."

Flinching violently, she tore from my embrace. The sweet understanding that had cloaked the room a second before snapped under the betrayal lacing her eyes.

She had never been able to say farewell. And she believed me to blame.

The pain in her expression was a knife to my heart. Unlike that first night in the forest, she did not try to hide her feelings behind a grin. *She thinks...* "Milady, I—"

She held up a hand and sank to the bunk.

The storm had passed as she cried, I realized. No longer did the vessel pitch and roll with the angry waves. The steady rocking motion meant we once more carved a path through the sea on our way to the English coast.

So she did not sit because she could not find the balance to stand. She sat because of the deep emotion travelling across her face. What surprised me was the lack of fury I had grown so accustomed to seeing. Instead, she seemed defeated. "So you confess it?"

I shook my head. "Confess it? Nay, I do not."

Her eyebrows pulled together. "But you just said..."

Ready to have this out once and for all, I knelt before her. She jerked away. She could have cut out my heart and it would not have caused me as much agony as to see her flinch.

"I said I am sorry. And I am. I am sorry for your loss. But I did not do it."

The puzzled look intensified. "You did not?"

"I did not kill your parents."

She leaned away from me. I tried to take her hand, but she snatched it away.

"Gwyn, I do not know who murdered them, but I assure you it was not I."

She leaned forward, and I dared to hope she believed me. But she only squinted into my face, eyes narrowing, look probing. She was trying to see if I spoke true.

I did not blame her. After all she had suffered, accepting the truth would be difficult. I kept my face intent, holding her gaze with my own. Praying she saw through to my heart, aching for her and longing for her to know the reality of what had happened that night.

"I do not believe you."

I kept my voice even by the grace of God. "Why not?"

She flung herself off the bed and took one step. Anger flashed in her eyes. I rose. She started to slide, not having her sea legs yet, and I gripped her elbow. She tossed off my hand and backed up against the porthole. "But I saw you!"

"Aye, you did, but—"

"*Nee*, I saw you. With my own two eyes. With my glasses."

"Gwyn, listen to me."

"*Nee!*" She fisted her hands and brought them up to her closed eyes. I wondered if she would scream, but she only punched the air in front of her. "I know what I saw. I may not see well, but I have no doubt I saw true that night."

I took a deep breath. "What did you see?"

She looked at me as if I had gone mad. "You know what I saw!"

"Think back to that night. What did you see?"

"You know. You were there. *You* were what I saw!"

"Tell me anyway."

She shook her head. "I cannot."

"Why not?"

"I do not wish to relive it."

"Are you not already?" I took a step closer, wanting nothing more than to draw her into my arms again and let her find comfort, but she reared against the porthole. She glanced out as if contemplating escaping.

I withdrew. "Tell me what you saw." My voice came out breathless and coaxing, a question rather than an order.

Her shoulders slumped. "You." Her voice cracked. "I came into the Great Hall, looking for them. After you had arrived, I was sent to my chamber. I did not like it, but Uncle Oliver told me to stay there."

"Why?"

"He said the four of you had urgent business to discuss, but I did not wish to retire until I had seen my parents. I wanted to know why you were there."

I kept silent, letting her speak. Knowing the reason I was there would only make her more upset.

Her gaze sought the ceiling. "I never discovered the reason. I never cared after that. I came into the Great Hall, expecting to see them laughing, talking, drinking wine with you and Uncle. But…" She swallowed. "But…"

She turned to me. To my surprise, no anger lit her gaze. Just defeat. "I saw them lying on the floor. *Moeder* was already gone…and I saw you. I saw you kneeling over Papa. You—you pulled a dagger from his chest." Tears filled her eyes. "And you looked at me. The blade dripped Papa's blood. You ran. I screamed."

Her hands reached up to cup her face, and the proof of her mourning slipped through her fingers. She swayed. I rushed to her, catching her before she fell to the floor. She did not fight. She did not even protest as I laid her on the bunk and tucked in every spare blanket around her, including my cloak.

"I have hated you for months because of what I saw that night." Her eyes probed mine.

"I do not blame you."

"I do not understand why you take such care, then. Why you rescued me from the convent, from the thieves, from the sea."

I looked down at her, feeling more tired than I ever had in my three and twenty years. "I did not do it, milady."

She waved her hand in front of her face, but her eyes did not dismiss my words. "I would like to hear what you saw that night."

My eyes widened, and hope began to burn inside my heart like a low ember. "I would like to tell you."

She blinked once, twice.

I smiled. "You have been through much this night. I will tell you soon." I could not keep my next words barred behind my teeth. "Mayhap then you will believe me."

Her eyes closed. "Mayhap." The word floated on a sigh. The most beautiful of sighs I had ever heard. The most beautiful of words, as well.

I thought about waking Agnes. For a long moment, in fact. But the women had each suffered such an ordeal the last few days that I could not bring myself to do so. They would be safe down here, in the cabin.

Though weariness weighed down my bones, I resisted the temptation to sink outside the cabin door and sleep. I needed to find Ian and Cade. I knew both probably had secured an empty hammock in the crew's quarters and were snoring now. Still, I would like to see for myself.

The motion of the ship did not make traveling the hall from the cabin to the crew's quarters overly difficult. Nothing like walking the route during the raging storm of hours ago. When I emerged onto the deck, surprise gripped me at how far daybreak had progressed. The sun still slept, yet the sky had lightened and morning hovered not far off.

I found Tudder leaning over a map on the quarterdeck, a candle in his hand. He looked up. "Dirk."

"How fares the ship?"

"She survived the storm." The man scrubbed his face with one palm, a small smile twitching at one corner of his mouth. "Blew us off course, though, I'm afraid."

I raised a brow. "How far off course?"

He motioned with the candle to a corner of the map. "We land in Portsmouth in a few hours."

"Portsmouth?" I blew out a breath. "That is off course." Miles from where Tudder had planned to make port in Portland. Miles away from my home. I shoved that thought to the back of my mind—I had not planned on going home, endangering the lives of my family…I could not.

"You are welcome to stay aboard whilst we load supplies. We will sail for Portland come evening." He punctuated his words by stabbing the map with a finger.

I grinned, knowing Tudder did not plan on my agreeing. "Nay, we will cause you no further trouble. You have been most hospitable as it is." Barrington Manor kept court farther inland. It made little difference whether or not we began our journey from either port. Mayhap it would cost us half a day of travel. But in my tired state, I cared little except for locating my men and catching a few hours of sleep.

Or did it have something to do with a wistful sigh and its owner sleeping in a bunk below that made me not mind the possibility of a longer journey with her? I shook that thought away.

"As you wish," Tudder said.

I opened my mouth to inquire after Cade and Ian when Tudder stopped me with his look. "Dirk, do you mind if I ask how you find yourself in your present predicament?"

Predicament. The same word he had used when I revealed the women's identities to him on the docks. "My men and I rescued them from a convent in Leiden."

Tudder nodded, eyeing me. "Two are nuns."

I cracked a grin, understanding his silent entreaty to know more than I had told before. "Aye, two are nuns. The other…" I ran my fingers through my hair.

"Ah." A chuckle tumbled from Tudder's chest. "So that is the way of it then?"

I froze.

His chuckle became a laugh. "Did your lady love flee all the way to the Low Countries after your spat?"

Recovering my wits, I shook my head. "Nay, that is not the way of it at all."

Tudder raised an eyebrow, looking none too convinced.

"We are not promised to each other." I nearly choked on the words, thinking of the memory I had pleaded with Gwyn to relive. "She—she is…a lady, that is true, but…"

His expression morphed from one of amusement to one of suspicion. "Why, pray tell, did you 'rescue' her from Leiden?"

I sighed. "It is a long story…" One I was not sure I wanted to share with my captain-friend.

"If you do not wish to share your long story just yet, I think there is one of my own that you would like to hear."

I waited.

"Mary is dead."

I drew in a quick breath. "What? What happened?" The image of Mary laughing while Tudder gazed at her, adoration in his eyes, sank into my brain like an anchor. That had been the first time I had seen her, soon after they married. The last time I saw her, she had been as vivacious as ever, glowing while their newborn son slept in her arms.

"She saved our boy from our house afire."

I put a hand on Tudder's shoulder. "I am so sorry, brother."

A curt nod. "I thank you. I am told she did not suffer."

I closed my eyes, hearing the grief and agony in the man's words. He had been told. So he had not been there.

"I came into port the next morn. Only hours too late."

I gripped his shoulder harder. "I have no words, my friend, save of the mercy of God."

Tudder's tension eased somewhat. His fists relaxed at his sides. "That has been the only thing that has kept me going these past few years."

I suddenly regretted the time that had passed in which I had not seen him. How much time? Three years? Four? "How many years now?"

"Two."

"I am sorry I did not know."

"Naught you could do. As for the years that have passed…" He chuckled. "Nature of our friendship, I suppose."

"I want you to know I appreciate it—our friendship, that is. And all that you have done for me." Tudder had been as wild as Cade and I had once been. My cohort in many less than honorable escapades. But he had shrugged off that life while I had yet languished in it. Changed by Mary, he had claimed. I had never doubted. I had never seen a stronger love. An echo of the pain the man must daily suffer twisted in my chest.

"You can count on me to save your sorry hide, Dirk."

I snorted. "Indeed. Do not forget to give my regards to your son for me."

His anguish vanished, and a look of pride glowed on his tan features. "You may do so yourself soon. He sleeps below."

I grinned. "Cabin boy, eh?"

"He calls himself that. First voyage. I could find no one who could care for him now that the widow who kept him is too frail for the task."

"Tudder…"

The man's brows rose.

"The lady thinks I murdered her parents."

Tudder's eyes narrowed. "'Tis not a predicament you have found yourself in. 'Tis a boiling pot."

I nodded and looked up at the sky above us. Light pushed in at the corners of the horizon, a harbinger of the sun's imminent arrival. "I must find some way to make her believe the truth."

"I do not think abducting the maiden is a good way to go about that."

I stiffened. "I abducted her to get her out of Philip's provinces."

Tudder cocked a brow, and I could hear his unspoken "*Philip's* provinces, eh?"

"I am sorry, brother. You know I am with your cause." The cause to free the Protestant Low Countries from Philip's Catholic clutches.

He folded his hands across his chest, waiting.

I laughed. "Netherland's cause."

Tudder cracked a wide grin. "We will win independence. William of Orange will make sure of it."

"'Tis only a matter of time before the Spanish king knows he's been bested."

"And, until he comes to that realization, I intend to make off with as much of his gold from the New World as possible."

Our guffaws lifted into the light air of morning. Then I sobered, my thoughts returning to Gwyn. As they had been doing often of late. "The lady has no part in the fight. She does not deserve to be a casualty of it."

"The lady is part Dutch, I can tell. Our independence is not her fight because she so chooses."

"She is Catholic."

"Exactly."

I pulled in a deep breath. "That is why I must return her to her uncle's manor, where she will be safe. And I must do so without being apprehended."

"How much trouble are you in, exactly?"

"A great deal. The evidence against me is quite incriminating."

"In this crime of killing her parents."

"Aye." A salty sea breeze wafted past us.

Tudder expelled a sigh. "Sounds like you will have quite the jaunt through the English countryside to return her. What do you intend to do after you restore her to this uncle?"

I ran my fingers through my hair. At one time I had known the answer to that question. *Restore my reputation. Prove my honor.* But now that mattered less and less to me. And a certain sleeping maiden who hardly ever cried and could barely see mattered much, much more.

"I do not quite know the answer to that yet, Tudder."

Tudder grimaced. "Keep your wits about you." His look told me he did not believe I was.

My sentiments, exactly.

Gwyneth

Chapter Seventeen

I awoke to sunlight streaming over the counterpane. I followed the slanted line to see the origin at the porthole. Glancing at that circular link to the outside world, a memory of backing up against it arose in my mind. The gold-painted casing had resisted against my back, but I had paid the pain little heed. A greater pain had overtaken me in that moment.

Tell me what you saw.

Those had been Dirk's exact words. Five short strings of letters arranged in such a way as to inflict the least possible discomfort, I was sure. Yet, in spite of his care and the compassionate look in his eyes, I had never wanted so little to do with him as in that moment.

Waves of grief washed over me as I remembered reliving the memory. I expected tears to spring to my eyes as the terror, horror, and denial took over my senses. But they did not. In a way, it was a relief. I had already wept myself dry.

With Dirk.

I rose to a sitting position and watched the fresh light of morning play on the floor of the cabin. What had possessed me that I would have disintegrated into a puddle in front of the man? He must now think me a lunatic instead of merely a crazed Catholic girl…

I shivered as I remembered his arms around me.

The pane of light bounced off the small chest in the corner opposite the bed, and rebounded back to splay golden fingers into the corner across from me. Dawn failed to penetrate that darkness. However, my eyes—eyes devoid of glasses—caught a slight movement.

I let my head fall back as a scream of rage boiled in my stomach. How could I have been so foolish as to fall into the sea? What maiden could claim she had *fallen* off a ship? The idea was preposterous. The urge to laugh collided with the pent-up scream. The sound emerged as a pitiful groan. I placed my bare feet on the floor. My brow scrunched. Where were my stockings? I groaned again. Probably at the bottom of the sea keeping my glasses company.

"Lady Gwyneth?" A sleepy sigh came from the corner.

My stomach unknotted, and my forehead smoothed. So Dirk had been telling the truth. Sister Agnes and Margried had slept in that corner while I had fallen apart in front of him.

"Margried? Did I wake you? I am sorry."

"Nay, nay, no need to apologize." Light from the porthole rippled into the corner again and illuminated Margried unfolding herself and rising. The sway of the ship's soft motion sent the light ricocheting away, but Margried stepped forward toward the bed, toward me.

"Sister Agnes must have gone above. I did not hear her leave." She blinked in the light. "How do you fare?"

"I am well, although my stomach still feels full of saltwater."

"I am so glad to see you awake."

"I am glad to be awake." I did not much care for sleeping. Not with the nightmares.

I noted her smile as she sat down beside me. "Lady Gwyneth…"

"Call me Gwyneth, Margried. I would like to think we are friends."

She nodded. The faint line on her forehead attested to the healing of one of the wounds she had received at the convent. "We are. And I will… Gwyneth."

I watched her press her palms together in her lap. "What is it?"

When she turned to me, her face was the most serious I had ever seen it. "What would you think if I said I wished to convert?"

My jaw unhinged, and I stared in wide-eyed amazement. Timid, quiet Margried who seemed so devout, so in tune with God, so…faithful. Convert?

A choked sound emerged from my throat. Immediately, Margried's gaze dropped to her hands, which twisted once more in the lap of her modified habit. "It is just that…" A long sigh. Her gaze lifted to the porthole, met mine, and focused on the ceiling. "I wonder if…if it is enough."

I waited for more, but she offered none. "I do not understand, Margried. If what is enough?"

She flung up her hands then buried them in her lap as if shocked at herself for making such a frustrated gesture. "If *any* of it is enough. Vespers. Celebrating the hours. Lighting candles. Meditation. I am not sure it is enough for me."

Frightened at the path I thought she led me on, I swallowed. "You mean you wonder if you can live the life of a nun? Margried, you are still

a postulant. You have not yet taken vows. If you wish to reenter common life, I am sure—"

Shaking her head, she looked at me with imploring eyes. "Nay, that is not what I meant. Gwyneth, you live such a life. You know what it is to be…Catholic and yet not married to the Church. Is that enough for you?"

The air of the cabin grew stuffier until my chest was heavy with seawater once again. So I deflected the question. "Is this because of Cade?"

She blushed. So it was.

"I—I have…feelings for Cade. He is unlike any man I have ever met."

I rose from the bed. "He is Protestant."

"He is a good man." Of this, she looked most certain.

"So you wish to convert so you can marry him."

She stood and strode to the porthole. "Nay, it is not because of him I ask you this. I have had certain questions since long before I met Cade. Since long before I came to the convent, actually."

"What kind of questions?"

"Questions about the Protestants. Questions about Knox and Calvin and even Luther. Questions about the Bible."

A shocked gasp escaped me. "About the Holy Bible, Margried?"

Her face swiveled toward me with an intensity that surprised me. "Aye. About faith and what it means to live by it. About salvation and how it is to be obtained. About Christ and what His work on the cross truly accomplished."

I slumped back onto the bed. "I do not know what to make of your questions."

She nodded, looking as if my reaction did not surprise her. "I know. I know you do not."

"What will you do, do you think?"

"The same things I have been doing, I suppose. Thinking. Praying. Hoping for an answer."

I looked at her blurry outline and could not understand why I did not feel anger. If she had come to me a fortnight prior and told me of her feelings, her *questions,* I would have erupted in righteous indignation. But now I was hollow, empty somehow. I did not want to hear more; I was afraid to.

I took a deep breath. "Do you believe you will?"

"Do I believe I will what?"

"Receive an answer."

Margried nodded. "Either that or the courage to convert."

Dirk

Chapter Eighteen

Boots clomped toward my hammock, and I spun out of the swinging cloth. Cade lifted his hands, a smile on his sideways face. "All is well."

I stood, righting the world and his image. "Then why the rush?" The man had been barreling through the belly of the ship as if another storm had descended upon us. I scrubbed a hand down my face, wiping away sleep.

"I thought you might like to know we have made port."

I turned my head to see out the lone porthole of the crew's quarters. No sunlight filtered through the opening. I surged toward the gray view.

"Another storm may pass over us this day."

I met Cade's eyes. "We have made port, you say?"

"Aye. Tudder is seeing his ship loaded with victuals and a few goods as we speak."

Blast, but I had slept longer than I had intended. The events of the night had taken their toll. Which reminded me that Cade had also taken a dunk in the storm that had sought to drown Gwyn and me. "Cade."

He stopped in the middle of the hall and put a hand on the frame that separated that space from these cramped quarters. The stench of the place stung my nose.

"You suffer no ill effects of taking a swim last night?"

One corner of his mouth lifted. "Nay, I do not, brother."

The image of Gwyn's pale face rose in my mind. "I thank you again. I do not know how I would have gotten the two of us out of the sea if it had not been for you."

He snorted. "You would have found a way, stubborn as you are."

I pulled my fingers through my hair. "Speaking of stubborn..."

Cade's smile vanished. His eyes narrowed as if guessing where my thoughts led. I did not doubt that he knew exactly what I was about to say.

"Last night, when we arrived, I sensed you were upset about something."

"I was." As matter-of-fact as ever, the mule.

"Why?"

He smirked and raised one eyebrow. "You have no need to fear me."

I grinned, amused. "What?"

Cade scoffed. "When you feel you do not have the upper hand, you act as if you do by perfecting your posture." His eyes dared me to deny it, but there was a gleam of humor in his eyes.

I blew out a breath through nostrils sore from enduring the stale air of below deck. I did indeed stand feet apart and shoulders rigid, the same position I would assume were I being attacked by an armed man. I strode forward several steps, forcing my body to ease up as I did so.

Cade's gaze never once flinched from mine. "The women are awake."

Gwyn. I pushed away thoughts of holding her last night. "How do you know this?"

"Their voices ring outside the door."

I nodded. "We will see them off the ship here in Portsmouth."

"Why not sail farther to Portland?"

A shrug lifted my shoulders. "Why not disembark here? Barrington Manor is miles yet inland. We will converge upon a central path once we have put the docks far behind us."

Cade stroked his jaw with his thumb and forefinger. "I suppose I am concerned about the approaching storm."

The sounds of cargo being loaded onto the upper deck echoed from above both of our heads. Men's shouts flung through the air.

"We will be no safer aboard ship than on land. Lady Gwyneth proved that last night. We will find a place to stay for the night." Or before nightfall, if need be.

Cade bobbed his chin once, as if satisfied, and turned to go. I put a hand on his shoulder, staying him. He swiveled to stare at me, but I knew he sensed the subject stirring within me.

"Why?" *Why the look of disapproval last night, Cade?* The man had been like a brother for years and knew me better than my own brother, Harold, did. To have fallen short of how he viewed me caused a pang in my chest.

He heaved a weary sigh and looked up at me with a half-smile. "For the way you are willing to compromise yourself for her."

"Explain."

"You know exactly of what I speak." And the trouble was, I did. He punched my arm lightly. "I worry for you."

So he saw what Tudder claimed to see—me falling for her. "I rescued her from the convent. She would have perished had we not been there. That is all."

Cade's smile disappeared. "Is it?"

My patience ebbed. "What else would it be?"

A guffaw poured from his chest. He shook his head. "You look at her as if the sun sets behind her. You cater to her every need."

I scowled. "That is chivalry."

"That is the action of a man in love with a maiden. But this maiden can never be yours."

"And what about the way you have been looking at Margried?"

A vein pulsed in his cheek. "And what about the way you lied for her when this entire *rescue* mission is to cleanse the stains marring your name by proving your integrity?"

Though a voice whispered in the hollow of my chest that I went too far, I pressed anyway. "Margried is a nun. To speak lowly to her as I have seen you do is unseemly."

"Do not talk to me of unseemly, brother, when it was you who conspired to deceive the good captain to secure our passage."

The tight words, spoken in an equally tight tone of voice, flowed between us. My voice lowered. "I did not lie. He knows all. And my aim for this mission is to merely see her to safety."

His eyes did not so much as flicker. "*Is* that your aim, Dirk?"

"Of course it is."

"Is it your *only* aim? At one time, you meant to return her to her home in order to see your name cleared."

My brows knit together. Cade had once followed on my heels to every nefarious deed. Adventures, we had once called them. And we had turned away from them at the same time, found God on the same day, as a result of the same death.

And on that same day I had made a goal. I had let go of my father's lifeless hand, hung my head over his dead body, and vowed to restore what my father had given me that I had squandered: the name Godfrey. *God's peace,* the name meant.

As if I had ever known such a thing.

Could I throw that away and make my goal Gwyn's safety alone?

"It is my only aim now." I tossed the words to Cade and pushed past him, not caring that my shoulder plowed into his.

"Be sure of that, Dirk."

I looked back at him. "I am." The only problem, of course, was that I was *not* sure that Gwyn's safety was my only goal in this journey back to England.

What I was sure of was that I had just fallen, nay, jumped into the pit of deceit as had once been my wont. The pit I had sworn I had turned away from when I found God on the day of my father's death.

Gwyneth

Chapter Nineteen

I praised God that Sister Agnes did not return until later. After I had said a dozen or so prayers. After Margried had washed her face and calmed. After we both worked to restore some order to my gown's hanging slices; Dirk had certainly done damage trying to free me from its weight. When Agnes returned pale-faced, Margried and I dashed to her side. I stumbled over the bunk, never seeing the protrusion that obstructed my way.

"Are you well, Sister Agnes?" Margried's soft whisper intoned worry.

"Of course I am."

I turned my face to hide my smile. The older nun would never reveal a weakness.

"How are you?" Sister Agnes's voice rang with concern.

I turned to Margried, whose cheeks blossomed crimson. My jaw dropped. How could I have forgotten? "Your arm! Has it worsened?"

Margried shook her head as the red siphoned from her face. "Nay, nay. It has not worsened. Merely…"

"Grown?" Sister Agnes supplied the word as she pushed up Margried's sleeve with gentle fingers. Indeed, the word fit the symptom. I leaned close, squinting. The bruises had faded on Margried's left arm, but the fingerprint marks had swollen.

My eyes met Margried's. "Who left these?"

She shook her head again, trying to pull down her sleeve. "I know not. It matters not."

"Milady?" A knock pounded on the cabin door, startling us all.

Margried swished her sleeve back into place. Sister Agnes flew to her feet and straightened her habit, modified to appear as a common gown, but a habit nonetheless.

I stepped to the door, shuffling my feet out in front of me to check my path. I had no desire to plunge headlong toward the floor. Not when it was surely Dirk who waited on the other side. After a quick glance at my friends to ensure they were comfortable with receiving company, I opened the portal.

He stood close enough for me to see that a few reddish curls hung over eyes almost bloodshot with weariness. Had he slept at all? My heart sank, realizing I was most likely the reason his rest had been stolen from him.

"Are you well?" It was the same question Margried had posed to Sister Agnes, but somehow it seemed different flying from my lips to his ears.

"It is time to disembark, milady."

So we were back to *milady* yet again. No more Gwyn. I missed the sound of my name even shortened. But I had not missed how he had skirted my question.

"Wait." I pressed a palm to the door he tried to close.

One eyebrow rose, resurrecting the wolfish appearance I remembered from our first meeting. A surge of panic took hold in the pit of my stomach, and I lashed out against the fear in the way I had grown most accustomed to. In anger. "You intend to take us from the safety of the ship when you are almost dead on your feet?"

His eyes narrowed. "I do."

I shuffled my gaze away lest he discern the fright that anchored me to the floor and induced me to lace my voice in rage. "Why do you not just leave us here and wash your hands of us? Surely we are no safer with you on the shores of England than on this heretic ship."

Two unrelated emotions crossed his face. Irritation. And compassion.

It was the compassion that sent me over the edge. "You should have left me to drown in the sea last night."

Now it was he who pressed open the door as I attempted—and failed—to shove it closed. Without taking his eyes from me, he addressed the women in the corner. "Leave us."

I shot a dagger-sharp expression at Margried and Sister Agnes as if daring them to disobey, as if I wanted to be alone with him. Which I most decidedly did not.

Unfortunately, my look worked too well, and the women left. Sister Agnes appeared only annoyed, while Margried, as she passed, touched my arm and gave me a glance rippling with concern. I trusted them to stay right outside the door. Yet…

When I turned my gaze back to Dirk, what I saw carved across his features made me swallow. I took a step back.

Big mistake. He took a step forward.

I took another step back. Bigger mistake. He took another step forward.

So I stopped, holding my ground, breathing in the tension clouding the air in the room, staring up at him as if he had grown a second head. Mayhap he needed to, for the one he had seemed absent of all sense. He did not appear to be acting with any amount of brain at the moment.

"What thoughts flit through that fair head of yours, milady?"

I blinked, unsure of how to answer. I did not wish for him to know of the fear sluicing ice through my veins. Yet, strangely, I was somehow as warm as cold. Odd. "I am thinking you twice the rogue you have ever been."

"Mmm." Did the man have any idea how handsome he looked while attempting to appear indifferent?

That cooled my fury, fueling confusion instead. "You will never be more than a disreputable rake."

"Aha."

This time he stepped first. I retreated, and a circular casing dug into my back through my rumpled and torn gown. My heart pounded. It was the second time in a matter of hours he had backed me up against the porthole of this cramped cabin. One corner of his mouth lifted as he laid a hand on the wooden wall above and to the right of my head.

"Do you have something to say to me, you wolf, or do you merely take pleasure in perusing your prey?"

A grin snaked its way onto his face. Genuine befuddlement pooled within me, withering my resolve. I steeled my expression when I realized I had been staring up at him, the emotions on my face unmasked. But he had caught that brief vulnerability. I knew he had.

He stood close enough now for me to measure the angle of his jaw with my gaze. In fact, he stood just close enough that I could reach up with one hand and brush the curls out of his eyes if I so wished.

Of course I did *not* wish.

I very much did *not* wish.

The scar at the corner of his eye beckoned to me, but his gravelly voice broke into my reverie. "A wolf, you say, milady? But a lioness is never prey to a wolf."

"A lioness?" To my consternation, my voice sounded like a young girl's.

"A lioness. For is that not what you are?"

Something snapped inside. Tears pricked the backs of my eyes. And in that moment, the spell was broken. The tension in the air cleared like a clouded sky after a long storm. I pulled in a shuddering breath in the silence that followed, watching as he released me from his gaze and

dropped his hand from the wall. He even took a step away.

His image blurred. I squinted. He took a small step forward. *Wonderful.* I could not see him if he stood too far away, but shivers ran up and down my spine if he stood too close.

To distract myself, I raised a hand in the direction of his right eyebrow. "Where did you acquire that scar?"

His brows rose. As did his hand. He caught my wrist within his grip before I could either touch him or pull away. "England. Which is where we are going."

Did he think I would let him off that easily? "How?"

"A story for another time, mayhap." His voice had not lost the gruffness.

"Must you always be so secretive?"

His eyes darkened. "Must you always be so angry?"

I willed the tears not to well. Alas, they did not obey. Remorse tightened his features. He rubbed a tiny circle on the back of my hand with his thumb.

"Did you sleep at all this night?" I tried to tug my hand free.

"Aye."

"Then why are you acting so…irrationally?"

Next, he did something even more irrational. He turned my hand in his ever so softly, his touch as gentle as winter rain, and kissed my palm. Waves of shock made my bare toes curl against the wide planks of the wooden floor. The scruff of morning whiskers scraped my skin as he pulled away.

I had nowhere to go, pressed against the porthole as I was. Dirk made no move to put distance between us. I was not sure what to make of that. Did I respect him for making no attempt to put an end to whatever had just transpired? I knew not.

What I did know was that something *had* just transpired.

I had to get away from him. I stepped around Dirk, and a raised plank in the floor tripped me. My knee slammed into the wood of the bunk as strong hands grasped my waist, pulling me against a rock-hard chest. I jerked free.

Dirk released a sigh. "I trust you are ready to disembark this ship, milady?"

I resisted the temptation to turn to face him. "I am."

"Without your glasses?"

I raised my chin. "I am." He was across the cabin and had one hand on the knob before I said, "You plan on returning me to my uncle?"

He turned. "I do."

I nodded. "I possess another pair of spectacles. They are in my chamber

at home."

"I will get you home, Gwyn."

Dirk, Margried, Sister Agnes, and I ascended and emerged from the hatchway into faint sunlight. I squinted against the glare and found myself taking in deep draughts of air. The deck smelled so different from below, but even better was the variety of sights—albeit blurry—that met my eyes. Members of the crew scurried down the hatch after we moved out of the way. They carried barrels and boxes on their shoulders, destined to be stored down in the hold. Many of the men who stayed above had ropes in their hands.

A cry turned my head, and I gasped to see a figure suspended high above us, on the mast. I could not be sure, but...was that a man? A sail slapped across my view, hiding the mystery from me.

"He will be all right." Dirk had come to stand beside my shoulder.

I marveled anew at how it felt to be so close to a man who towered over me. "A man is up there?"

"Repairing a tear the storm gave the sail."

"How did he...?" The sail slapped away again, revealing the blurry figure once more.

"He climbed."

And he would have to climb all the way down again. Such a height! The thought sent my stomach whirling. A raindrop plopped onto my cheek, and I reached up to wipe it away.

Watching my motion, Dirk frowned. Tudder emerged from the corner of my eye. Sister Agnes, standing on my other side, stiffened. Margried shrank behind her.

"Allow me to introduce my son, Titus." A young lad who looked to be about four or five stepped out from behind Tudder, who laid a hand on his shoulder.

It had been such a long time since I had seen any children. This one looked straight at me; did he smile?

"It is an honor to meet you, Master Titus. Your father has told me much about you." Dirk's voice brought my gaze to his. Emotion arrested his features.

I crouched to the boy's level. "I am glad to meet you, as well, Titus. My

name is Gwyneth."

The lad's grin widened. "You look like my *moeder*." His English lilted with the way of the Dutch.

I stored away the sound of both Tudder and Dirk catching their breaths.

Sister Agnes shuffled closer. "Rise, Lady Gwyneth. 'Tis unseemly."

I ignored her. "What an honor to have you say that, Titus. I am sure your mother was a sweet, kind woman." *And that, I am not.*

His head bobbed up and down as his face assumed an expression full of sorrow. My heart broke for him in that moment, certain that he had endured much in his short life. That I could sympathize with.

What made me do it, I had no idea. But I opened my arms. Titus hesitated but a moment, raced toward me, and burrowed into my embrace.

Dirk

Chapter Twenty

How long had it been since the boy had known a woman's arms around him? I could not fathom it, but the sight of Gwyn cradling small Titus close to her brought a rush of emotion to my throat. She turned her head to whisper some sweet something in his ear while her hand stroked the blond curls bursting from beneath his small cap.

And what the lad had said was true. She did resemble Mary. Fair hair, small features evenly spaced in a heart-shaped face. No wonder the boy had been drawn to her and clung to her even now.

Did she like children? Generally? I found myself wondering if mayhap she even wanted many of them pulling at her skirts someday. I knew of few women who did not long to be the wife of a privileged lord, who did not desire to rule a keep...but motherhood was often relegated to nursemaids, nannies, and governesses. My sister Susan liked children, but of the majority of women in my acquaintance, how many would have reached out to Titus, a young boy who had known much sorrow?

The truth arrowed into my heart. Of course. Gwyn knew his sorrow—that of losing a parent. She had weathered that storm two-fold. Because of me, or so she believed.

I almost staggered with the weight of the realization. I turned to Tudder and saw his shock. Grief pulled at the corners of eyes rich with unshed tears. The same look I had oft beheld on my mother's face resided on his—the look of love lost.

Titus pulled back but still rested in the safety of Gwyn's arms. She crooned to him, her eyes lighting with a smile that rivaled the sun in the sky. She did want children. I could see it in her eyes. As did I. *Where did that thought come from?*

I pulled my gaze away to frown at Sister Agnes, who watched the display with a disapproving stare.

113

RACHELLE REA

"He is a fine boy, Tudder."

Tudder nodded in my direction. "That he is."

"Tudder?" Gwyn looked up then back at the boy. "Titus Tudder. What a strong name you possess."

Both father and son puffed out their chests in pride. "His mother picked it."

"*My moeder* picked it. 'Tis a Bible name."

Gwyn nodded. "That it is."

Young Titus glanced at his father, and Titus walked to stand beside Tudder. He grasped the tail of his father's captain coat. Tudder righted the cap twisted on the boy's head and directed a grateful gaze in Gwyn's direction.

A cool pink dusted her cheeks, and she looked away. Did she suddenly remember the boy she had held belonged to a Protestant father? A captain of a Sea Beggar ship? That the Tudder name stood for all that the Barrington name disdained?

Nay, I did not see that in her eyes, in the tilt of her head, in the feathering of her lashes across her cheeks. If anything, at that moment, she appeared as if the barrier had come down, as if the wall between her world and the world she called *heretic* had fallen.

Had it?

That was a question best saved for another time. Mayhap a question to which I would never know the answer. Mayhap a question I could never even dare to ask. More than any differences our warring religious waged between us, Gwyn considered us separated by the bitterest of betrayals. And yet I was losing my heart to her. Just as I was beginning to lose hope that what I had set out to do—restore my name, my reputation, my honor—would ever lie within my grasp.

Gwyneth

Chapter Twenty-One

My arms ached to hold the child again. How long had it been since I had held a babe, much less the weight of a strapping boy of five in my arms? Too long. I had never had siblings, and our family, recusant Catholics such as we were, had never been very social beyond venturing out to neighboring estates. I rued the loss of community.

Heavy footfalls brought my attention to the hatchway, just in time to see Cade and Ian—I could not tell them apart without my glasses—emerging, a satchel over each shoulder.

"That is all." Cade's voice.

"Will you be leaving us now, Dirk?" Tudder's tone boomed loud and hearty. He seemed to have recovered from the emotion of a moment ago.

Dirk clasped hands with the captain. "Aye, we will." He forced a smile and cast a worried glance at the sky, which had just sent another raindrop spiraling onto my hair.

"Be sure to refill your canteens before you go."

Dirk nodded. "We appreciate all that you have done for us."

Tudder's head turned toward me. He lowered his voice from less boisterous to almost quiet. "Keep your wits about you, man."

A grin played at the corner of Dirk's mouth, and I was just close enough to see it. Oddly, he looked at me next, a depth in his gaze that I could not decipher. Before I could look away, his eyes narrowed on something past me, beyond the ship. His grin disappeared. "Cade."

Cade surged forward to where he could better see. He nodded at Dirk.

I spun to see what had captured their attention. The port bustled with shadowy figures, despite the fact that it was early morning and a cloudy one at that. "What do you see?" My words vanished in a peal of thunder that made me flinch.

Margried grasped my left arm at the same time that Dirk did my right.

"We are leaving. Now." His tone brooked no room for argument. Ian and Cade burst into motion. Even Tudder caught the fever that consumed Dirk. He called for a longboat and the lowering of the swing that would see Sister Agnes, Margried, and me into the boat.

"No time." Dirk pulled me to the rail, and Sister Agnes and Margried followed.

"No time for what?"

As Ian disappeared over the side, climbing down a rope ladder, I understood. No time for the swing.

Dirk went next, but when I stepped aside for Cade to go, he shook his head and helped me over. My stomach flipped at the swaying of the ship—and the ladder. I stopped climbing and clutched the rope, watching my knuckles turn white, imagining my face turning green.

"Gwyn, come." Dirk's plaintive tone set my feet moving again. He sounded so close. I looked down. And immediately regretted I had done so. My stomach flopped again, but instead of being put to rights, my insides were now even more out of sorts.

I scurried down the ladder, eager to be inside the safety of the longboat, angry at myself for feeling seasick now when I was *off* the ship. I had not felt this way even when I was immersed in the roiling waves.

My foot missed the rung. My hand grappled for a hold. The palm of my other hand burned as I fought for my grip.

"Gwyn." Something brushed my skirt, and I looked down. Dirk's eyes met mine. I read the message in them.

I let go.

And he caught me. The boat rocked as he took a step backward, steadying both of us. I scrambled away from him and lurched for a seat. Leaned my head out over the water as I breathed deep, trying to stop the churning inside of me.

Sister Agnes and Margried climbed down without incident, although I quirked a brow at how Cade jumped into the small vessel. The boat rocked, and so did my stomach. I could not discern Cade's reaction to my glare.

The men grabbed oars and set out for shore. Just in time, for the rain began in earnest, plopping into puddles that quickly grew in the bottom of the boat. I watched the blurry hull of the Sea Beggar ship move away from us. Tudder and his son stood at the rail and waved. The little boy's expression was lost on my eyes, but the ache of *farewell* lodged deep inside my heart. Such a stout heart the young one had. I admired it. Even envied it, in a way.

Dirk's anxious expression stamped out what little conversation Sister Agnes, Margried, and I might have had in the rain that slanted across our faces. His dark cloak stretched wide as his muscles strove against the current to see us to the docks. The men oared toward a quieter area. What—or *who*—had they seen that had made them flee the ship as swiftly as we had?

One glance at the Sea Beggar ship had me squinting, trying to make out the name on the side. "Margried," I whispered. "What is the name of the vessel?"

She studied it a moment. *"Rijke Ziel."*

I gasped then shook my head at Margried's concerned look.

Rich Soul.

What an odd name for a treasure ship that looted galleons returning to España from the New World. All because the Dutch Protestants sought to send a message to King Philip II that they *would* pursue freedom, that they would rule themselves.

Was that what Tudder had considered when naming his ship as he had? That a rich soul was a free soul, a soul unbound, unfettered?

I watched Dirk's hair coil in the rain. That would explain why the men were such good friends, of course. Dirk valued freedom. Always had. Which was why he had been such a scandal for as long as I could remember. Always the subject of the titters behind gilded fans and fancy gloves in the corners of dances and dinners.

The boat docked at a narrow wooden plank. Ian jumped out to anchor the vessel to the dock with a thick rope. Cade got out next and reached for my hand. Margried sat closer to him so I motioned her ahead. She went without hesitation. Interesting.

"Go, Sister Agnes."

The older nun frowned at me, but obeyed. *Unseemly,* I could hear her thinking. Still, because of my station she obeyed. She tripped on the hem of her habit as she stepped out. Cade caught her with able arms. My stomach twisted as the boat rocked, and I grabbed the side for support.

"'Tis well, milady." Dirk's voice held a smile. "I will not let you fall in again."

I eyed the water then reached out to take Cade's hand.

Dirk tossed our things at our feet, and exited the boat. As the men tossed satchels over their shoulders, they each glanced up at the busy port, at the bustling people.

"Are we running from someone?"

Dirk met my eyes. "We are in England now." Which meant yes.

Cade chuckled. "Are we not always running when we have you ladies with us?"

My mind spun with those two statements as we hurried through the crowd lining this place on the docks. A new aroma swallowed up the smell of the sea. The stench of people, animals, and unkempt coast made my stomach twist in knots. It was probably a good turn of fortune that I had eaten naught this morning.

We are in England now. The smoothness of the language swirling from people's mouths and into my ears attested to that undeniable fact. Not as smooth as my grandmother's Spanish, but not as chunky as my mother's Dutch.

I glanced at Margried and Sister Agnes, following closely. I supposed I should have felt a measure of relief at knowing the riots of the Low Countries were now completely behind us. Religious upheaval had traveled to England, of course, and had even tainted the streets with blood before, but not now, not anymore. Recusant Catholics—those who did not attend Protestant Book of Prayer Services—were only fined.

Are we not always running when we have you ladies with us? Cade's statement swam through my senses…and it hit me.

Dirk. Ever the nefarious rogue I had accused him of being just this morning, here, in this land, was wanted for murder. And he risked being caught, risked certain hanging by setting foot on English shores. For me. To return me home.

The thought—the truth—no sooner crashed through my mind than I heard his shout. "Run, Gwyn!"

And I picked up my skirts and ran after him. Clasping my hand in his, he led me down a deserted patch of street. My shoes sloshed on the muddy ground, and the rain picked up its pace, as if it sought to cloak us from our pursuer. Our pursuer. The mysterious sight Dirk had seen that had compelled him to leave the Sea Beggar so soon? Was it a man? I chanced a glance back. *Who is chasing us?*

But I saw no one. That scared me more than if a rabid wolf had been on our trail.

I pulled up short. "Dirk!"

He pulled me in between two buildings and clamped a wet palm over my mouth. I stiffened against him, sensing the need for silence, reliving the terrifying moment—had it been only two days ago?—when he had done the same at the convent. An ache built in my chest. The rough wall

at my back scratched through my dampened dress.

Finally he removed his hand and ducked his face close to mine. "What is it?"

"Where are the others?" I forced my whisper to remain as low and controlled as his had sounded.

"Safe."

I turned my head, eager for him to go on. Where were Margried and Sister Agnes? Ian and Cade? Had they found a hiding place as we had? Or had they been caught in our pursuer's clutches? Seconds stacked upon seconds as I stared into Dirk's face, my peripheral trained on the entrance to the alley that revealed an empty road. No one passed by. My heartbeat steadied, though the dull ache intensified.

He was close. Close enough for me to see that scar that always stood out to me, right above his eyebrow. Close enough, too, to see the tension in his expression. He met my eyes. Trapped—that's what I was. Why did I not feel threatened? With his arms around me, one hovering at my shoulder should he feel the need to muzzle me again, I was ensnared. But not only by the height and breadth of him. By his gaze. Flecks of hazel danced in those brown eyes.

Remember who he is, Gwyn. Devon Godfrey who now went by a dagger's name, Dirk. The rebellious second son of Lord and Lady Godfrey, bane of all who knew him, wolf in wolf's clothing, my enemy…murderer.

My rescuer. This was madness, feeling my heartbeat quicken at the way he refused to look away, as if…as if I captivated him somehow. But that was impossible.

So was feeling safe here, in his arms. I should not. Yet I did.

I drew in a shuddering breath right before he leaned down, a hairsbreadth from my face. At that distance, I could see each feature of his face. He touched his forehead to mine. Before I could speak, draw a breath, or think a single thought, he leaned closer but hesitated, as if asking silently for permission.

I did not pull away.

And he kissed me.

My eyes closed. His hand at my shoulder moved to my face, and I was treasured, cherished. I expected to feel fear, but instead expectations shattered and only warmth cascaded through me, up my spine, in a hurricane of knowing. Knowing that this—kissing Dirk—was ridiculous and yet right.

He was gentle. Cautious, though not timid. I could not feel my lungs,

though I felt my fingers quiver. All I cared about was reaching one trembling hand to his chest, as though the kiss was not enough and I needed to touch him to reassure myself he was solid, real, here.

He was. Oh, how he was.

Dirk

Chapter Twenty-Two

I pulled back and tightened my arms around her, pressing her head to my shoulder. My ears tuned in to the faint *clip-clop* of a man's boots against cobblestone.

She inched back and gazed up at me from beneath hooded lids. I swallowed hard, fighting the satisfaction of knowing the kiss affected her as it did me, fighting the desire to draw her back again for another. But I had to remember my purpose. To keep her safe. *My only aim,* I had told Cade.

Grabbing her hand, I pulled her deeper into the narrow enclave between the butcher's shop and the apothecary, pushing her behind me, protecting her body with my own. If anyone glanced down this way, they would see nothing. Or at least I prayed that was true. *Lord, will You cover us in shadows?*

I knew He was capable. Of course, I wondered about the likelihood of the Lord listening. After all, I had just kissed Lady Gwyneth Barrington, daughter of deceased parents whose blood she believed stained my hands.

I was not altogether certain the Lord would be inclined to grant me any favors at the moment.

The footsteps halted and so did my breathing. I squeezed Gwyn's fingers, lying so small in mine, willing her not to make a sound. A dark form blocked the little light that pervaded this space. *For her sake, Lord? For her sake?*

The form passed. The *clip-clop* resumed. The man walked on. I breathed a sigh of relief for the second time in the span of two minutes.

I turned. Braced myself for a glower intended to melt my brain. Or the slap of her pretty palm across my cheek. Mayhap even stony silence and a skittering gaze. I deserved all of that and much more. I prepared myself for all of it, expected all of it even. I did not know how the woman would pull off glaring at me and ignoring me at the same time, of course, but if

anyone could, it would be Gwyn.

Face turned toward the ground, she sniffed. My stomach flipped backward, collided with my spine, and sank back into place with a plop. I caught her face in my hands and turned it up.

No glower. No slap. No stony silence. Or skittering gaze.

Raindrops pelted both of us, but they could not disguise the single tear that trailed down her cheek and off her chin. Not given the sob that accompanied it. Her lower lip wobbled. Which only made me want to kiss her more.

Slowly, tenderly, as compassionately as I knew how, I drew her to me and embraced her. She rested there and calmed.

But I did not. I lifted my face into the rain, hoping the cold water would douse some sense into me. What kind of lout was I that I had made a woman weep? What's more, I had made *this woman* weep. This woman who needed precious few things from me: protection, escort, mayhap a bit of understanding.

Certainly not a kiss.

She did not cry after that single, wracking sob and lonely tear. How different from any other woman she was. So many used hysterics as a routine method of procuring their way…but not Gwyn.

She pulled away, and her absence caused an ache in my bones. "Forgive me. I should not have…" I ran my fingers through my dripping hair and studied her. Could not this rain abate for one moment so I could see into her eyes? Nay, her expression was unreadable.

Her arms folded. "There is naught to forgive. I know you were just trying to keep me quiet."

I schooled my features just in time.

What if I allowed her to think that? To reason that the only intent behind that kiss had to do with the man who had passed us by? Instead of being the intent of a man swept in by her beauty and mesmerized by the vulnerable look that swam in her eyes?

But then…"Why are you upset, milady?"

"Margried. Sister Agnes. I worry for them."

Relief sluiced through me. As did frustration. Not exactly the reaction I had expected, when I had just claimed her lips with my own. Tears. Fright for her friends. Had that kiss meant nothing to her?

Of course it did not. Not when she believed my only purpose for it was silence.

"They are well." I knew I could not promise such a thing, but I suspected

it was true.

Unlike the lie I was allowing Gwyn to believe. I could not bring myself to correct her. The decision fit like an old shirt, snug, warm, unused for a season, but still good and worthy of wear. After all, deceit had once been my everyday apparel.

I studied the stones that surrounded us. Except that now I lied to Gwyn to protect her from knowing the truth. Used to be, I deceived in order to save *my sorry hide*, as Tudder had put it. In the end, though, how was it different? In both cases, I escaped embarrassment, shame, and the consequences of my actions.

She stared up at me. "How can you know that?"

"Cade and Ian will protect them until we meet up again."

"Why did we run?"

I cringed. Saw *his* face in my mind framed by black hair and a thin beard.

"Dirk?"

"We need to go. We will meet up with the others at the woods." I reached for her hand.

She pulled away from my grasp. "You will tell me why we fled from the port in such a scandalous fashion."

I fought it. Truly, I did. But the grin found lodging on my face anyway. "Because I live in a scandalous fashion, milady."

She huffed but let me tug her out of that alley. Which was a good thing. A very good thing. Because that huff had me seriously contemplating kissing her again. And not because I wanted to keep her quiet.

Although that would be nice.

"And are you fulfilled by your scandalous life?"

My brows rose. I sensed her frustration with me, but I thanked God for the reprieve. With her angry with me, I would be much less likely to pull her close again.

We sidled past the butcher shop, and I caught the faint whiff of the place. Glancing at Gwyn, I saw that she did, too. I quickened my pace when her face assumed a pale green pallor. The smell of blood in the convent had given her the same pained expression. As had the stench of the English port. I had noticed the saint had an unusually sensitive stomach. There was no need to aggravate it now. Not when we needed to meet Cade and Ian in the woods as soon as possible.

Before I sighted Arthur again.

"Dirk?"

I tore my gaze from her face and scanned the area, an isolated part of town where few ventured. Before darkness fell, anyway.

"I am sorry, milady?"

"Did you hear my question? I asked if you are fulfilled with your scandalous life."

"And what if I ask if you are fulfilled with your own?"

She huffed again. "Stop!"

Immediately, my gaze probed our surroundings. My footsteps ceased, but hers did not. She stood right beside me now and pulled me along. Raising one brow, I resumed walking. "Are you well?"

Concern pounded within. Did she feel ill? The last thing I needed was for her to retch right here in the street.

"I am."

I shook my head, making my confusion known. *Then why command me to stop?*

"Whenever you are asked a question with which you are uncomfortable, you turn the tables and ask an equally probing question. Stop."

"I do not do that."

"Aye, you do."

Thinking of how Cade had called attention to my guarded stance, I snorted and tugged her along for several paces. Few buildings lined the sides of the street, if indeed this muddy slush could be labeled a street. I flicked a look at Gwyn. The hem of her gown—what was left of it after I had sliced at random during our time in the Channel—plodded through the mush as if it weighed more than she did. A smile tugged at my lips as I wondered what she would say if I scooped her up and carried her to the woods.

Plenty, I was sure.

I could not risk her reputation with that type of behavior, however. Not even here, on the edge of town, where not a soul lingered. There were always eyes everywhere.

I stamped down the smile and assumed a scowl. Anger burst within my veins and oozed into every pore like the juice of a punctured tomato skin. My gaze never stopped probing the area. It frustrated me that no sooner had we landed on the English coast than I had seen *him*. Arthur. Right-hand man of Oliver Barrington, Gwyn's uncle.

He had not seen us from the shore, I was certain of that. But I had seen him.

"Are we almost there?" Gwyn blinked, making me aware that the rain had stopped; our cover had deserted us. I fought against the desire to tug her along faster. The need to get away from the town—and Arthur—pulsed deep.

"Aye. Almost." I sent her my most reassuring look. Her lips looked chapped. I had a sudden urge to slap myself as Gwyn had not in the alley. We had fled the Sea Beggar ship so quickly we had only procured food for the journey through the woods to Barrington Manor—not replenished our canteens.

Gwyn stumbled, and I caught the wince. My hand twitched for my knife, but I knew she would never let me shorten that hem and ease her battle sloshing through this odorous muck.

"There." I pointed.

She followed my gaze. "Where?"

"Behind that small shack is a copse of trees." I led her around the meager excuse for a building and watched her eyes widen. The tiny bit of sunlight playing chase with the clouds glinted off her hair until it glowed.

When I lifted a branch for her to step beneath, she released my hand. I mourned the loss.

"Will we find the others here?"

The words stung for some foolhardy reason. What did I expect? For her to enjoy my company? It was too late for that. Far too late. "Cade and Ian will have the sisters here waiting for us."

"Sister and postulant."

My head swung around. "What did you say?"

"Sister and postulant. Margried has not yet taken vows."

I stored that sliver of information away to be dissected later.

"And if they are not?" Her gaze meeting mine harbored a challenge.

I could have reached out and touched the invisible stones stacking up between us, forming an effective barrier between my heart and hers. "We wait for them."

"And if they do not come?"

"Then, milady, we decide what to do."

Surprise brightened her features. I could not have pinpointed which of those dire words caused her joy if my life depended upon it.

But she blessed me with the bliss of her smile, and my throat dried at the sight. I could not decide what was more beautiful—the smile on those red lips that turned up her cheeks or the one sparkling within her green eyes. *Lord, did You fashion her after an angel or a lioness? I am having the hardest time deciding.*

Gwyneth

Chapter Twenty-Three

A thrill of pleasure rippled through me when he used the word *we*. As if we were friends. The thought delighted me to no end.

Until I reminded myself who he was. It seemed I was having trouble doing that lately—remembering just who had killed my parents, abducted me from the convent in Leiden, dragged me through the forest of the province all the way to the coast, and lied in order to procure my passage across the *Kanaal* on, of all things, a Sea Beggar ship.

Nee, instead, my mind stubbornly centered around whose strong arms had lifted me from the hard stone floor when the smell of blood had overtaken me, whose gentle hand had helped me rise from beside the Rhine, and whose whispered words in my ear—"You are going to be well"—penetrated my unconscious ears after he plucked me from the sea.

I touched a finger to the rosary around my neck. My distraction provided my foot with the opportunity to slide on the muddy forest floor, emitting an aroma I fought to ignore. I righted myself and prayed Dirk had not noticed.

"Are you well, milady?"

I rolled my eyes heavenward. "Yes."

One corner of his mouth rose. The aching pain that had taken up residence in my chest in that alleyway right before he kissed me had not lessened. Now it blazed inside, threatening to become a raging inferno. Spanish spewed from my mouth before I could clamp it back. I was not even sure I wished to.

Dirk's smile disappeared. "What was that?"

More words flew from my lips to be carried by the wind upward into the cloudy sky. I called him a fool, a wolf, a lout, a rogue.

He shook his head as if in annoyance. I stopped my tirade when the call of a bird resonated from somewhere to our right. Louder than usual, the sound made me pause. What type of fowl stretched its feathers in this dismal weather?

A grin blossomed on Dirk's face before he puckered his lips and made the selfsame sound. I gaped at him.

"Close your mouth, milady. It rains."

I swallowed my rage when Cade, satchels over each shoulder, came into sight. I smiled before a tempest of fear swept from my stomach to my throat. "Where are the others?"

Dirk

Chapter Twenty-Four

"Right here." Margried's voice preceded her appearance.

"Margried!" Gwyn wrapped her friend in an embrace.

"Gwyneth!"

Postulant. The word tossed around in my mind, inviting further contemplation.

I glanced at Cade, wondering if he knew the woman had not yet married the Church. Further contemplation of *that* would have to wait, however, for the next person to come forward was Agnes. And she was injured. She limped with one hand pressed to her side. Her scrunched brow attested to pain. Ian appeared behind her.

"What happened?" Gwyneth asked the question before I could.

"She slipped and fell in the street when we separated." Cade's gruff voice revealed none of the compassion his eyes contained as he looked at Agnes. His gaze slid to me, and we exchanged a look of responsibility.

If we had been on better alert, Arthur would never have been able to sneak up upon us as he had. I could still feel the icy sensation that came with the realization of his nearness. Doubt needled. What if he *had* seen us? Seen Gwyn?

Then he would know she was in my charge, and he would be relentless until he discovered why. For a moment, a sliver of respect for Lord Barrington arose within me. Did the reason Arthur loitered at the docks this morning have to do with a journey across the Channel? Had he been on his way to fetch Gwyn home?

The sliver shredded. Her uncle should have brought her home long before now. In fact, he should never have allowed her to go away.

Ian lifted a hand in the air, palm up. My brows rose as I realized why. The rain had begun anew. The brief respite we had been granted was now over. "We must make haste."

Gwyn turned and looked at me. "But Sister Agnes is hurt. You cannot expect her to walk."

"I will be well." Agnes smiled, as if to reassure the other women.

Gwyn stepped to stand in front of me and put her finger in my chest. "We should rest."

"You have forgotten where you are, milady. In England, there is no rest for criminals."

Her eyes darkened.

"He is right, Lady Gwyneth," Agnes said.

Gwyn's head whipped around so fast her wheat-gold locks brushed my chest. "Are you sure?"

In answer, Agnes turned to go. I looked to the west. "We will find a river after an hour."

Gwyn looked at Margried, relief written on her features. With that, we set out. Cade fell into step behind me. The women followed him, and Ian took up the rear. I glanced back at Cade. "I want to tell you the truth."

"About time you discovered that deceit is never the answer."

We exchanged glares. I stepped over a log, held out a hand to Gwyn, and kept my gaze locked on Cade. He reached for Margried's hand and never looked away.

We walked in silence for several minutes. I could not give the blockhead what he wanted—tell him I was not falling for Gwyn. That I could not do because I wanted no more lies between us. Which meant I must tell him about my conflicting motives. But Gwyn and Margried walked far too close to us for that confession. Unless I spoke in code. "There is one more thing."

He cocked a brow.

"I am not certain that it is my *only* aim."

That gleam of humor returned to his eyes. "You never convinced me of that in the first place."

I stifled the sigh that fought for escape. Silence settled over us, save for the sounds of the forest, the rustling of the women's hems, and the occasional sucking sound of their shoes vying for traction. The rain fell steadily now, drenching my cloak.

I turned up my face to catch the falling droplets and quench my thirst. *Lord, will You help me lead them? Help me get them to Barrington Manor, whole and well?* For I well knew the dangers of traveling whilst cold and wet. The lung fever had killed my father, after all. I could not let any fall ill now, while in my charge.

The sound of rustling skirts drew closer, and I turned my head to see Gwyn at my side. "Dirk."

"Aye, milady?"

Her eyes loomed wide. If she looked up long enough, the rain would have to cease completely so that the sky could mirror the depth of those green orbs.

"Can we not rest a mere moment? Sister Agnes…" Her words trailed off as her gaze also trailed behind to cast a glance at her friend.

"Aye." I agreed not only for Agnes's sake, but also because of the gray pallor of Gwyn's face. I caught Cade's eye and nodded toward the wood, intending to do some scouting. Strange that I should feel reluctance to leave Gwyn for the short time it would take me to examine the surrounding area.

Thoughts of her followed me into the thickening wood. Did she feel poorly? Did she even notice, as concerned as she was over Agnes?

I was thorough but quick at reassuring myself no one followed us or lurked ahead. After returning to the others, I held back, out of sight of all but Ian, who glanced at me and grinned. I glared, and he turned away.

Gwyn stood in front of Cade with one hand resting at her hip, the other tucking her wet hair behind her ear. They spoke, and he let drop one of the satchels he carried. Without waiting for him, she pulled free a blanket. Rain pelted the rich fur, darkening it in spots.

She motioned to Agnes and helped her sit at the base of an elm tree, where the roots, albeit uncomfortable, would provide some protection from the muddy ground. I expected Gwyn to drape the blanket over the nun's shoulders before I remembered it was summer. I watched Gwyn smile at Agnes and coax her into leaning against the tree trunk. She lifted the blanket over the woman's head, creating a shield against the rain, even as she stood a victim to the falling droplets herself. *Aye, Lord, I understand now. An angel.*

Gwyneth

Chapter Twenty-Five

Dirk reappeared, a determined look on his face. At least, I hoped it was a determined look. The rain prevented me from being sure.

"Let me." Without waiting for my answer, he plucked the blanket from me with gentle fingers. A small part of me wanted to protest, but it was useless. He could shield her much more effectively than I. His superior height lent him more favor when it came to the distance between Sister Agnes's head and the blanket. So I said nothing, only moved away.

Dirk called Margried over and gave me a pointed look, nodding toward the canopy Sister Agnes rested beneath. I shook my head. "There is not room underneath for the three of us."

Margried settled at the base of the tree. "But it feels heavenly to sit down."

I sat tentatively, aware of the pain in my chest that had risen from an ache to a pounding rhythm. Mayhap I was just hungry. Or thirsty. Or both. As I had seen Dirk do, I had lifted my lips to the heavens in order to catch the falling rain, but my mouth was still too dry, so I gave up. Dirk lifted the blanket higher and all at once, the rest of me became dry. Well, not entirely. I was soaked through. We all were. But the beat of the rain against my hair and skin had stopped.

I looked at Sister Agnes. "What are your injuries?"

Her brows collided. "I am well."

Margried blew out an exasperated sigh. "And that is all I have been able to get out of her all morning."

"Sister Agnes." I tried again. "You must tell us what ails you so we can help you."

She shook her head. "'Tis no more than I can bear. Do not concern yourselves about me."

I perused her, wishing I knew more than I did about the healing arts

and what roots eased pain, but it was the cook who managed the herb garden in our keep. I cast a glance around us at the wet forest. I had no idea whether or not what Sister Agnes needed grew but a foot away.

She had limped earlier. Now she pressed a hand to her right side. "Are you bleeding?"

She glared at me. I merely raised my eyebrows. Fiery looks would not intimidate me. I used them too much myself.

"Nay, 'tis only proof of my fall."

I smiled and sought to gentle my tone. "What did you fall against?"

Margried knew the answer. "She plowed into a hay wagon when we spun to flee from…" She shrugged. Whatever—or whomever—we ran from.

I turned back to Sister Agnes. "Which hurts worse, your limb or your rib?" At my use of the word *limb,* she flicked her gaze away, toward Cade and Ian, who stood a respectable distance away.

"Which hurts worse?" I insisted. Mayhap if she would just tell me, I might focus on doing what I could for the most serious injury.

"Sister Agnes…" Pleading bled through Margried's tone.

The nun huffed. "You must believe that I speak the truth. My side will bruise and my limp will ease. Upon the morn, I will be well. 'Tis no more than I deserve."

My gaze snapped to hers. "What do you mean by that?"

"I will be better on the morrow. Do not concern yourself."

"Nee, what are you talking about, 'tis no more than you deserve'?"

A shard of pain shadowed the light of annoyance in Sister Agnes's eyes. "I mean what I said."

I wanted to throttle the truth from the woman. If she were not so hurt, of course. Margried, ever the gentle one, laid a hand atop Sister Agnes's fingers lying against the roots of the tree. "'Tis not your fault what happened."

The truth tore the breath from my lungs. "Sister Agnes…you cannot… it is…" Words whipped around my brain like the wings of caged cardinals.

Margried glanced at me and smiled. Then she turned the full light of that smile on Sister Agnes. "God saved us that night. You must believe that. He called the others to His heaven for His purpose, just as He kept us here for a purpose."

I nodded.

Sister Agnes shook her head. "Nay."

Margried patted the older woman's hand. "Aye."

So Sister Agnes blamed herself for the events of two nights ago, when the convent was raided. I leaned forward. "The Fury has swept northward through every province. There was naught you or any of us could have done to prevent it from reaching Leiden."

If you want someone to blame, blame the Dutchmen who did the deed. My blood boiled at the thought, but I ignored the anger for Sister Agnes's sake.

Sister Agnes studied the ground. "I should have heard. I should have known. I should have warned them. The three of us barely escaped with our lives."

Margried took the woman's hand and raised it to her lips. Kissed it. "It is not God's way to share with us every detail of His magnificent plan."

Sister Agnes's throat worked, and I saw she struggled to believe Margried.

That made two of us.

Dirk

Chapter Twenty-Six

The women's words affected me. At times, anger washed through me with more force than the rain pelting my back and shoulders. Then the awareness of Agnes's grief pounded into my heart. She blamed herself. She thought she deserved punishment, even the pain she suffered now.

Margried's lilting voice echoed through the forest, speaking of truth, mercy, and God's will. At first I had expected her and Gwyn to agree with Agnes. Offer her some penance with which to soothe her soul. Prescribe prayers, plan to light candles, accept the burden the nun carried.

Margried did all the talking and Gwyn could not string a sentence together, but her agreement seeped into my bones despite the fact that I could see nothing of her face for the blanket I held over them. Most unusual, for anyone other than a Protestant to speak of God in such a personal manner. Most unusual, indeed.

Listening to the conversation—spoken in English, though they could have conversed in Dutch for privacy—had intrigued me as to the depth of the beliefs of the devout trio who sat below me. Mayhap I would be able to discover more later. I shook my head. What was I thinking? I must reach Barrington Manor with the women well and whole. Then leave.

To roam the world for the rest of my life—that was my fate. Margried's words rang in my ears: *It is not God's way to share with us every detail of His magnificent plan.* And the details He did give were sometimes hard to swallow. *Lord, will You help me complete this mission?*

"We had best be going." We had tarried at the trunk of this tree long enough. If we wanted to leave Arthur far behind—which we did—then we had better walk a few miles today.

Gwyn stood and stepped from beneath the shelter of the blanket first. Conflict drew her brows together. Margried exited next and helped Agnes stand. Peace resided in Margried's eyes, while Agnes looked only mildly troubled, as if she were still in the process of mulling over Margried's words, but near accepting them. Strange. Why did Gwyn look so afflicted?

I snapped the blanket into crisp folds. Had I misinterpreted Gwyn's garbled words for something they were not? I stuffed the blanket into the satchel Cade had relinquished. Without a word, Cade turned and led us to the west.

My next thought turned my stomach to stone. Did Gwyn *not* agree with Margried?

As I had promised, we reached the river in little over an hour. The rain had ceased, depriving us of even the small blessing of lifting our heads and receiving a few drops. Margried and Gwyn, with matching chapped lips, dropped to their knees beside the riverbank at the same moment. Ian helped Agnes sit while I pulled an empty skin from my satchel. I sank beside Gwyn and plunged the opening beneath the water, but I was unable to relish the sensation of the river rushing over my hand once I saw Gwyn had stopped drinking. "Milady?"

She looked up at me through heavy lids. Blinked. "Dirk."

"Are you well?" Bubbles ceased to decorate the surface over the skin. Meeting Ian's eyes, I lifted it up.

"Merely tired."

Ian took a step toward the river and reached for the now-full skin, then returned to Agnes.

Gwyn closed her eyes, and her chin lowered. Alarm slammed through me. Margried stopped tossing handfuls of water into her mouth and pinned her gaze on Gwyn. My thoughts whirling, I exchanged a worried glance with Cade, who had sunk into the muddy bank on Margried's other side.

I thrust my hand beneath the surface of the water again and let the river ripple through my fingers. My eyes probed the opposite bank, searching for something, anything. Birdsong lilted through the trees. Squirrels scurried up a high branch. The sounds of clawing and chattering alerted me to other creatures' presence. Whatever bothered Gwyn had not come from the river.

Gwyn's eyelids drooped heavier now. As I watched, she stretched out her hand, as if she struggled to maintain her balance even as she knelt.

Dizzy. I shot to my feet.

The skin of water Ian had handed Agnes halted halfway to her mouth. "Lady Gwyneth?"

By her side by then, I caught the hand she held out. "Are you well?"

Margried's voice turned shrill. "Gwyneth?"

Gwyn's lips moved. Although I could not understand the Dutch words, I understood well enough the paleness of her face. I could not be sure what ailed her. One thing I could be sure of was that we needed to get her out of the woods. As quickly as we could.

"Come. We must go." I stood, pulling Gwyn up with me. She swayed on her feet, and I did not let go of her hands. She pulled one away to press to her dress. Surprise and confusion burned in my brain as she curled her fingers against her bodice instead of her stomacher. She had a sensitive stomach—I had expected cramps, stomach pain, even retching…but this? Did she struggle to breathe?

"Cade." I need not have said the man's name. He already had Margried by the arm. Ian helped Agnes stand.

"I am well." Margried touched Cade's hand holding her sleeve.

"Are you sure?" he asked her.

"What is wrong with Gwyneth?" Whether she asked the question of me or Cade, I could not be sure. Her eyes flicked between us both and Gwyn.

My mind echoed the question.

"Dirk."

I rested my hands on her shoulders. "What is it, Gwyn?"

"I—it hurts." More Dutch words I could not decipher.

I lifted her and gathered her close against my chest. "Leave it to me. You will be well again soon."

She closed her eyes and did not answer. I turned and trooped to the west.

"Where are we going?" Her voice rang weak in my ears, but that she had the strength to ask the question filled me with determination. She *would* be well. She would be whole. I would not lose her now, not after everything else she had survived.

"To a friend." It was my sincere hope that the man would still consider himself as such.

She had sunk into delirium by the time we reached Saint Benet's Abbey, although in truth it was no longer a monastery; the only such structure saved from King Henry's Dissolution nearly thirty years earlier, it had been merged with the bishopric of Norwich. The structure loomed above us in the waning light of evening, tall and imperious. As it had always done when I approached it, the sheer strength surrendered to a peace and tranquility that testified to the purpose of its walls. It was a place of healing. A sanctuary.

More than ever before, I prayed that it would be so. *Lord, will You not heal her?*

No longer conscious, Gwyn had slipped into a dream-like state from which I was rendered powerless to free her. And just as every other time I had seen her sleep, her face crumpled as if with unease. She was feverish and restless, crying out and thrashing in turns.

"Who goes there?" a deep voice called out from behind the large door.

"Travelers journeying past, desperate for food, drink, and care."

The door creaked open, and a figure stepped out. I recognized him at once. Joseph. Just as tall and intimidating in form as the place in which he lived, he nonetheless wore a spirit of peace that mirrored that of the monastery. It made me believe Gwyn might just find healing here. "Is that you, Devon?"

I nodded, the sound of my Christian name unfamiliar and unimportant. "Aye, Reverend."

"Who are these with you?" The man's gaze swept the group, his eyes growing wide at the sight of the woman in my arms.

"Friends. In need of care. Desperately."

"As are we all. Come in, come in." His voice grew urgent on those last words. I stepped inside as he stretched out his arm, opening the edifice to us. "Here."

Joseph's long, dark robe rustled against the rushes on the floor as he walked past us. I followed, trusting Cade and Ian to stay on my heels. "You may bring them inside."

He opened the door to a small cell, unoccupied, with three bare cots pushed against the stone walls.

Meager light drifted in from the hall as I filed in and gently laid her on the naked bed. Agnes hovered near my shoulder. "I am well enough to care for her." She looked at Margried. "Sister?"

Joseph's brows shot to his hairline, and he looked straight at me. "These are nuns in your charge?"

Discerning as ever. "'Tis not what it seems."

He shook his head, and the hint of a smile stretched his chin. "As it always is with you."

With that one statement, he gave me grace. The sense of acknowledgement of my past crimes, and his absolving me of them in his eyes, grew almost palpable in the small room. I met his eyes, gratitude rising out of the depth of my soul.

Gwyn moaned and tossed on her narrow bed. I stared down at her. Every finger longed to reach out and smooth the hair from her forehead, damp with sweat and hot with fever. Every fiber of my being longed to see her glowing and vibrant again.

Agnes stood and limped over to stand between the beds of Margried and Gwyn. "Shoo, all of you."

"Nay." At my word, Agnes turned and pinned me with a glare.

I did not relent. "You are not at your best. You will need help."

"What will you need, good sister?" Joseph already stood in the doorway, ready to fetch whatever she asked for.

"Water. Cool water to soothe her fever."

Joseph disappeared. Ian followed him.

Cade shed the satchel he carried in the corner and came to stand by Margried's bedside. "What can I do?"

Agnes looked at him then at me. "Find me clean bedding and more garments, if you can."

Cade beat me to the door of the women's room, but only by a second. He went to the left. A chill going through me, I cast one last glance at the small room, wanting to see Gwyn one more time. Agnes stood over her, shielding her face from me. The mystery shrouding the woman's illness took over the beat of my heart. I flung open every door in the hall, seeking linens of any sort.

My search proved fruitless. I made my way down the dark corridor, lit with no more than a stub of candle, left over no doubt from church services. Every portal revealed naught but another room, each empty of any scrap of fabric. Until the last.

Arms loaded, I swiveled and strode back the way I had come. *I thank You, Lord.* Coming to the cell in which I had left the women, I made certain my boots sounded on the stone floor, alerting them to my presence. I heard the whisper of voices and stepped into the doorway.

Joseph sat a bowl of cool water on a rickety chair beside Gwyn's bed. Agnes reached for a rag from my pile and plopped it in the bowl. I laid the rest of my burden on the table between the two beds, on which a lone candle lent light.

I got my first good look at Gwyn. Little wisps of her long hair, darkened a shade by sweat, stuck to her forehead. But she was calm, neither moving nor moaning. That was a good sign, was it not?

I looked at Agnes to be sure. She neither met my gaze nor made any comment about my hovering, an obvious announcement that I would be helping. She leaned toward Margried, speaking in low tones to her. Then she straightened. "Where is Ian?"

As if summoned by her query, Ian stepped into the doorway, looking hesitant to come any farther. He had a pear-shaped jug in one hand and a cup in the other. "From the well. 'Tis quite cool."

I had never before seen a smile on Agnes's face, but she beamed with one now as if she had just witnessed a sunrise. She dipped some into the cup, but Gwyn's lips would not part. She turned her head away, eyes still closed. Agnes sighed.

Cade appeared in the doorway. A flicker of surprise flashed in his eyes, no doubt at seeing so many gathered in the small cell. His gaze touched on the cup Agnes had returned to Ian. He strode forward, poured water into the cup, and handed it to Margried. I frowned at that. *Postulant,* I reminded myself. She drank eagerly.

A few quick steps took me to the far side of Gwyn's bed. "With what is she afflicted?"

Agnes shook her head. "I fear lung fever."

I wobbled on my feet and sank to the stone floor, my hands grasping for the thin blanket beneath which she lay unmoving. I dared to touch her hand with my own. Her skin blazed. I looked up at Agnes, unable to keep the desperation from weighing down my tone. "Will she live?"

She sighed.

I looked at Gwyn lying senseless, unable to hear us. I had seen her like this before, still, silent. She had recovered then, after I had pulled her from the depths of the ocean.

But I had seen my father like this, as well, skin afire, suffering. A lance of fear pierced my heart. He had not recovered.

In the next hours, I bathed her face and neck, her arms and hands.

I smoothed the hair from her forehead and lifted her shoulders while Agnes coaxed cool water from the well between her chapped lips. Dark circles ringed Gwyn's eyes. When she moaned, the sound shaved off a chip of my heart.

Sounds were important to her. I knew this. I knew it had a little to do with her eyes betraying her at times, blackening a world that should have bloomed bright for her. Her love of the lilt of wind whispering through trees, the splatter of rain, or names on her tongue went beyond being deprived of so many glories of the sense of sight.

As I dipped the rag in the cool water once more and washed her hands, I recalled the way she often tipped her head to better hear. And the way her lips had so carefully formed the letters of Titus's name. *Titus Tudder. What a strong name you possess.*

At once, I wondered what she thought of my name. *Dirk.* I had not always been known by the name of a dagger, but it was the only name by which she knew me. Joseph called me Devon. If given the choice, which would she prefer?

She would probably say Dirk suited me.

Agnes sagged against the side of the bed, resting her head inches from Gwyn's hand as if her very closeness could help heal her. Joseph had gone to fetch any garments he could find. I did not know where Cade had gone. Margried, curled on the bed next to Gwyn's, slept soundly.

The rock in my chest grew heavier as the hours passed. If only Gwyn would awaken and look at me with that glare of hers.

"Gwyneth Barrington." The whisper wrapped around the room, thudded off the walls, and pierced my soul. It received no answer. Only deserted me, fled the empty cell, and wandered off to wherever unanswered words and whispers go.

I would not give in to the despair. *Lord, will You not heal her? I promised You anything once if You would only save her, but I cannot do that now. I am powerless to promise You that. I was then, as well. I always was and always will be.*

I stared down at her face.

But, I beg of You, touch this woman. Save her. Will You please make her well and whole again?

"Gwyneth Barrington."

Wonder of wonders, her hand moved beneath mine.

"That is right…your name is strong because you are strong. You deserve a strong name. You…" *You deserve better.* She deserved to do more than lie in a bed, oblivious to the beauty she inspired in the world around her. She had lain abed twice since I had taken her from the convent across the Channel. "You must fight. Fight for hope." I leaned in and spoke into her ear. "Hold to hope, Gwyn."

She shifted on the bed, and her fingers squeezed mine. Her eyes remained closed, but it was enough.

Jubilant happiness stole through my being, surprising me with the burst of relief, affection, and something stronger, something deeper that caused my heart to beat wildly and my hand to shake as I held hers. *I have done it now, Lord.*

I was no longer falling in love with her. The deed was long done.

I love her. Wholly. Completely. Unconditionally. I, Devon Godfrey, second son and converted rogue, had given possession of my heart to a Catholic maiden who knew me as nothing more than a scandal…a murderer.

I laid my head down on her hand. What had I told her? *Hold to hope.* But for me, there was no hope to hold.

Gwyneth

Chapter Twenty-Seven

I dreamed I sat overlooking golden fields, green forest, and glittering sunset. The peach and amber haze of dusk lent the landscape I surveyed a lazy air. Or perhaps it was just that I was old. Somehow, without looking down at my age-spotted hands or touching the wrinkles on my face, I knew the years had passed, a lifetime had fled, and I was old. The knowledge did not scare me.

In fact, nothing scared me.

It was that total lack of fear that brought the smile to my face. I knew I was dreaming, but I wondered just the same why I dreamt such a thing. Why not dream that I was young, romping over the grounds extending beyond Barrington Manor on the heels of my grandfather? Riding on one of the many mares in our stables, my father at my side? Eating that new plant, potatoes, that had been brought from the New World five years after my mother's birth? Even looking into her worried eyes and reassuring her that some adventure gone awry had taught me something? Why did I not dream that my grandfather and my parents were still alive?

Instead, I dreamed I was old. My life nearly gone. My last candle nearly snuffed out. Peace reigned in my heart, oddly enough, as I sat there and watched the sunset. Then I realized why. Someone was holding my hand.

But when I awoke, my hands lay on the coverlet, alone. I opened my mouth almost as soon as I opened my eyes, desperate for a drink.

"Lady Gwyneth!" Sister Agnes leaned to hover over me, an expression of joy on her face. She disappeared, only to return again a moment later with—mercy of mercies!—a cup in her hand. She helped me sit up and take a sip. The water tasted cool, refreshing.

"What happened? Have I been ill?"

Sister Agnes placed the cup near a pitcher. "Lung fever."

My eyes widened.

"Either from the dip you took in the sea or being out in the rain."

I smiled. "Or both." My gaze scanned the room. "Where are the others?"

"Cade took Margried for a walk in the courtyard. She needed some fresh air."

I stored the information about Cade and Margried in the back of my mind. "And Ian and Dirk?"

Sister Agnes hesitated then sat on the side of the bed. Dread built in my chest. She met my eyes with her own. "They are well."

Anxiety flowed from my heart, and freedom took its place. Not even the dull ache that had plagued me pained me any longer. "Then why do you seem worried?"

She laid a hand on my forehead. "Your fever is broken. Praise the Lord. It has been three days."

"What of Dirk...and Ian?" I added the second man's name as an afterthought and chided myself for it.

"They are in the chapel."

My brows rose. "The chapel?"

"They are Protestant through and through, but Dirk wished to spend some time seeking solace."

I let one brow slide down and kept the other aslant. Sister Agnes could certainly prolong the telling of the truth when she needed to. "What are you not telling me? Why does he seek solace?"

"He just heard that his brother is dead."

And when she decided she no longer needed to prolong the truth, she spoke bluntly. I sank back into the bed, letting my tired muscles melt into the rope supports. "His brother?"

"Harold Godfrey."

Just as soon as I had gone limp, I stiffened and shifted, trying to sit up, but Sister Agnes laid a hand on my shoulder. I glared at her. "I must go to him. See how he is."

From the doorway, a shadow cast over the foot of the bed. "He will be well."

I looked up at the large man filling the frame. Who was he to tell me Dirk would be well? "But he may need—"

My words cut off, but what I had been about to say swirled in the air around the three of us. *Me. He may need me.* What had I been thinking? How was I intending to comfort the man in such a loss? Except for having experienced grief myself, I could be of no help. Unless Dirk wanted candles lit, prayers for release from purgatory said. Which I was entirely

sure he did not.

"He needs no one now save God," the man said. Who was he?

I pulled away from Sister Agnes's hand and surged to a standing position. "He may need a friend."

"He will find such a friend in God."

I swayed on my feet and had the good sense to relent before I fell. I groped for the bed again, and Sister Agnes helped me beneath the covers once more. A blush climbed to my cheeks as I realized I had stood in a man's presence in nothing but this meager shift that had come from… *somewhere.*

So I lay in a strange bed, in a strange room, in a strange garment. While Dirk sought solace in the chapel…. The chapel. I cast a glance around the room…which strangely resembled a nun's cell. *Nee.* It could not be. Had I awoken in the convent at Leiden? Yet how could that be? Had I been ill that long? Had we once again crossed the *Kanaal?*

But why was a man in the doorway of my cell? No men save priests and popes had ever been admitted within the convent. The former, rarely. The latter, never.

I shook the thought from my mind, searching first Sister Agnes's face then squinting to search the stranger's. Sister Agnes remained uncharacteristically silent. The stranger merely stood there, too far for me to discern his expression. How I wished for my glasses so that I could better see him!

But there was one thing even my poor eyesight could not hide from me. The replaying of his words—English words—in my mind assured me we were still in England. And there was but one monastery left in England, though it was not a monastery any longer. Saint Benet's. Managed by the bishops of Norwich.

I stared at the man, aghast. He spoke of God as a *friend.* Heresy! Such as could be expected from a Protestant clergyman.

I pulled my gaze away from the man to watch Sister Agnes pour more water, clear as the diamonds I wore around my neck. I drank the entire cup dry. My fingers reached for my rosary, and a strange trio of words leapt into my brain as if I could see them clearly imprinted on the air in front of me. *Hold to hope.*

Where had I heard that?

I shook off the question and looked to the man in my doorway once more. "God has no need of seeking the friendship of sinners."

"Only the friendship of saints?" A glimmer of a smile lit the man's voice.

I shook my head. That was *not* what I meant. 'Twas heretical even to think such things. "God in His heaven does not desire to mingle with the stained souls that roam upon the earth. He is holy."

The man's head tipped back as if contemplating my words. "A holy God…in His heaven…"

Sister Agnes dipped a rag in a pitcher of water and touched my forehead with it. The coolness of it bade me close my eyes. His voice bade me keep them open, watchful, trained upon him. "He *is* holy."

I settled into the bed. He agreed with me then.

"But is that not what He did?"

I frowned. "Is what not what He did?"

"How did you put it? 'Mingle with the stained souls that roam upon the earth?' I ask you, is that not what He did?"

I opened my mouth, closed it again. Reached one hand, trembling with fatigue, to the rosary at my collar. My fingers trailed over the diamonds to the cross in the center, whereupon the crucified Savior stretched out His arms.

"Is that not exactly what He did?"

Sister Agnes frowned. "There is a difference."

I nodded in agreement with her and looked to the man again to see what he might say. It galled me, but I hung upon his words.

"What difference, good sister? I fail to see it."

I found my voice once more. "God judges the way of the righteous and the wicked. He upholds the cause of the just and brings destruction on those who sin against Him. Lightning is under His feet, and justice is in His hand."

"You speak of God as a judge."

"Are you saying that He is not?" To admit such would be blasphemy. None of it was truth. None of it could be truth.

The man's voice lowered. "I speak of God as a friend."

"Who are you?"

"I am Joseph."

I looked at Sister Agnes, squinting to see her expression. She had the same wary look upon her face that I knew resided on mine.

"Cannot the two be one? Just as the three are one? Cannot there be various facets to the character of God?" Joseph did not speak in an accusatory manner. Rather, he confirmed my suspicions. He was speculating. Wondering.

Fool.

145

Still, his talk of different facets stayed with me. God could not have varying facets to His character, as the diamonds beneath my fingers had facets and edges…could He?

'Twas not possible. If it were so, then His will would be impossible to understand. His magnificent plan, as Margried called it, impossible not only to know, but to accept. For all of His decisions would arise from a mind as convoluted and complicated as…my own.

To dare to believe such a thing would be calling into question the character of the one thing in all Creation that I could trust. And that I would simply not allow. Sinners made decisions out of their sinfulness; God passed judgment out of His holiness. To entertain the idea that in some instances God would…choose to be a friend…

That I could not fathom.

Dirk

Chapter Twenty-Eight

Walking out of the chapel, I found Cade and Joseph waiting for me. Mercifully, they had given me the time I asked for, in which I had knelt and tried to pray. But I could not get Cade's bloodshot eyes out of my mind. His face had looked haggard as he stood in Gwyn's doorframe, as if he had aged ten years with the news. I had risen from her bedside, steeling myself for whatever terrible tidings he came to tell.

I had not succeeded. No amount of steeling, no method of preparation, could have protected me against the punch his words delivered. *Harold is dead.*

I had turned and given Gwyn one lingering look. Agnes saw and murmured words of assurance that she would care for her in my absence. A gracious gesture, since from the first I had only been intruding on Agnes's care, anyway, desperate to be near Gwyn, to touch her hands, her hair, to hear her breathing.

Then, when Cade told me, I did not wish for her to see me fall apart.

I had not seen my brother in nigh unto a year. Just as I had not seen my mother nor either of my sisters in all that time. In the months since I had been running, I had not been home. I had not looked into my mother's eyes. I had not embraced my sisters. I had not clapped my hand onto Harold's thin shoulder.

Harold had always been thin. The Lord knew he had caught every ague and fever that had dared come anywhere near Godfrey Estate. *Lord, You know. You know.*

"How?" Now, looking at Cade, I croaked out the word from a chest constricted with sorrow.

His gaze never wavered from mine, grief for me pouring from his look. "He was thrown from his horse. He never awoke."

My hand reached up to find steadiness on the chapel's doorframe, the rough wall reminding me I lived. I closed my eyes, seeing the faces of my mother and sisters grief-stricken and sobbing. No warning. Harold, who had so often succumbed to the most trifling of sicknesses, who had spent so much of our childhood abed with the books that meant so much to him…weak, scholarly Harold had died so suddenly, Mother, Susan, and Millicent never even saw it coming.

There had been no opportunity to say farewell. My grief—that of a brother separated and denied one last look, one last word, one last clasp of the hand, one last embrace—was their grief. Alive one moment and gone the next. At least when it had been my father's time, we had the opportunity to whisper farewell.

Joseph, shadowed in the meager light, held something in his hands. "This came just now by messenger."

He held it out to me, and I took it, though I had no desire to read the missive. Why stab myself anew with the sight of the truth written on the page? The pain had been blinding enough when I heard it spoken.

> *Lady Rohesia Godfrey, by the grace of God to Joseph of Saint Benet's Abbey, The Broads, Norfolk, her most kind greeting.*
>
> *I beseech thee, if the whereabouts of my son, Devon Godfrey, are known to you, send him my plea for his homecoming. Harold Godfrey, thrown from his horse this twenty-eighth day of August, went to be with his Lord and Savior.*
>
> *Yours, Rohesia Godfrey.*

My mother's coarse script scrawled across the page and thrust the dagger deeper into my heart.

"I am sorry, Devon."

I swallowed. "I thank you, Reverend."

"The messenger waits at the door. Would you send a reply?"

With all of my being, I wanted to say aye and send a message in my own hand. Wanted to give my mother more tears, tears of relief this time, and assure her that I was safe and well. "Nay. To send her my own words would be of no help to her. It would only put her in danger."

Cade took the letter from my hand before I dropped it. He skimmed it quickly. "Let me write something. Assure her—assure them all—I know where you are, that you are well."

I shook my head. "She would know you are with me."

"She would say naught of it."

"But she would come here."

Cade sighed and folded the message. "Aye, she would."

I knew my mother. He knew my mother. She knew us. She would not doubt for a moment that Cade's saying he had seen me, seen me well, meant he was with me. She would bring my sisters across the miles and meet us here, caring not a whit for the danger. I could not allow that.

"Then I will tell her such." Joseph turned to go.

I stayed him with a hand on his arm. "Do not. She will only wonder where you had seen me and when."

"I will not tell her I have seen you. Only that I have heard from you and know that you are in good health."

Cade cleared his throat. "And tell her you will make every effort to contact him with the news." The reminder made me draw a breath.

Joseph nodded, his features solemn, and disappeared down the hall. The shadows pulled him into their lair, and his image was lost to me.

Just like Harold.

"Come." Cade put a hand on my shoulder and steered me straight back into the chapel.

I remained silent, not caring where I was except that it not be far from Gwyn. Gwyn! Earnest prayers rose from my heart to my throat to my tongue that God be with her, that He heal her. I could not lose her, too.

Fool. I would undoubtedly lose her in the end.

She had never been mine and never would be. Never, even if it were possible, consent to be. If the lung fever did not steal her now just as it had stolen my father from me, then my returning her to her uncle at Barrington Manor would surely lock me out of her life forever.

Cade led me back into the chapel, and I uttered not a word of protest. Merely dropped to my knees in a pew and let the sorrow lodge in my chest as if taking up permanent residence. Mayhap it *was* settling in to stay. What had I now? Not a father, not a brother, not the woman I loved… not a home. Not a way to provide for my mother and sisters. They had no one now. With my father gone, Harold had come into his inheritance. He had excelled at maintaining the keep, managing the men in employ on the estate, ruling his small kingdom as our father had before him.

I had once envied him the security of not being second son.

Now the responsibility for my mother and sisters fell to me. And I could not live up to it. Could not return to Godfrey Estate. I was an accused man. Having fled, I was as good as a condemned one.

With my face buried between my arms, my only view was of the cold stone floor of the chapel on which I knelt. But though I could see only that, I knew that God could see much more. I heard nothing save the sound of my breathing in that space, but it was as if the voice of God had spoken directly to me, the words so imprinted themselves upon my brain. *I know.*

And I knew He did. He knew Harold. He knew me. He knew the firstborn son of my father had so often been my example. He knew I had fallen so far short of that example. He knew all.

I had not experienced the peace I knew now since my conversion, since that moment outside my father's deathbed where I had surrendered all to the Christ who offered—nay, promised—to forgive. A groan wrenched from my chest, and I lifted my head. Saw the sight of Christ, crucified on the cross, above me as the point of focus for the entire chapel.

After a time, Ian entered the chapel, and I bid Cade to leave. From the look in his eyes, he understood that it was not from my not wanting him near. I needed only time. Ian knelt near me without a word, but not as near as Cade had been. I did not mind. Mayhap I needed to be alone again. With my prayers. With my God.

But He seemed distant somehow, until that rush of peace. Mayhap it was my inability to string together any coherent prayers. The words tumbled from my brain in an insensible mass, even as the groaning of my heart doubled, tripled, and multiplied. If only I could convert the rush of emotions into prayers…

Ian laid a hand on my shoulder, and I was grateful for that touch. It seemed as if the hand of Christ touched my soul with assurance and peace—though the grief in no way lessened.

Then I realized that though I could not, Someone could.

God knew. He knew the suffering of a stained soul lifting equally stained hands high to His heaven. He knew the muttering of the heart and thought it eloquent. He knew the anguish that brought beads of sweat to my brow as I wondered if Harold had known pain, had suffered. He knew the collision, seeming conflict, and in the end, the clear mingling of sadness and peace, of grief and trust, that came with the pouring out of my heart before His feet.

I closed my eyes again, not wanting to see the cross, not wanting to see Ian, not wanting to see even the cold floor that caused my knees to ache. I wanted to see nothing, so that I could feel everything. For if I pushed out the pain, I pushed out the peace. If I protested against the agony of knowing I would never see my brother again, I would never see my Savior bending low, hands outstretched to receive me. If I locked out the misery

and the grief, I would lock out God's mercy and grace.
And that I simply could not bear.

Gwyneth

Chapter Twenty-Nine

I lay awake, staring at the ceiling, scoffing at Sister Agnes's words that I must remain abed this night. After hours of doing just that, restlessness pulled at my legs. But I obeyed. Because I knew if I rose, my head would cause the room to tip and turn. Because I doubted my legs would hold me. Because the fever still attacked me intermittently, and when it did not, the chills came.

But moreover, I obeyed because that was what I always did.

I had always fancied myself utterly unlike everything my mother was, but I began to see the untruth in that as I studied the ceiling above me. The shadows moved and melted according to the desire of the candle flickering beside the pitcher of water on the small table between Margried's bed and mine.

My mother had always obeyed, as well. Timid, quiet, she had rarely smiled, rarely laughed. Only when she looked at my father did any kind of joy pass across her expression. But that was just it—it passed.

Was fleeting joy true joy at all?

I had always taken pride in Grandfather telling me I reminded him of my grandmother. I had never met her, but I had known her through his telling me of her. Of her spirited laugh. Of her teasing. Of her waking each morning, eager for the good, and willing to look for that good in those around her.

I looked up at the blurs of light and dark caught in a rhythmic dance, completely at the whim of the candle flame. I was caught, completely at the whim of life. When had been the last time I had laughed? When had been the last time I had been eager to awaken? I had lived so long in hate and anger.

I had hated Dirk. Hated him from that moment I saw him in the Great Hall, the knife in his hand dripping blood. And I had been so angry at him ever since he burst into the cell so like this one across the *Kanaal*. Why could he not have left well enough alone? Why did he have to chase me across a sea when all I wanted was to be free of him, to be free of the great crushing grief I had known for all these many months?

A sob escaped me though I tried to choke it back. I coughed and shifted on the bed.

"Gwyneth?"

I closed my eyes. "I am sorry, Margried."

"'Tis well. Did you have an unpleasant dream?"

"I am sorry I woke you."

"Do not worry yourself. But what woke you?"

I winced. "I have not been to sleep."

The sound of movement hit my ears, and I turned my head to see her lying on her side, facing me. The expression on her face would have been visible in the candlelight if it were not for my blurry vision. "Margried, do you ever wonder if you are seeing clearly what is before you?"

Laughter invaded her voice. "Not nearly as often as you do, I suppose."

"'Tis not what I meant." I did not feel defensive, but neither did I laugh. My nighttime musings had thrust me into a somber mood.

"What did you mean?"

"Have you ever looked at someone and saw who you thought they were, only to find they were someone else?"

Silence lingered for a moment. I began to regret my words, wished I could bar them once more inside my throat.

"Aye."

My eyes widened. "Aye?"

"Aye."

"Who?"

"One."

I turned over, too. Rose up on one elbow. "One."

Silence. She only turned to meet my gaze.

"Who, Margried?"

She released a shuddering breath. "Cade."

My jaw unhinged. I closed it again, swallowing my shock and my… lack of shock. Somehow her answer surprised me and failed to surprise me at the same time. The depth of that confusing emotion kept me silent a moment more. Then, "What did you think him at first?"

Another sigh sounded from her bed. "The same as you thought Dirk at first, I imagine. Much the same."

"And what is that?" The thought of Dirk's face brought a twist of uneasiness to my stomach. How was he? Where was he? Did he find solace in sleep or did his grief keep him awake?

"A monster. An enemy. A man to be feared."

'Twas exactly what I had thought Dirk to be. At first. But no longer. That thought nearly scared me senseless. "When did your estimation of him change?"

"That first night."

The shadows pulled my gaze to them. They danced a merry jig upon the ceiling. "That first night? Truly?"

"Aye. When he turned me in his arms to protect my hurt one."

I remembered Cade's calm after Sister Agnes's telling of such a terrible tale, remembered his quiet insistence that Margried disclose which arm was injured. Though I knew I tread on dangerous ground, I could not keep back the question my tongue begged to ask. "And what do you think of him now?"

"I think him a man above men. A friend. To be respected, admired, trusted."

"So he has earned your trust?"

"Aye."

I heard more than saw her shift to her back. Silence stole over the room we shared for several long moments. In fact, part of the reason I asked my last question was that I was almost sure Margried had fallen asleep again. As for me, I was more awake than ever. "He earned your trust by what he did, how he acted, Margried?"

"Aye." Her voice sounded soft, weak, nearing sleep, but her words crossed the distance between us, strong and steady. "He did. And he earned it, as well, by what he did not do, how he did not act."

Her breathing deepened not long after, but sleep did not claim me until after many more hours of staring at the shadows on the ceiling.

When I awakened, Margried had left. Where, I knew not. Was it morning yet? I stayed on my side, facing her bed, examining the blanket smoothed over the surface. Not a wrinkle marred its perfection. No blemish could I find though I stared for a good while. I told myself that the reason might lie with my glasses not being on my nose, but I knew

better. Margried was that neat, that tidy, that clean.

Had I ever produced such a perfect blanket in all my days?

Certainly never at my uncle's castle. As the daughter of a nobleman, I had filled my days with tutors and womanly arts. The former only because Grandfather and Papa, too, indulged me. The latter because I always obeyed my mother, whom in my entire life I had seen adamant about only that—that her daughter would be raised a gentlewoman.

At the convent in Leiden, my lack of familiarity with caring for my things surely expressed itself in my three months of housekeeping, or cell keeping, as it were. But, to my shame, I had not noticed this until, in the forest, Margried had taken my blanket from me and refolded it. Even then, I had not even realized the careless job I had made of folding that blanket until she had repaired it.

"You are awake."

I startled and turned over to find Dirk at my side.

"What are you doing here?"

"I was watching you sleep." Shadows hid his face but could not mask the quiet tone of his voice.

I knit my brows together and glared at him. "Why are you in here? 'Tis not proper."

"I wanted to know how you fared."

I looked at the ceiling. "I am well."

"Every time you have said that to me, I have not believed you."

"I do not—"

"You do not lie, I know." He rose from the stool that sat on that side of my bed and took a step away. At once, I was small, staring up at him, wishing I could discern his features.

"I do not." My protest sounded weak.

"Neither do I." His form passed in front of the end of my bed. I shifted to a sitting position, gathering the blanket to my chin. He came around and reached out a hand to the candle on the table between Margried's bed and mine.

But he did. He had. For me. To get me back to England.

Yet I remained silent as I watched him light a second candle I had not yet seen. He lifted it, held it to his face. A hazy glow surrounded his shadowy features. Did his eyes hold sorrow? I held back the words rising in my throat. Who was I to offer comfort to the man who had torn my family from me? I knew the pain of such a loss as he suffered, knew that words could do little to appease it. I pulled my knees to my chest, hugging them beneath the blanket, staring out the open door of my room into the dark hall.

"Milady, I..." His head turned toward Margried's bed. He crossed back to the stool, plopping into it as if a great burden rested on his shoulders. Mayhap one did.

"Say it." The two short syllables emerged from my mouth in a commanding tone that I did not feel.

"I did not lie to Captain Tudder."

My body froze. I refused to look at him. But somewhere deep inside, a seed of hope took root.

"I did not tell him you were Protestant."

Had he lied by omission, then? The small seed that wanted to sprout in my heart faltered. "Did he know?"

He expelled a short sigh. "He asked, and I told him the truth."

"That we are Catholic and against his cause?"

"He would say it is not his, but Netherland's cause. But, aye, he knew of your religion. He even knew that two of you were nuns."

My muscles melted, and I turned my head until my cheek rested on my knees and my eyes could stare straight into his. "He knew that?"

"He did."

"And still he allowed us to board." My voice held only half the wonderment my heart held.

"Still he sought to save you when you fell from his ship."

He could have let me drown. He could have tried to keep Dirk from diving in after me. He would not have succeeded at that. But he could have refused to allow Dirk aboard again with me. A shudder passed through me. We both would have drowned.

"Do you catch a chill, milady?"

Milady. How I longed for my name to fall from his lips. *Say my name.* I buried my face in the hollow made by my knees being pressed together and refused to open my mouth lest I let those words slip through. What could I say instead?

"Has the fever departed?"

I shook my head against my knees. As I stilled, I realized that I offered him my back. I did not watch him lest he brandish a knife. If he intended to do me harm this night, I offered him the perfect opportunity. I heard his boot grate against the stone floor. One leg of the stool lifted and landed with a clang. My head popped up to see him step toward the open doorway, candle still in hand.

"Stop."

He turned back. His dark cloak blended in with the shadowy surroundings, but his shock of red hair pulled from the light. The effect? His hair looked aflame. "What is it?"

I opened my mouth, closed it.

"Are you well? Shall I awaken Sister Agnes?"

"I am sorry about your brother."

The candlelight wavered on his chest as it expanded and deflated again. "He was…"

"Were you close?" *Why did I ask him that?*

"Aye. I had not seen him in many months, however. Not since…"

I clasped my knees tighter, feeling each letter of his unspoken words. *Not since the night my parents died…* He had been separated from his family for as long as I had been separated from mine. Grief for the both of us found lodging deep in my chest, and I fought against the terror that threatened to pull me down. *I cannot trust him.*

But he saved me.

I wished I could see his face. I longed to reach out to him. To touch that flaming hair of his. To be so close that I could see into his brown eyes. With no blur. To hear him say just one more time that he did not do it. "Aboard the captain's ship, you asked me what I saw that night."

His chin dipped down once in a nod.

"I told you."

He did not move.

"And you said you wanted to tell me what you saw."

So slowly that I never felt uncomfortable, never felt threatened, he moved to occupy the stool once more. I remained in the center of the narrow cot, huddled, waiting.

"You said something after my words," he whispered. "Do you remember?"

I did, but I allowed the single word to fall from his lips. Lips that had kissed mine.

"*Mayhap.* I said mayhap you would believe me if I told you what really happened and you replied, 'Mayhap.'"

I turned away from him and groped beside the water pitcher on the table to my right. My fingers searched until I realized I had no glasses to grasp. I raised my eyes to his and rued the fact that the blurred edges of his features refused to sharpen.

My fingers reached for the rosary at my neck. I clasped it so tightly

that the diamonds' sharp edges imprinted themselves on my palms. I recognized the pain from the night Dirk had come for me at the convent.

I was ready now to hear the story.

Mayhap.

Dirk

Chapter Thirty

She held on to that necklace as if it were her salvation, as if she were once again drowning in the Channel and that diamond-studded string was the rope that would see her safely aboard ship. *Lord, will You give me the words?* I shouldered a single chance. If I could help her see the truth this night, she might believe, might trust me…if I failed, all could be lost.

"I have one request."

I nodded, trying to keep my face open for her perusal. "Anything, milady."

Her gaze switched between my eyes as if she wondered if I could truly be trusted to tell her the truth. After all these many months of believing me a murderer, of hating me, could anything I said now turn the tide of her heart?

"Begin with why you were there." Tears already hovered in her eyes and voice.

I wished I could take this cup from her, shield her from reliving that night. "I came at your uncle's summons. He sent a missive to Godfrey Estate requesting an audience with me after we had a conversation in a neighbor's keep."

"Which neighbor?" Her tone did not sound strident or intrusive. She wished for details, then. I would give them.

"The Earl of Cushborough. I had taken my sisters and mother to call upon the countess. Frederick took me to see his new falconry when Oliver arrived. We talked…" My voice trailed, but I never looked away from her.

"Of what did you speak?" Her voice seemed hesitant, small. She had no inkling of what I was about to reveal.

"We spoke of you."

Her shoulders straightened, and she leaned away from me. I winced at the motion and fought the urge to rise, to go to her, to wrap my arms

159

around her and protect her from the blow I had delivered and the ones yet unspoken.

"Why would you speak of me with my uncle?" Anger flared on her face.

"Your uncle spoke of you to me, Gwyn." I kept my tone steady, soothing. Or so I hoped.

"I do not believe you."

"You are not required to believe me, but 'tis the truth."

She grabbed the other candle and held up the flame as if needing the extra light to search my face. Her chest heaved up and down as she took great gulping breaths and struggled to see.

"Mayhap you are not well enough to—"

"*Nee,* I am well enough. I merely…merely must force myself to listen."

"If you cannot withstand the whole, it will keep."

She studied me a moment. "It has kept long enough. Go on."

"That morning, your uncle sang your praises. He called you beautiful, wise, and learned. He mentioned you knew several languages, how to read and write in all of them."

Her chin lifted. "'Tis true. My grandfather taught me the tongue of my grandmother's España. Said that I was like her."

"He was a Spaniard?"

"*Nee,* but he loved her and learned it from her. She died before I was born."

"I am sorry."

Her throat worked, and she placed the candle back on the table. Did she deem herself no longer in need of it? Mayhap she would believe me. "My mother taught me Dutch."

I nodded. "Your uncle acknowledged the unusual circumstances that lent you such learning. He considered it an asset, as well, to possess such a legacy."

Her eyes widened. "Did he call it a legacy, my mixed heritage?"

I sought to remember. "From the way he talked of it, I assumed as much. I think the words he might have used were 'advantageous bloodline.'"

She seemed to slump as if this news disappointed her. "So he was attempting to make me look favorable."

I remained silent, knowing she would come to the conclusion on her own.

"So he could… marry me to you." Her hands balled into fists. "How dare he! 'Twas never his place to try to arrange such a match. That duty rested with my father." She looked up at me. "What did his message contain?"

"He sent me the missive three days later. All he asked was my presence at the keep that night."

"That was all?"

"That was all."

She looked as if she wanted to say something more.

"Milady?"

She looked up at me. "I was just thinking that is Uncle Oliver. Simple. Direct. To the point."

Did she miss the man? I inwardly shook myself. Of course she missed him. He was her only remaining family. The grandfather of whom she spoke had died several years ago, I recalled, in the plague outbreak of three years past, along with her uncle's wife. She was probably most eager to be in her uncle's presence again. To be in his safekeeping, under his watchful eye. She no doubt considered herself safe with him.

Only a few more days of travel and she could be home.

I did not want to take her.

At Barrington Manor, she would no longer be in my care. The lord that I distrusted would have authority. The thought caused bile to churn in my stomach. Could I, for the sake of restoring my reputation, relinquish her to the man who, because of the very night I told her about, I trusted not one whit?

"How do I know you will tell me all?" she asked, her voice small, her eyes wide.

With that question sour in my mouth, I promised, "You look into my eyes. Do not look away. See the truth, and hear me when I say I will leave nothing out. I may want to, but I will not."

The haze of torchlight cut through the haze of twilight and the tension that escaped from the open gates. My gaze swept over the solemn faces of the men in the courtyard as I dismounted my horse and stepped forward, toward the entrance to the castle.

Oliver's smile slithered onto his face as he greeted me. "I am most pleased that you could come, Godfrey."

"I thank you for inviting me to your home." Something seemed wrong here. A somber mood cloaked the keep in gloom. No servants scurried in the shadows. None but Oliver stood near.

"Let us convene in the Great Hall. My brother and his wife await us."

He went ahead of me. I followed at a short distance, not willing to lose sight of the man as the castle was dark, but also not wanting to be too close. Something about him made me uneasy. I had not experienced this heightened awareness when in the earl's company, when Oliver had ridden up to turn the conversation toward his niece. I had thought him rude for changing the course of our afternoon in such a way…but now, this night, a wily air hung about him.

Then I saw her.

Tall and striking, hair hanging in a long curtain over her shoulder, she turned her head to look at me, eyes widening with surprise and something else. Her small white hand rested on the stair rail, and her moss-colored gown flowed behind her. Her other hand rose to a glittering necklace with a cross dangling from the center. She broke her gaze away from mine and hurried up the stairway, lost to my sight not a second after.

I trained my gaze on Oliver's back. The man had never turned, never noticed.

I detected something different about her. Haughty air. Cold green eyes. And yet something about the way she at once reached for the cross at her neck and swallowed…as if she was as taken with me as I was with her.

But I knew even from that brief moment that she thought me below her. And she was right. The night's proceedings no longer held any illusion for me. Whatever Oliver's scheme, such a lady could never be mine.

I passed through the entrance to the Great Hall after Oliver, instantly relieved to find that light abounded in the expansive space. Candles, torches, and hanging lamps brought ease to my eyes and gave me a perfect view of the other Barrington brother and his bride.

The man stood and smiled. His features denoted his relation to Oliver, but appeared less sharp and angular than his brother's. Though thinner than Oliver, the two men were of the same height. "Welcome to Barrington Manor, young man."

I nodded my head and extended some shallow greetings as expected.

Simon Barrington swept his hand toward his wife. "Please meet my wife, Louisa."

I bowed to the petite woman, who looked uncomfortable with the attention. Her glossy white-gold hair caught the light enveloping the room and glowed.

I took a seat in the lone chair, resting my hands on the carved arms and leaning into the rigid back. Simon and Louisa shared a horsehair couch in a warm shade of red, while Oliver chose the hard settee. He crossed his boots in front of him.

Simon looked at me. His smile had not yet dimmed. "I have not yet had the pleasure of making your acquaintance, Devon. How does your family fare?"

"Well, sir. I thank you for inquiring. I believe tonight my mother and sisters planned on a quiet evening with Chaucer's Canterbury tales."

Simon turned to his wife and patted her hand. "Louisa, did you hear that?"

The worry lines etching her forehead eased when her husband looked at her then reappeared when he fastened his gaze on me once more. "Louisa owns every one of the volumes. You must extend an invitation to Lady Godfrey and your sisters to come and discuss it with her."

"I am sure they would take great delight in that, sir. I thank you for your hospitality."

"Also, if they have not yet had the privilege of reading John Stow's edition, they may borrow it from our library. Louisa thinks Lydgate's telling of the history of Thebes rivals Chaucer's excellent storytelling."

My brother claimed Lydgate pirated off of Chaucer's tales by adding his own, *The Siege of Thebes*. But I could not say that to Simon. And I had not yet read it, so how was I to know whether Louisa's literary opinion was correct or not? "You are most kind. I am sure they would appreciate that and take great care in the handling of the volume."

Simon waved his hand as if he was perfectly comfortable entrusting the book to me. The thought made me feel more at peace in this keep. I had liked the man at once, and his easygoing manner only increased my respect for him. Though we had never before met, I knew he must be well aware of my besmirched reputation. My former escapades were no secret to the nobility in the lands near Godfrey Estate, but Simon made no mention of them.

My gaze turned toward Oliver. He had not mentioned my record that left much wanting, but each time I looked at him, I was reminded of the deeds that stained my family's name. Mayhap that was why I did not completely trust him. Because it seemed almost as if he held my former life, the life I had embraced before Christ, against me and reveled in the knowledge that he was perfectly entitled to do so. Which, of course, he was—but then why was I here?

Oliver leaned forward. "The reason I brought you here tonight, Godfrey, is to continue our discussion from three days ago." He turned

to his brother. "I talked with Godfrey at the Earl of Cushborough's castle."

"How is Frederick?" Simon cocked his head as if genuinely interested.

Oliver looked annoyed by the interruption. "Well. Now as I was saying, I talked with Godfrey about Gwyneth."

A serving maid appeared at Oliver's side. She did not meet my eyes, which I did not consider unusual. What was unusual was the way her hands shook as she held out a tray to Oliver. He never looked her way, but merely took a goblet and raised it to his lips. The maiden crossed to extend the tray to Simon, Louisa, and me. I took a small sip of the rich wine.

"How did our daughter's name enter your conversation?" Louisa's timid voice broke the silence. Her brows collided in a confused expression that did not detract from her pretty features.

"I merely told Godfrey here of her many wonderful attributes. You have done an excellent job with her, Louisa."

Louisa looked not at all appeased. In fact, she appeared wary.

Simon set down his goblet and turned his head to the side as if to probe his brother's face with his eyes. "Merely?"

"I outlined her beauty and her wit. Surely you cannot deny your daughter possesses not a few charms?" Oliver punctuated his last words with a clipped laugh.

I shifted in my seat, watching the goings-on with wary eyes. Like a spectator at a game of cards, there was naught that I could do but witness and wait for them to remember I was yet present.

That happened none too quickly. Simon turned to me—revelation dawning on his face—then fixed angry eyes on his brother. "Oliver, you must desist from this—this fraud of a plan."

Oliver raised an eyebrow. His relaxed posture gave me the impression that this was an old argument. "Brother, how long have I been telling you that it is high time Gwyneth was given as wife to a man worthy of her?"

Simon shot from his seat. "And how long have I been telling you that her mother and I are capable of handling such arrangements?"

Oliver said a one-syllable word that elicited a gasp from Louisa. Simon's eyes flashed.

His mouth curved in a sardonic smile, Oliver raised a hand to wave his brother back into his chair. "How long will you tarry before beginning to make the arrangements?" He tossed his fingers, laden with gleaming rings, in my direction. "I have brought you a suitable son tonight. He is wealthy enough."

He conveniently left out my shattered reputation, pursuits only turned away from for the few months since my father's death.

Time for me to speak. I remained seated, but leaned forward. "I must protest." My eyes flicked to Oliver's. "You cannot force them to give their daughter's hand in marriage to me. Furthermore, you cannot force me to ask for it."

The man's face turned purple with rage so fast I worried for his health. But I refused to relent, turning instead to Simon. "I am sorry. I was not certain of his plans for the proceedings this night, and I was unaware you had not been consulted."

"Proceedings?" Simon regarded me with a cautious eye.

Louisa lifted a hand to her face. She had gone pale as she listened. Simon saw me look her way, followed the direction of my gaze, and sat beside his wife once more. Taking her hand in his, he closed his fingers over hers and addressed his brother. "Our father would be ashamed of you. Your impatience astounds even me."

Oliver's purple face contrasted with the placidness of his brother's and the pallor of his sister-in-law's. He pulled in a deep draught of air, as if searching for calm. His honeyed voice drifted through the air. "I merely want what is best for my niece. Godfrey would keep her comfortable, would be able to give her the life she is used to."

"I am but a second son."

Oliver pierced me with his gaze. "The second son to a wealthy man. Forgive me, but I am aware that your inheritance is no pittance."

I clenched my jaw. He was right, but the audacity of the man tempted me to lay a fist across his jaw. *Lord, my old wicked ways are wrestling with what I am witnessing here. Will You provide me with self-control?*

Simon shook his head. "Nay, 'tis not right, what you attempted, no matter what your motivation." His face softened as he exchanged a look with his wife. "Louisa and I have decided that we will not force a match upon Gwyneth. She is to choose the man who will be her husband."

Oliver propelled himself out of his chair. His face purpled again. "What a preposterous notion you speak of, brother."

"'Tis none other than the notion that prevailed in the marriage of our father and mother and of Louisa and me."

Oliver plopped into his chair once more, studying his brother's face. "Our mother did not live long after she married for love."

Simon cast a glance at me as if he did not wish to have this conversation in front of me.

"I should take my leave now. I thank you—"

"*No.*" Oliver pronounced the word with a heavy Spanish accent. "Stay."

Simon's face assumed a look of indulgence. "You have heard as often as I have, brother, the story of how our mother came to write letters with our father. They loved each other."

"Yet what benefit did love bring her? Or me, when my wife and child died of the plague when our father did?"

Simon looked taken aback, and he glanced at Louisa. "Love is everything." His features hardened. "Which is why we want it for Gwyneth, why we even named her what we did."

"I still say she would have been a beautiful Maria," Oliver murmured.

One corner of Simon's mouth turned up, as if he had this talk with Oliver often before. "Gwyneth means happiness, and that is what we want for her."

"Happiness is less important than an advantageous match."

"You could marry again, brother."

Oliver made a scoffing sound. "Unlikely. No woman would put up with me except the fair Louisa."

Louisa shrank back against the couch at his words, looking none too pleased. Simon's mouth flipped into a frown. I thought it odd that the man did not name his deceased wife.

Oliver looked at me. "Forgive us for subjecting you to our family squabbles, Godfrey." His white knuckles on the settee's arm belied the relaxed expression he forced upon his face. "Allow me to see you to the door."

Simon and Louisa brought their faces close together as I rose and followed Oliver from the room. Once in the hallway, I maintained no small distance between the other man and myself. How could he act as if he held authority over his brother in such a manner? At the expense of the maiden whose virtues he expounded?

Though the white-gold hair of her mother hung straight over her shoulder, Gwyneth had inherited more of her father's height, and she could in no way be called plain. My heart warred against the thought, but I supposed it was possible that Oliver could be lying about her virtuous, pious nature. That could be part of the reason he was so eager to be rid of her. But, nay, I did not believe that for a moment. In the brief second in which that look had passed between us, I had seen her soul, stained with pride, mayhap, but not with any more wrongdoing than that.

Unlike my own soul.

And what of Oliver's desire to wash his hands of her, see her in a proper marriage with even one such as I? What had he been after? The pathway of the older man's mind made little sense.

Silence hovered in the air between us. At the castle doors, Oliver spoke unintelligible words of farewell before closing the door and shutting himself off from my sight.

When I reached the stables, I heard the muffled scream. I raced back, threw open the door once again, and hurled myself down the hall.

Silence reigned. My steps slowed as I weighed what might await me. The uneasiness I had sensed earlier now burdened my shoulders. What had happened? Who had screamed?

I stepped inside the doorway. What I saw scarred my eyes. Two figures lay on the ground. Twin crimson pools formed near. I raced toward them and knelt. Louisa's sightless eyes stared at the ceiling. Her chest neither rose nor fell. *Lord, have mercy.* The blood spilling from the side of her gown attested to her fate.

A shallow breath brought my gaze to Simon. His body lay crumpled on the floor, turned away from me. One last exhale of air, and his life left his body, as well.

My chest clogging with a myriad of emotions, I gently rolled him toward me. My gaze latched on the knife in his chest, and I shook my head. Sorrow that I had not reached them a moment sooner collided in my soul along with questions. Who had taken their lives? And why?

A bloodcurdling scream came from the doorway; I pulled on the knife and jumped to my feet, ready to defend the lady I had seen so briefly before against whatever enraged killer had murdered her parents.

But there was no enemy in the doorway. Only her. Gwyneth.

Gwyn.

My heart crushed at her look, shattered into a million mites of dust that would have blown away in the slightest breeze. Silence stretched between us for the shortest of seconds, palpable, deafening. The silence breathed as her parents, lying on the stones at my feet, no longer did.

A single drop of blood fell from the knife to burst into ten before the toe of my boot.

The stark hurt in her eyes, quickly consumed by pure hate, made my blood still like ice in my veins. My only route was to flee before guilt was pinned upon me. I had never been an innocent man. Far from it. But I refused to pay for a crime I did not commit.

As I made my escape, I listened to the castle come alive with her cries and those of others joining her in that blood-soaked room. Her look

haunted me. Something behind the pain slicing through the clear cool emerald river of her eyes caused me to want to stay. But there would be no turning back now.

As I fled, running through the woods like a crazed animal, prayers flying from my lips and catching in the branches above me, I knew. I knew there was no hope of ever going back, of ever convincing her of the truth. I knew utter hopelessness that night. As if nothing would ever be the same. Just like my life. I had thought, in the short time since my father died, that I was succeeding in changing, becoming the man he had wanted me to be, that my family needed.

All undone in a moment's mistake.

So I kept running.

And that was all.

Gwyneth

Chapter Thirty-One

As the last word fell from his lips, I looked away. I wished I had sooner, for then mayhap I could have doubted. But he had been right; the truth was clear in his eyes. And it stabbed.

Wails poured from my throat unchecked, and I rocked back and forth upon the narrow bed. I was aware of Margried stumbling through the door to wrap her arms around me. I even saw Sister Agnes appear in the open doorway, looking at me with a dazed expression. She stood behind Dirk, who, with anguish in his eyes, hovered near as if he could not bring himself to leave, but neither could he come close.

As if it were that night once more and he was torn between staying and leaving, between remaining at my side and running for his life.

My wails transformed into keening and my keening into screams that I could not control. Out of myself, I grieved. Rocking back and forth, huddled in the cocoon of Margried's embrace.

"Gwyn." I heard Dirk's agonized whisper before he said my name in stronger and stronger tones. Just that one word came from his lips, but I heard so much more. Then what I heard he put into voice. "I am sorry. So sorry. You are well, Gwyn. You are well, whole, here. Here, with me. You are well."

Throughout it all, he stood at the foot of the cot, neither near nor far.

Moeder!

Papa!

"Gwyneth." Margried's gentle voice accompanied her kiss on the top of my head. Her long fingers stroked my hair. Still I could not stop the dry sobs from attacking me. No tears came. Not a one. But I could not cease screaming, keening, crying out. Or rocking. Back and forth. Back and forth.

Mayhap if I burrowed deeper into Margried, I would never have to come out again. Never have to face this body-wrenching grief again. Back and forth. Back and forth.

How I heard the sound of hurried, frantic footsteps coming down the hallway, I never knew. But I did, and soon they stopped as a new figure stepped through the doorway. Joseph took one look at me and circled Dirk, passing him to get to me. I shrank back, not eager to be anywhere near a man's touch.

Dirk made a sound so near a growl I lifted my gaze to him. He focused on Joseph. "Leave her be. Can you not see she fears you?"

Joseph did not cease his approach. He merely leaned closer to me, though he did not touch the bed. I made a mewing sound between my moans of anguish.

"Reverend." Dirk's sharp bark made me flinch. Seeing my movement, he looked stricken.

"What she fears is neither me nor you."

"Then what does she fear?"

I had nearly forgotten Sister Agnes stood close by, but it was she who held the candle that lit the room.

Back and forth. Back and forth.

"The pain. The grief. The possibility that she might feel such again." Joseph's eyes trained on mine, and I buried my head in Margried's shoulder, unable and unwilling to meet his piercing look. It had not been a look of anger, that much I could tell. But neither could I discern just what lay in his eyes, whether determination or truth or something else.

"Lady Gwyneth, look at me."

For mayhap the first time in my life, I disobeyed. Unable. Unwilling. Back and forth. Back and forth.

"Lady Gwyneth, I am going to pray for you now." Without waiting for my acquiescence or protest, he bowed his head. "Father God, we are gathered here in fear, in grief, in heartbreaking pain. Our hearts crack and splinter with the pain we hear pouring from Your child, Gwyneth Barrington. We can hear it, and we can see it, Lord, and we cringe at the enormity of it."

As did I. My wails and moans increased in intensity until I could barely stand the sound in my own ears. My chest threatened to rip from my ribcage. And my heart—I had nearly given up on it—it beat so wildly, so erratically, so quickly.

Back and forth. Back and forth.

"Heavenly Father, we cannot understand the scope of the pain and

grief we are seeing and hearing now, but we know You can. Your hands stretched the heavens wide, Your fingers splayed the forests tall, and Your feet stand on the clouds. You are mighty and powerful, and we praise You for that. We are most unworthy to come into Your presence now, but by the blood of Your Son, Jesus, we do so in light and without shame."

My groans lessened, but the sound still rang in my ears. I wished it would go away! How I wished it would just go away. I wanted to hear more of Joseph's prayer...the word *blood* sent a shudder traveling through me, but *without shame* caused my head to rise.

"Aye, without shame and *in light* we come before You, O Most High. We give You praise for Your magnificence and give You praise that You see us, mere mortals. We are gathered here, clinging to the hope we have in You. We are eager for Your complete healing and restoring love to rest upon Your child, Gwyneth. Her heart is scarred with what she has seen and what she has experienced. Our hearts break for her, and hers, most assuredly, is cracked in the deepest places."

I choked on a dry sob. No tears. Why did I have no tears? Was I cursed to be a tearless woman for the rest of my days?

"God, we pray You would touch Your daughter, Gwyneth, and restore her to wellness, not only from the lung fever, but from the wounds in her heart to which we bear witness. Though the heart may be cracked wide, grace can still seep in."

I pulled in a shuddering breath, desperate for air to fill my pinched lungs, desperate for the grace of which he spoke to appear. But when the breath was over, I closed my mouth and was no different than before. Tortured moans tumbled from my tongue, and no power within me could stop them.

Margried patted my back and started to hum. The sound broke through the ringing in my ears, drowning it out until I heard naught but the soft notes of a hymn. What did grief sound like? A scream? What about healing, restoration? Humming?

How then was the sound of healing louder than a scream? Yet it was. Margried's melody washed over me until I noticed I was no longer keening, no longer wailing, no longer sobbing. My body was devoid of energy, devoid of everything save one terrifying, undecipherable thought.

Hold to hope.

Joseph released a heavy sigh. Dirk's features relaxed into an expression of awe, his gaze warm on mine. I laid my head on Margried's shoulder once more, unwilling to look into his eyes for long. Not when I felt so cold, so incapable of receiving warmth. My parents were gone, their deaths final, their murders a mystery. The raw pain that thought brought nearly sent the flood bubbling from my mouth again, but I held it back and focused on Margried's humming. *Hold to hope.*

No doubt remained in my mind that Dirk had told me the whole and complete truth. His account of the night ripped open my core, but it also released me from the fetters of hatred that had chained me.

Or did it? Or did it merely redirect my loathing onto the person responsible, though I knew not his identity?

A whimper pulled from my throat before I could hold it back. It left me and landed on each of the four walls of the small space, but no other sound followed. Mayhap I was under control now. Mayhap the effect Dirk's tale had on me was finished.

Nay, the effect of his telling me the truth could never be finished. After all, his disclosure of the events of that night had a catastrophic effect on my spirit. And I finally knew that what I thought I knew all along had been false. Would forevermore be false.

Dirk had not done the foul deed.

Margried's words about her growing respect for Cade echoed in my mind. *And he earned it, as well, by what he did not do, how he did not act.* Had Dirk ever acted as a murderer might? *Nee.* And after all he had done for me, had he ever given me any cause to…to doubt him to be my parents' killer? Aye. Time and time again.

He was innocent.

Instead of the relief I had at first expected, a surge of contempt rose within me. Who *had* killed my parents? The monster! The beast! Expressions of repugnance and abhorrence stumbled over each other within my mind—

I cried out and placed my hands over my ears, sacrificing the soothing sound of Margried's song on the altar of ridding my head of those horrible thoughts. *Nee.* I would not hate again. It had nearly destroyed me the first time. No more!

A fuzzy feeling overtook me. I no longer heard Margried humming, but I sensed Joseph, Sister Agnes, and Dirk stirring around me. What they were doing, I did not care. I closed my eyes. But it did not work. Shutting myself away from the outside world of that cramped cell only exacerbated the grating noise of my own hatred in my ears. If I hated the man who had murdered my parents, I would bar my heart against that kind of pain again, would I not?

A lightning strike inside my mind caused me to gasp. My thoughts shifted. My hands fell away from my ears, and I heard once again the sound of Margried humming a tune I did not recognize but knew to be a hymn. I heard also the sound of voices praying. Unintelligible words, all, but prayers nonetheless. In Sister Agnes's passionate tones. In Joseph's powerful manner. In Dirk's pleading voice.

I could not allow myself to hate again.

I had hated once. I hated Dirk once. And it had nearly been my undoing. How many wrong choices had I made as the result of being imprisoned by my revulsion? Nay. Hatred would not bar my heart against pain. Hatred would only bar my heart against healing, redemption, love. My eyes opened.

But more importantly, in that moment, my heart opened.

Dirk

Chapter Thirty-Two

The sounds of her screams stung my mind every time I sought to close my eyes and seek the solace of sleep. At last, I surrendered the hope of rest and left my bed for the chapel once more. Mayhap here I could find peace. After several long moments of staring at the cross and stumbling over stuttering prayers, I put my head in my hands. *Lord, You know. You know.* Even when I knew not where He was leading, He had the way planned. Even when I knew not why He allowed tragedy, He supplied the living water that quenched my thirsty soul.

"Could you not sleep, Devon?"

I lifted my head and turned to find Joseph standing a few steps away. The candle in his hand sent light cascading over his face, a face full of compassion.

"Nay, Reverend. And you?"

"I had no desire for sleep this night."

I narrowed my eyes at his strange words.

After Gwyn had calmed, Margried insisted we leave. I had not thought to inquire after where Joseph headed, only assumed that he would be as eager for rest as I. Although, in truth, I had not been *eager* for rest, merely ready to try to convince myself that if I fell asleep, it stood to reason that Gwyn rested as well. And I wanted to know that she rested.

Of course, the consolation of that thought crumbled when the image of how fitful and uneasy Gwyn looked while slumbering surfaced in my mind. I focused on Joseph once more. "I had no desire, either."

"Are you not weary?"

"Weary and ready for sleep are two different things."

A smile cracked Joseph's face. "Indeed."

"Why are you not ready for rest?" The man had surely expended considerable energy in the powerful prayers he had poured out on Gwyn's behalf. My entire soul had ached just to listen to him beseech God for her healing. The man's closeness to the Almighty baffled me this night,

as it always had

"I have other avenues of replenishment than sleep." He knelt beside me but did not seem in any hurry to pray. I nodded my head as if I knew of what he spoke. But other than a vague suspicion, I had no idea. Slow seconds passed as his smile stretched.

"Are you going to make me ask?"

Joseph chuckled. "I suspect you already know my answer."

"God."

"Aye."

I studied his features for a moment then trained my gaze once again upon the cross, the focal point of the entire chapel. "You remind me of another friend of mine. He is the captain of the vessel which brought us across the Channel."

Joseph's slow nod formed his sole response.

"He is Protestant." I looked at him, expecting a sigh, a sad frown, or at the very least, a shake of the head. After all, he had not converted from Catholicism by choice, but by necessity. I had been under the impression that at the core, he remained Catholic.

But Joseph exhibited neither annoyance, irritation, nor surprise. Instead, he nodded again.

"Is this the friend who led you to the Lord?"

"In a manner of speaking. He was not physically present when I gave my life to God, but a few years earlier he said farewell to Cade and me. He married a good woman. The only reason he gave for changing his ways was that Christ had taken hold of him. Seeing that, I could not stop wondering what the draw was."

Joseph turned his face to the cross. "And I remind you of this friend because…?"

"You speak of God as if He were a friend."

"Is He not?"

I grinned, caught. "You know I believe that He is."

"Why does it surprise you that I believe the same?"

Without blinking, I answered the truth. "Because you were once a monk."

"The lady wonders the same."

I started. "Gwyn?"

"Aye."

"What did she say?"

"She struggles with seeing God as holy yet near, loving, a friend. She expressed disbelief that I see multiple facets to God's character."

I closed my hands into fists. Opened them again. Turned them over and studied my palms, still streaked with rope burns from the night I had pulled us from the sea.

"She has been hurt." Not until the words left my mouth did I realize how superfluous they were. The man had heard her screams just as I had. The memory of them echoed in my mind, slicing my soul with each agonized sound.

"She has. Deeply. But not irreparably."

"Praise God."

Those two words settled in the air between us for a long moment. I lifted my gaze from my hands to settle again on the cross. It seemed I could not tear my eyes away from it for long.

Joseph spoke first. "She is convinced God's holiness predisposes Him to be a righteous Judge. She views Him as residing in His heaven only."

"Instead of looking upon Him as a loving Father—near to her, with her?" From what I had seen, from her reaction to Margried's words, I could well believe that.

"Exactly."

I closed my eyes. "I want to show her He is both."

"Start here."

I opened my eyes and saw Joseph's smile. When he bowed his head, I did the same. *Lord, show her Your love. Show her Your peace. Show her Your hope...*

Gwyneth

Chapter Thirty-Three

Hold to hope.

The words would not leave my mind. Such a strange phrase. I could not unravel its meaning any better than I could smoothly fold a blanket, yet it stayed with me, stuck with me, even as I fell into an exhausted sleep and dreamed. I dreamed again that I was old, sitting, looking over a lovely land, with someone beside me, holding my hand.

I dreamed also of my parents, that they were alive, well, and laughing. Why did God give me such cruel dreams? For the thing with dreams was that eventually one must awaken.

I woke to find Margried's head resting on my bed. Her tousled curls hid most of her face. My gaze latched on the shrinking bruise at her elbow. Did it still pain her? The memory of our conversation aboard the Sea Beggar ship came back to me. Did she still intend to convert? And what of Cade? He had taken her on a walk in the courtyard yesterday. Had he been whom she had been with earlier when her bed had been perfectly pressed?

With great care, so as not to disturb her, I slid out from the blanket and placed my feet on the floor. A wave of dizziness swamped me, and I waited for it to pass. Unfortunately, the ache in my throat never did. I may have torn something after all the screaming the night before. My head throbbed, too, but I ignored the discomfort and reached for my glasses before I remembered yet again that they were not there.

I frowned. Where were my clothes? I could not walk through the monastery in naught but this thin shift.

I rose from the bed on trembling legs and made a slow, slow circle searching for signs of the gown I had been wearing at the river. At last, my feet stumbled over it, folded neatly in a corner. As quietly as I could, I slipped into my chemise and torn overdress. I struggled with the sleeves but finally succeeded in lacing them in place. Running my fingers through my hair, I bemoaned the lack of a wimple, but there was naught to be done about its absence.

With one last glance at Margried, who slept with nary a snore, I stole through the doorway and into the dim hall. Tallow candles flickered in small alcoves in the stone walls but did little to cut the darkness of the space. I had assumed that I had woken near morning. Had I been wrong? No matter. The hour was of little consequence.

The direction of my thoughts surprised me. After all, a few short months ago I would never have dreamed of walking through England's last monastery's inner halls in the dark watches of the night.

The way curved, and I turned the corner to find yet another long passageway stretched out before me. The path sloped downward beneath my feet. The air warmed. I rubbed my tight sleeves to revel in the feeling, at the same time wondering at the silence, at the complete and utter lack of persons coming or going this way. Indeed, the morning must be new.

Just as I had begun to wonder if I had taken a wrong turn and would soon come out at a dungeon or some such equally unappealing destination, I turned one last corner. The smooth stone of the floor broke off to the left into crumbling steps that appeared much older than the rest. My brow folded as I frowned and stared at the door at the bottom of the steps. A heavy latch barred the slats of wood.

From behind it, I could hear rustling. What could this place be? What did this cave hold? I peeked my bare foot out from my hem and placed it on the first step. A pebble loosed from the slab and rolled. I heard the rustling stop. I froze, half on the step, ready to flee if I heard anything more.

Then I heard more rustling. For several moments, I waited, listening. The rustling flowed and ebbed like the waves lapping against the hull of the Sea Beggar ship, rhythmic, melodic, almost…soothing. With as much care as I could manage, I tiptoed down the last several steps, avoiding any pebbles that looked inclined to alert whoever was inside of my presence.

At the door, I pulled in a deep breath, suddenly wary of what I might find on the other side. I pulled the latch, watched it release, and pushed open the door.

"Welcome, sister."

I jumped at the sound of Joseph's voice. Squinting, I saw his face held a smile.

"I…if I am interrupting, I—" My voice sounded gravelly.

He rose from the rickety chair he had occupied and turned to face me.

"Interruptions are oft more the true work than the work itself."

"Forgive me for intruding." I spun on my heel.

Joseph's voice stopped me. "Lady Gwyneth, I am glad you came."

"You are?" I faced him again.

"I am."

The temptation to ask him why arose, but I caught sight of where he had been working. A small desk sat in front of the lone window in the room. The first streaks of dawn informed me of the early hour and provided meager light by which I could see the items arranged on the desk: a vast assortment of writing instruments. I stepped closer to be sure of what I saw. An inkpot. A small knife for scraping off mistakes. And, of course, sheets of paper.

Joseph swept his arm in the direction of the desk, an unspoken invitation for me to step even closer. I accepted with eagerness. Grandfather had explained to me the process by which we had been able to procure our library, but never had I been this close.

I looked at Joseph. "You are a scribe?"

"Gutenberg's invention is magnificent and will change the world. Still, there is work yet for scribes."

I studied him. "The first book was printed in English nearly a century ago."

He smiled. "Not as much work as there once was."

"What are you copying?"

"The Holy Writ."

I perused the page. In strong, bold script the verses lay before me. God's Holy Word, so beautifully preserved, so reverently handled. I thought of the vastness of the book collection at Barrington Manor. Grandfather had told me scribes had worked hard to provide us with such a wealth of knowledge, though Gutenberg's press was indeed changing things. "Do you copy other books, as well?"

Joseph nodded, smiling down at his work. "I still adhere to the Rule of Saint Benedict and spend two hours a day reading, and during Lent I read a book in its entirety."

Shock pulsed. The clergyman had been a *monk?* "You were a Benedictine?"

"Until such became illegal."

My eyes widened. "You converted?" Most priests fled to the Low Countries. Most Catholic noblemen became recusant, paying the shilling for not attending the Book of Common Prayer services at their parish

churches on the seventy-seven annual days of obligation.

"I did."

"Heresy," I whispered.

He stared at the sacred pages before us. "If there be skilled workmen in the monastery, let them work at their art in all humility."

"Saint Benedict said that."

His smile returned. "You are a learned woman."

A blush crept up my cheeks. Following his example, I did not reply.

"Who taught you?"

"My grandfather provided me with excellent tutors." I did not wish to speak about myself, but about him, the monk who had returned to common life, like Luther had done. Had Joseph wed a nun, as well?

Joseph laid his hand on the desk and turned his full attention to me. The sun had begun to rise over the horizon and sent its rays through the window to glint off his hair. He may have been a handsome man once. "Your grandfather must have seen great potential in you, to invest so much."

I looked down at the pages, the pot of ink, wondering at his words. "Someone must have seen the same in you for them to teach you how to be a scribe, to entrust you with the Holy Word of God."

Misplaced trust. For he had turned his back on the Church. "We all make our way by following others' footsteps at first."

My curiosity got the best of me. "Why did you become a monk?"

Joseph took a moment in answering. His head turned toward the sunrise peeking through the small window. "I felt called."

That was it? "How did you know?"

"'Tis a question I am asked often."

I made my voice as gentle as possible. "Do you have an answer?"

"Nay, 'tis a worthy question. The reason I hesitate in sharing my answer is that my words seem so shallow, so incapable of containing the depth of conviction with which I entrust them."

I pressed my lips together into a thin line, determined not to speak another word until I had allowed him his piece. As I waited, a surge of weariness stole over me. Mayhap my long night tugged on me or a part of my spirit did not wish to hear his answer. I forced myself to wait.

"Somehow I just knew."

"Knew what?" I had never had a talent for waiting.

"I knew that God had called me to a life of service, of supplication, the life of a scribe. At first I did not wish to accept it."

"Because you thought it would be too difficult?" How many times had I thought the same about my suddenly becoming an orphan? That it was too difficult, too much of a challenge? How many times had I cried myself to sleep these last months, the pain gnawing at my soul until I could hardly bear it?

"Nay."

My eyes flicked to Joseph's, and I wished I wore my glasses because his features were indiscernible to me.

"Because I thought it would be too easy."

My shock must have shown on my face for Joseph held up a hand, as if asking for permission to gather his thoughts before he put them to voice. He need not have done so. I had no words. Only surprise and incredulity.

"I thought that God calling me away from the world was too small a sacrifice to make for Him. A monk's life is not truly that demanding. There is labor, but there is also great contentment, great security even, to living in a monastery, surrendering oneself to the benevolent mercy of the Church. Living a life of prayer seemed to me a joy, becoming a scribe a privilege. At first, I hesitated to accept His call because it was exactly what I wanted to do."

My forehead wrinkled as I pondered that.

"And then I hesitated to accept His call to convert when England saw no more need for monks."

Blasphemy, that God would call someone to Protestantism.

"The other night, Lady Gwyneth, you expressed disbelief in my saying I believe God to be a friend. Despite your doubt, it is true. God is a friend to us. It is that friendship and the thought of reveling in it for a lifetime that almost made me turn away from both calls."

"I have never heard of such an experience as yours."

Joseph's cheeks stretched as he smiled. "I am not sure what to say about that. It is my suspicion that experiences such as mine happen more often than many think."

I took a deep breath. Joseph's view of God contrasted with the one I had grown up with, the one I had trusted in all my life. He seemed so sincere. Yet the thought of God not being as I had always thought rocked me to the core.

"Is it your desire to take vows, Lady Gwyneth?"

I shook my head. "I want a home, a family. My uncle's wife and babe died, and my parents had no other surviving children. I cannot remain at Barrington Manor forever, unable to inherit…" My voice trailed off in

the breeze that swept in through the open window.

So much in my life had changed so recently, so quickly. The mad rush to the convent in Leiden had only ever been temporary, Uncle Oliver and I had agreed. He had promised to send for me soon, after the danger had passed. The danger that bore Dirk's name. The danger that seemed pointless now.

I shook my head, retracing the course of my thoughts. Dirk was innocent of the murders of my parents; he had abducted me from the convent and, in the process, he had saved my life. I would have perished that night at the hands of the Dutchmen if he had not been there.

"What are you thinking, Lady Gwyneth?" Joseph's tone was gentle.

I met his gaze with mine.

"God is able to do the impossible," he said. "I would not count your life as a lost cause just yet."

"You speak in riddles." And why was I confiding in him, listening to him?

"Nay. In truth."

The gratitude fizzled. Anger took its place. Anger at this man for always having the answers. For always smiling. The headache I had nearly forgotten about increased in intensity until I was tempted to hold my head in my hands. I had not yet fully recovered. "I tire of you speaking of the Lord our God as if He were naught more than a companion to offer us comfort and consolation. You sound like one from Luther's camp."

His smile faded. Finally. "Did I not just say that God is mighty by saying He is able to do the impossible?"

My anger melted into shame and pooled in my pulsing brain. Aye, he had. I had to get out of here. I took a step toward the door and reached it just as a knock rang through the room. I wrenched it open and gasped. "Margried!"

She stood close enough for me to see her eyes close as the expression of anguish on her face dissolved. "I am so glad I found you."

"Why? What is it?" Speaking fast hurt my throat.

She looked at me and laughed. "You! I knew not where you were."

The concern in her voice blared through my mind. "I am well."

But was I, really? The dizziness that had swept over me when I first awoke rushed through me again.

Margried pulled me into a fierce embrace that bespoke of her worry for me. "I am glad." She pulled away and tugged on my hand. "But I do not believe you. Back to bed."

I gave an unladylike snort and stopped her from dragging me through the door. "Wait."

She turned back, brows raised, determination written all over her features. I flicked my gaze between the beautiful picture she presented, all afire with purpose, and Joseph, standing in the sunlight. "Joseph has spent the morning talking to me of God." I spoke before I could talk myself out of it.

Margried's eyes widened beneath her perfect black brows.

"Mayhap you should ask him some of your questions."

For a moment, I thought her eyes would fill with tears, she looked at me with such appreciation. In that second, I saw how important this was to her—to find the truth. Shame roiled in my stomach. For I had not been pressing for the truth lately. I had been content with merely surviving, merely arriving at enough sustenance to see me to the next dawn.

Was I finally ready to live again? Not in hate, but in love? Not in fear, but in confidence?

"Mayhap I should." Margried's eyes filled with intent. "If you promise to return to your bed."

I shook my head and chuckled at Margried's clamping her hand on my arm again. "I desire to break my fast first. After that, I will. I promise."

I closed the door behind me with a thud of wood against stone. Placing my feet on the stone steps with care, I managed to keep any stray stones from slipping. It would not do to take a tumble down these stairs.

"Good morrow."

That deep voice wrested my gaze from the ground. A gasp escaped me as I stared up into Dirk's face. Still two steps below the smooth floor upon which he stood, I had a better view than usual of his broad chest and strong shoulders.

The look in his brown eyes lashed my gaze to his. Uncertainty tugged on his features, as if he was not sure how I would react to seeing him this morn. After last night. But all he said was, "I wondered where you were."

Concern in his voice inspired an entirely different reaction than Margried's anxiety had. Warmth streamed through me. No residue from the night before. Just warmth.

"Good morrow." I heard the gravel in my voice and winced.

Dirk reached out one hand. I took it and allowed him to help me up the last two steps.

"You should not be out of bed."

Why could he not have asked me how I fared or what I had been doing in that cave of a room? Instead, he spoke to me as if I were a disobedient child. I glared at him. "You should not accost maidens in a monastery."

"Is that what I am doing? Accosting you?" The rumble beneath his words sent my stomach into somersaults. A spark lit his eye, as if he were pleased by my acidic tone.

I jerked back my hand, ashamed I had let him hold it so long. "What do you call it?"

When one corner of his mouth turned up, I braced myself. That had been the wrong question to ask.

Dirk

Chapter Thirty-Four

What had possessed her to ask that? I stared down at her, pleased to see the pink lacing her cheeks and the fire in her warm green eyes, the color of the sea before a storm. She looked better this morn. Much improved. Strong. And she did not seem repulsed by my presence. The realization exhilarated my senses until my body no longer reminded me I had not slept in two nights.

Yet I was painfully aware that she was not herself. Not entirely. Not yet. The whiteness around her mouth sent a pang of alarm through my system, and I wished she had not taken back her hand. I wanted to support her. I wanted her to lean on me.

And that question! Good Lord, what could she have been thinking? Normally so witty, so skilled in verbal sparring, she should have known not to open herself up like that. I was tempted not to honor the foolish question with an answer. But I could not resist. "I would call it most anything save such an unsavory word as accosting. Mayhap flirting."

The pink in Gwyn's cheeks blossomed into the color of mature red roses. My pulse sped up at how delightful she looked. Enchanting.

Grinning, I took a chance and swept her hand into mine. Led her away from the stairs. It would not do to have her grow so impassioned that she fell backward. And it did appear as if she were racing down the road to becoming so angry with me that anything was possible.

"How dare you impugn my honor with such words!" Scratch that. She no longer raced. She had arrived at the corner of livid and enraged.

I kept her hand imprisoned within my own and steered us down the hall. "I have done no such thing. Are we not speaking of me, Dirk Godfrey? I have no honor, do you not remember?"

I looked away from her for one second to bring us around the corner. When I brought my gaze back to hers again, the candlelight flickered on her tight expression. I sobered at once and brought us to a standstill. Cad! She was not well, could I not see that? And I had goaded her until her eyes bore a pain that nearly sent me to my knees.

Slow as the sun's course across the sky, I brought my hands up to cup her shoulders. Her head lifted. My heart rocked at the look in her eyes. She trusted me. Drawing in a breath to replenish my suddenly empty lungs, I stamped down the shout that rose to my heart. *She trusted me.* And I had pushed too far. "Gwyn, forgive me. I should never have—"

She shook her head so vehemently that golden hair swished against my fingers, soft as silk. "Nay, I—I should never have said that to you about you not having any honor. I am sorry."

"Shh. You were right."

"I was wrong."

One corner of my mouth quirked. "Look at us. We have our roles completely reversed. It was not that long ago that *both* of us were right."

"In our own eyes." She swallowed. "You are a man of honor, Dirk Godfrey. I should have seen that from the beginning."

My chest swelled at the tone of her voice, the sincerity of her words, the look on her face. I freed one hand from beneath the blanket of hair on her shoulder and raised her chin. I liked how tall she was, how the top of her head came almost to my jaw, how when I lifted, her gaze seared almost straight into mine. Liked it too much, in fact. That trusting expression swimming within the luminous orbs staring into me worked like a sweet elixir, taunting me, pulling me in. My head descended toward hers until a mere inch separated us. I hesitated. Just as before.

And just as before, sweet merciful heavens, she did not pull back. Did not make a sound. Did not even blink.

Reason took hold of me then and cooled the warmth traveling through my blood. Well, mayhap not cooled so much as mingled until logic overpowered love.

Like the crack of a thunderbolt had sounded in my ears, I pulled away. *Love.* I never took my gaze from her, though. If I could not taste, I could yet look. At the woman I loved.

Her lashes swept down to stroke the satin of her cheekbones. Faint circles ringed the undersides of her eyes. And the whiteness around her mouth had yet to color.

And I had almost kissed her. Again. The first time she had been frightened beyond wit's end. Now she was yet weary and weak. A surge of protectiveness welled within me. The irony struck; I wanted to protect her. From myself.

"I am sorry, Gwyn." My hands slid from her shoulders. "I should not have—"

She swayed on her feet, her eyes still closed. I reached for her again, this time cupping her elbows. "Are you well?"

She moistened her lips. "Cold."

I kept hold of one elbow while I shrugged out of my cloak. After draping it over her shoulders, I swept free the silk that was her hair. Nay, satin. Whichever. I was *not* thinking about it.

She wobbled on her feet again. I put an arm around her and took one hand in mine. "I will take you back to your chamber."

"*Nee!*" Her golden lashes vaulted open, freeing the green of her eyes to set fire to my insides.

I stilled.

"I—I need to break my fast." Her eyes pleaded with me. "Walk with me."

I stared at her, unsure, not liking how the roses in her cheeks had wilted. "Are you sure you are well enough to walk to the kitchen? I would be happy to bring you—"

"I am. I am well enough." As if sensing my hesitation, she started walking.

I went with her. For support. Not because I liked her beside me, but for support. "Gwyn."

"Mm?"

"The kitchen is this way."

She allowed me to turn us around, and we walked in silence for several moments. We passed the stone steps that led down to Joseph's scriptorium.

"I do not hear…" Gwyn did not finish her sentence, even when I gave her a quizzical look.

"What do you not hear?"

"When I first approached that room this morning, I heard the rustling of paper."

"Joseph may be elsewhere."

She nodded, but her gaze stayed on the wooden slats of the door. Though I acquiesced and let her slow, I would not abide her stopping. Not when the kitchen was so close. She needed to sit. Rest. If not for her own sake, then for mine.

"Did you know he was once a monk?"

I winced.

"Of course you did." She rolled her eyes heavenward.

I drew in a deep breath as we neared the ovens. My stomach reacted to the smells pouring from the place. My thin cambric shirt registered

Gwyn shivering against my side. I frowned. She should not be shivering. Not when beads of sweat had formed on my forehead as the warmth from the kitchens spilled into the hallway we occupied. Not on a summer morn in the English countryside. But she had been ill for days.

I threw open the door and ushered Gwyn inside. "Come."

The sweet smell hovering in the air above us grew even stronger. Was that cinnamon? I saw Gwyn sneak an appreciative sniff. Having an appetite was a good sign, was it not?

I guided Gwyn to a chair that looked half my age and took the one across from her that had to be a century old. She slipped into her seat and closed her eyes. Throwing every vestige of nobility to the wind, she drew a deep draught of the smell wafting about our heads.

I chuckled, watching her and wondering what was better: the anticipation of whatever it was that was cooking or seeing that anticipation play out on the angelic face before me.

"Smells good, does it not?"

"It smells divine." Her eyes popped open, her mouth formed an adorable oh-shape, and her long, white fingers crept up to cover her gasp.

My chuckle grew into a full belly laugh at her discomfiture. "Hungry, are we?"

She glowered, an incredulous sniff forming her only response. The lioness had returned. A wave of gratitude storming through my soul threatened to sweep me away. More than hunger, more than delight, more than amusement, I felt intensely thankful to God in His heaven for sparing this woman before me. From the Dutchmen, from the highwaymen, from the sea, from the lung fever, and lastly, from the grief that had torn her spirit—and nearly mine—to shreds the night prior.

I saw her settled at the table and took quick steps into the kitchen, determined to serve us before we were forced to take bites out of the air around us because of that heavenly aroma. Just as I expected, I found Joseph had left a pot to simmer. I filled two bowls with steaming porridge and returned to Gwyn, surprised at how much I had missed her in the mere moments required to fetch our meal.

I placed one bowl in front of Gwyn and one in front of me on the table that separated us. Sitting, my eyes closed as I breathed in the plume of vapor rising from the concoction.

When I looked up again, Gwyn's eyes had closed, too, as if she were drinking in the scent.

Despite the dizziness, the weariness, even the glares she shot my way, she seemed different this morning. Lighter. I loved it. *Love.*

"What do you suppose it is?" Her question snapped me back to the present and sent a thrill through me. When was the last time I had been happy? When had Gwyn ever addressed me without my having to tug the words from her? The thought sparked through me until I was warmed.

"I know not." I plunged my spoon into the thick confection, releasing a ribbon of cream that curled around the utensil.

A giggle brought my head up. Gwyn held up a thick glob of the goo on her spoon. I grimaced. Could something emitting such a *divine* aroma be gluey? Nay. I shook my head. Nothing that tasted terrible could smell this good.

I lunged forward and wrapped my lips around Gwyn's spoon. The heat of the stuff brought tears to my eyes, but no matter, for the sweet, maple taste closed my eyes, anyway.

Gwyn let out a laughing shriek. I opened my eyes to see her hand diving for my spoon. I pulled it from the bowl and away from her reach. Mirth turned to horror as my action flung the sticky concoction straight into her wide-eyed face.

Time stood still as shock registered upon her lovely features, then restarted as she released a gasp in perfect timing with the lump traveling from her cheekbone to her chin.

I stood. My chair's legs scraped against the stone floor. Where was a cloth when I needed one? "Gwyn, I—"

"I know. You are sorry." Her tone whipped my eyes to hers. The arresting gleam in her gaze gave me pause. It was a look I had never before seen on her face.

"I am."

"That makes three times in the past half hour you have apologized to me." With precision, she pushed her chair from the table and stood. A slow grin raised one corner of her mouth. The thin trail of porridge traveled to the end of her face, but before it could drop, she lifted my cloak from her shoulders and rubbed her cheek against it, cleaning her face of the mess.

I gave a throaty chuckle and reached for the spoon I had tasted from. Gwyn had let it plop back into her bowl during her mad dash for mine. Which meant it was reloaded. I raised the utensil high and watched her eyes widen at the amount of creamy, sticky substance piled upon it.

"Are you trying to ruin my cloak, woman?"

One corner of her lower lip tucked beneath her teeth. "*Nee.*"

I smiled at the way she had drawn out the word. "That is too bad."

Her brows cinched together. "Whatever do you mean?"

Just as with her earlier question, this one should never have left her lips. She was definitely disarmed in wit today. A twinge of guilt stayed my hand for a single moment as I debated whether or not she was up for this teasing. But the porridge she had deposited on my cloak caught my eye. My smile stretched into a grin. "Because, my fair maiden, I am trying to ruin your cheek."

I flung.

Porridge flew.

Gwyneth

Chapter Thirty-Five

I shrieked.

Porridge plopped.

A hearty laugh tore from Dirk as I stung him with a look. The daggers I threw with my eyes would have laid him flat if I had not had the sudden urge to laugh along with him. So I did. I slapped our meal from my face—the man had remarkable aim—and wiped my hand on his cloak. I laughed. It was glorious.

When our mirth dissolved, a cloak of embarrassment shrouded the room. I looked down. Such a shameful way for a lady to act. I sank into the chair, weary once more. My headache returned. A blush heated my neck, and I pulled off Dirk's cloak. I dared to look at him as I handed it back. He took it, a somber expression clouding his eyes.

"Do not say it." My words surprised myself.

And him as well, from the look he sent my way. "Do not say what?"

"You are sorry. I have heard enough apologizing from you in the last half hour. Indeed, in the last day."

He sat directly across from me, so I saw the edges of his mouth lift, a smile half of amusement and half of sincerity. "And do you believe me, at last?"

I thought of the answer I had given him on board ship when he spoke of telling me what he saw that night. *Mayhap*, I had told him. A single word. One that he had latched onto and treasured until last night when the story had spilled out of him. I groaned and shoved the memory away.

He crouched before my chair, putting one hand on the table. "What is it? Are you in pain?"

His earnest look burned with hurt. For me. For what I suffered. A suffering for which I had at one time blamed him. Ignoring his other questions, I answered the first. "Aye, Dirk. I believe you."

His eyes closed. His fingers on the table trembled. My jaw dropped open at seeing that hint of weakness stem from this strong man. The same

191

strong man who now knelt in front of me. The same one who had saved my life multiple times.

I stared at him. "Does that please you?"

He opened his eyes. Moisture glistened in them. I clenched my teeth lest my mouth fall open again. Such a dichotomy he was, the epitome of strength and yet caring at the same time. He seemed all the more human for it.

But Joseph had said God possessed complexity of character, as well. Just as I had done with the memory of Dirk's telling me the truth, I pushed all thoughts of God and Joseph away. I could not handle walking down those paths now. Mayhap I would never be able to.

Dirk nodded. "Aye, it pleases me."

I smiled and drew in a deep breath. My gaze flitted over our bowls of porridge, still steaming.

"You missed a spot."

I swiveled my head to look at him. He reached up and swiped my jaw with his finger, leaving a tingle in the wake of his touch. I looked at my hands folded in my lap and heard him withdraw, stand, move away. I heard more than saw him sit, pull his chair up to the table, and still. When I at last gained the courage to raise my gaze to his, I found him looking at me. A spark of something I did not recognize flickered in his eyes. A smile both kind and roguish tipped his lips.

That smile I recognized. His wolfish look.

I shook my head and grabbed the spoon from which he had not eaten. Plunging it into my porridge, I watched the cream purl in a rivulet to the edge of the bowl, as if freed from its imprisonment below the surface by that single, short break.

And I wondered if it was somehow symbolic.

After we broke our fast, Dirk laid aside his spoon. He had scraped his bowl empty and finished mine, too, after I could not eat another bite. Still, the spices that had lent this porridge a heavenly quality lingered on my tongue. I frowned at my own thought. Since when did I call a meal heavenly? It reminded me of earlier when I had labeled the aroma *divine*. Such lowering of sacred terms, the use of them for common things, was… was…

Protestant.

I gasped. Dirk looked up, a furtive glance pulling the corners of his mouth downward. I waved away his unspoken question and stood. He rounded the table and took my elbow. "Time for you to rest."

"I am well."

His look revealed his annoyance with that word.

I bit back a giggle. "Truly, I am."

He ignored my protest. Could I blame him? The words had emerged laced with laughter. Dirk steered me toward the door, his hand at my back. I blushed. But why? What did I have to blush about?

Unless. Unless this ease in Dirk's presence was what had emotion warring within, knotting my now-full stomach to the point of pain.

"You are pensive." The observation sliced the air of the hall through which we walked, reminding me I did not walk alone. Dirk took my hand and tucked it in the crook of his arm.

I searched my mind for something to say but came up empty. What could I say?

"Are you in pain?"

I blew out a sigh. "I do hope that someday soon I will not hear that question as often as I have heard it since you abducted me."

Mayhap it was the many mishaps I had managed to fall into during the last few days that now confused my mind. Surely I would return to my former self presently. Yet did I wish that?

He sent me a sidelong glance. "As do I."

I looked away, uncertain how to take his words. A small part of me wanted to hold those three short utterances close. I turned my back on that part of me. When Dirk returned me to Barrington Manor and Uncle Oliver, he would leave. He was a wanted man—the thought flitted through my mind before it came to a sudden standstill. Dirk *was* a wanted man, but he was wanted for a crime he had not committed.

The injustice of it all crushed my tangled insides of a sudden. All the suffering he had endured over the last few months, all because he had been presumed a murderer when in fact he was innocent. But now I knew the truth. I lifted my chin. I would tell Uncle Oliver that Dirk had not killed my parents. He would see Dirk free from the allegations.

"Things will be different now, Dirk." I squeezed his arm, feeling his strength. "When you return me home."

I felt him stiffen. "Do not concern yourself with me. I need you to focus on regaining your strength."

I need you... A thrill shot through me before I stamped it back. "I can focus on both at the same time. My mind has not lost any strength, I assure you."

There. He had no proper way to reply to that without insulting me, which he was too much of a gentleman to do. A gentleman, indeed. And why had I never before opened my grief-clouded eyes and seen it?

"Be that as it may, I find it hard to believe that you wish to focus your efforts on me, milady." The grin he sent me punctuated his words with good-hearted mirth.

I smiled in return, but was not yet ready to bury our serious topic. "I owe you a debt."

Dirk stopped us in the middle of the hall. "Nay, you do not."

"I do. I accused you of a crime you in nowise committed. You have suffered much these past months because of it. You have run from your accusers. You have not seen your family." My tone lowered. "You missed your brother's death."

"That is not your fault." His gruff voice smacked into the stone that surrounded us.

"If I had not jumped to conclusions, if I had just let you speak, listened—"

Dirk took my arms in his big hands. "Stop."

I shut my mouth. His fierce look vanished, and his grip loosened. "This does no good."

"What? Apologizing?"

"Nay. Blaming. Regretting. Such things only imprison us in the past."

"Dirk?"

He met my eyes.

"I know all about being imprisoned in the past."

He could have sighed in sympathy. He could have nodded, for most assuredly he knew it to be true. He could have smiled and lightened the mood. But he did none of those things I feared he would do when those words, unbidden, left my lips.

Instead, he gathered me in his arms, tucked me close against him until I could hear his heart beat against my ear, and did not say a word. I let myself relax against him. He was right. I had been blaming myself. Truly, I still felt responsible. But he probably felt responsible for what I had been through, as well. Was that why he had done what he did? Fetched me from Leiden, rode beside me through the forest, carried me across the *Kanaal*, only to see me fall victim to lung fever and despair here in these once-holy halls?

"Dirk?"

"Mm?"

"Why did you do it?"

"What do you mean?"

"Why did you rescue me?"

He pulled away just enough to smile down at me. "You usually call it an abduction. Now I rescued you?"

My cheeks bloomed with color. "Rogue."

He tilted back his head, let out a laugh, and embraced me again. I could hear both his heartbeat and his low voice as he said, "The Low Countries are dangerous for such a devout Catholic." He winked at me. "You needed me."

I fought the flutter of my heart. What were these feelings I had never felt before? Slowly, gradually, reluctantly, I stepped away. My gaze lifted to his. "And you need me now. To help you clear your name. To tell all of England that you are innocent."

He shook his head, so I did the only thing I could do. I plopped my hands on my hips and scowled up at him.

Dirk

Chapter Thirty-Six

The woman had no earthly idea how angelic she looked when she was trying to appear angry. I fought the urge to draw her into my arms again, surprised and strangely enthralled by how right it felt to have her close. Almost as if she fit.

She was trying her hardest to look upset at the moment. But I knew she was not truly angry. Her eyes did not flash fire. Her brow did not crease. Nay, I had seen the woman enraged. This was not it.

A devilish thought slithered into my brain, and I latched onto it. I would play along.

I folded my arms and stared down at her, mesmerized by the glower she tried to give. Her eyes looked luminous. Her words echoed in my mind. *You are innocent.* Of a sudden, the plan to goad her evaporated as shame took the place of the game. "Nay, Gwyn, I am not innocent."

Shock lit her eyes. "But you did not kill my parents."

I sighed, glad she believed me, trusted me, even. Yet afraid that if she only knew—

"What have you done?"

"Lived a coward's life—that is what I have done."

Her hands fisted at her sides, and her head shook from side to side. "I heard the rumors. I know the stories. Your reputation is not unknown to me."

"They are not just rumors, not just stories."

"You were rowdy and rambunctious. You got into scrapes." Her tone made it sound flippant and I knew that she had *not* heard all. Her parents and her uncle must have shielded her from the truth. And rightly so.

"You do not know all. Do not make excuses for me."

"I am not—"

I put a finger to her lips, a smile tugging at my own at the way her eyes widened. "Listen to yourself. You are defending me when I do not need defending. I was not a boy, Gwyn. I was a man. A man who made mistakes, who took the wrong path."

I ran my finger down her jaw, in the same place where earlier a dollop of porridge had resided. Just as then, her ivory skin was soft to the touch. Soft. Protected. *She* was the innocent.

"How did you get that scar?"

I stiffened, knowing the mark of which she spoke. Knowing I did not want her to know. "What scar?" My voice sounded more gravelly than I intended.

"This one." She reached up and tapped the spot, just below and beside my right eyebrow.

"A scuffle." I hoped my tone brooked no room for argument.

"What kind of scuffle?" This *was* Gwyn I was talking to.

"One I should never have been a part of in the first place." I rubbed my jaw, remembering the metallic smell of blood, the crack of fist colliding with bone. It was a night I had succeeded in forgetting. For the most part. Just like every other night when I had played the prodigal.

"I rode my horse against my mother's wishes." Gwyn's words came quickly.

I raised a brow. "What?" Surely she jested…

She nodded, dislodging my finger from her chin. "She did not want me to ride, but I did. Sometimes even my father did not know. Sometimes I even went without a saddle."

The image of her, younger, smaller, commanding a steed without even all of its tack, was a punch to my gut. She could have broken her neck. "Did no one know you went out?"

"My grandfather did." She bit her lip as if *ashamed* to offer this tidbit of information that acted as a balm to my racing heart. Thank God, someone had known. Thank God, He had protected her foolhardiness.

Yet she did not offer those three words to appease me, she offered them with reluctance. She did not want me to know she had gone off alone on a horse with someone knowing because that might discredit her rebellion in my eyes.

I grinned. "I would not have credited it to you, you little minx." Her eyes flashed, and I could not resist going on. "To see how saintly you are now, I merely assumed you were the perfect daughter."

She shook her head. "I had to grow up in my faith."

My smile slipped. "As did I. As do we all."

A thoughtful look dawned on her face. "Your faith…"

I sighed. "It is not as different from yours as you might think."

She frowned and shifted her gaze down the hall, in the direction of the cell appropriated to her. As if she longed to escape. But I did not want to end this just yet. I wanted to know why she struggled to see God as a Father, as a Friend.

She surprised me by speaking before I could. "Joseph…he is…different."

Most interesting statement. "He elected to convert and stay here, rather than flee as most did."

I took her hand and placed it on my arm. Started walking with her down the hall to her room. Though I felt no hurry, I did feel it would help her if we moved while we spoke—if she did not have to look into my eyes and instead could focus on her feet. But she did not. Delightful nymph, she stared up at me as we walked, imbuing my heart with warmth. Not only did she trust me enough to reveal the emotions flitting across her face, she trusted me to guide her where to go.

If only guiding her heart would prove so easy a task. "He is a man of God, through and through. I have never known him to speak a falsehood or shy away from earnest questioning."

Her brow wrinkled. "He is Protestant."

"Some Catholics are not always men of integrity and honor." The many examples of corruption, lies, and extortion in the Church flew through my mind. Priests offering penance to those they had commissioned to sin. Monks lying about tithes. 'Twas what Martin Luther had warred against until his death two decades ago, before Gwyn had even been born. Now his followers continued the fight.

"Explain." Her voice, like a newborn bird's wing, sounded soft in my ear.

I looked down at her. Did she really wish to know? And how could she not already? I reminded myself of the sheltered upbringing she had enjoyed, safe and set apart from the injustices and crimes of the world in which we lived. Just as they had not told her of my dark past, her parents and uncle would never have told her of the crimes committed by the Church in which they put their faith.

"Are you aware of Martin Luther's disgust with indulgences?"

"I have heard of his Ninety-Five Theses, in which he called the Pope a false witness." Her eyes sparked.

"In that document, he argued against the sale of pardons."

Her head tipped. "The sale of what? But indulgences are offered for sins forgiven, for good works and prayers."

How could I soften the blow? And yet, how could I deny the power behind the truth? "Christ paid the price for all of our sins, those we have already committed and asked forgiveness for, as well as the ones we shall commit tomorrow. There is nothing in God's Holy Word about earning merit for good deeds and prayers."

"He is right."

I looked up to see Joseph standing before us in the hall, a lit candle in his hand. The light flickered off of his serious expression.

Gwyn's gaze transferred between the man and me, a look of incredulity on her face. She fastened a disbelieving stare on me. "You have read the Scriptures?"

"I have," I answered. "My family owns a portion of Tyndale's Bible."

She shook her head then speared Joseph with her gaze. "And you?"

"God's Word is meant for all His children."

Gwyn shook her head. "How can you say that, you who were once of the Order? 'Tis heresy."

I reclaimed her hand when she pulled it from my arm. When her gaze swung back to me, I spoke gently. "'Tis what Luther taught, that all saints have the Spirit of God in them to help them interpret the Word of God."

She looked at Joseph again, triumph shining in her green eyes. "Luther taught it? Exactly why you should not believe it."

"But I do."

"How can you say that?"

Joseph smiled and swept his hands out as if to embrace his austere surrounding. The former monk in the former monastery. "Just as it was for Luther to leave the monastery to proclaim God's truth, it is for some to stay and do the same."

Gwyneth

Chapter Thirty-Seven

My ears barred entrance to Joseph's words. What was he saying? 'Twas unheard of, unthinkable, the highest form of hypocrisy!

What purpose had he claimed? *To proclaim God's truth.* Like he thought he was doing now? My heart burned within me to rail against them both, to convince them of their wrongdoing, to show them the falsehood of their beliefs. But my strength deserted me. My limbs became deadweights. I looked at Dirk, begging with my eyes. "Take me to my room."

He looked at Joseph, who looked straight back. I turned my gaze away, refusing to meet their eyes. How could they say such things, believe such things? It made no sense at all.

Once back in the cell, I sank onto the cot that I had left rumpled from sleep and screams. Pulling the blanket over my body, I closed my eyes, but I doubted sleep would come. What need had I of sleep anyway? The weariness that had nearly overcome me in the hall had deserted every muscle. In its place, though, it had left the pounding headache. No doubt I had not fully recovered from the lung fever, not to mention last night.

I pushed away thoughts of Dirk's story and focused instead on an interesting truth. I had no trouble believing him when it came to his retelling of that fateful night. But I could not believe a whit of what he said in regards to his faith. Faith? Bah! It was hogwash, all of it.

An hour later, Margried ran in the door. I leaned up on one elbow. "Margried?"

She pulled off her makeshift wimple and plopped onto her bed beside mine in a most unladylike manner. Worry fell like a stone into my stomach. "Margried, are you well?"

Then I saw the smile on her face and knew the answer she would give me. She looked beyond well. She looked extraordinary. The question was, why?

"I feel as if my eyes were just opened."

I cocked a brow. "With whom? Cade?"

She shook her head. "Nay." She vaulted to her feet and clasped her hands to her chest. "Oh, but I must speak with him directly!"

"Wait!" The sound of my voice halted her footsteps racing to the door. "Can you not tell me first? I am worried for you."

That anxiety must have shown on my face, for she turned around and retraced her steps to her bed. I noticed not a wrinkle or crease marred the surface, even after her ungraceful landing a moment ago.

"Do not worry over me, Gwyneth. Never again need you worry over me." Her tone lilted exultantly.

I took a deep breath, stamping down my impatience. "What happened? Who were you with?" A frightening thought clawed at my heart. What if it were Dirk?

"The reverend. And after him, I spent a long time in the chapel."

"Tell me all."

"After you left, I did as you suggested and asked him some of the questions that have been on my mind."

"Where did you start?"

"I asked him what he thought of the Protestant movement as a whole."

I resisted the urge to scoff at her wording. Movement! More like a revolution. Both were distasteful words that brought with them the force of change, the latter more explosive than the former. "And what did he say to that?"

"He said he respected them, admired them for standing up for what they believe in. He even conceded that they are right on certain points."

"Such as the sale of indulgences?"

Margried blinked. "How did you know?"

I waved away the question. "What did you ask him next?"

"I asked him his opinion of the fathers of the new faith. Does he agree with Knox and his preaching of violent revolution? What does he think of Calvin and his Geneva? And, most importantly, what of Luther and his turning away from monkhood to marry a former nun?"

"How did he react?"

"He seemed quite pleased, actually. He says that Knox is a powerful tool in the hand of God, although Joseph personally advocates peace. He also says that he finds Calvin's Geneva fascinating. However, he has to keep his interest to himself."

"And what of Luther?" Speaking the man's name reminded me of the look on Dirk's face as we stood in the hall. His words echoed in my mind. The Spirit of God living in each of us, teaching us how to interpret the Holy Scriptures? I could not fathom the thought.

Margried's smile dimmed, but her eyes remained intent. "Joseph says he agrees with him."

I jumped from the bed. "He said what?"

"He thinks Luther was right."

I sat down again and leaned toward her as if closer proximity would pull the words from her. "How so?"

"Joseph has studied the passage pivotal to Luther's preaching. *The righteous shall live by faith.* He agrees with Luther on the point that Christ's saving work on the cross paved the way once and for all for the children of God to come to Him, to come to faith."

My shoulders slid forward as if a burden had been deposited on my back. The last few words caught my attention and forced me to stare at her. "Come to faith?"

Margried avoided answering by rising and walking to the door. I thought she would leave and was just about to turn my eyes away when she stooped to grasp the wimple she had discarded when she had first entered, then stood. "That is what he called it."

I rose. "*It?*"

"I did it, Gwyneth. But, what's more, God did it."

My eyes widened. I waited for her to go on, speechless.

"God answered my questions this morning, just like I have been asking Him to. And He gave me the courage to convert. So I did."

The breath left my lungs.

One corner of her mouth tipped in a smile. "And the best part, Gwyneth?"

I could not imagine.

She looked down at the wimple in her hands. I rose from the bed and took a step closer just in time to see her knuckles turn white with the force of her clenching the fabric, almost as if she wished to rip it, but did not dare. Her grip relaxed, and she smoothed the wrinkles she had created. I watched as if in a stupor as she placed it on the table beside her bed and then put her arms around me. I woodenly returned her embrace.

"The best part is, it is enough."

I at last found Sister Agnes in the garden. My ears caught the faint sound of her humming under her breath, what I recognized as a liturgical tune by Hildegard of Bingen. After I knelt beside her, I watched as she plunged veined hands beneath the soil to pull free the roots of weeds choking the abundance of plants she knelt among. A pungent scent, not quite pleasant or unpleasant, assaulted my nose.

"What is it?"

She looked askance at me. "It is garlic."

"Garlic?"

"A flavoring herb that comes from Greece."

"Ahh." I examined the odd-shaped, whitish plant then transferred my gaze to the beads of sweat beneath the line of Sister Agnes's wimple. "Have you been here all morning?"

"Aye." She pulled up a weed and tossed it into a pile at her side.

I glanced down the row I assumed she had been working all this time. "You have accomplished much."

"That does not mean I could not use two more hands."

I tunneled my fingers beneath the loam, searching for the stem of the weed that had broken the surface to threaten the garlic. After finding it, I tugged hard. The sound of tearing roots beneath our hands punctuated the weeds' surrender. Other than that, we worked in silence. I focused my mind on the task at hand and, to my surprise, found it not altogether unpleasant. Almost like the scent of the garlic.

Which made it even more unnerving when Sister Agnes disrupted the quiet. "What is on your mind, Lady Gwyneth?"

And I had been so close to *not* thinking about the events of the morn. "It has been a most interesting day."

"Oh?" Her tone betrayed mild curiosity, but just like the smell of the garlic, what once seemed weak and powerless belied an urgency. I wondered if she had any idea that this day was coming.

Margried had given me permission to tell her. She had almost asked me to do it. "It will sound better coming from you," she had said.

"It will not sound better coming from either of us." Poor argument on my part, but it was the truth.

"I am much too excited to reveal it in a manner in which she will be able to accept it."

With that I could not argue. Sister Agnes needed the fact of the matter without Margried's glowing face and exuberance. I was not even sure Sister Agnes would be able to handle the enthusiasm later; she definitely could

not take it now. "Margried has converted."

Sister Agnes's hands stilled. I watched her face whiten, though her features remained expressionless.

"She has been thinking about it for a long while and made her decision just this morning. She is happy." I regretted the croak in my voice.

"Happy?" Sister Agnes turned blazing eyes my way. I fought the urge to flinch. "Is this because of the man?"

Cade. "*Nee*, she made her decision independent of him."

"But he persuaded her to it, did he not? I do not believe for a minute she has been thinking about it for a long while, and neither should you. He has misled her, lied to her, filled her head with myths of marriage and making a life together!" She rose and swiped with dirty hands at her habit, only worsening the streaks of dirt.

I stood, too, and stayed her with a hand to her shoulder. "He did not persuade her. And she *has* been thinking about it."

"How do you know?" Her voice rang sharp and caustic.

"Because we talked about it on the ship."

Shock lit on her face, and she swallowed hard. I could see the disappointment there, the sadness over Margried having come to me and not her.

"Please, Sister Agnes. She is happy."

She sighed and raised still-struggling eyes to meet mine.

"You will not dissuade her." I sought to gentle my voice, but it did no good.

"If not Cade, who? Who was with her? Who led her to this? It was not you, was it?"

I flung aside the hurt that spiked through me at those words. "*Nee*, of course not!"

"Who?" She sounded hysterical.

"A friend."

"Give me a name, Gwyneth."

My eyes widened. She had never before used my Christian name. The depth of her pain struck me between the eyes until I almost staggered beneath the weight of it. *Margried, why? Why now? Why here?* Yet how could Margried have seen how this would affect Sister Agnes? Neither of us had thought that far.

She looked upon us almost as daughters, Sister Agnes did. I saw that now. Daughters in the faith. The faith that she now considered Margried to have deserted.

Sorrow for Sister Agnes welled within me, but strangely enough, I did not share the woman's sentiment. The confusion that pummeled me over *that* almost made me miss the fire in Sister Agnes's face.

Almost. "Joseph."

Sister Agnes gasped then let out a shriek. She picked up the skirt of her habit and ran through the garden. I watched her blur and disappear, drawing in a deep breath and almost gagging on the strong scent of the garlic.

Dirk

Chapter Thirty-Eight

The sound of flying footsteps made Cade, Ian, and me turn. We stood in the courtyard, discussing our plans. The morning sun beat down upon us without repentance, but we had agreed we wished to escape the confines of the monastery. A structure of hope and healing, I had called it when we had first arrived five days ago. I still considered it to be so, but sometimes a man needed to be under the September sun, breathing in warm air and freedom.

My eyes widened in shock as I recognized the figure that now raced toward us. With her long black habit billowing outward like a bat's wings, Agnes ran. Upon sighting us, she pulled up short.

Liquid dread pooled in my stomach at the wild look in her eyes. My anxiety caused my words to come out a bellow. "What is it?"

She glared at me. "Where is Joseph?"

"Probably in his scriptorium." 'Twas his favorite place.

She started to turn, stopped, and faced Cade. "As for you, I regret ever entrusting her to your care outside the convent when we were both falling. I will speak with *you* later."

With that, she fled with as little decorum as she had come.

Cade, Ian, and I exchanged glances. Ian, his eyes wide, spoke first. "Any ideas?"

I raked my fingers through my hair. "None."

Cade said nothing, only stared in the direction Sister Agnes had gone.

"Cade?" Ian scrubbed his hand down his face. "Do you know what that was all about?"

Without answering, Cade broke into a run. Ian and I followed close at his heels, calling his name to no avail. We gave up our shouting about the time Cade led us down the inner hall in the direction of the cell the women shared. I skidded to a stop, nearly bowling Cade over despite the

fact I had expected him to pull up here.

Cade knocked once. We all heard the soft voice that belonged to Margried. That was all the permission Cade needed. He barreled through the door.

I caught a glimpse of Margried, sans wimple, black hair swirling about her smiling face, running toward him, before he slammed the door. His muffled oomph confirmed my suspicions that Margried had catapulted herself into his arms.

Ian looked at me. I looked at Ian. He broke into a grin first, but I was not far behind. We ambled down the hall in silence. My ears strained to catch any sound coming from the room, but either the walls were too thick or talking had been put off for a moment.

"Now what?" Ian's grin had not slipped an inch.

But mine had. "We had better see if Joseph needs rescuing. If I am right and Agnes's anger is directed at him, he might need reinforcements."

Ian nodded, a serious expression clouding his eyes. "Where is the scriptorium?"

I led the way, following the warmth emanating from the kitchen. The shouting could be heard long before we came to the stone steps I had not wanted Gwyn to stumble over. Agnes had traversed the rocky terrain just fine if the trouble she was giving Joseph was any indication.

"Good sister, you are accusing me of something I did not do." Joseph sounded placating but firm.

"You are most certainly at fault. Do not even try to dissuade me from speaking my piece and making known just what I think you are! How dare you plant ideas in the girl's head!"

My hand stilled on the knob. Girl? Of which one did she speak? Gwyn? Or Margried?

"I merely answered the questions that have brewed in her mind for months. God—"

"Do not invoke His name." Agnes's voice lowered. I could almost picture her in Joseph's face, finger wagging. "It was not to God that you submitted yourself when you made her believe that it was good and well to doubt, to question, to betray the religion of her family and her choosing."

"Was it of her choosing, sister?" Joseph spoke loudly enough for every letter to be heard a mile away. "I imagine not. Circumstances beyond her control, a situation that should never have happened, forced her into the life she leads. If she doubted the love of God after what happened to her, who can blame her?"

I winced, the knife twisting in my gut. It was Gwyn they spoke of, then. What else could he be referring to except the murder of her parents?

Ian nudged my arm. "Should we go in?"

Agnes's next words erased all thought of an answer from my mind. "How could you, you who once dedicated your life to the church? Though perhaps I should not be so shocked, since you abandoned your vows!" Footsteps pounded in the direction of the door, and I made to open it.

But before I could, Joseph barked, "Agnes! You should be ashamed of yourself." His voice softened. "You are reacting out of anger, pain, and cold shock. What you need is a quiet hour in the chapel. There you can ask for God's help in understanding her decision. This is a joyous day in her life, and you need to understand that."

I expected Agnes to scream more threats as before, but instead, tears invaded the tone of her next words. "How can I understand her converting to a false faith? This is heresy! She will be excommunicated!"

I backed away from the door, almost pushing Ian down in my haste. Converting? Gwyn had converted?

"Dirk?" Ian's whisper sliced the air, but I did not have time to give him an answer for my strange behavior. I had to find Gwyn. I had to see her face.

At the end of the hall, I stopped. Where could she be? It had been obvious she had not been in the room with Margried. I hurried to the courtyard, hoping to find her there. When a scan revealed that space empty, I broke into a sprint and ran through the gate.

And straight into her.

"Dirk?" Her surprised expression turned to pure shock when I scooped her into my arms. I pressed her head to my shoulder, no longer needing to see her face, needing only to hold her.

"Gwyn, is it true?" My heartbeat increased until it almost brought pain.

"Why are you acting like this? Is what true?"

"Joseph said—"

She went nearly limp in my arms. "It is true."

I swallowed the warrior's whoop. "Praise God."

She looked up at me, tears in her eyes.

"How...?" I asked. "What changed?"

Her shoulders lifted and fell. "I..."

"Later," I whispered. All I needed in that moment was *her*.

Then her eyes narrowed.

And I said, "I have been praying you would come to faith."

She reeled from my arms with all the force of a winter gale.

The look she gave me told me all I needed to know. I rubbed my jaw. "So it is not true."

Judging from the icy shock and confusion on her face, the answer was nay. Slowly she shook her head. *"Margried converted."*

The image of Margried running to Cade made my chest ache. And I suddenly realized why. My joy over what I had thought was news of Gwyn converting had been twofold: I had been delighted that she now pursued a relationship with God. But I had also been delighted at the possibility that *I* might be free to confess to her my love, to forge a relationship between *us*. That was why Cade had been so joyous.

"Ah. Well, then, that is… that is wonderful news."

"Is it?" She looked so uncertain.

Idiot. I mentally kicked myself. Of course she did not think so. Sister Agnes's words came back to me. *Heresy.*

Gwyn pressed her lips together. "I—I am happy for her. She is happy."

I studied the strained features, the forced smile. "And you, Gwyn? Are you happy?"

"What kind of question is that? I was abducted from the middle of the Beeldenstorm by my worst enemy and dragged across half the world in the last fortnight. I had lung fever and almost screamed myself to sleep last night." Her face crumpled. "And my worst enemy has become a friend. So, of course, I am not happy."

I dragged her to my chest and clasped her close, resting my chin on the top of her head as she struggled against the dry sob that shuddered through her. Despair. I heard it in her voice, and that knifed through me even more than Joseph calling the murder of her parents a *situation*. Of course, I knew now that had not been of what he spoke.

And I knew now that this woman in my arms had not been the one of whom he spoke. She steadied herself and stiffened, obviously uncomfortable at almost weeping in my presence once more.

Lord, will You not touch her heart and help her see You love her?

Time was running short. Ian, Cade, and I had agreed that Gwyn seemed healthy enough now to travel the day's ride to Barrington Manor.

That meant I had less than a full day before I would be forced to relinquish her into her uncle's care—for a time. Just enough time to determine whether my suspicion of Oliver was well founded. Just enough time for Gwyn to fetch her glasses.

I would not leave her in his clutches if I feared for her safety at his hands. Though once I might have.

For the first time since I had set out for the Low Countries in search of Gwyn, I realized the depths of my sinful soul. How selfish I had been.... I saw now that though God had ordained my mission to find her, had used it for good, I had approached it with the wrong motives.

I had been willing to rescue her only in order to restore my reputation. I had been willing to sacrifice her safety so that the end result would yield my name cleared, my life renewed.

Standing there with her in my arms, I surrendered. No matter what the cost to my reputation, the plan to use her rescue for my own selfish gain was long gone.

With great reluctance, I allowed Gwyn to step away. "I am sorry, Gwyn. For everything. All of it. It will all end soon."

She looked up, her brow wrinkling.

"We leave on the morrow for Barrington Manor."

A myriad of emotions streaked across her face. Acceptance. Apprehension. My brow furrowed as I waited in vain for any hint of joy to reach her eyes. Why did she feel anxiety about returning home?

"I will be ready." That was all she could say? After this whirlwind of a journey to save her from her countrymen in the Low Countries and deposit her safely on English soil again, she promised to *be ready*?

"Gwyn, I am honored to be called your friend."

An adorable blush bloomed on her cheeks. "I am sorry—"

With one finger, I stroked the rosy hue. "Nay, do not apologize. I merely wish you to know that *you*"—I cupped her cheek in my hand— "are very dear"—and kissed her forehead—"to me." The words I could not say slammed against my ribs. *I love you.*

The kiss I had given her in the alleyway and the one I had almost given her this morning pressed to the forefront of my thoughts. But, nay, I would not force my affections upon her. How could I? She was far too precious for that.

So I remained silent and watched the most beautiful woman in the world walk away.

Gwyneth

Chapter Thirty-Nine

I had never felt so plain in all my life.

Once before the man had kissed me senseless, but it had only been a method to procure my silence. This morning, I had almost thought he might kiss me again, but he had not. Instead, right there in front of the courtyard, he had said I was dear to him. And he kissed my forehead. My forehead! But I had wanted so much more.

My blush returned. I had tried to deny it, but there was no use. It was hopeless, just like so much else. I was falling in love with Dirk Godfrey.

And he thought nothing of me.

Oh, he had said that I was dear to him, but how his eyes had been guarded when he said it! And I had forced his hand, really. Without meaning to, of course, but that didn't change the fact I had admitted an inkling of my feelings for him—that he had become a friend—and he had merely felt the compulsion to say something kind in return.

I considered banging my head against the wall.

When had it happened? After all, I had so recently hated him to the core of my being and back again. When had he arrowed his way into my unsuspecting heart?

I shook my head as my feet hurried down the hall to my room. It mattered not when it had happened. The truth was, it had. I was pitching over a cliff with no way to stop. After all, now everything the man did only served to endear him to me. His kindness to me. His patience with Sister Agnes and Margried. His way of going to God whenever anything grieved him. Even with something as wrenching as the death of his brother.

His sure and steady way of always being there when I needed him. Even when I did not know I did. Even when I did not *want* him there. Though I was gradually beginning to *want* him there. I shook my head again, determined to stop the mental list of his finer attributes. I knew

them all by heart. Literally.

Voices brought my attention to where I was. The low tones refused to allow me knowledge of their owners, so I knocked on the door of the room Margried and I shared.

She opened the door. "Gwyneth!"

My brows rose. "May I come in?"

She tossed a glance over her shoulder then smiled at me.

I stepped in, unsure of what I might find. Cade came forward, a smile in his blue eyes. My attention flicked between him and Margried. "Am I interrupting?"

"I was just leaving." Cade spoke to me, but his gaze had fastened on Margried once more. He did not look away until he was out the door and Margried had closed it after him.

Margried pressed her back against the solid wood and let out a small sigh.

"You two have come to an understanding?"

She nodded, lifting her chin and smiling. "We are betrothed."

A flutter in my stomach warred with the confusion I had felt since she first told me of her and Joseph's conversation. "I am happy for you."

She rushed to my side. "You are? I am so glad. I thought mayhap you might be…"

I shook my head. "You are my friend, and now you are getting married." I put my arms around her. Her tinkling laughter fell across my ears. The pleasant sound made me close my eyes. I wished I could be as happy.

Margried released me and stepped back. "Thank you, Gwyneth. You mean so much to me. It is beyond joy to have your approval."

"You said so yourself. Cade is a good man. He will make you a good husband."

She nodded, at once solemn and uncertain. "Would that I would make him a good wife."

"You will. There is no doubt in my mind of that." *Only of far different things.*

Margried skipped to the door, exultant. "There is no doubt in my mind of anything at all! Not anymore."

A grin tweaked the corner of my mouth. "Margried." I put a hand to my head.

She stilled. "Did you tell her?"

"Aye."

"And?"

I bit my lip.

"That bad?"

"Aye."

"What did she say?"

I tucked my lip tighter between my teeth.

Margried let out a groan. She plodded to her bed and fell against the blanket. Staring at the ceiling, she shook her head. "She will never understand." Her eyes dropped closed.

I remained silent, because I feared she just might be right.

One eye popped open. "This is where you tell me she will. Eventually."

But how could I do that? I did not believe it myself.

Margried sat up. "Tell me exactly what she said."

I sank to my bed. "She thought you converted because of Cade."

Margried released another groan and fell to her back once again. "This is worse than I thought."

"Mayhap not."

"*Now* you offer encouragement?" She smiled.

"Only because I know for a fact that she will let Cade alone. She has bigger dragons to slay."

She cocked a brow.

"Joseph."

Her eyes widened. "Oh, no. You told her that he…?"

"What was I supposed to do? She was going to go after Cade! You know *he* would not have handled it well."

She winced. "Nay, he would not have." A smile tore through the wince.

The picture of Cade towering over Sister Agnes, glaring and going off in Margried's defense sent me into a peal of laughter. No doubt imagining the same thing, Margried joined in.

"Do you have any idea of Joseph's reaction?"

I shook my head. "I came straight to you." Then I remembered that I had not, in fact, come straight back to the cell. I lowered my gaze.

"What is it? You look troubled."

I could always count on Margried to notice my shifting moods and express concern. "I am troubled." I met her gaze. "I misled you. I did not come straight here. Dirk stopped me first."

"What did he say to you to cause such a longsuffering expression?" Margried rose and sat beside me. Her arm warmed the back of my shoulders.

"He said I was very dear to him."

She blinked. "He said what?"

I put my face in my hands. "I called him a friend, so he said I was dear to him."

A sound flew from Margried's mouth, and I looked up to see her smile as wide as ever I had seen it. "Gwyneth! That is wonderful! He loves you!"

I gasped. "Margried." Her name came out a hiss. "Keep your voice down. And he does not."

She shook her head. "How do you know he does not? I have seen the way he looks at you. And he is always there to save you when you need him."

Exactly the problem. He *was* always there. That was one of the many reasons I was falling for him.

"If he loved me, he would have told me so. When he kissed me, mayhap." My fingers careened toward my mouth.

Margried's mouth fell open. "He kissed you?" Her face broke out in a grin, and she clapped her hands to her heart. "He does love you!" She jumped from the bed and twirled in a circle in the scant space afforded to her.

"Margried, what are you doing?"

She flung her arms wide. "Reveling in the glory of it. Is it not a beautiful thing to be loved?"

I swallowed.

"I never thought I would know the feeling. Never. Not after…" Her face sobered in an instant. Her grin splintered to pieces, her cheeks paled, and her arms drifted to her sides. Everything about her seemed less lustrous somehow.

The sight made me rise. "After what?" But I suspected I knew already. She had been betrothed once before. She had said as much, but no more, when I learned she was a postulant and asked her how she came to be at the convent. "After your betrothal?"

She clasped her hands in front of her waist. "Aye."

"Would you like to tell me about it?"

"Nay."

"Well, you do not have to—"

"Aye."

Stillness shrouded the room until the heavy cloak seemed to weigh down both of us.

Margried slumped back to her bed, whispering an earnest prayer. I shook my head. For all the times she had sat down and risen again, her coverlet still appeared smoother than mine.

I waited for her to feel comfortable enough to speak. "Margried, you do not have to tell me anything you do not wish to."

"You are one of the best friends I have ever had. I treasure our friendship. For that reason, I need to be honest."

I reached forward and patted her hand, trying to project with my eyes the compassion rising in me. I saw this was not easy for her. "I treasure you as well. I am listening."

"My father sought to see me married. At first, I thought he meant well, that he wanted only what was best for me, to see me well provided for with a home and a husband of my own. My mother died when I was young, bearing my sister." She took a deep breath.

"Thus, I expected to be subjected to countless rounds of suitors. But that was not what happened. Instead, my father came to an agreement with a noble who owned land far from ours. The man had recently lost his wife to the plague, and he was eager to marry again and sire an heir. His property was such that my father was highly pleased with the offer. But when I learned I was betrothed to the man, I told my father I would not go through with it." A tear slid down her cheek. "I would not marry a man more than twice my age."

I closed my eyes and moaned. "Oh, Margried." What had she done? Under law, she had no power to refuse marriage. How had she wrung herself free of such a distasteful match?

"I ran away."

I gasped. "You what?" I had thought she had been *sent* away.

Her chin lifted. "I stole a horse from my father's stable and rode it to the coast. There I stowed away upon a ship that crossed to the Low Countries. It did not take long before I was discovered, but the ship's captain protected me. He helped me get to the convent at Leiden, far enough away that I was safe."

Timid, shy, beautiful Margried was that defiant? That strong? That courageous?

A shy smile tipped her lips. "You do not believe me."

"I believe you. I just...do not...believe *you*." I shared her smile.

She rolled her eyes.

"What did Cade say when you told him?"

Those eyes closed.

Dread, cold, caught me unaware. "Margried? You told him, did you not?"

"I did not have the opportunity."

"When do you plan on making the opportunity? A man has the right to know his betrothed has been promised once before." Surprise that she had not already shared her story with the man prevented me from feeling anything resembling judgment. Surprise at the fact that I felt no such sanctimonious surge swept through me. I was the judging kind, after all.

"Aye." Margried's lips thinned.

"Are you frightened?"

"Nay. Cade will not think less of me, I am sure of that."

My brows bunched. "Then why not tell him?"

"I did not say I would not tell him."

"Why have you not already?"

"There simply was not time."

I raised a brow. "How long were you two in here alone? What *were* you talking about all that time?"

A soft, dreamy smile floated onto her face, and her cheeks pinked.

"Ahh. I see."

Her head shook from side to side. "He was a perfect gentleman."

I nodded, smiling, then sobered. "You will tell him?"

"At the first opportunity."

"You will have to make the opportunity, Margried. You realize that, do you not?"

She sighed. "Of all the times for you to remember to be an advocate for the truth."

"The truth—the lack of it—destroyed a part of me for far too long. I will not let the fear of it hurt you."

"I told you I am not afraid. The man my father chose never even met me. He would not recognize me should we ever…meet."

"Then why—?"

"I am not afraid! I am ashamed!" She cinched her eyes tight, and her hand flew to her mouth as if to hold back a sob.

I flinched at the volume of her words, as well as the terrifying possibilities her words presented. "Of what do you have to be ashamed? It is your father who arranged the match. He alone bears the responsibility. Margried, you are innocent." *Please, God, let her still be innocent.*

She did not answer, so I asked a question that I did not truly care about. A mere distraction—that was all it was meant to be. "What was the man's name?"

She looked at me with sorrow pouring from every inch of her. "Oliver

Barrington."

Some distraction.

Dirk

Chapter Forty

Gwyn never met my gaze as I lifted her onto her horse. The rebuff stung, but not nearly as much as her walking away from me the day prior. I would have given an eyetooth to know what had been brewing in that pretty blond head whilst she whisked away from me, as if she could not bear to be near me much longer.

And directly after I had admitted how dear she was to me. It made no sense.

Cade mounted his horse as I mounted mine. His grin looked too wide for his face. Of course, for a newly betrothed man, it might be normal. I would find no sympathy for my plight there.

"I am well, young man." Sister Agnes's snapped words turned my head. Ian backed away from her horse, mounted his own, and gave me a significant look. At last, someone else who understood that the workings of women could not be understood. Best the boy learn that now rather than later.

I steered my horse beside Gwyneth's. Cade brought his beside Margried's. Ian shot me another look as he pulled up beside Sister Agnes.

One last glance at Joseph and the small smile on his face, set against the strength of the monastery, and I knew the time had come. I lifted my arm and we were off, but I could not quite escape the words Joseph had left me with that morning as I packed the horses. I had shrugged off breaking my fast with the others and so we had the courtyard to ourselves.

"She will believe."

I had raked my hand through my hair. "I am praying for healing."

"As am I." He laid his hand on my shoulder and launched into a prayer that held just as much power as the one he had spoken in the womens' cell when she had frightened years off my life.

When he had finished, I looked at him.

218

"I know," he said.

"Am I that easy to read?"

"Like a book copied by my own hand." His lopsided grin did nothing to loosen the serious planes of his face. "She is not that difficult to decipher, either."

I stiffened at his words, unsure of his meaning.

"I imply only that she is near to coming close to the God she has pushed away."

I blew out a breath.

"And that she returns your feelings for her."

Turning to my horse, I lugged the last bag, laden with supplies, to its back. Tying the rope tight, I fought the questions in my mind. "You are wrong, Reverend. She hated me not a fortnight ago. No woman is that fickle. Especially not Gwyn."

He chuckled. "Your journey has softened her heart toward God. Why should it not soften her heart toward you?"

That single sentence replayed in my mind again and again as I led the others on the path west, toward Barrington Manor. The sun shone through the canopy of leaves on the quiet road we travelled.

When that same sun ascended to the center of the sky, I chanced a glance back at the others. "We will stop here."

We ate cheese, bread, and apples in silence. I thought of the meal Gwyn and I had shared the day before. Though I watched her throughout the meal, she would not meet my eyes. I expected to hear Cade and Margried's whispers, but even they seemed tense somehow. Could the unease Gwyn felt at the prospect of returning home have infected us all?

Lord God, will You not give her peace? At last?

We rode the rest of the afternoon in silence. My every attempt to engage Gwyn in conversation proved fruitless. The sun sank low, the air turned chill, and we neared the manor.

And I knew it was now or never.

I exchanged a meaningful look with Cade. From the way he glanced to his side at Margried, I knew he gathered my meaning and had plans of his own. I put distance between him and me, praising God when Gwyn did not seem to notice or resist. At last, there was enough room where I could talk to her with a modicum of privacy.

"Milady, I need to ask you something."

She looked up at me, surprise shining in her eyes. If she had assumed I would allow her to return to her uncle's home without any more attempts

to draw her out, she had been sorely mistaken.

How to phrase my question in a way that would not offend her? "Are you looking forward to returning home?"

Her brows rose, and her eyes widened. She trained her gaze forward. "I will no longer be your responsibility soon enough. I am sure I have been a burden, but after I talk to my uncle, he will see reason and reward you for seeing me home safely."

The words thudded one by one through the recesses of my mind. Was that what she thought? That I saw her as a *burden*?

Sunlight glinted off her hair. All at once, I remembered the rain falling around us in the alleyway and her reaction to the kiss I had stolen. She had said she thought I meant to keep her quiet. *Your responsibility...*

Realization struck like a brick to the head. My gaze rolled to the darkening sky. How could she think such a thing?

Yet how could she not? When had I ever presented myself honorably, intentionally, respectfully? When had I offered her a glimpse of the way I wanted to cherish her? By the way she looked at her hands, I knew that I had allowed the silence to stretch for too long.

"I never want to hear such foolishness from you again." My tone was gentle.

Her glare was not. "How dare you—"

"I do not see you as merely a responsibility. And I have never seen you as a burden." Ever. Not even when I carried her from the convent.

She looked askance at me, dubious. "You pursued me out of your sense of honor. You sought to make amends for the way I hated you."

"Gwyn, you are wrong." *I did not seek to make amends for your hatred. I sought to mend only my name.*

Doubt etched her features, not doubt of her sentiment, but doubt of me. "I am only sorry I blamed you for so long and forced your hand."

I drew in a breath and refused to give voice to the fiery words that rose within me. "Confound it, woman, how could you think such a thing? You did not force my hand. I rescued you because your safety is more valuable to me than my own life." *And now, more than my name.*

She blinked. That was all. The expression on her face went blank and all she did was blink. My heart sank like a stone. Joseph had been wrong. She did not return even an ounce of the intensity of affection I felt toward her. I trained my gaze straight ahead, but my peripheral vision worked just fine as I watched her mimic my movement. Silence settled heavily.

It had been too much even to hope for. I could see that now. She had been too hurt, too broken, by me, no matter how false the allegations, to ever consider letting me into her heart and soul.

I should have been wise enough to see that from the beginning and bar her from mine.

Dusk had disappeared by the time we broke through the trees to see Barrington Manor sprawled in front of us. I frowned at the way the eerie silence of twilight cloaked the land and reminded me of the night Gwyn's parents died. Looking at her, I longed to reach for her hand, offer her reassurance.

For, unlike that night months ago, this time I would not leave her to the terrors of this place. She had never answered my question earlier. And I knew from the frown on her face that she did *not* look forward to returning to her uncle's keep.

I wanted Gwyn to get her glasses, and I wanted to be sure my suspicion of Oliver was correct.

If I was right, we were leaving again.

As I led our small group closer, my senses tuned in to the sounds of men shouting and laughing. I guided my horse to the front gate. Stealing glances at Gwyn did not prove difficult. She stared at the formidable structure before us as if it might open its mouth and eat us alive. The wrinkle between her brows and the white knuckles clenching her horse's reins only strengthened my resolve to stay beside her.

The last night I had been at Barrington Manor had been enough to plant in me a wary distrust of Oliver; his niece's reaction to returning to his care caused it to sprout a mile high.

I came to the gate. Gwyn led her horse close to my side. Though torches flickered above us, I knew darkness shrouded our faces. A voice called out over the wall. "Who goes there?"

"The niece of Lord Barrington and company." I kept my voice neutral.

Frenzied whispering ensued. I glanced back at Cade, but he shook his head, unable to make out any words, either.

The clomp of footsteps receded. Good. Mayhap someone was going after the lord of the manor. Tense moments passed, and I did what I had wanted to do for the last hour. Under the cover of the night, I reached out and laid my hand over both of hers. At first, they stiffened on her horse's reins. Then they trembled. If she trembled out of fear… *So help me, Lord, if she reacts like this when we are in the man's presence, I'll—*

"Who is it that disturbs the night?"

Oliver had come to the wall. His resounding baritone tumbled over the distance and into my ears. Gwyn's hands remained still; that fact alone gave me the strength to answer with self-control. "The company of your niece."

His scoff scratched the air. "Liar! My niece is away, out of England entirely."

"It is me, Uncle." Gwyn's voice sounded steady, strong. And I knew she had her chin in the air and fire in her eyes. My heart swelled in my chest.

"Gwyneth." Shock failed to invade the man's tone. Much disdain, however, did.

The urge to break Oliver's nose made me glare at the stone wall separating us. Gwyn's hands moved beneath mine, and I loosened my grip on her, hoping she had interpreted my fierce hold as a protective instinct and not disgust for her uncle. No matter that it had truly been both.

"What a nice surprise, my dear." False delight rang out in Oliver's words. "Go on, Gerald, allow them in."

The creaking of the gate opening drowned out any other speech. I flicked a look at Cade and Ian, giving them each a warning look. Turning back, I rested a hand on my baldric. My good hand covered Gwyn's, but I could pull my dagger with my left if need be.

Gwyn had other ideas. She pulled her hands from beneath mine just as light slipped under the ascending gate and broke the blackness.

"My dear, I am so happy to see you." Oliver approached his niece's horse. It took everything in me to stay seated and not block his path. One of Oliver's men stepped forward, holding a torch high.

She smiled a wide smile that bespoke of conflicting emotions. "Hello, Uncle. I am glad to be home."

"To be home," she had said, not "to see you." His smile slid a fraction of an inch then froze in place.

He swept his gaze past her. "You must introduce me to—" The corners of his mouth dipped, and a growl emerged from his throat. "Godfrey! How dare you show your face on Barrington land!"

Men descended from every direction. I heard the ring of swords being pulled from scabbards and freed my own weapon.

"Stop!" Gwyn flung her arms wide. "Uncle, he is innocent."

Oliver stared at his niece. "How can you say that? He killed your parents."

"He did not. Now call off your men."

The lord's face reddened. His glower revealed his displeasure, but he nonetheless flicked his fingers. Swords sheathed all around us. I followed suit.

"Come." Oliver swiveled on his heels. "You must be in need of food and drink. We can talk in the Great Hall."

Aghast at the way the man turned away without offering his niece any assistance, I slung myself off my horse and put my hand on the side of Gwyn's mount.

Oliver pivoted. "Get your hands off her."

"Uncle, he is not touching me."

I disproved her words by reaching for her. Or rather, she disproved them herself by letting me lower her to the ground.

"I merely helped her." *As you did not.*

"There are men for that."

And why did he think himself above helping a lady from her horse? The man was a powerful, proud one. I would do well to remember how cunning was the creature with whom I now dealt. And he would do well to remember the same.

Gwyneth

Chapter Forty-One

This was not going well. Dirk crumbled a piece of bread in his hand and kept a steady gaze on my uncle, who sipped his wine and glared in return. Cade sat close to Margried, who never once looked at Uncle Oliver. She had reassured me again after our revelatory conversation that they had never met; he would not know who she was as long as her name was not spoken aloud. Yet tension reigned.

Sister Agnes looked wary. Ian, too, seemed on guard. His eyes flicked between every other person in the room. When he looked at me, he widened his eyes, as if to ask how I fared. But I did not know how to tell him I was miserable without giving it away to Dirk, who had somehow seated himself so that I sat in his periphery and Uncle Oliver in his direct line of vision.

At least I had had time to retrieve my glasses from my chamber. The ability to see clearly lent me a sensation of strength I had missed.

I smiled at Ian, and he smiled back his boyish smile. I would not let on to Dirk about my anxiety because the impending explosion between him and my uncle looked imminent and, well, there were innocent bystanders. At the wall, the two men had argued about who helped me off my horse. That had been only the beginning. Inside, they argued about whose arm I held while walking to the Great Hall. I could only imagine what had happened while I hurried up the stairs to fetch my glasses. Lastly, while we waited for the bread and meat to arrive, the men argued about who sat beside me.

Dirk had won each time.

I did not want to admit to the triumph that had filled me when he had. And I did not care that his success came about more by sheer force of will—and a fierce glower—than any choosing on my part. Although, if it had come down to my choosing, I would have chosen Dirk.

That thought scared me. But I had gone from loathing the man to loving him in a matter of days. Mayhap I was entitled to a sliver of fear.

Uncle Oliver put down his wine goblet. "I am waiting."

My uncle's gaze fixed on me for the first time all night. I met his look, anxiety weighing down the few bites I had managed to swallow. I straightened my spine, unwilling for him to see me cower. "For what, Uncle?"

"For you to tell me what you are doing here, of course, dear." He punctuated the slap of the words with a slight chuckle that failed to ease my discomfort.

And why that discomfort? I had seldom felt this way around my uncle before; he was a strange man, but he was family. "I came home. The Beeldenstorm came to Leiden. I was no longer safe there."

"You should have written to me. I would have sent men to escort you home safely, properly. There was no need to engage the services of an outlaw."

Dirk stiffened. His jaw worked. Before he could say anything, I stuffed words into the air between the three of us. "There was no time for such measures. I regret that propriety may have been compromised—"

"Nothing was compromised." Dirk turned his look on me.

I raised an eyebrow at him. "—but these men have kept me perfectly safe."

Sister Agnes turned to address Cade and Ian. "I believe they need a moment to themselves."

Margried jumped to her feet, not waiting for either man to help her. My eyes widened as I realized why. How selfish I had been, thinking only of myself and coming home, when I should have been most worried about Margried. After all, she had been subjected to sitting in the room with both her former and present betrothed. She must be quaking.

"Of course we are all exhausted from our journey. Uncle, shall Joan see them to their rooms?"

Joan stepped forward to do my bidding, but her eyes went to my uncle. Uncle Oliver raised a brow as if he meant to feign disinterest. "They are staying the night?"

"I thought we could offer them lodging for several days, actually. They have traveled many miles to see me safely home." I emphasized the word *safely.*

Dirk and Cade exchanged a look I did not miss. Cade caught Margried's arm. She stumbled on her way out, and Cade righted her. Sister Agnes

and Ian also left. I almost volunteered to go with Margried, but thought better of it. Cade would take care of her.

And Dirk and Oliver needed someone to sit between them.

"You claim they saw you safely home, my dear, but the truth is that you arrive in the dead of night—"

"I would hardly call this soon after the evening meal *the dead of night*."

"—unexpectedly, with no word by messenger whatsoever—"

"If there had been time, we would have seen to it you were aware of our whereabouts, but we assumed you would welcome us."

"—looking quite the fright in a bedraggled gown, your hair mussed."

I gasped, my hand went to my hair, and I winced down at the slices Dirk had given my gown. I should have changed when I fetched my glasses from my bedchamber.

Dirk made a sound I could categorize only as rude. "This is uncalled for. The lady is weary from her long journey and has suffered much."

"So you admit you dragged my niece through deplorable conditions."

"He took exceptional care of me, Uncle. I insist you stop insulting him."

Uncle Oliver glared at me until I realized I had leaned away from him. Toward where Dirk sat slightly behind me and to my right. I shook my head in disgust at myself and shock at my uncle's behavior. "I do not understand why you are acting like this."

His face softened, and his tone turned pleading. "I am concerned for you, my dear. You arrive at the manor in the middle of the night, and you appear as if this man has acted less than honorably with you."

I leapt to my feet. My quick intake of breath sounded like a wave crashing against the shore. "How dare you imply such a thing!"

Uncle Oliver reached to lay a hand on my arm. He ran it down my wrist to pull my fingers to his lips, but I swung them away from him before he could plant a kiss. His face purpled with a rage I had never before seen on his features.

Dirk had risen as well, I realized. He pulled me back to stand beside him. He did not say a word. He did not have to. His dark look said it all.

I stared up at him in wonder, aghast at the thought that I not only trusted him, a fact that would have made me faint in this same room months ago, but that I trusted him more than my own uncle. The man I had known since birth and loved, despite his moods, seemed different tonight.

"Dirk." At the sound of my voice, he turned to me, his expression softening, his eyes searching. "I want to go to my chamber."

He did not spare my uncle as much as a glance. Merely tucked my hand in his arm and drew me close to his side. Together we left the room.

Scant candlelight offered us clear vision down the hall, but my mind was murky. What had come over my uncle?

Then there was Margried. Once betrothed to my uncle, she was now frightened of even looking at him. What if someone slipped and called her by name? How could I protect her?

And Dirk. He looked ready to draw his dagger on my uncle every time the man opened his mouth. Of course, Uncle Oliver insulted me nearly every time he spoke. I could not fathom either man's behavior. Despite his words earlier, I had been certain that Dirk would see me to Uncle Oliver's doorstep and ride into the night, eager and glad to be rid of the burden of caring for me.

As we traversed the stairway that led to the second floor of the keep and my bedchamber, I wondered how I could have ever believed that. How could I have ever fathomed that this honorable man would rescue me, save my life, and then deliver me over to…over to…?

What *had* gotten into my uncle? He seemed so little like himself; I failed to wrap my mind around a reason for his strange behavior.

And I knew all the facts. Dirk did not. But he should. I hoped Margried would forgive me for telling him about my uncle's past with her. "Dirk."

He stopped at the top of the stairs and turned to me. I loved when he did that, gave me his full attention and turned those bottomless brown eyes on me.

Loved it too much. "Margried was betrothed once before."

The light of surprise in his eyes said he had not been expecting that, but he nodded and waited for me to go on.

"To my uncle."

The shudder rippled through him and into me. He tossed a glance around and pulled me forward. "Is there somewhere we can speak privately?"

The whispered words ran through the hallway as if lit on fire, they were so loud, and I suddenly realized what he meant. The knowledge shook me as I took his hand and led the way forward and up the turret stairs. A small round room at the top looked over the land to the east of the keep, with naught but trees and a small sliver of moonlight visible.

A smile appeared on Dirk's face. The man was entirely too handsome when he sported that grin. "Somewhere where we could speak privately, not somewhere I'd be tempted to kiss you."

My blood ran hot and cold, boiling up to my cheeks and into my hairline, icy to the tips of my toes. I looked away, out the window, uncertain of where to begin to scold him for such talk.

He touched my cheek and brought my face around. "I am sorry, Gwyn, for the things he said."

I nodded, a lump in my throat preventing me from speaking. My uncle's brash words had sliced deeper than I cared to admit. How had Dirk known that?

"The marriage was arranged by her father." The words came out a croak.

Dirk nodded. "I suspected Margried had no say in the arrangement."

"That's just it. It was merely an arrangement. My uncle never even saw Margried. He did not recognize her tonight."

"But that is why she was tense in the Great Hall."

"You noticed that?"

He slanted his head as if amused by my lack of faith in him.

"I only assumed you were watching my uncle too intensely to observe—"

"Hush."

My brows knit together. "Do not tell me to—"

"And there's another thing we need to talk about."

I raised a brow. "What? Your habit of interrupting me?"

He chuckled. "Your belief that I kissed you only to hush you, keep you quiet."

My ready retort died in my throat. He said it as if my *belief* were only that: belief. Not truth. Then why *had* he kissed me?

My lungs, filled with air from the breath I did not know I had been holding, threatened to collapse. I could not bear this. This awareness of him, standing so close, hand still resting against my cheek and hair, saying things I could not possibly fathom…coupled with all else that had gone on this night.

I turned away. My cheek chilled when Dirk dropped his hand. I closed my eyes. My hands rose of their own volition to cover the sound of the sobs that would be held back no more.

A strong chest moved against the arms I had drawn up to hide my face. I swayed on my feet. Dirk's boots planted themselves beside mine. Without hesitation, I leaned into him, scared and shocked and furious that I no longer had either the desire or the strength to stand on my own.

Wrapped there in his embrace, I felt my heart break. Because this was what love felt like—safe and warm and luminescent with the knowledge

that he was there for me, whenever I needed him.

And this would be the last time I knew it.

So I let the tears come, overflow my eyes, flood my fingers, soak into his shirt. I sank into the hands on my back that rubbed and soothed, the chin that rested on the top of my head.

What did love sound like? Like sobs in the night drenching Dirk's shirt, like the soft shushing sounds he made that became a balm to my battered soul, like the way his heartbeat accompanied the way he rocked me back and forth.

What did a breaking heart sound like? Like the last choked breath thick with tears as I bottled myself up once more. Like the barrier I erected between us thudding into place as I pushed against his chest with my hands. Like every emotion, every nerve, every drop of blood in my body ripping apart as I stepped away.

"Gwyn."

"Nay. Do not say a word. Please." Keeping my eyes closed tight against the pain avalanching through my soul, I turned my back to him, the movement as final as a death knell.

Dirk

Chapter Forty-Two

"I just wanted you to know about Margried."

That was what she said. Tears still clogged her voice and shone in her eyes as she swiveled away to stare out the window. And she spoke of Margried. I raked my fingers through my hair, done with talking about the newly converted woman. Cade would care for her. But Gwyn had no one.

Her uncle was a fiend. That much was obvious from the way he behaved toward his niece tonight. My shirt was damp from the tears she had shed over the hurt. My right hand clenched into a fist as I remembered her stricken expression when he had insulted her. I wanted to strike the ever-present insolent look off of Oliver's face.

"Gwyn…" I blew out a breath and readied to say the words I was not sure she would want to hear. Even now, would she be willing to listen to reason? "You do not have to stay."

Her shoulders stiffened. Her breathing became so rhythmic it silenced. I waited.

"But I do. This is my home." So final.

"You should not be forced to stay with an uncle who cares so little for you."

She turned, her rueful smile piercing my heart. "You said 'should.'"

"I said 'should not.'"

"*Nee.* You said: should.' Not I *will not* be forced to stay with my uncle, but that I should not. There is a difference."

Regretting the choice of words that had distressed her, I took one step toward her. "I will take you far from here. To my mother and sisters. You will be safe there." Would she? "I give you my word." With every breath in my body, I would see to her safety.

Her head shook from side to side, and I wanted to growl at the hopelessness I saw on her face. "You cannot promise that." She reached for the cross dangling at her neck. "Promises are meant to be kept."

"I keep my promises. Do you not know that after all this time?"

Her eyes shone emerald-green in a sea tossed by a monsoon. "My father told me that once."

"Did you believe him?" Simon had seemed the kind of man in whom she could put her trust. In fact, if he were still here, I most likely would not be discussing stealing her away.

"I did." She covered the cross with her fist. "But in vain."

I touched her arms. "Tell me what happened."

"They gave me a Welsh name because it means *happiness*." She smiled. "*Moeder* always said she liked Gwyneth better than Adrina or Edith, Spanish and English for happiness."

I waited.

"This belonged to my mother. It was given to her by my grandmother when my parents married. *Moeder* wore it every day." She drew in a deep breath. "A fortnight before their deaths, they gave it to me, and I have worn it ever since. The moment my father fastened it around my neck, he said it came with a promise. A promise that, as my parents had chosen to marry for love, so would I be free to do the same."

"How did they break that promise?" My blood boiled at the thought of what she might not be telling me. Had she been betrothed before as Margried had been? Mayhap even wed and widowed?

"He promised he would be there." Her words filtered into the space around us as softly as a breeze. "He promised they would *both* be there to rejoice with me on my wedding day..."

A single tear fell from her eye. The temptation to gather her close once more proved too much. I folded her in my arms and waited for her to weep for the second time that night. But silence wrapped around us. Mayhap she had already spent all of her tears.

"I am sorry, Gwyn. So sorry." I kissed the top of her head. She pushed away. My arms dropped to my sides.

"I cannot go with you, Dirk. I cannot trust you."

My gut twisted. "You trusted me to get you safely here." Albeit not quite smoothly, but surely safely. She had survived every mishap, after all: the thieves, the near-drowning, the lung fever.

"And you did. I am grateful and in your debt."

"Nay, Gwyn. It is I who am in your debt. You believed me."

"Cade, Ian, and Joseph all know you did not murder—"

I put a finger to her lips. "They were not there. They did not see what you saw. They believed me on the basis of the man they knew me to be. You and I had never even met before that night. You believe me in spite of seeing what looked to be evidence to the contrary."

A wince and she looked away. "'Tis a miracle. I am not prone to certainty in much."

"What do you mean by that?" But I already knew. Her religious fervor, the foundation of her life, had been rocked by all that had happened.

She backed away and leaned against the small window, the sole opening in the tiny space we shared. The night's wind whipped around us of a sudden, as if tossed by the tumult passing between Gwyn and me. "You know my struggles, Dirk."

"I pray for you."

"You do?"

Her look of surprise stung. "I do. For healing."

Tears pooled in her eyes. The scant moonlight made her hair sparkle silver. Her beauty tightened my chest. Young… fragile and delicate. But with the strength and resilience of a lioness.

"You will find healing, milady. I know it." In my heart of hearts, I did. "Allow me to take you away from here so that you might find it."

She wrung her hands. "Do not ask me again, Dirk. Please do not. I cannot go with you. My place is here, at Barrington Manor."

"With an uncle who could hurt you."

She gasped. "He would never hurt me. How can you say such a thing? He is merely in one of his moods this night."

I hesitated, not eager to bring forth the doubts that had plagued me for months. "Did you ever think about the full implications of my innocence?"

"What is that supposed to mean? You did not do it, but what's done is done. They are gone." She stroked that cross.

"If I did not do it, who did?"

Her eyes rounded, allowing me one single, brief glimpse into her shocked soul before icing over. "How dare you imply my uncle could have killed my parents! Why, his own brother!"

I strode forward and clapped my hand over her mouth. Her voice had elevated both in pitch and volume. Anger invaded her face.

"We do not wish to be overheard." I pulled my hand away. "Listen to me. I was there that night. I saw the way your uncle acted, the way he treated your father. They were not close, were they?"

Her arms crossed. "But they were blood."

"Are they, really?"

Her mouth dropped open. "Of course. My grandmother was the widow of a Spaniard who fled to England, but my grandfather loved her."

I nodded, rubbing my jaw as I followed the bloodline.

She narrowed her eyes. "They may not have been close, but I never knew them before my father married. They might have been better friends before my father's devotion belonged to *Moeder*." Her hands flung out in front of her as if she struggled to understand where I led—or she did not wish to understand. "*Het maakt niet uit!*"

"Look at me. It *does* matter. Very much." I thought of my own brother, and my heart squeezed in pain. "Let me take you to my mother. You will find comfort in each other."

The look in her eyes changed. The war within gave way to comprehension. She remembered my grief, respected it, and saw what I was trying to do. Still, she shook her head. "I will stay."

My eyes closed as I pulled in a deep draught of the night's air. But when I opened them again, eager to impress upon my memory the way she looked outlined by the moonlight, her hair tinted silver, green eyes sparkling with strength…she was gone.

Gwyneth

Chapter Forty-Three

I hated to hurt him, for that was what I had done. But I would hate even more the day he looked at me and saw me for the burden I was. How could I have agreed, plunging myself into his hands completely, surrendering to be his responsibility for the rest of his life? He would take me to his mother's, he had said, and would see to my safekeeping. How could he do that as a man on the run, an outlaw, a criminal? He could not. Not without relinquishing his freedom.

But, oh, I wanted to agree. To take his hand and see his smile and flee as fast as I could from this place that held such bitter memories.

I did flee, only I was alone, instead, and I left him with a look of such pain on his face that I wanted nothing more than to put joy in those eyes again. But to give myself that, I would have to steal from him his freedom. And he had always been a free man, a rake, a rogue, the most honorable man I had ever known. To be constrained would be his undoing. I refused to be his shackles.

The clatter of my footsteps on the stairs hurt my ears, but I did not stop. Could not stop. If I stopped, I would look back. If I looked back—

"Gwyneth."

My breath caught in my throat as I looked up at Uncle Oliver. One hand at the railing, he stood in a casual stance, as if he had happened to meet me at the bottom of the stairs. A niggle of suspicion made me think otherwise. "Uncle."

"Why are you flying through the night? You could hurt yourself."

"I am well, though I thank you for your concern." Did I sound as stilted as I felt?

"Is not an uncle naturally inclined to be concerned for his niece?" A smile stretched across his lips. I had never noticed how serpent-like he looked when he smiled that smile.

"I understand your concern, Uncle, but I find it somewhat misplaced."

His brows rose. The muggy air within the keep suddenly smelled cloying. Had Uncle not allowed the servants to perform proper airing out of the rooms in the long months of my absence? Surreptitiously, I slid my leather shoe, hidden by my skirt, across the floor. The rushes felt fresh. Mayhap only anxiety clogged my lungs.

"I must insist you treat Dirk with respect."

"Insist? What a strong word for a weak woman."

My hands tightened at my sides, but I forced myself to remain calm. Prove my strength. "He is different from what I thought. I am sorry I ever sought to tarnish his name."

Uncle Oliver shook his head. "You saw what you saw, my dear. You cannot tell me he dissuaded you from that, made you doubt the events of that night."

"He told me the truth." My heart pounded a staccato beat in my chest. "Something you never did."

What a powerful frown filled his face. "He fed you lies."

"He told me you wanted to marry me to him." I flicked my gaze between his narrowing eyes and the knuckles going white from gripping the rail.

"You know not of what you speak, my dear." Fury infected the words.

A frission of fear shot up my spine at the sight, and I remembered Dirk's warning that my uncle might stoop to violent measures. We were alone here, yet Dirk had no other way out of that turret save for these stairs. *Please, Lord, send him down.*

"You must learn to tame your tongue if you are to please your husband."

Shock pebbled my arms. "Husband?"

A chuckle spilled from Uncle Oliver's mouth. "You will spend the rest of your life in luxury, and one day you will lavish your gratitude upon me, the man who made it all possible. I have plans for you, my dear."

I shook my head from side to side. "I do not understand."

"Grand plans your parents could never have envisioned."

Swallowing hard, I remained silent, willing him to go on. What plans?

"They would have denied you your true heritage, the benefits of your bloodline. But we come from Spanish nobility, Gwyneth. You are going to be even more. Wed to royalty."

He was mad. I took a step backward. My foot fumbled at the first stone stair. I gained my footing and stood tall, but still I was nowhere near eye-to-eye with my uncle.

"My parents promised I would marry for love." Or never at all. And at

the moment, the latter seemed the more likely possibility.

The cold diamonds at my neck pressed against the collar of my gown, weighted with hope...and despair. Suspicion arose.

Uncle Oliver's eyes looked wild in the light. "And who is your guardian? Your parents are dead and buried. You will never see them again. I have made all the arrangements. Almost everything is settled. You will see. You will like España."

My gasp rang in the quiet of the night. *You will never see them again... arrangements.*

"And you will behave." His arm swung up, lifting his coat until the dagger at his side lay exposed to my eyes.

I flinched away.

Dirk must have been as quiet as death on the stairs. He surged to my side, knocked my uncle's arm away before he could deliver the blow, and tucked me behind him all in the space of a few seconds. "Lay a hand on her, and I will kill you."

"Like you killed her parents?" Uncle Oliver's voice held a sneer. *Her parents,* he had said. Not *my brother.* Not *Louisa. Her parents,* as if they belonged to me alone. As if I alone was of their blood, was of their family. My uncle's blade flashed before my eyes just before he lowered his arm, concealing it from view.

Heritage. Bloodlines. Royalty. That dagger...the same I had seen months before, bloody, in Dirk's hand.

My palm lifted to my mouth. Dirk's arm tightened around me. He was right. My own uncle had killed my parents.

"I am not guilty of anything except fleeing that night and leaving her to you," Dirk said.

"You have been spinning lies, under the pretense of rescuing her. You have probably made her doubt me, the Church, the very Pope! I have plans for her. And upon the morn, I plan on *you* being gone." His footsteps receded, cool clicks on the stone floor. Nowhere near as monumental or massive as they should have sounded. He had killed them. And then given my hand in marriage to a man I had never even met. *You will like España.* A man who lived in a country I had never seen. Royalty, apparently.

I sank to sit on the stairs.

"Are you well?" Dirk turned and knelt in front of me. His hands hovered over my head, my hair, my cheeks, as if hesitant to touch me, lest he do me harm.

"I am. Now. Thank God you came." Thank God, indeed. For had I not asked this rescue of the Lord? The truth of it amazed me. And caused a seed of hope to take root in my heart. A tender, fragile seed, it was, but it was there. That was all that mattered.

That and the way Dirk looked down at me now. "Let me take you away from this place."

I had no desire to argue. But there was that one lingering desire that had not been vanquished even by the fear and horror evoked in Oliver's presence. I slipped my hand into Dirk's. He smiled. At last, that smile I loved.

They had named me Gwyneth for a reason. *Happiness.* What does happiness sound like—even in the midst of a painful truth? A smile at the foot of the stairway.

Dirk

Chapter Forty-Four

I hurried her through the halls, pressing into the darkness, unafraid of what we might find. Her hand in mine filled me with inexhaustible strength as we searched for where Joan might have led the others. Her gaze on me was steady and warm, and I could not help but hope this meant she trusted me, truly trusted me, to see her to safety.

We found them at last. The sound of Agnes's voice was unmistakable. "Why did you not tell me who he was? Now we are trapped here for who knows how many days!"

Margried's soft voice prevented me from deciphering the words that made up her answer. I knocked on the door and hesitated. As much as I wished to invite myself in, I waited.

Agnes swung the portal wide.

"We are leaving," I said. "Ready yourselves."

I turned away and took Gwyn with me, but not before I saw the open-mouthed look Agnes gave. That expression almost cooled the fire in my bones that had ignited at seeing Oliver's intention to strike his own niece.

Taking a chance, I rapped on the door across the corridor from the women's. A gruff grunt and a minute later, Ian cracked it open. I pushed my way in.

"What's the plan?" Cade met my eyes, sensing my intent. He looked at Gwyn, huddled next to me, clearly uncomfortable about standing in this room. It was then that I noticed both Cade and Ian were shirtless.

I dipped my chin toward the door, and she stole away.

"Who's ready for another abduction?"

Ian cracked a grin. "When do we leave?"

"Right now."

"Finally made you mad enough, did he?" Cade pulled on his shirt and baldric. "Took you longer than I thought."

I opened and closed my fists. I was far too tense. We had to depart in silence, with deliberation. Oliver's talk of his plans for Gwyn had made bile rise in my throat. He was a lunatic if he thought she would just acquiesce to his machinations for her. And he did not know her at all. "Took Gwyn longer than I thought."

"Ahh. Is that the way of it?" Ian's smirk disappeared as he ducked his head in his shirt. Lucky man. Otherwise I might have had to wipe that look off his face.

Cade's voice brought me back to the task at hand: our need of a method of escape. "That has been the way of it from the beginning."

I scowled. "And it was not with you and Margried?"

He glowered back, but I saw the edges of his frown sneaking into a grin.

Ian huffed, looking perturbed on purpose. "Why could not Agnes have been younger?"

Cade chuckled. "Age is no factor with that one. She was probably as sour then as she is now."

I rolled my eyes heavenward. "Not to mention the fact that she is a nun."

Ian shrugged. Nodded. Grinned. "Too true."

I looked out into the hallway and saw the women's chamber door remained closed. "We will not be able to just traipse out of here."

"Do we need a distraction?" Ian rubbed his hands together.

Looking at Cade, I jerked a thumb in Ian's direction. "What's gotten into him?"

Cade shrugged. "He's always been one for a good abduction."

Ian snickered.

"A distraction will not be necessary," I said. "*If* we can remain quiet enough and purchase the guards' silence."

"And when you say 'purchase,' you mean—" Cade cracked his knuckles against his palm.

"If necessary."

The two men, men who had served by my side for years, brothers to me, looked ready, eager, even.

The reputation I had worked so badly to restore seemed unimportant now. And that was a good thing, because I was about to trample it into the dust.

Gwyneth

Chapter Forty-Five

I slipped on a simple dress to replace my journey-worn, sliced one then I draped the blue gown over the counterpane on my bed. Sentiment struck, and I stroked the skirt, marveling at how much *living* had been done in that dress. Margried sat beside it and put her head in her hands.

"What is wrong?"

She shook her head and looked at me. Relief streamed through my being. In her eyes I read not anguish, nor despair, but frustration. My gaze darted to Sister Agnes, who fumed and muttered to herself while stashing the few things they had pulled from their parcels right back into them. "You told her?"

Margried nodded. "I told Cade earlier, too, while you and Dirk talked. He deems it of no importance, except for the fact that he hates your uncle."

"I can see why."

"It was one of the hardest things I have ever done, to sit there and watch him, knowing who he is, knowing he does *not* know who I am."

I hugged her. "I am sorry. But we are leaving. You need never see him again."

She pulled back and searched my face. "Why are we leaving? Did something happen? You seemed eager to come home."

I sighed. "Not so eager as I once was, before I realized Dirk was not guilty as I thought. Oliver has always been rather…"

She raised a brow. "As long as you are willing. I would rather not be involved with any more abductions during my lifetime."

"I am certain that Cade echoes your feelings on that subject."

Sister Agnes shouldered one small pack and held out another in our direction. "I am finished."

I took the burden from her before Margried could rise. "Thank you, Sister Agnes. For all you have done for me."

"For us." Margried came to stand beside me. Though tension still radiated between the two women, as it had since Margried's conversion, I sensed a clearing that promised the eventual healing of their friendship.

Promise. There was that word once more. It seemed to be chasing me.

A soft rap on the door sent me lunging in that direction. I opened it to see Dirk's face on the other side, determination in his eyes. I had at one time picked arguments with and goaded this man. No more. I could not even speak when he looked at me as he did now.

I should have packed. Something. Anything. I was leaving, after all, the only home I had ever known. I should have done more than changed my gown. Grabbed another pair of shoes. At least slipped on an overskirt, a safeguard against the roads while we traveled. But all I could do was stare into his face.

"Are you ready?"

"We are." The answer came from Margried, who came up behind me and opened the door fully. My heart started up again and raced, as if to make up for all the seconds it had stopped while I stared into Dirk's eyes, as if to remind me that this night I would be leaving everything I had ever known for the second time, for him.

I was more fearful than I cared to admit.

As I stepped out of the room, I drew in a deep breath, ready to leave, but thinking of what I left behind.

Wrapping the silence around us, we descended the stairs. My shoes, worn from travelling, the lacings tatty, let the stone scrape my feet through the rushings. I embraced the discomfort, relishing the thought that my parents had walked this very path, loathing that it would be the final time I did so. Dirk led us in the direction of the kitchen, and I was glad for his wisdom. Destined to be empty this time of night, the kitchen would form the perfect escape and allow us a direct route to where the horses were kept. Dirk swung wide the door.

A small squeak alerted me to the presence of a woman. At the sight of me, she paled, and her eyes rounded. Her throat bobbed as she swallowed.

"Joan." I held out a hand to her. "Tell no one you saw us. Please. Let us go."

Understanding lit her face, and she nodded. "God go with ye."

I smiled. "I thank you." For I knew she meant it, but, furthermore, I felt it quite possibly could be true. Had not God answered my desperate prayer spoken on the stairs? I had not truly thought He would send Dirk to rescue me, but He had. And now, as the cool night air swept over my face and we hurried to the stables, my uncertainty seemed to melt away.

Mayhap Joseph had been right. Mayhap God indeed possessed a kind spirit, a gentle soul. Mayhap He loved me, personally, not for what I did, but for me.

I could feel the pleasure rolling off of Dirk as we rode away. He and the other men had dispensed of only three guards, felling each of them with a blow that bespoke of a terrific headache when they awoke, but sparing their lives. Our easy escape put a smile back on Dirk's face.

"Why did you do it?"

He looked at me, curiosity playing on the planes of his face.

"Why did you save me from the convent?" I fought to keep my expression even, but I feared I failed. I needed to hear him say it again.

Hurt entered his eyes. "I told you once before, because you needed me. Would you have rather I left you there?"

"At one time, my answer would have been aye."

"And now?"

"*Nee.*"

"What has changed?"

I swallowed, accepting the reverse of the conversation. Away from his motives. To mine. "My understanding of the man you are. You are a man of honor. I know that now."

A small smile surfaced on his face. "Your opinion of me has most assuredly changed. My motives did, as well."

Surprised, I pressed, "What do you mean?"

He sobered. "The truth is that I wanted to clear my name."

Wanted? "'Tis an honorable pursuit. But you speak of it as if it is in the past."

"It is."

Oh.

"Yours is an honorable pursuit, as well, milady." His tone lowered.

"What pursuit is that?"

"Your pursuit of God."

I drew in a quick breath and took the words along with it, letting them settle deep within. Did I pursue God? Or did I pursue sainthood, godliness, the label of a perfect Catholic? How twisted it seemed when I posed the

question to myself in that fashion. I said I wanted godliness, but what was that if I knew not the God I wanted to emulate? And after this journey, I wondered how much I really knew God, after all.

I led my horse even closer to Dirk's, not yet ready to probe my heart. "How does rescuing me from Leiden restore your reputation?"

Dirk winked. "Saving the damsel in distress."

I shook my head.

"I wanted to have the chance to tell you the truth."

"And you did." I shuddered as the memory overtook me. I refused to allow it lodging in my brain. This night I would allow sufficient room in my thoughts for one thing and one thing alone: the answer as to why this journey had even begun.

"And I am grateful to God that you believe me."

I nodded but did not meet his eyes. "I am grateful you saved me that day. And for telling me the truth." I smiled. "Though I daresay, next time you need to prove yourself, consider a less lawless way."

He chuckled. "I will. As for yourself, consider a different method in your pursuit of the truth. God does not desire us to come to Him with our minds so much as He is interested in our hearts."

My eyes narrowed, taking that in.

We rode for an hour or two. The moon seemed to widen and expand. At one point, Dirk gripped the reins of my mount and whispered to me. I obeyed, taking my glasses off and handing them to him. I rubbed the bridge of my nose and let my eyes close.

"We stop here." His deep rumbling voice seemed to be part of my dream. But his lifting me down was not; neither was my feet touching the forest floor and refusing to hold the rest of me. He caught me as I stumbled against him.

"I am sorry."

"*Het maakt niet uit.*"

My gaze swung to his in an arc that sent a stab of pain through my neck. "Did you just say it doesn't matter? In Dutch?"

"I listen to you." He steered my steps toward where Ian and Cade were depositing Sister Agnes and Margried. They looked as weary as I felt. He applied gentle pressure to my arms. "Now, sleep. Rest. The distance to my family's estate will keep us journeying for a few days."

I dropped to the hard ground. To my surprise, I found a blanket beneath me when I lay back. The last thing I thought was how nicely my mother's language had sounded in Dirk's voice.

A scratching noise awakened me. A flash of light to my left punctured the darkness of the monastery's cell. But the table—and the candle—sat to my right…

The light vanished.

How had the candle moved…?

Oh. There had never been a candle. I had not been in the monastery. Instead, I lay on the forest floor—but what then had been that flash of light? A hand clasped my mouth, and my lungs filled with a captive scream.

I bit the gloved fingers. A word not often spoken in my presence hissed in my ears. But the hand held fast. I moaned, trying to make as much noise as possible so the men, sleeping near, would hear me. *Dirk!* I received a blow to the side of my head for my trouble.

Where had the moon gone? Light! I needed light. To see my abductor. A thick arm pulled me to my feet. I stumbled and stood as clumsily as I could, trying to make it seem like I still remained groggy from sleep rather than that I was acting rebelliously. For I did not want a repeat of that slap. I dragged my feet as I was pulled along beside my captor. Alas, what shuffling I managed to create in the dry leaves sounded miniscule to even my own ears.

Awaken, Dirk! God, help me!

The man tugging me suddenly stopped. He lifted his hand from my mouth for a brief second. I gulped in air but was muzzled again before I got the chance to shout.

"Be silent." The harsh whisper hit my ears, and my heart picked up in pace. Up till now I had assumed the abduction would be stopped, that my captor would be overtaken by Dirk or one of his men. But Arthur's voice in my ear put an end to that hope.

Throughout the many years Arthur had worked for Oliver, his skill in hunting had never been matched. He knew how to leave a trail that would take Dirk and the others in the opposite direction of where he intended to take me. He had probably already laid the false trail before he had stolen me from slumber.

We walked for a while before he leaned low. "If you scream, I'll slit your throat right here."

He shoved me on a horse and climbed up behind me. As we rode into the blackness, I could think of only one thing. I had been right all along. The thought brought no satisfaction.

For now Oliver would win. Win me. And harm Dirk when he came looking for me. *Oh, God.* I clutched my diamond rosary in my fist and stared with dry eyes into the night.

I *had* become a burden to Dirk. By relinquishing my life over to him and becoming his responsibility once more, I had hurt him in more ways than turning away from him and surrendering to a life underneath Oliver's heavy hand could ever do. For he would come after me. And both men could not triumph.

Several minutes passed before I realized I had left my glasses with Dirk.

Dirk

Chapter Forty-Six

She had come. That thought beckoned me to open my eyes to the morning. Only when I opened them, dawn had yet to fully arrive. I turned over on my blanket, wanting only a glimpse of her. Did she sleep with wrinkled brow and fitful fidgeting this night, as she had since I had first known her? Or did she sleep soundly, peacefully? I squinted into the pre-dawn haze, up at the tendrils of light breaking through the trees' colorful leaves, allowing me just enough of a view of her blanket…her empty blanket.

I shot to my feet and bellowed. Cade and Ian jumped up, weapons drawn, eyes scanning our surroundings for the threat that had made me holler. Fear frosted every nerve as I realized the threat was long gone. And so was Gwyn.

Sister Agnes and Margried had both shrieked when I roared. They untangled themselves from their blankets and knelt, staring down at the empty space where Gwyn had been.

When she did not emerge from the woods, the last sliver of hope I had clung to evaporated. I raked my fingers through my hair and took a jagged breath.

"She is gone! Who would have taken her?" Margried's crying catapulted Cade to her side.

Sister Agnes's stony expression cracked and let her concern show. "Do you think 'twas her uncle?"

Had Oliver come and stolen her away in the dead of night? I shook my head. "I know not what to think."

A chilling thought raced through my mind. Or had she gone willingly? Deserted us? After hours ago sending the smallest seed of hope burgeoning in my soul, could she have decided to crush it all? My thoughts swam, rushing to keep up. She had seemed eager to escape her uncle last night. She had not said a word when I had declared I sought to get her out of Barrington Manor, so I had taken that as acquiescence. She would not have gone back again, would she?

Ian stepped to my side and whispered in a voice too low for the others to hear. "Shall we go after her?"

I keyed in on the younger man's choice of words. "Do you think it was her choice? That she ran?"

"I think you know her better than anyone."

The slightest bit of tension exited my shoulders. He was right. I knew her hurts and her longings. The way her green eyes sparked fire when I teased her. The innocent way she kissed. The troubled way she gave in to sleep. The way she guarded her glasses.

Her glasses.

She had not run. For her glasses remained with me.

I bent and scooped her spectacles from the ground where I had left them the night before. "We ride for Barrington Manor."

In an instant, everyone sprang into motion, gathering their things, readying the horses. For a small, insipid moment I studied her round lenses, the strong arms that were meant to hook over her ears, as if her glasses could provide me with answers to the mystery of where she was. I tucked them in my pocket. *Please, Lord, will You keep her safe? And give me swiftness?*

I launched into motion. Wherever she was, with whomever she was, Gwyn was more vulnerable than ever.

Gwyneth

Chapter Forty-Seven

Arthur carried me, kicking and screaming, inside the large stone doors of the entryway and dropped me to the floor. Oliver—I refused to call him uncle—spat at my feet and expelled a slew of Spanish expletives. In shock at his outburst, I stilled.

"Niña tonta!"

I glared as he circled me. Squinting, I met his eyes until I was forced to look away and stare straight ahead. "I am *not* a foolish girl."

"Gallivanting off in the dead of night, after having only just arrived home! And with a murderer, no less. What were you thinking?"

"He is no murderer." *Unlike you.*

He hauled me to my feet and sneered in my face. "He made you believe that, did he?"

"He taught me to believe in many things." Like trust.

His fingers dug into my arm, and I looked down at them, aware of the leaf that had attached itself to my gown while Arthur rode me back here on his horse. Aware of the way Oliver did not seem to notice either that or his harsh grip. Aware of the way the clammy air of the entryway entered my nose and clogged my throat.

No servants dared show their face. Only Arthur waited in a candlelit corner, his face shadowed.

My eyes returned to Oliver, whose expression had changed from stark rage to something else. I might have called it a softening except for the hard glint in his eyes that, if anything, had only become sharper. "Have you fallen in love with him?"

I did not deny it, but neither did I look down or away in shame. The old Gwyneth might have, but she no longer lived. I did not miss her. A woman who believed in love and mercy had taken her place.

"Have you?" Oliver grasped hold of both of my arms and pulled me

even closer against his scowling face. His hot breath swirled around me, wrinkling my nose and making me want to gag. I had to get away. I had to get back to Dirk! What would he think, waking to find me gone? *Please, God.* But I knew not what to ask, what to pray, save for that. *Please, God.*

A hollow, harsh laugh spewed from Oliver's mouth. "You have! Incomprehensible! You, a stalwart saint, and he, a common criminal."

"There is nothing common about him." I spat the words and received a slap to the cheek for the effort.

He smirked. "I have wanted to do that for hours."

Gasping, I brought my palm to my face, feeling the sting of tears at the backs of my eyes. But I would not cry. Not now, not in front of *him*, this monster I had once called family. I would not allow him an honor I had heretofore allowed only my father and mother to see.

And Dirk, I suddenly remembered. I had wept with Dirk, many a time. Why had I never realized that before? The walls I had built around my heart always crumbled in his presence. Could that mean anything less than that I loved him?

I pinned a stare on Oliver that could leave him in no doubt about my loathing. "He is no criminal."

"We sheltered you too much, my dear." The endearment sounded more like a jeer. "Your parents sought to protect your sensibilities and, in doing so, cost you insight."

Denying myself the urge to ask him why he had killed them, I instead said, "My parents loved me." Which was more than I could say for him. What had happened to the uncle who had been my friend?

"Your parents were near-sighted. They might have loved you, but they never had the vision for you that I have. They denied you access to your true heritage, as well as denying you knowledge of who Devon Godfrey is."

"Was. In any case, it does not matter." What was he talking about, my true heritage? The Spanish nobility he had earlier claimed? "I know he is twice the man you are."

He caught my chin in one rough hand. "And how do you know that?"

I ignored the slur and answered with the truth. "He is good. Kind. He is willing to fight for what is his. When he gives his heart, he gives his all." And I had given him my heart.

If only I could be sure he loved me in return. Not just as his charge but as a woman who would stand by his side.

"He has deceived you. You have known him for, what, a fortnight? He is naught but a wolf." Oliver waved his hand, dismissing me. Before

I could shout that he was wrong, he turned away and grabbed a blurry candle from the wall. "Bring her."

I had forgotten Arthur stood near. He swung me up against his chest again. Though I struggled and fought, I presented no match to Arthur's massive form.

When Oliver did not take the stairway that would lead to my chamber, I scrambled to understand. Stopping in a secondary hall, he opened a door I had entered only once before, through which we descended into the bowels of the castle. Meager light from the approaching dawn curled fingers of hazy warmth through the open windows. Until we left level ground and went deeper into darkness.

"Where are you taking me?" But I knew the answer before I asked. Once, years ago, I had opened that door; Grandfather had stopped me before I got too far, but that glimpse had been enough.

"The dungeon."

"Why?" I just wanted him to begin talking again. If he did, mayhap I could make him see reason, convince him—

He turned. The candlelight revealed a grin on his face. "I must keep you safe until I can secure passage for us to España."

To my Spanish *royal* husband. "I thought you said you had made all of the arrangements already."

His grin faded, illuminated by the flickering flame of the candle in his hand. He continued focusing on the stairs. "I have. Your marriage to the king is not for many months, however."

My blood turned to ice. The soreness that had settled into me—consequence of being hauled onto Arthur's horse and tossed at Oliver's feet—faded as a new, shocking pain took its place. "King?"

Oliver laughed a full, madman's laugh. "King Philip."

"Of España?" My words came out choked.

A heavy sigh. "Have you not been listening? You must improve upon that, my dear, if you are to make a good wife, a good queen."

Somehow, some way, I had to stall him, stall this….this foolishness! "I cannot be queen."

"Of course you can. A marriage to Godfrey's second son was only a diversion. This love you think you feel for him…you must forget."

My head reeled. "King Philip already has a queen."

The truth was he was on his third. But unlike the father of our own Queen Elizabeth—Henry VIII—Philip's wives had died.

"An unsuitable one."

"How is she—?"

"Her twin girls died two years ago. A miscarriage of her first pregnancy! 'Tis most unsuitable. And girls! *Two* girls." Oliver shook his head as he put his candle into an opening in the wall. A door with a single small square of a window called for my attention.

So this was the dungeon. My eyes strained to take in the stone floor covered with straw. One of the stone walls looked moldy, but I could not be sure from this distance. The stone ceiling loomed heavily, as if the weight of the castle had descended on my head. The musty smell made me want to gag.

But not as much as Oliver's insanity.

"So you would have King Philip divorce Elisabeth of Valois?"

An expression of longsuffering convulsed on Oliver's face. "No. She is pregnant once again, but of course neither she nor the child will live."

That the man cared so little for the life of the queen and her unborn child sent a chill down my spine. I pushed against Arthur. "You may let me go now."

Oliver nodded to Arthur then returned his gaze to me. "You will stay here where I can protect you from the likes of young Godfrey until we set sail."

I wrestled away from Arthur and forced air into my lungs. "You cannot do this. Listen to yourself! You gamble with God, taking for granted the death of both the queen and her babe. Even if Elisabeth dies, mayhap the child will be a son and will live. Then what need will the king have of another wife?"

"A man can never have too many sons, a king too many heirs. Look at Carlos."

The king's firstborn son, who was rumored to be mad. Like I was sure the man before me was. I searched for another argument and found the perfect one. "Why me?"

Oliver chuckled. "Why you, indeed? You are not a princess of Portugal, like Maria Manuela was. You are not a queen, like Mary of England was. Neither are you related to the king, like they both were."

At last, he was coming to understand. But his tone did not betray comprehension, only the fervor of a man coming to the cusp of his grand explanation. "You see now why I will not be suitable. If he is in need of a queen, he should marry a princess."

"Ah, but that is where you are wrong. You have something much more desirable than royal blood in your veins."

He hesitated, but I refused to give him the satisfaction of asking. Still the question vibrated in my brain. *And what is that?*

"You have English, Dutch, *and* Spanish blood in your veins."

Ah, yes, the bloodline he had mentioned. My father had been both English and Spanish. My mother was thoroughly Dutch. But, "Why would that be of import to the Spanish king? Would he not want a full-blooded *mujer Española?*"

"Are you truly that dense, my dear?"

Apparently.

Oliver huffed. "Having a queen with English blood will sway the Catholics under England's Queen Elizabeth to support King Philip. He will be able to restore Catholicism to England. This country has languished in the throes of Protestantism for too long."

My voice sounded weak to my ears. "Our Queen Elizabeth has procured peace, never mind the fines for missing Book of Prayer services. Both religions coexist."

Oliver looked at me in horror. "Catholicism is the only true religion."

I did not speak the thought aloud, but it thundered through my soul with the force of a mighty gale. *And Protestantism is the only true faith.*

"And you must never speak of Queen Elizabeth as *yours.* Consider yourself Spanish."

"I am more Dutch than either English or Spanish."

A devilish glint lit his eyes. "And that, my dear, is another reason why you will be such an asset to Philip."

He spoke of him as if he knew him, as if he had spoken with him. Had he? If he had corresponded with the king, what had he said? What had the king said?

Oh, God, would the king truly listen to this madness? And if he had, would he manipulate the situation? Assassinate his wife so that he could marry me? I shook my head. I refused to give in to Oliver's nonsense, however persuasive he might be. "This is ridiculous. You cannot be serious. The king would never listen to such folly!"

"You have not even heard the best part."

I quirked a brow.

"From whence did you just come, my dear?"

I mashed my lips together.

He glared. "Fine, then. Be obstinate. You saw it yourself and cannot deny it. The Iconoclastic Fury races across the Low Countries like a runaway blaze. It is rumored to be dying down, but the Dutch are setting fire to their own country and rallying behind William of Orange. They intend to revolt."

"Mayhap they do." A small niggle of light burst in my brain. The man could not mean…?

"The situation is out of control. Philip is pressing to put a stop to it before things progress further. If left to themselves too long, the Dutch may go too far and it will be too late. But Philip will not let that happen. Because he will have you."

"Me?"

"You said it yourself. You are more Dutch than either English or Spanish. With you as his wife, as his queen, Philip will be able to assert his power once more. The Dutch will flock to you in droves, starting with the Catholics and ending with the rebel Calvinists."

He meant what he said. Every word. I saw that truth reflected in the candlelight illuminating the fire of passion in his eyes. He intended to ship me to Philip with a note that read "for you." *Para usted.*

He was that mad. That insane. That determined and devoted.

He came toward me. I forced myself not to flinch, but he only laid a hand on my shoulder. For a moment, I thought I saw in his eyes a speck of the old uncle I had known since birth. The one who had laughed when I had returned, filthy, with leaves in my hair, from running my horse over our lands. My mother had cried. My father had been livid.

But my uncle had laughed. And I suddenly wondered just how long he had been concocting this plan.

He smiled down at me. "Trust me, Gwyneth. This will all work out for good. You will see. You will make an excellent queen."

The image of Oliver laughing shattered in my mind. In its place rose an image of him as he looked at that moment, the candle's flame lighting up his face. He looked alive with purpose. But such a dark, dark purpose. A purpose that included the death of a queen and a babe yet unborn. A purpose that hinged on my being the fourth wife of a man more than twenty years older than I.

And ushering in the overhaul of not one country, but two. According to Oliver, with me on the throne beside Philip, not just the Low Countries, but England, too, would be swift to fall into Hapsburg control.

Oliver's hand fell from my shoulder, and he turned his back to me.

Arthur set down the candle and retrieved something from his cloak. Something that he outstretched as he strode to the door.

A key.

"Wait—"

"Silence." Oliver's hand rose, but still he did not face me. "It is necessary. The fool will almost certainly come after you. Until then, you must be secured. I must know you are safe."

"You mean trapped."

He remained silent.

Oh, God, please do not let Dirk come. Oliver was mad. He would kill him. Another person I loved.

The urge to ask could not be denied a moment more. "Why did you kill them?"

My words caused Oliver to halt. Then he turned toward me, anger on his face. "Because they would never have agreed to my plan for you, my dear. The plan that will ensure I can forever leave England and return to my native land, the place where I should have been born."

I blinked. "This is your land. You are half English."

He smiled. "That is what my mother allowed everyone to believe, though I suspect your grandfather knew the truth. That I am the son of a Spanish noble who was disinherited before he died and left my mother penniless. Not a drop of English blood flows in these veins."

So many secrets kept over so many years. They crumbled around me.

"But in your veins flows not just Spanish blood. And the world depends on it."

With that, he left. He must have taken my stunned silence as acquiescence, for he ascended the stairway without ever looking back.

Arthur swung the door wide, capturing my fragmented attention. Lifting my chin, I took a step toward the door. I halted; Arthur's face had changed.

The cold expression had melted, and a leer had taken its place. "Come." He motioned with his hand.

Revulsion pulsed through me. My breathing quickened. With all the dignity I could muster, I stepped past him, into the cell, and swiveled around. My skirt's billow died as I met Arthur's gaze again.

He did not close the door and lock me in. Not immediately. Instead, he leaned close until I tipped my chin to avoid him. But I did not look away.

"You are even more beautiful than when you left months ago."

I said nothing. When he raised a hand to my cheek, I turned away. But I could see the key dangling from his finger.

"I could take you away from here."

Arthur. Truth slammed into me with such force I almost cried out.

Oliver would never dirty his hands. It had been Oliver's dagger, but it had been Arthur's hand that had stabbed my parents.

I spat at him.

His face contorted. "You have made your choice." He shut the door and peered through the bars of the window at me. Arthur held the key high, taunting, threatening. I held his gaze, for he was right. I had chosen. And I would live with that choice now.

The key slipped through his fingers and clinked against stone. He looked down. "Oh. Pity, that. Down a crack. I suppose you are locked in here for good."

Or I would die for that choice.

Dirk

Chapter Forty-Eight

My conclusion was confirmed when I found the trail someone had laid for us to find in order to buy himself some time. Cade grunted at the level of skill, but my anger only burned hotter. *Arthur.* We turned the horses toward Barrington Manor and covered the land in a hard gallop. I regretted pushing Margried and Agnes so hard, but I could not leave them so deep in the forest for fear they themselves would be captured or rendered helpless against animals.

We tied the horses a safe distance away from the castle just as the sky began to lighten.

"I am coming with you." Arms crossed, Margried glared up at Cade, as if trying to appear fierce, and failing.

"As am I." Agnes stood tall, her gray eyes flashing.

Cade shook his head. "We cannot search for Gwyneth and keep you safe, as well."

"You need us." Agnes looked too smug for the words.

"Why?" Though I had not intended it, the word came out a growl.

"Have you ever been inside Barrington Manor? Really inside?" Margried pleaded with me with her eyes.

My head pounded with the effort of seeking to understand what she meant and keeping at bay my desire to lay a fist alongside Oliver's jaw. "Just last night."

"Do you know where Gwyneth's chamber is? Or the place she goes to be alone?"

Ian expelled a sigh. "And how would *you* know where such places are?"

Agnes smiled at Margried. "Margried has a memory that works in pictures. Gwyneth once described her home to her. Margried will be able to lead us where we wish to go."

Cade looked at me. I met his stare then Ian's. "Fine. Come."

Our return to Barrington Manor transpired far too easily. We encountered not one guard, which was too bad, because my fist itched to lay into something. The entryway stood empty. Too late, I realized the hair on the back of my neck stood at attention. I held up a hand to the others. Something was not right.

"So the murderer has returned." Oliver's voice preceded his footsteps. He came from the Great Hall. "You made better time than Arthur expected. It seems I won that wager."

"Where is she?"

"Are you referring to my niece? I assure you, you have no business with her. She is a betrothed woman, after all."

I strode forward with a speed that he did not expect. The sliver of surprise in his eyes bore witness and gave me great satisfaction as I took hold of his collar. "Where is she?" I ground out each word.

The ring of a blade exiting a baldric echoed on the high ceilings of the room. I jerked away from Oliver and drew my dagger just in time to meet Arthur's weapon.

"Next time be quicker, Arthur." Oliver mumbled the words as he straightened his cloak.

Arthur and I stood there, weapons extended. My peripheral vision assured me Cade and Ian stood mere feet away.

"You are outnumbered." I threw the words at Oliver.

"Ah, but I hold the hostage." He flicked a hand at Arthur, and the man stepped away.

I did not move. "What is stopping me from disposing of you both and saving her?"

"Saving?" Oliver tipped back his head and laughed. "I am the one saving her life! She would die here a recusant Catholic, but I can make her a queen."

I faced him, weary of his games. "Tell me where she is or I will run you through."

A feminine gasp sounded behind me, but I did not regret my harshness. I knew Oliver intended to kill us all before the hour chimed.

"You will do neither the killing nor the *saving,* as you call it. I hold all the cards here, and we both know it."

I leveled my gaze on him, thoughts whirling as I sought to guess his next move. In order to distract, I tossed a different subject in his face. "Why did you kill your brother?"

His face changed. Darkened. "Because he would never have agreed to my plan for Gwyneth. And he killed my mother."

Gwyn had failed to mention that. Suspicion of his reasoning irked. "How?"

"She died giving him life. He stole the spirit from her."

Each muscle in my body went on high alert. How long had this man harbored such a notion? The grief had leaked his rationality drop by drop over the years. Not only did I have a controlling uncle on my hands, I had an insane one.

The grin he gave looked otherworldly, evil. "But enough of all that. I must say, you stepped into your role quite nicely. I am almost grateful to you for playing your part so well."

My blood ran cold then ran not at all. So he had orchestrated it all from the very beginning. I had been naught but a pawn in his plan. And so had Gwyn. "Did you send her away for her own good, then? Or did you intend for her to be hurt or killed by her own countrymen?"

He scowled. "You must think better of me than that. I would not want my niece killed. She is to marry King Philip!"

My brows rose.

"*No*, she was the one who wanted to be away. She wanted to be as far away from you as possible."

Even after all this time, it still stung. The slap of rejection. Knowing she had once distrusted me, even feared me. Suddenly I had to know she was well, rescue her from the clutches of this madman, take her far away where she could never be harmed again.

The light blinded my heart.

It was not possible.

I could never protect Gwyn like I wished to, never shield her from hurt and sorrow like my heart demanded I do. In rescuing her from the convent, she had fallen. In seeing her to the shore, she had been attacked. During our journey across the Channel, she had nearly drowned. And by delivering her home, I had given her into the hands of a man who had murdered his own flesh and blood.

It was impossible to take matters into my own hands. I saw that now. Pain ripped through me. *Oh, Lord, will You protect her?* A soft whisper of peace cloaked my soul in the assurance that He would. I could not, but what I was too weak, too human to do, God could.

I stared into Oliver's face. He rattled on about bloodlines and benefits, but I heard little. I could retrieve those words from the abyss of my memory later. In that moment, I reveled in the love of God that shone light into my darkened heart. Until the light pierced the deepest place.

I was just like him.

The realization almost took me to the floor. I was just like the man I did not listen to now. He had plans, grandiose plans, and he intended to see them through. But they were ridiculous, flawed in impossible places, beyond a sliver of hope of coming true.

Had I not once had a magnificent plan that would restore me to my family, purify my name, and save Gwyn from all danger? And how had I gone about that plan? I had abducted her. Taken her against her will, nearly frightening her to pieces in the process. The truth bit deep.

Oliver and I had both been willing to do anything to secure what we wanted.

In trying to clear my name of a sin I had not committed, I had committed so many. By seeking to use his niece for his own selfish gain, Oliver had surrendered to the powers of darkness. Gwyn's words about my motives being honorable lit up my soul—as did her teasing about finding less lawless methods next time.

By God's grace, I would.

"Enough!" I cut my hand through the air.

Oliver glared. "I quite agree. Enough insolence. Enough time has passed that I am sure Gwyn is in need of nourishment. I have no more time for you or your companions." He snapped his fingers, his rage turning his eyes a sickly shade.

Arthur came forward, a blank look on his face.

"Halt. I would rather finish him off myself." Oliver pulled a small dagger from his cloak. I recognized it as the same blade that I had pulled from Simon's chest that fateful night months ago.

Roars sounded from behind me as Ian and Cade rushed forward. They would not make it in time. I deflected Oliver's hurried slash. Arthur smacked my weapon away with his. Oliver's dagger dug into my side, but not deeply enough. Still, a wild burn chased through my gut.

A blond man entered my vision and struck Oliver away from me. Oliver's face twisted, contorted in terror. His eyes, so dark before, filled with fear and a rage quickly dimming.

It was then that I saw Arthur had been felled by Cade.

And Oliver by Gerald, the man from the gate.

Oliver sank to the floor, and I pressed a hand to my side. Ribbons of red drained from the both of us, mixing into rivulets on the floor. I knew not where my blood ended and his began. Time froze as I stared at the

way our blood looked so much the same. Just like our characters had once looked similar.

But no more. Now I would aspire to be like another Man who had once shed blood—blood that had cleansed my soul and set me free forever.

A cacophony of voices rose all around me, but I ignored them all. I strode away. And started shouting her name.

Gwyneth

Chapter Forty-Nine

Arthur had taken the light with him. Darkness swathed the small space I now occupied, and I heard a scratching noise. So I was not alone. I was to share the dungeon with the rats. For some reason that fact alone did not cause the tears to overflow my eyes and slip silently down my cheeks. *Nee,* I cried not for me. But for the uncle I had lost.

Now I had no family at all.

I took as few deep breaths as possible. Despite the fact my nostrils did not acknowledge the foul smell after a while, I knew the filth that surrounded me, and that was enough.

Hopelessness trudged through my soul as the seconds stacked into minutes and the minutes into hours. I fought to stand, but my legs rebelled. I finally sat, huddling my knees close. Time marched through the darkness of the dungeon, unable to penetrate any corner, any inch of space. How I longed for light. Just a meager amount of light to remind me I lived, not in this horrible blackness, but in light, glorious light.

Pressing my hand to my thundering heart, I stroked the rosary. How the diamonds would sparkle if only I had a speck of light to cast upon them. Feeling their imprint in my palm, I heard my father's words. His promise.

"Your mother and I bequeath this to you, in faith that you will find the man who shares your soul. We promise you that, when you marry, it will be to a man of your choosing, as it was for us. And we will be there, smiling upon you."

Pain ripped through me as I remembered his smiling face. *Moeder* had watched with tears of joy in her eyes and a sweet smile glowing from every feature. I looked like her, I had been told. If I had light and a mirror, I would hold my image in the glass and imagine it to be her I saw.

A rat came too close. I aimed a kick, shrieked, and missed. It scurried off. I tore the rosary from my neck, feeling it click apart. Sobs shook me as

I grieved the promise my father had given me with such assurance that he would be there to keep it. Neither of my parents would ever see me marry.

I might never marry at all. I would fight my uncle until my last breath. Even if King Philip were as mad as he, I would rather die than enter into a loveless marriage.

Especially now that I had known love.

Dirk's smile…those brown eyes dark with teasing, even glinting with anger…all those red curls… Memory after memory assaulted my mind until I held my hands to my face and wept.

"God, watch over him, please. Do not let him try to save me. The risk is too great, the danger too overwhelming. He knows not what he would face. *Please* keep him safe. Do not allow him to try and rescue me."

The prayers rolled from my heart until, at once, they stopped. I drew in a deep breath, never minding the stale air that surrounded me. When had prayer become so easy that I did not realize I was talking to God? When had saying the rosary become not enough for me? When had speaking to Him as a friend become the only thing that satisfied the gripping pain? When had I allowed myself to cry with Him?

Margried's words echoed in my mind. *"The best part is, it is enough."* She had spoken those words right after Joseph had led her to "come to faith."

Joseph—such a strange man. The oddest man I had ever met. His eyes always seemed at peace. His bearing spoke of contentment. And he spoke of God as a friend. Not as a judge, not as a holy Lord, but as a friend. I could not fathom it.

As I shook my head, I wondered. Could I? After praying to God like that just now, could I not fathom what Joseph meant, what he had been trying to tell me?

My thoughts whirled with the opinions Joseph and Dirk had presented about Luther and his followers, the Holy Spirit indwelling the children of God… Dirk's words returned to the forefront of my mind. *"God does not desire us to come to Him with our minds so much as he is interested in our hearts."*

Something snapped inside me. I still had questions, just as Margried had questions. But need there be this great chasm between me and faith for merely my questions' sake? Could I not approach God as a friend, as I had been doing just now, and see if the chasm could be breached?

"God, I know not what to say. I know not what to pray. I know only that my heart is changing. Here in this pit of darkness there is none I can turn to except You. I have fought against it for so long. I told myself it could not be right, could not be holy, to view You as a God with facets to Your character. It could not be right, what Luther and Knox and Calvin have begun, the revolution of all we have ever known."

The labels swam in my mind again. Protestant. Catholic. Of a sudden, the separation between the two ways seemed far less than the separation between God in His heaven and me.

"I want You to be here with me now, when I have no one else. No one else."

A rush of peace and love and grace brushed over my soul, as when I had surrendered to the tug of the *Kanaal*. I made not a sound. I could not move. But, unlike when I had nearly drowned, I knew I was not alone.

Dirk

Chapter Fifty

Gerald called out to me. I stopped. Turned.

"She is this way, in the dungeon," he said.

Cade looked wary, Ian even more so. After all, this gatekeeper had been in Oliver's employ. But he had also saved my life. "Lead me to her."

"Wait," Cade said. He turned to Margried. "Does he tell the truth?"

Margried closed her eyes, as if summoning the keep to her memory. When she opened them again, she nodded.

We reached the stairs, and Cade and Ian exchanged a look. Ian stayed behind with the women. As we walked down, Gerald took the lead with a candle in his hand. Fear made my heart pound. What would I find? Was she alive? It had been Oliver's plan to marry her off to the Spanish king, and that alone proved his insanity. Who could tell how he had treated her when she fought back? For I knew she had fought back. My lioness.

Lord, I cannot save her. I cannot. But You can. Please let her know You. There in the back of my mind was the prayer I did not dare pray, but I was sure He heard anyway. *And please let her be well and whole. Alive.*

"She is locked in there." Gerald's words fell like stones into the stairway we descended.

My hands formed fists. "How long?"

"Oliver and Arthur took her down a few hours before you arrived."

My steps picked up in pace. *Let her be alive.*

The smell and cold accosted us before I saw her, crumpled in a corner. If Oliver had not already been dead, I would have killed him. I lunged for the door and gripped the bars that punctured the small open space. "Gwyn?"

A gasp.

My eyes closed. *Praise God.* She lived. "Gwyn?"

"Dirk?" A rustling as she rose. The sound of dainty shoes against stone. A stumble. "Dirk, is that you?"

Curse this door that stood between us! I ducked down, my fingers seeking the latch even as Gerald's words tugged at my mind. *Locked.* "It is me. Are you well?"

The sound of a single sob echoed in my every drop of blood. "You found me."

"Gwyneth-mine, of course I did. You doubted?" I straightened.

Finally, she was there. Her face lifted to the opening in the door. I jerked toward Gerald, grabbed his candle, and searched her face. No signs of bruises. No blood. Tearstains.

"You came." She sounded afraid rather than pleased.

I pushed my fingers through the bars. "I could do nothing less."

"You must get out of here. Oliver—" The words died on her lips, and her expression betrayed more brokenness than ever before. Her trembling hand reached up to mine.

I clasped her palm and caressed her skin, trying to coax warmth into her cold fingers.

"You are here…" Gwyneth's voice drifted off as I watched the pieces come together in her mind. "That means that *he…*"

I took a breath to cool my anger, but it failed. I met her gaze. "Oliver will never hurt you again."

At my words, she sighed and closed her eyes. They popped open again. "Do you have blood on your face? You are hurt! What did he do to you?"

Beautiful, wonderful, angel of a woman. Here she was, locked in this hole, and she asked about me. "Do not worry yourself." I drank in the way she looked at me. "You are my only thought for the moment."

Oliver had known I would come after her. If he had doubted, he would have placed her under guard in her chamber. Instead, he secured her here. My eyes roved the little I could see of her prison. Small space. No shackles. No chains.

Another thought invaded. Where was her rosary? I tossed away that question, for more pressing matters called for my attention.

Tears filled her eyes when my examination brought my gaze back to hers. "I came to faith."

Joy collided with the terror that rushed through me at seeing her like this. "I will get you out of here, Gwyn." I was wasting time. I would find the key and—

"There is something you do not know."

I rubbed small circles on the back of her hand. "Do you trust me?"

Chapter Fifty-One

I did not hesitate. "With all my heart." I poured all the love etched in my soul into my gaze.

He stared straight back. A vein twitched in his neck. I hated the distress he felt for me. *You must not worry,* I wanted to say. *God has given me joy and you have given me your love. I see that now.* But I would not say those words. To do so would only cause him more pain. He needed this, now. The thought that he could free me.

These walls were stone, this door as thick as ice. Still, hope surged within. The hope God had given me. The hope Dirk had helped me see was there all along. At last I could hold back the words no longer. "I am well, Dirk."

"I will find the key. Where would Oliver have kept it? On his person? Among his belongings?"

"Dirk," I whispered.

"If Oliver intended to marry you off, Gwyn, he would not entrap you here with no way out." He leaned closer to the bars that separated us.

"Dirk."

"Gerald, Cade." He tossed the words over his shoulder. "Can we get another candle down here?"

"Dirk!"

His gaze met mine.

I swallowed, wanting to tell him gently. "The key—"

"Where is it?"

I blew out my breath. "It's gone!" I winced.

His eyes narrowed. "What do you mean it's gone?" One curl fell over his forehead, and I wanted so badly to be able to reach up and touch it. But that would mean I would have to let go of his hand holding mine.

I opened my mouth and closed it. Tried again. "Oliver turned his back

while Arthur put me in this… Arthur hates me."

Dirk's lips thinned.

"I think he may have thought…" I searched for words. "He offered to take me away, but I refused. I never trusted him." I took a deep breath.

"Gwyn, did he hurt you?"

I jerked my gaze to his. "I spat at him."

He snorted, sounding pleased.

"He dropped it. The key. After he locked the door, he dropped the key down one of the cracks in the floor. He never intended for me to get out."

He released my hand and disappeared from view. He must have begun to search along the stones on his side of the door. "I will find it. I promise you. I will get you out."

Promise. A single tear fell down my cheek as my hand dropped once more to my side, cold without his warmth buoying mine. "It is hopeless, Dirk. It is gone. But, listen."

He stood. I gazed up at him. Oh, how once his way of towering over me had made me feel safe. He still made me feel safe. And loved. This good man was willing to kneel in the dirt of a dungeon for me, to set me free.

My eyes widened as the expression on his face changed. The desperation had departed. Instead a cold, calculating look came into his eye. "Arthur wanted you to run away with him?"

I nodded. "It matters not. I know God now, Dirk. I am well. Let me go."

"Never." His brow rose, and I saw that scar that reminded me he was a rogue. He grinned. "Have you learned nothing?"

Mouth agape, I watched him sprint from the room.

Dirk

Chapter Fifty-Two

Arthur wanted her to run away with him.

I raced up the stairs and didn't stop to spare Ian, Agnes, or Margried a glance. I halted in the hall and stared down at Oliver's and Arthur's bodies. My grin faded. A gasp brought my head up. Two servant girls stood in a doorway, hands over their mouths, wide eyes staring straight at me.

With my back to them, I crouched in front of Arthur's lifeless form. "She said you wanted her to run away with you," I whispered.

His weapon lay close to him, as if it waited for him to pick it up again. If he had had his way, he would have. He would have wielded that blade for a good many more years. And though I was no longer a betting man, I was betting he would have thwarted this wild scheme of Oliver's.

He offered to take me away, Gwyn had said. She had been mistaken about Arthur extending that offer only once. Arthur had not intended to leave her in that dungeon if he had wanted her for himself. So, in order to break her, he had taken the one thing that he knew meant the most to her: her hope.

I reached beneath Arthur's shirt and pulled out the key on a cord around his neck.

I had a dungeon to unlock. And glasses to deliver.

Gwyneth

Chapter Fifty-Three

I rose to the tips of my toes and pressed my face to the bars. Cade and Gerald came thundering down the stairs, a candle in every hand. They looked at each other before looking at me. Gerald shifted from one foot to another as if wary, so I stared instead at Cade's confident smile.

The sound of another set of footsteps caused my heart to soar even as I ordered it not to. *It is hopeless,* I had told Dirk. And it was.

His words echoed through my being. *Have you learned nothing?*

Dirk came into view, his grin having grown wider. He rushed over to the door where I was imprisoned. His expression turned serious as he reached his hand through and brushed a stray strand of hair off of my cheek. "Hold to hope, Gwyneth-mine."

I froze. He smiled and held up the key Arthur had dropped into a crack in the floor. I gasped. "How did you…?"

"*Het maakt niet uit.*"

If the bars had not been biting into my face, I would have laughed. I settled down onto my feet. My hands fell to my sides and started to shake.

Dirk's eyes bore into mine with a look that branded itself into my mind. I heard the key find the lock, a grinding, a release. I was free. He swung open the door and engulfed me in his arms.

His breath tickled my ear as he held his hand to my head. I closed my eyes.

"Would you like your glasses now, milady?"

My head turned, and I stared at Dirk. "I can see you quite well."

A smile tipped the edges of his lips.

"You saved me."

He looked at me. I saw then he had feared this night that he would be too late, take too long. His smile widened.

I flung my arms around him, laughter spilling from the joy

overwhelming my soul. Tunneling my fingers into his thick red curls, I hugged him, unable to get close enough. All I wanted was for the moment to last forever.

When he gently guided me from my prison and into the candlelight, I looked back. "My rosary."

The diamonds sparkled from their bed of stone. Dirk stopped me when I tried to turn. I watched him enter and kneel to retrieve my parents' gift.

Cade shoved one of his candles at Gerald and came toward me. He kissed the back of my hand. "It is good to see you, milady."

I laughed again.

Dirk stepped to my side, punched Cade playfully on the shoulder, and handed me my rosary. He picked me up in his arms. Which I was grateful for. Would my legs even hold me, wobbling so? I closed my eyes then popped them open again to look around.

My gaze went to Dirk. Every inch of my body hurt, but I ignored it and nestled my face in the curve of his neck, listening to him breathe as he carried me from that dark, horrid place.

But it was not all horrid. I had met God there. "Dirk."

"Gwyneth-mine?"

I shivered at the name. "Would you be disappointed in me if I did not wear my rosary anymore?"

He turned his head to give me a worried look. "As for your parents' promise—"

I put a finger to his lips. "'Tis not that. I will keep it for the promise it represents, but I no longer need it to pray."

One eyebrow lifted.

"And…it does not bring me pain to think of their promise. I know they *will* be with me, in spirit, when I marry the man I love."

The other eyebrow joined the first. He stopped while the other men walked on ahead. I heard a shriek of joy from Margried, then hurried whispers, and imagined that Cade had told the women I was safe, but was not to be disturbed quite yet.

I watched Dirk's gaze fall to my mouth and smiled. *Nee*, not quite yet.

"I would not be disappointed in the least. But I would be upset with you if you did not wear it on your wedding day."

I cocked my head, a thrill going through me when he said *wedding day*. "And why would that be?"

He shook his head. "Nay, I changed my mind. I care not what you wear. As long as you marry me."

I pressed a hand to my throat. "Are you asking me to be your wife?"

"Aye, milady, and that was most assuredly not an answer."

My smile widened as I watched that wolfish grin come over his face. "How is this for an answer?"

Ever so slowly, I leaned in and watched his eyes darken. I placed my mouth on the scar beside his eyebrow. He moved his head and mine until he captured my lips with his own. It was clear his intent was *not* to keep me quiet.

The kiss was rich with promise. A promise that would never be broken.

We would have many more obstacles yet to face, but I determined then and there to let my diamonds shine on my wedding day. Dirk might not care what I wore, but that day, like every day following this one, would be a day of love and hope. What better to wear on such a day than the sound of hope?

The sound of diamonds.

Historical Note

The Iconoclastic Fury really happened.

During the summer of 1566, the tension between Protestants and Catholics in the Dutch Low Countries—ruled by the Spanish king—had begun to boil. In August, what was commonly called the Beeldenstorm began. Villagers desecrated Catholic churches and destroyed art and decorations. They saw to it that statues and ornamentation, such as icons of the Virgin Mary or stained-glass windows depicting biblical scenes, were rendered unrecognizable. Protestants considered such icons idols—profane. Thus, the name Iconoclastic Fury.

The aftermath swept through Europe, and King Philip II of Spain would later send an army to calm the chaos. In conjunction with the Fury, the Sea Beggars came to be a symbol of the rebellion, led by William of Orange. At first, Philip's regent in the provinces, Margaret of Parma, was told not to worry about "those beggars." What was meant to be a derogatory dig at the rabble who were rebelling against the most powerful Spanish dynasty of that era, the Hapsburgs, came to be embraced as a compliment.

King Philip II had a complicated home life and marital history. He became a widower three times. His first wife, his cousin Maria Manuela, died in 1545 after giving birth to a son, Carlos, who was mentally ill. Next, Philip married his second cousin Mary I, also known as Bloody Mary, Queen of England, in order to gain the English throne. He never secured power over England, however. When Mary died without producing Philip a suitable heir, her sister, Elizabeth I, became queen of England.

Whereas her half-sister Mary had been staunchly Catholic, Elizabeth was Protestant. England had flipped between Catholicism and Protestantism ever since Elizabeth's father, Henry VIII, had declared himself the head of the Anglican Church in order to begin the first of *his* marital mishaps. Under Elizabeth, Catholicism was technically illegal. Everyone sixteen years of age and older was expected to attend Book of Common Prayer services on at least seventy-seven days a year. Those who did not were fined a shilling. Catholics who continued to practice their religion—and skipped Protestant services—came to be called recusants.

Philip sought to court his late wife's half-sister, Elizabeth, but the English queen refused to receive his suit—as she refused to receive anything more than promises by any other man who wanted her hand in marriage. Still in need of an heir, Philip married Elisabeth of Valois. Sadly, Elisabeth's first pregnancy ended in a miscarriage of her twin girls. She would indeed later die in childbirth, but not until 3 October 1568. (Philip would remarry one last time, to Anna of Austria, whom he loved.)

At the time that Oliver was calculating to use Gwyneth's heritage to further the cause of Catholicism and bring nearly all of Europe into Hapsburg hands, the news he had received was correct. Philip's wife, Elisabeth, was pregnant. However, his information, as was the case with most information in that pre-Internet era, was also outdated. Elisabeth gave birth to a healthy baby girl, Isabella, on 12 August 1566, before Dirk and Gwyneth ever left the Low Countries. Not a son, but a successful birthday for both mother and baby. So the scheme Oliver concocted was entirely in vain. Good thing, too, or else Protestantism might, *just might* have been stamped out forever...

Acknowledgments

A thousand thanks…

To Jesus: for calling me to rise (Matthew 17:7).

To Mama: I lost track of how many times I asked myself what you would do, then wrote Gwyn doing it. You are the inspiration behind her, height and all. Surprise!

To Daddy: for saying Catholicism is the only true religion. With a grin. You sparked the idea. So, really, this is your fault.

To Grandma: for all you've taught me.

To my clan of a family: for supporting me.

To Sarah Fisher: for first calling me Phoenix, being my favorite INFJ, and your late-night editing help with *that* scene.

To Meghan Gorecki: for changing my mind about Yankees, fangirling, and introducing me to *Once*. So much Hook went into Dirk, aye?

To my Journey Church Missional Community: because you're awesome. Especially Leah Russell and Chelsea Bouknight, for asking me to bring excerpts to Bible Study. Ya'll bless me.

To Chelsea Mauldin: for catching that history mistake I almost made!

To Linda Gooding: for knowing this would happen.

To Amber Stokes: for first polishing the diamond.

To Stephanie Morrill: who first told me I had voice. GTW is one of the reasons I thought I could do this.

To Joanne Bischof: for loving the names. And reading those contest entries that never did get sent in because I was signing a contract instead!

To Tiffany Titus: As soon as Titus stepped onto the scene, I knew his name. And that was because you had a ring on your finger that would soon give you the same name! Thanks for letting me use it!

To Susie Vahala: for daring me to dream when I got off the uneven bars that day.

To Kim Branham: for letting me use your son's name. Sorry, Cade, you do kiss a girl.

To Kim Howell: for calling me your author friend!

To Koryn Yarosz: for loving my nun.

To Erica Vetsch: for saying I was ready.

To Lisa T. Bergren: for writing *The River of Time*.

To Siri Mitchell: for writing *The Messenger*, which made me think first person point of view in a historical just might work. It did. It really did.

To Shannon Primicerio: for answering all those industry questions.

To Anne Mateer: for saying I struck you as a writer who would not quit. You win.

To all the Word Weavers: who said they knew it was only a matter of time.

To Tiffany Briley: for every single time you said, "Me, too."

To Rachel Blom and Jennifer Bishop: for translating Dutch and Spanish for me. (Readers, all mistakes are woefully mine.)

To Roseanna White and everyone at WhiteFire: for taking a chance on me. I am so glad to be working with all of you!

To the Doctor: Geronimo!

And, finally, to the reader who made it this far… *Be daring.*

CPSIA information can be obtained
at www.ICGtesting.com
Printed in the USA
FFOW04n1720110615
14180FF